lost ranch
books

XS

www.lostranchbooks.com

# WHITE WINTER

## To Walk Humbly

Laurie Marr Wasmund

*The White Winter Trilogy,* of which this book is a part, is a work of fiction. Apart from the well-known actual people, events, and locales that figure in the narrative, all names, characters, places, and incidents are the products of the author's imagination or are used fictitiously. Any resemblance to current events or locales, or to persons living or dead, is entirely coincidental.

Copyright © 2019 by Laurie Marr Wasmund

All rights reserved.

Front cover photograph:
The James Marr Family, 1919
Wollaston, Massachusetts
Personal Collection of Author
Back cover photograph:
The Official Klan Band of Colorado
Personal Collection of Author

Cover design by Laurie Marr Wasmund

Published in the United States by lost ranch books
www.lostranchbooks.com
ISBN 978-0-9859675-7-4

He has showed you, O man, what is good;
and what does the Lord require of you
but to do justice, and to love kindness,
and to walk humbly with your God?
Micah 6:8

# ONE

The summer of 1923 arrived in beauty at the home of Mr. and Mrs. James A. Graves. Situated on eleven acres in the Denver Country Club, the house was a modern day marvel: a Tudor castle built on dusty prairie, with a three-story façade fronted by an entrance that mirrored Hampton Court in London. Canted bay windows lined one wing of the house, while mullioned windows dominated the other. Fourteen chimneys rose from the roof, bundled together in threes and fours, and a round turret graced one end of the building. White gables jutted from the main section of the house, decorated with wattle and daub designs. A home of this size, complexity, and stateliness had not been built in Denver since the 1890s, when the great gold and silver magnates of Colorado constructed stone fortresses as testaments to their wealth.

At the back of the house ran a full-length stone patio, surrounded by graceful white balusters. Beyond the carefully tended shrubs and trees at the patio's foot, close-cropped lawns meandered down to a shimmering pond. Reeds and cattails grew along its banks, while a cluster of lily pads floated on its mirror-like surface. Japanese goldfish, imported at the price of five dollars each, swam in the peaceful waters. Gravel walkways, lit by strings of tiny electric lights, led through beds of vibrant flowers. An assortment of outbuildings completed the estate: a garage large enough for six cars; a stable ample enough for a herd of horses; a guest house; the servants' quarters; two gazebos, and a studio, tucked back in a corner behind a hedge of graceful shrubs.

At the far end of the estate, guests combed the shrubbery and trees for clues in a treasure hunt. Kathleen stood in the shade offered by one of the gazebos with Stephen at her side. Almost three years old, he was too young to go chasing after the guests. Anyway, this was an adult treasure hunt, something which had become popular after the war in Europe, as wealthy "bright, young people" raced around London or Paris in pursuit of pleasure. Tonight, the prize was a bar, set up in a clandestine corner of the garden. It was fully stocked with the makings of alcohol-free Prohibition treats such as fruit cocktail, shrimp cocktail, and oysters shipped directly from New York by Express. An assortment of pre-Prohibition liquor spiced up the watermelon balls and pineapple rings.

"Oh, look!" Marie Grissom, a friend of Jim's from college, shouted to Evan Lockridge and his friend, Perry Travers. "The clue has something to do with frogs. It's back to the pond, boys!"

"Can we go with them, Mommy?" Stephen asked.

"Let's see what they find."

Evan, Marie and Perry stumbled toward the pond, where feather-light red, white, and blue beach balls floated lazily in the nearly still water. Even the slightest breeze was strong enough to make them skim along the surface like swans. Here and there, balls the size of car tires tumbled over the grass, kicked or tossed or shooed aside by the partygoers in another nod to the child-like pursuits that had obsessed the young since the war.

Marie kicked at a ball, sending both her sandal and the ball flying. Beside Kathleen, Stephen giggled.

"Wait! Wait! I've lost my shoe!" she shouted.

Perry scooped her up in his arms, carrying her toward the pond as another team sprinted out of a stand of Ponderosa pine trees. One of them grabbed Marie's shoe from the ground and yelled, "You'll never see this again!" Their evening would end in unbridled drunkenness, no matter who found the treasure.

"Can I have a ball now?" Stephen asked as the teams thundered off toward the stables in search of the next clue.

"Tomorrow," Kathleen said. "But you must wait until Mr. Terrance takes them out of the water for you. And remember, you are to save one for your sister, and for Alice Colleen and your other cousins."

Stephen's face closed in a pout, but he did not complain. Even at his young age, he knew that whatever he asked for was guaranteed.

"Let's go back to the patio," Kathleen said. "It's nearly time for bed."

With Stephen toddling beside her, she made her way up the sloping lawn. The theme of the party—something required in this new age of revelry—was America and Britain and the close ties between the two. Buntings of the Union Jack and the Stars and Stripes hung suspended from the gleaming windows of the house, and tiny flags outlined the gravel paths, attached to sparklers that would be lit after dark. On the patio, Jim's parents, Victoria and Arthur Graves, sat at a round table topped with a red, white, and blue tablecloth, along with their close friends, the Fallowses and the Crawfords. Beside them were Jim's sister, Eleanora, and her husband, Thomas Lloyd-Elliot, who had served in the British Expeditionary Force during the war. Earlier, Jim had welcomed the Lloyd-Elliots to Colorado from England, where they had lived since the war: "We welcome you home again, Ellie, and we hope you won't be blinded by our sunny days after England and France, Thomas."

"You forget I was in India for years," Thomas countered.

"Of course." Jim laughed. "Then, let's hope you aren't parched by our dry weather. Welcome to the Queen City of the Plains and the great state of Colorado."

At the patio, Thomas offered Kathleen a chair. "Lady Graves."

"Thank you." She lifted Stephen onto her lap. By the laws of high society, children weren't allowed at evening gatherings, but Jim had wanted to show off Stephen to his sister and her husband. Upstairs, Susanna, only seven months old, slept, attended by her night nurse.

Dressed in an elegant tuxedo with white tie and tails, Jim was telling a story. His specially-tailored pant legs tapered smoothly into his cowboy boots, which were made of full ostrich quills with goatskin uppers sporting flamboyant hand-stitched swirls of golden thread. The sunset, brilliant in the western sky, glistened in his blue eyes. His hair was closely-cropped, curling back from his forehead in neat rows. He was still a sought-after and convivial guest at social events, but now he was much more: successful businessman, husband, father, politician, a man in his prime.

"Wildcatters come in all shapes and sizes," he said. "There's a woman in Wyoming who is seventy-three years old, Mary White Wing. No teeth, just a dirty strand or two of hair, and the most god-awful smell you could imagine. One morning, she arrived at my site, riding a half-starved nag, with a pack of mangy dogs weaving in and out of its hooves, and bet me fifty dollars that her well would shoot higher than mine when it came in."

"Did you take the bet?" Mrs. Crawford asked breathlessly.

"I didn't arrive where I am by passing up a gamble."

"What happened?"

"She won." Jim shrugged. "By about eighty feet. We sat on a boulder and drank her homemade hooch and watched it spill—"

Eleanora leaned toward Kathleen. "Listen to him talk. The world is his oyster."

It certainly was. Since the Armistice, the world had exploded with opportunity. Jim's oil wells pumped furiously, and money poured into the Graves home. His political aspirations had borne fruit as well. Just last November, one month before Susanna was born, he had been elected to the office of State Senator. He had finished presiding over his first legislative session in April.

It was hard to believe that nearly five years had passed since the end of the war. Kathleen had returned from France with Jim, after Eleanora— Mrs. Brently, as Kathleen had known her during their time in France— had chosen to stay behind in Paris. After her arrival in Denver, Kathleen returned to Graves Oil, now known as Graves Industries, as a typist, and she moved once more into Aunt Maury and Uncle Seamus's apartments above Sullivan's Grocery. The apartments, already limited in size, were even more cramped with Kathleen, Seaney, Maggie, and Maggie's daughter, Alice Colleen, in residence.

Returning had been much harder than leaving. The girls at the typing pool wanted to hear about Kathleen's experiences. Day after day, Mavis and Annabel, whom Kathleen had known before she went to France, and Edna plied her for details. Oddly, Mary Jane Grayson—who might have understood— rarely asked Kathleen about it. The only constant was the enduring censure of Miss Crawley, her supervisor. Nothing Kathleen did pleased her.

On a warm day in early June, 1919, Kathleen and the others from the typing pool were on their way to lunch when they spied Jim's Silver Ghost at the curb in front of Graves Industries. His chauffeur held the door open for him.

Kathleen's heart had lifted. "Wait for me," she said to Mavis.

Mavis, Annabel, and Edna had gawked, and Mary Jane had stood a little behind them, as Kathleen skipped a couple of times to catch up with Jim.

"Mr. Graves!" she called.

He had turned toward her, brandishing the insouciant smile that had both infuriated and charmed her in the past. "Why, hello, Miss O'Doherty," he said. "What a pleasant surprise. Are you on your way to lunch?" He nodded toward the girls, and they waved flirty, gloved hands.

"We're going to the Woolworth's counter."

"I've heard it's quite popular. And you and your father are well?"

"Yes, he is. He's living in Denver now."

"Not at Red—, what was it?"

"Redlands," she supplied. "No, since my mother's death, he's had no heart for ranching."

She said no more about the heartbreak of seeing Redlands abandoned by her father, Gerry O'Doherty. He spent his time now in billiard halls and men's clubs or with the proprietor of the boarding house where he lived, Mrs. Bennett, whom he knew a little more familiarly than Kathleen thought proper.

"And your cousin Sean's exploits were in the newspapers, if I'm not wrong," Jim said. "It was said he acted quite bravely."

"That's right, and he came home without a scratch on him, as my Aunt Maureen likes to say."

He lowered his voice. "And you, Miss O'Doherty, I hope the sorrow of your suitor's death in France has passed."

His words silenced her. She could hardly tell him of the hours that she had lost to grief for Paul Reston—sobbing as she sat on the rock formation on the ridge above the farm house at Redlands; tortured by the memory of the wild horseback ride through France every time she rode Napoli; broken by the thought of his touch on her skin whenever she bathed or changed her clothing. She could hardly tell him how she paged through her sketches, wishing that she could leap into one, that it might carry her back to France. Weakly, she replied, "I'm doing better. My mother also passed away from the flu."

"Of course, I recall that," he said. "I'm very sorry. And Harriet Mills, who was mourned as much here, in the office, as she was by you and my sister in France."

Oh, Hank, with her toothy grin that would never be pretty, but which outshone every smile around her, and her melodic voice as she sang to the soldiers. In losing Paul and Hank to war, America had squandered so much. And there were thousands more just like them—their futures and intelligence and wit lost before their time.

"How is Mrs. Brently?" Kathleen asked.

"Mrs. Lloyd-Elliot and the Colonel are doing well and living in London."

"Oh, so they married!" Kathleen rubbed beneath her eyes to clear the tears. "I'm so happy for her. If you write to her, would you please tell her that I said hello? We always imagined we would all stay in touch, but—"

"I'll pass on your greetings and well wishes to my sister," Jim said. "And now, you should go. It looks as if your friends are getting restless. It was nice to see you."

"Oh, yes, thank you."

As she had walked away, she wished she had been able to say more, about how every day was a struggle to return to a life where little changed, where the days passed in an expected, comfortable rhythm. She hated the routine, the boredom of "normalcy," which President Harding was so keen to establish in America. She could never go back to any kind of normal life, although everyone around her seemed to embrace it with great relief. In France, her life had been purposeful and fulfilling. But it had all been a lie—she had only gone to France because of the war, which had destroyed an entire generation of men.

"Miss O'Doherty!"

She turned back toward Jim. "Yes?"

"In case the Woolworth's counter isn't as filling as you expect, would you care to have dinner with me tonight?"

"Yes," she had said. "Oh, yes."

That evening, they had dined at the Royal Restaurant on the "Great White Way" of Curtis Street. Even on a Thursday, the streets overflowed with theater goers, newspaper boys, and girls in beaded dresses advertising the offerings at restaurants and shows. Cars honked and swerved up and down the street, crossing the tracks within inches of the trolleys.

They had dined in a private room and had danced to the music of Gould's Orchestra. The maître'd and the waiters had shown no disdain for Kathleen's green baize dress, which was faded from too much washing and ironing. Instead, they had crowded around, seeing to Jim's every comfort and desire.

When Jim had dropped Kathleen off at Sullivan's Grocery that night, he had asked her if he might see her again. As she had climbed to the shabby apartments of Sullivan's Grocery, she had felt relief—a release, almost—that she would, again, be among her own kind, although she knew that Jim Graves and Eleanora Lloyd-Elliot were nothing of the sort. But neither did she belong at Sullivan's Grocery, where the war had drained away its vitality, or in the typing pool, where the girls talked about nothing more than hats and movies.

So began a summer of evenings at the theaters and restaurants along the Great White Way that Kathleen immortalized by mounting the playbills and tickets and pressed flowers from her corsages into scrapbooks. She and Jim fed the zoo animals at Elitch Gardens, took wild flower excursions into the mountains, and boated on the lake at City Park. The days passed, happy, carefree, without a sorrowful memory in the world.

Stephen picked at the intricate pink and silver cherry blossoms that were beaded from waist to hem onto Kathleen's white chiffon dress. She kissed her son's head. Born in October of 1920, he was the spitting image of his father. His hair was a soft, fly-away white blond and his blue eyes burned with curiosity and intelligence.

Now Samuel Fallows asked Jim, "What's all this about Teapot Dome? You don't have any interests in that area, do you?"

"I have leases throughout Wyoming," Jim said smoothly, although his body stiffened as if in preparation for battle. "But I had nothing to do with Teapot Dome."

Kathleen stroked Stephen's hair. Since the spring, the scandal had consumed more and more print in the newspapers. Oil that had been held in reserve for the Navy had been leased to Harry Sinclair and others by the Secretary of the Interior, Albert Fall. Much had been made of Fall's sudden wealth, including a cattle ranch and other prominent business ventures.

"All that fuss," Thomas said. "It even reached the newspapers in Britain. Harding and the Republican Party of America were accused of turning every scrap of land in the western United States over to oil and coal companies."

Jim laughed. "That's an exaggeration—"

Stephen rubbed his eyes, and Kathleen whispered, "Do you want to go to bed?"

The child nodded, and Kathleen urged, "Tell Daddy goodnight."

Stephen slid from her lap and went over to where Jim stood. Spreading his arms, he said, "Goodnight, Daddy."

Jim lifted his son. "Goodnight, young man. Tell your grandparents goodnight."

He set Stephen on the floor, and the boy ran to kiss his grandmother on the cheek. Less certain of himself, he told his grandfather goodnight. Arthur merely nodded.

"Oh, isn't he adorable," Mrs. Crawford said.

"Tell your aunt and uncle goodnight," Victoria instructed.

Stephen went to shake Thomas' hand, but Ellie said, "I believe I'll accompany young Master Graves to the nursery, if that's all right with you, Kathleen."

"Of course."

Ellie rose in a shimmer of light. Made of black georgette crepe, her dress was ornamented by strings of tinsel-like beads hanging from her breasts to her waist and from her hips to below the hem. Around her neck, she wore several strands of pearls.

They left the patio, and Kathleen turned Stephen over to the uniformed nurse, Miss Brown, who picked the boy up and went ahead of them. Pausing at the end of the forty-foot foyer, Ellie looked up at the stained glass window that graced the landing where the grand staircase split in two, each secondary set of stairs leading to a separate wing of the house. "Jim told me that he designed the stained glass windows based on sketches that you made in France."

"My favorite is the one modeled after the window at Saint-Sépulchre in Montdidier."

"Ah, yes, that would probably be my favorite as well," Ellie sighed. "It's no surprise that Jim built the most outrageously ostentatious house in Denver, but to build it so obviously for you—well, that is extraordinary." Reaching the landing where the grand staircase split into two, she asked, "Which way to the nursery?"

Kathleen gestured toward the stairs to the left. Stephen's nursery was four doors down the hall. Filled with every toy or stuffed animal or novelty that a child might want, it was painted a bright blue with a rocking horse mural on one wall. Miss Brown was helping Stephen to change into his pajamas behind a trifold screen.

"Did you paint that?" Ellie nodded toward the rocking horse.

"I did." Jim had given her free reign with the decorating of the house. Susanna's room had a soft rainbow and cloud mural on one wall.

"You always were talented," Ellie said.

"Mommy!" Stephen ran out from behind the screen, and Miss Brown turned down his blankets. Kathleen said, "Let's say our prayers."

Stephen knelt beside the bed. Kathleen knelt beside him, while Eleanora took a step backward, as if afraid she might be asked to join them. Kathleen prayed, ""Protect us, Lord, as we stay awake—"

Stephen chimed now and then. "Pwo-tek us, Low . . . stay away—"

"Watch over us as we sleep that awake we may keep watch with Christ," Kathleen continued, with Stephen brokenly echoing her. "And asleep, rest in His peace."

"Amen," Kathleen said, making the sign of the cross over her body.

"Amen." Stephen imitated her motion before crawling into bed. "Now, sing the song."

Kathleen sat on the bed, pulling the blankets close around him. *"Gee, I'd like to be a monkey in the zoo, You'll never find a monkey feeling blue—"*

Eleanora's laugh tinkled as she recognized the song. Kathleen, Hank, Helen, and even Mary Jane, who had stayed in France for only a short time, had called the song the anthem of the Graves Family Foundation Relief Society.

Kathleen kissed Stephen's forehead. "Goodnight."

He touched his hand to his lips and held it out for her to take. "Goodnight."

Kathleen gathered the kiss. "Say goodnight to Aunt Ellie."

He touched his lips again and offered the kiss to Eleanora. "Goodnight."

Ellie laughed as she accepted the kiss from him and followed Kathleen into the hall. As they moved out of earshot, Ellie said, "That's quite a bedtime ritual, from the sublime of prayer to the ridiculous of Broadway."

"We promised each other that we would sing that song as a lullaby to our children," Kathleen said. "It was Hank's idea—"

"Of course it was." Eleanora took her arm in sympathy. "What a loss this world suffered when she died. And your friend, Paul. I'm so sorry."

"That's all in the past," Kathleen said weakly. How could she mourn Paul here, in this house, where her children and husband suited her so well? Only in the privacy of Redlands did she pine for him openly. She stopped near another door. "I'd like to look in on Susanna."

"Of course."

They tiptoed into the adjoining nursery, which was dimly lit by a single bulb inside a frosted glass owl on a lantern base. Susanna slept in the wooden-slatted crib, a flaming fuzz of red hair on her head, her tiny hands clenched in fists. Every once in a while, she shivered as she dreamed.

"She's lovely," Ellie whispered. "Why did you choose the name Susanna?"

"It felt young and fresh. It didn't remind either one of us of the war or of"—she faltered at the mention of Elizabeth, who, along with Jim's and Ellie's brother, Stephen, had drowned in a lake in the mountains—"anyone we knew or had known. We agreed that her middle name would be Eileen after my mother."

"Jim says that you asked him to marry you. Is that true?"

"I asked him when I first saw this house."

Ellie laughed, then clapped her hand over her mouth.

Kathleen remembered the evening late in August of 1919, when Jim had driven her from Berkeley Park to open prairie south of Cheesman Park. At the end of a well-traveled dirt road, he parked the car.

"Close your eyes," he said. "I'll help you out of the car."

With a laugh, Kathleen had allowed him to lead her by both hands over uneven ground. Standing behind her with his hands on her shoulders, said, "Open your eyes."

The edifice rose up before her with the sunset-washed sky as a glowing backdrop. Streaky clouds of orange and red reflected in the mullioned windows of the façade. Parked nearby were wagons loaded with lumber and brick, and gasoline-powered cement mixers, and a strange vehicle that looked like a military tank with a steel blade attached to its front. Piles of lumber and stone and berms of dirt spread over the property.

"What is this?" she had asked. "A hotel?"

"Hardly. Follow me."

He had taken her to the back of the house, where the lovely patio with its stone balustrade was beginning to take form. Gossip had it that Mr. Graves was building a mansion for himself, although some grumbled that it had been financed from the spoils of the war that had taken so many lives. "Is it yours?" she had asked, although she knew the answer.

"I'd be remiss in showing it to you if it wasn't, don't you think?" He led her to a deep depression that had been dug into the dry soil. "There will be a pond here. If my calculations are right, the reflection of the house will appear there."

"The chateau where we stayed in France had a stream where a dam had been built to form a lake with an artificial island—"

"I'm afraid I'll have to pass on that. Cherry Creek was damned up long ago by Robert Speer to build the country club golf course."

She had laughed, but she was uneasy, too. All the money that had gone into it, that would continue to be spent to maintain it. The chateau in France had housed hundreds of people at one time, but this, this home had been built for only a handful of people. It was shameful, embarrassing—or was it? Wasn't this what America lauded in its citizens: the self-determination and industry that allowed for this? And Jim must have hired dozens of workmen and masons and carpenters and others to build it, giving them all employment.

"It has eleven bedrooms and nine baths," Jim said. "And a total of, I believe, somewhere around fifteen thousand square feet of interior space. There are three dining rooms."

"One each for breakfast, lunch, and dinner?"

He had laughed. "For entertaining purposes. One is intimate, for family, while another seats twenty for small gatherings. The third will fit a table that can seat fifty at once."

"Why does one person need all this?" she asked.

"I don't intend to be 'one person' for my entire life," he said. "At some point, I intend to have a large and flourishing family. And, as I am on the Board of Directors at the Colorado and Western Railroad and the Colorado Power Company and have shareholder stakes in other corporations as well, I need a place to host my business associates, as well as a place to hold political functions—"

"Political functions?"

"I'm casting my hat into the ring to run for State Senator next year." His arms had slipped around her waist, drawing her against him as they both faced the house. "If you lived in my district, I'd be plying you with dinner and wine right now in the hope of winning your vote. You are my severest critic, you know."

"I am not—"

With a kiss to her cheek, he had said, "Oh, yes, Miss O'Doherty, you are. I am Icarus and you are the sun, melting my wings and casting me into the sea to die a slow, cold death."

She had laughed, but something blossomed inside her. A warmth, a sweetness, some kind of longing tinged with anticipation. She felt happy in Jim's presence—free from the memories of the war and the pain of Paul's death. Jim had moved forward, toward less complicated or less dreary times.

"Are we going inside?" she asked.

"You must allow me to have some secrets from you." He turned her around with gentle hands on her shoulders. "I have a picture in my mind of you sitting beside this pond—once it's filled with water—and sketching. Very pastoral or bucolic, *très chic, très plein air, très Parisienne.*"

The image took hold in her mind: the house and clouds mirrored in the still water of the pond and the dragonflies that skimmed along the top, sending ripples through the reflection. In the spring, frogs would spawn iridescent tadpoles in the water, and the red-winged blackbirds would trill in the cattails along the edge, and wild mallards would lay their eggs in pockets of reeds along the shore. All brought about by the power of Jim's will.

"When we were in Paris, you told me you wouldn't talk to me about marriage again," she said.

"And I've kept that promise."

"You said that, well, if we ever spoke of it again, it would be because I mentioned it."

"As you are now."

She realized that he wasn't going to help her. "I would, I wouldn't, well, if you wanted to talk about it now, I wouldn't mind."

"And I thought you were going to propose to me. But I suppose I'll have to continue to weep over my empty hope chest."

She laughed. "Will you marry me, then?"

"Why, yes, Miss O'Doherty, I believe I will." His answer was immediate. "You've made me wait two long years for this, and I'm not going to take the chance that you'll run off to another war." He sobered. "Kathleen, I promise you that I will love you as you should be loved for the rest of your life. It will be my privilege. All this"—he waved toward the house—"I've done with the hope that you would deign to marry me."

After that, it was remarkably easy. Kathleen had left her job at Graves Industries the following week, amid wild speculation from the other girls, and in December of 1919, she and Jim had married before a justice of the peace. From England, Eleanora had sent Kathleen a wedding ensemble and trousseau that was as generous as it was glamorous.

Now, Ellie said, "Well, I'm very glad you proposed to him. After knowing you and Hank and Helen in France, all I wanted was for the three of you to be safe and happy. And then Hank . . . I'm so pleased we were together in France. I am so happy it's over."

"Do you sometimes think . . ." Kathleen hesitated. Do you sometimes feel that you aren't able to completely settle down in this world because of the war? If we hadn't gone, if I'd stayed here and kept working, I would have married someone I met at Mass, I suppose, and I would have lived like—"

She stopped. She had nearly named her mother and Aunt Maury. They were fine women, respected and welcomed in their communities. Yet their lives had revolved around babies and housework and trying to scrape together enough money to buy what they needed. They would never see the lights of Broadway in New York, or the Eiffel Tower, or the Mediterranean coast in Nice as Kathleen had.

"Our time in France feels to me like something that I tossed in a bin with the thought that I never wanted to see it again," Eleanora said. "But once it was gone, I wanted it back, with an almost physical anguish, because nothing that I have done since quite measures up."

"That's how I feel," Kathleen whispered.

"It is a terrible way to live. To long for such a vile thing. A thing that caused so much misery and hardship to so many millions of people." Eleanora touched Kathleen's hand. "Have you heard from Helen lately?"

Helen Parsons, a member of the Graves Family Foundation Relief Society, had stayed in Paris after she fell in love with a Frenchman whose face had been badly damaged during battle. Helen had taken a job as the assistant at the Studio for Portrait Masks, where Anna Coleman Ladd created elegant masks for French soldiers whose faces had become disfigured during the war.

"She's at an art shop in Paris," Kathleen said. "Henri is still working at the Sorbonne."

"It's a shame that the Portrait Studio closed," Ellie said. "But I don't fault Mrs. Ladd for wanting to return to America with her husband. Besides, once the Red Cross withdrew its money from the project, she would have been forced to start all over again to find funds."

"We would have funded it," Kathleen said. "At least, part of it."

"Yes, and Thomas and I also would have contributed. But she still would have needed more, as well as a sponsor organization of some sort."

"Why not the Graves Family Foundation?"

Ellie laughed. "Mother told me that you've kept that going. She said that Jim turned over all the charity work to you."

"He did, and I enjoy it so much," Kathleen said. "Who knew that giving away money would be so much more fun than spending it?"

Ellie laughed. "I am so happy for you. These beautiful children, this glorious house, Jim's position in the Legislature—the two of you have been able to live out your dreams."

Kathleen caught herself from replying, Jim's dreams. Of course, they were also her dreams. Stephen, Susanna, Jim's love for her—of course, they were.

Light flooded into the room. "So here you are, Ellie! You'll never believe what happened! Evan fell in the pond during the treasure hunt, and Perry jumped in after him—"

Susanna awakened with a cry, and Kathleen gathered her up in her arms. "Don't cry," she soothed. "It's all right."

"Oops!" Marie swayed in the doorway. "I'm sorry! Was that too loud?"

"You're sloshed, dear," Ellie said, taking Marie's arm.

Miss Davis, Susanna's nurse, rushed into the room. "What's going on?"

"I'm sorry," Marie said in full voice. "I woke the baby."

"Come with me." Ellie led Marie from the room.

Marie's voice echoed down the hallway. "So, Evan fell in the pond, and Perry went in after him, but he slipped and fell, too, and they just wallowed in the water together, and they killed one of those goldfish, so we had to have a funeral for it—"

"Was it a burial at sea?" Ellie asked.

Their laughter rang through the hallway.

Miss Davis reached for Susanna. "I'll put her back to sleep, Mrs. Graves."

"That's all right. I'm not needed downstairs just now."

Once she was alone in the room, Kathleen sat down in the rocking chair, Susanna cuddled against her. She listened to the chatter of guests, some of it loud and slurred; the occasional shouts and laughter from near the pond; the music of the all-Negro jazz orchestra, complete with saxophone; the click of glasses as more liquor was consumed; someone—undoubtedly Evan and Perry and maybe even Jim—singing the Princeton fight song, *"And Nassau's walls will echo with the Princeton Tiger's roar—"*

It was true that no one would miss her—the mouse, the quiet one, the young girl that had managed to capture Jim Graves' heart. Few of Jim's acquaintances saw how such an attraction might last. At times, Kathleen wondered herself. They had never truly talked about her experiences in France, including her love for Paul, and she had never asked Jim about romantic loves he might have had before her. By some unspoken agreement, they had both discarded their pasts and replaced them with a headlong dive into marriage and family.

She kissed Susanna's cheek, laid her in the crib, and left. Outside, Miss Davis waited for her.

"She's asleep," Kathleen said. "I'm sorry about the intrusion—"

"Oh, it was no problem, Mrs. Graves. No problem at all—"

Downstairs, Kathleen paused at the foot of the stairs. The sun had set, and the multitude of artificial lights had come on throughout the grounds. Outside, people were still roaming about the lawns, or lying on chaises on the stone patio. Yet she could hear the words of a serious conversation taking place in the parlor.

"It's no mystery why so many are joining the Ku Klux Klan," Samuel Fallows was saying. "It is a bona fide organization, not like the Masons or the Knights of Columbus. It was given a charter by the state of Georgia."

"But how many members are in Denver?" Thomas asked.

"I'm not sure," Samuel said. "All I know is that representatives from Atlanta arrived here a couple of years ago to organize, and they released a statement about their permanency—'We were here yesterday, we are here today, and we shall be here forever.'"

"You're quite the spokesman," Thomas observed. "I assume that doesn't mean that you have any connection with it."

"Of course not—"

"Why is it so appealing, Jim?" Ellie deferred to the expert.

"I'm not entirely sure. But the members seem to be unskilled laborers and those in service—"

"They're average men who've been left behind," Samuel corrected. "Just about every good job's been taken by an immigrant who doesn't even speak English, but who will work for less pay. And these immigrants have brought with them crime and filth. The Italians and their bootlegging, the Chinese and their opium, the Irish and their betting and brawling. All the Klan wants is a return to some semblance of order in this country. If immigrants want to live here, they should abide by the rules and understand their place. We all know that Catholics and Jews can't live in neighborhoods such as Park Hill or Cheesman Park or this one—"

Kathleen stepped into the room, and Samuel fell silent. It was well-known among Jim's friends and associates that she was a practicing Catholic. Father Keohane—Brendan—allowed her to attend services at Blessed Savior on Thursdays.

Jim stood beside the sprawling white marble fireplace, one tensed hand laid on the mantel, the other near his waist, a cigarette between tightly-clenched fingers. He looked as if he might murder Samuel.

"Oh, this is deadly," Marie said from the cushioned chair where she lounged. "Jim, ever since you went into politics, you're far too serious! We should put up a tombstone for Fun, just like we did for that poor little fish."

"Agreed." Evan strolled to the grand piano, sat down, and made a dramatic show of pushing up the cuffs of his shirt, which were far too long. He wore an ill-fitting tuxedo, which he had evidently borrowed from Jim while his own clothes dried. His friend, Perry, wore another of Jim's tuxedos, which was far too tight on him. His neck bulged from the shirt collar.

Floating an arpeggio over the piano keys, Evan began to sing, *"Jimmy was a soldier brave and bold, Kathy was a maid with hair of gold—"*

Everyone laughed at the change of name from "Katy" to "Kathy." Perry started to sing as well, and Marie danced over to Thomas, grabbing his hands and hauling him out of his chair. "C'mon, Colonel!" she shouted. "Ellie, you too!"

*"K-k-k-Kathy, beautiful Kathy,"* Evan sang. *"When the m-m-m-moon shines, Over the cowshed—"*

He rolled his eyes to indicate the house, and Marie shouted, "Some cowshed!"

The others joined in, stuttering along with the lyrics of the song, which had been popular during the war. White light shimmered from outside, reflecting in the high, arched windows.

"Oh, look!" Marie called. "They're lighting the sparklers! Let's go! Quick! Before they burn out!"

As the group rushed outside, Kathleen went to the window. The lawns snapped with hundreds of fiery sparklers, lit by the gardeners. Guests plucked the lit fireworks from the ground and danced off with them, some of them writing their names or drawing pictures in light in the sky. As they frolicked, fireworks flew upward from the corners of the estate. "Oohs" and "aahs" swelled up from the gardens as the darkness of the night disappeared in thundering sheets of white, red, and blue.

Standing behind Kathleen, Jim put his hands on her shoulders. "What do you think, Mrs. Graves? Another success?"

It looked so much like that first night in Montdidier when she had met . . .

"Another success," she said.

# TWO

In uniform again, Sean tugged at the starched white shirt collar around his neck. On his head was an officer's hat, with a badge in the center that read: Denver Police Department. An identical emblem covered his heart on his jacket. In the warmth of this June night, his black woolen trousers clung to his thighs, and sweat sopped his armpits. Around him, Berkeley Park slept in silence. When he came to Sullivan's Grocery, he tested the front door to see if it was locked. As always, it was.

He leaned against the brick wall of the store and lit a cigarette. It had been a long journey to this quiet night in the place where he had always lived. When he'd come home from France in May of 1919, he had found himself lost as to how to take up his old life again. Oh, there'd been plenty of problems to tackle. Ma lay in bed all day, while Pa huddled in the corner where he once cut meat and drank. The shelves in Sullivan's Grocery were nearly empty, and the customers had fled to something called a "supermarket." The brick storefront looked shabby and neglected, the outbuildings and corrals behind it nearly all derelict.

Dutifully, Sean had taken up the yoke, cleaning, repairing and refurbishing the store. Just when he thought it might be possible to salvage what was left of Sullivan's Grocery and its reputation, Liam, Maggie's husband, had come home.

On Thanksgiving Day, 1920, Liam had been released from Fort Leavenworth after President Wilson pardoned the remaining thirty-three Conscientious Objectors who had served time under the Sedition Act of 1918. At the news, Colorado exploded in rage. One after another, letters arrived at the Sullivans' apartments, crudely addressed to "Slacker Keohane" or "Yellowbelly" or simply "Coward." The Denver newspapers, including the one Maggie worked for, the *Denver City Daily News,* published outraged articles about the insult to Americans who had lost their lives or their loved ones in France. More than one post of the American

Legion claimed that the "pardoning of arch slacker Liam Keohane" defiled true honor and sacrifice. Veterans called Secretary of War Newton Baker un-American and unpatriotic. In one newspaper Liam was warned that he had better not show himself in Denver.

In December, a brick had flown through the plate glass window of Sullivan's Grocery, effectively putting an end to revitalizing the store. The drapes of the apartments upstairs were pulled shut, drenching the rooms in darkness. Long after the new year of 1921, the Sullivans hid, more or less prisoners in their own home. The fervor had cooled, but even now, more than two years later, Liam went outside.

With her husband home, Maggie was soon expecting again, and in August of 1921, the twins, Frankie and Declan, were born. With so many vying for space, Sean began searching for employment. That was when he had come across a recruitment poster for the Denver Police. Former soldiers were encouraged to apply. Sean had no trouble passing the elementary police exam and proving his marksmanship at the shooting range on the prairie north of Denver. As soon as he was hired, he had taken a room at a boarding house nearby. It was clean enough, although it smelled of its ancient landlady, Mrs. Potter. He gave whatever extra money he could to his parents.

Maggie kept her job as "Mrs. James, the Thinking Woman" even after the arrival of Kieran, only fourteen months after the twins. Instead of supporting his family, Liam spent his days writing his story for posterity, in the belief that the people of the United States should know how its government had treated its own dissident citizens. But how many of those who went to war would never have the chance to write their own stories, as Liam had? Sean wondered. How many of them would never have a darling daughter and two rough-and tumble boys and a sweet baby, or a wife like Mag who hung on every word her husband uttered? Berkeley Park had plenty of boys who would never come home: Donnell and Frank MacMahon—for whom Liam's boy Frankie was named—and Gordon McKenna, and two of the Sheas, and others.

For Sean, the worst insult was that Liam had been offered an administrative job and a sergeant's rank during the war even though he refused to serve. The only way that Sean had gotten a Sergeant's stripe on his uniform was to kill like some wild animal. Where was the justice in that?

He crushed his cigarette butt under his heel as he stepped out from the shadow of Sullivan's Grocery. Once beyond the building, he glanced toward the back of the lot, behind the store. In one of the sheds, a light blazed.

Maggie had long ago given up trying to work during the day, with Ma, Pa, Liam, and the kids to tend to. So Sean had helped her to set up an office in the garden shed. After hauling her heavy Underwood typewriter down from the apartments, he'd insulated the walls of the shed with cardboard and puttied the window frame to stop the wind. He had also installed a pot belly stove to keep her supplied with hot tea. She worked during the precious hours between bedtime and baby Kieran's feeding. Barring nightmares, soiled diapers, and childhood illnesses, it was the only time she had to herself.

The sound of her fingers on the stiff keys of the Underwood resounded into the street, and Sean decided against stopping in to say hello. She had enough to do without pandering to him. Besides, since his return from France, he and Mag didn't always see eye to eye. She resented his decision to join the police, and he could barely contain his criticisms of Liam. His senses ruined by his imprisonment, Liam demanded darkness and silence, and it fell to Maggie to make sure that the apartment was free of light and sound. Poor little Alice Colleen, who at five years old was as pretty as Kathleen, had had to grow up far too quickly. She listened for the boys at night and reported to Maggie in the shed if they woke, and she had learned to play silently, never running or jumping or shouting as Kathleen and Sean and Mag had as kids. But the twins were not so easily reined in, and Mag had her hands full trying to keep them from annoying their father.

Sean moved past the store and down the street. When he rounded the corner onto Tennyson, the modest, brick silhouette of Blessed Savior came into view. A lone figure sat on the steps beneath the yellowish porch light. Father Keohane held a book at an angle, trying to read. A citronella candle burned at his side to keep away the mosquitoes. He seemed not to have aged in the past few years. Still slender and pale, with wire-rimmed glasses that resembled President Wilson's, he had once been a ghost of his hearty, athletic brother, Liam. Now, Brendan looked healthier than his brother.

"What are you doing out so late, Father?" Sean asked.

Brendan closed his book. "It's too hot to sleep tonight." He waved his hand toward the rectory behind the church building. "And Father Devlin's bothered by the light under his bedroom door if I read in the parlor."

"Well, good luck reading by that light," Sean said. "Want me to fetch a kerosene lamp for you?"

"Thank you, but no, you've your duty to do." Brendan removed his glasses and wiped them clean with a handkerchief. "I'm glad you're in this neighborhood. I think it gives us all peace of mind that one of our own is protecting us."

Sean quailed. He still felt uneasy with living a normal, quiet life. Even though he had daydreamed of home as he waddled through the mud in the trenches or shivered under a thin blanket in some barn in France, now that he was here, it seemed dull, petty, a fool's errand. The slightest thing—a fly buzzing against a window pane, the honk of a car, the distant firing of a gun—took him back to the battlefield, to the stench and fear and brutality, but it also made him long for the excitement of defying death, or the sense that every nerve in his body was ready. He missed the camaraderie of soldiers, the knowledge that they were all in it together, that they had the same goal: to stay alive.

Suddenly, a brilliant flame split the dark night high on Table Mountain west of Denver. Sean stepped into the street to gain a better view. Father Keohane followed, his book abandoned on the porch. Three large crosses blazed in the clear night, the flames white and fierce against the black of the mountain.

"I don't see how anyone can feel safe with the shenanigans that lot is pulling," Sean grumbled.

"I attended a Klan recruitment meeting the other night."

"What? When?"

"I went to the one at the Denver Auditorium, the one that our newly-elected Mayor Stapleton let them have, even though every notable politician in the state, including Governor Sweet, objected to it."

"Why did you go?" Sean asked. "The Klan's named Catholics as public enemy number one in America!"

"I know, but they'd posted handbills on every Catholic church or Jewish synagogue in town, including this one." He gestured toward Blessed Savior. "I assumed it was an invitation."

Sean chuckled. "Ah, Brendan, that was a dangerous conclusion."

"I was in good company. Father Walsh and Father Kelly from the Cathedral of the Immaculate Conception were with me, although they both wore their army uniforms. I was the only one to wear clerical garb. I concealed it until I was seated in the Auditorium."

Sean shook his head. The meeting had caused a row in Denver. Because the Auditorium belonged to the city, a loud protest had gone up when the mayor announced that the property had been rented by the Klan. Stapleton had defended his decision by claiming that he had been assured that no attack would be made by the Klan on color, race, or creed. All the same, Brendan was taking a terrible chance in showing up at the event.

"We fought the war to make the world safe for democracy only to come home to a country that doesn't believe in it," Sean said.

"Democracy hasn't been safe in America for a long time."

It was an argument that Sean had heard from Maggie. She—and evidently Brendan—claimed that Liam had had his rights as an American taken from him. The great democratic principles of freedom of speech and freedom of religion had proven meaningless against Wilson's war machine.

"I need to be on my way," Sean said.

"Goodnight, Sean. Take good care of yourself."

"Aye, you, too, Father."

As he went about his beat, Sean wondered if the Keohane brothers were the true heroes. After all, Liam had taken on President Wilson and the United States military, and now his brother was challenging hundreds of white-hooded Protestants. All Ma could—or would—talk about was how her blue star son had returned from war with not a scratch on him, not a hair lost from his head, and a chest full of medals, besides. But Sean felt none of the pride or sense of worth that a hero should. He couldn't forget the eyes of the men he'd killed, or seen die, or watched as their wounds took the breath from them with agonizing slowness. Even now he had nightmares about the rampage through the German trench that had won him his chest full of medals.

The cross on Table Mountain flared, jangling his nerves. Brendan was right—the Ku Klux Klan had made it clear to everyone in Denver that Jews, Roman Catholics, Negroes, and foreign-born immigrants were the enemies of America. There were Klan followers in the Denver Police Department who said that the Pope aimed to destroy America's hard-won Christian values by arming the Knights of Columbus against goodly Protestants. The Klansmen vowed that they would be better armed when the time came.

He remembered how angry he used to get at Danhour for his slander against the Church. Now there were thousands of Danhours everywhere in the country, wearing white robes and calling whoever wasn't with them evil.

# THREE

The morning dawned bright and cloudless, the heat already stealing in through the open windows in the Sullivans' apartments. Maggie stood over the ancient black stove, scrambling eggs in a cast iron pan that dated back to Grandpa Sullivan's grubstake days. With the back of her hand, she pushed back a damp lock of hair from her forehead. She'd long since left off yearning for the neat kitchen with gas stove and ample shelves that had been in the Erwins' house, which she and Liam had rented when they were first married. It was probably for the best that she was left with Ma's old monstrosity to cook on—matches, gas, and four children didn't always go together well.

Alice Colleen sat at the kitchen table, singing, "Toot, Toot, Tootsie," again and again. Her dove-soft hair was the color of Maggie's and her grandmother Maureen's, a reddish-gold with a tawny sheen befitting an African lion. Her eyes were her father's—flecked with green, gold, and brown, and always watching, always inquisitive. Tenderness rushed up Maggie's throat as she marveled at how lovely Alice Colleen was, with her sweet Clara Bow mouth and pale skin.

She was fitting together a wooden puzzle that had been passed down from the Graves children to Maggie's. Kathleen was always hauling over a sack of toys that Stephen didn't like, or that she didn't like. The puzzle was made of blocks of wood that fit together into simple buildings—far too bourgeois for the Graves children, Maggie suspected. If blocks allowed for the turrets of a castle, Kathleen probably would have kept them.

She scolded herself. Envy was a sin, one of the deadly seven. Maggie said a quick prayer and made the sign of the cross over her body. "Toot, toot, Tootsie, don't cry," she sang.

Alice Colleen looked up from her blocks. "What's the rest?"

"*The choo choo train that takes me away from you,*" Maggie warbled. "*No words can tell how sad it makes me. Kiss me, Tootsie, and then, Do it over again . . .*"

Frankie and Declan waddled through the door from the parlor. At almost two years old, both boys resembled their father. Frankie's face carried the same roguish rosiness in his neck and cheeks as Liam had, while Declan was thinner and paler, more like his Uncle Brendan. In personality, they fed off each other. If one was sleepy, the other was wide awake. If one was playing quietly, the other was tearing through the apartments.

"Oh, look," Maggie said. "It's Toot Toot and Tootsie themselves." She bent to kiss each on the top of his head. "Good morning, you two."

Declan crawled onto a chair at the kitchen table and watched Alice Colleen assemble something that looked like a Japanese pagoda. She was nearly finished when Declan reached out and dislodged a piece.

"Stop it!" she protested. "Mommy, he ruined my house!"

"Shhh," Maggie said immediately. "You'll wake up the baby and Daddy. Give Declan a couple of pieces so he has something to play with."

Alice Colleen sniveled, but obeyed. She began meticulously reassembling the blocks, slapping away Declan's hand whenever he reached for a piece. Frankie stood beside them, his eyes and forehead all that were visible to Maggie over the table top.

"I hungwy." Declan banged his two sticks on the edge of the table.

"It's almost ready," Maggie assured him. "Quiet now, stop that."

She turned back to the stove. She should have expected to have twins; after all, her mother and Auntie Eileen, Kathleen's mother, had been twins. Maggie had become pregnant within a month after Liam had returned home, as if she only had to look at him to conceive. But two babies—two hearty, hungry, demanding boys—had come as a surprise to her.

But, then again, just about everything that had happened since the war had surprised her.

She'd been counting on everything being back to "normalcy," as President Harding called it, but evidently Harding hadn't taken the Sullivan family into account. Maggie had been sure that Seaney would have Sullivan's Grocery up and running soon after he returned from France, but her biggest surprise was his joining up with the Denver Police Department.

When he had abruptly announced it at dinner, much as he had shared his the news of his enlistment years ago, Maggie had forgotten all decorum and manners. "The police!" she had shouted. "Do you know what they did to Liam? They starved him, and they beat him, and broke a rib. And then, they turned him over to the military for court-martial—"

While Seaney had glared at her, Ma had warned, "Maggie, you must forgive—"

"Maybe so. But I will never forget what they did to an innocent man."

"He wasn't innocent." Seaney fumed. "He chose to disobey the law."

Seaney had accepted the job, and soon after, he had moved out of the Sullivans' apartments. At least, he gave Ma and Pa part of his paycheck every week or so, which meant that Maggie was not the sole provider.

And that was another mind-boggling surprise. Her mother, who had refused to leave her bed for most of the time that Seaney was at war, had shown no inclination to get up after his return. She took most of her meals in bed, and she only graced the parlor for a few hours a day. She didn't even bother to attend Mass. Brendan stopped by daily to offer it to her and to Liam.

The overflowing boxes of ribbon and tulle, the treadle sewing machine, and the antique vanity in Mrs. Sullivan's Millinery, where Maggie had once written stories, were forgotten until Maggie gave in to Alice Colleen's pleas to let her play dress-up in the attic. After all, someone should get some use out of it.

But the most shocking surprise was Liam's return. Maggie had resigned herself to living without him, even though the war had ended. But two days after Thanksgiving, in 1920, Brendan had called Maggie and asked her to come to Blessed Savior. Maggie had known that whenever Brendan asked her to come to the church, it was dire news. So she had fallen back on her solace: Evelyn, the character from her short stories. That day, Evelyn walked along the sidewalk, the leaves dancing a merry quadrille—Maggie didn't know exactly what that was—around her ankles, the dainty heels of her well-polished calfskin boots clicking along in a smart rhythm.

It was Evelyn who breezed confidently into Blessed Savior, and Evelyn who tapped politely on the door of Brendan's office, but it was Maggie who fell on her knees at the sight of Liam, Maggie who had to be helped by both men into a chair, and Maggie who wept without restraint.

"Maggie, Maggie," Liam had said, his hands on her hair. He kissed her forehead, her cheeks, her lips, even though they were wet with tears. Unable to speak, she had breathed out nonsense: "When did . . . How? . . . I've missed . . . I can't—"

He had laughed. After all he had been through, he had been capable of laughter.

He came home filled with stories of brutality suffered at the hands of the military, but no one wanted to hear them. Pa left the room when

Liam came into it, and Ma's face turned stone-like if he spoke of his imprisonment. Two of the dissenting German Hutterites from South Dakota had died from injuries and illnesses racked up during their time in the pits of Alcatraz, and poor Ralph Hunt from Pueblo would be locked up forever as a lunatic.

Liam burned for justice for them. Throughout the day, the portable Corona typewriter that Maggie had once borrowed from Judah Rapp, Liam's lawyer, clattered away in the back bedroom, which had once been Seaney's. As well as a chronicle of his time in Fort Leavenworth, Liam typed pages and pages of philosophical and theological suppositions, trying even now to prove to the Catholic Church that the war had, in no way, been "just." He asked Maggie to read his work, and he expected her to be able to argue its finer points. She wanted to protest: *I have spent the last three years raising Alice Colleen on my own, and taking care of Ma, and trying to earn enough so that we don't starve. I haven't the time to read about the war or Catholic theology or anything else.* But that was unfair.

Liam's faith remained as strong as ever. Every night the Keohane family knelt at their home altar and prayed: Liam leading the prayer, while Alice Colleen nestled close to the father she adored, and Maggie struggled to keep the twins from wiggling, and held baby Kieran in her arms. But Liam's physical needs had changed dramatically. His appetite had vanished, and he slept in spurts, ten minutes now, twenty later, something which had become habit after being doused with cold water whenever he slept soundly. Light bothered him, as did any kind of noise, whether it was the clank of pans as Maggie cooked or Alice Colleen's sweet singing or the twins crying for their dinner.

He ridiculed Maggie's work as Mrs. James, The Thinking Woman, a job that she had won after the previous advice columnist at the *Denver City Daily News* had died in the influenza epidemic. Looking over the piles of letters that came for Mrs. James, Liam said, "You have the opportunity to turn these people to God and the Church and urge them to save their souls."

"Mr. Ledbetter would have my soul if I tried that."

Liam fanned through the letters. "A man whose mother-in-law cooks what he says is no better than trench food, a woman who thinks it wrong for girls to bob their hair—not one of these people has done anything to honor their God—"

"You don't know that," Maggie argued. "Maybe the girl with the bobbed hair goes to church every Sunday or serves meals to the poor—"

"The only answer is God," Liam said. "To be completely subservient to His design. The rest is vanity. *Vanitas vanitatum et omnia vanitas.* Vanity of vanities, all is vanity. Ecclesiastes 1.2."

"In the meantime, Mr. Trench Food still has to eat. And evidently, nothing his mother-in-law cooks is 'new under the sun.'"

She expected him to laugh, to praise her clever reference to Ecclesiastes, but he had scolded, "You need to be more respectful of God in your answers to these questions."

Why? she had wanted to ask. What has God done to earn that from me? A failed business, parents who were aging before their time, a husband who seemed more aged than her parents. Yet when she looked at Alice Colleen and Frankie and Declan and baby Kieran, she knew. Four children—each healthy and strong, not one of them simple-minded or sickly, not one lost before it took its first breath or to a childhood ailment. Maggie had carried and given birth to them with ease, unlike her mother, who had buried as many as Maggie had delivered.

"Circulation is up because of me, Liam," she had said. "I know the *Denver City Daily News* isn't the *Post* or the *Rocky* or even the *Express*. But people—and especially women—like Mrs. James."

"Why can't you use your own name? Why must you hide behind a false one?"

She would be lynched if she used the name "Keohane." Liam had to know that—he was just being difficult.

"Do you think that Dorothy Dix was born with that name?" she countered. "Or Pinky Wayne at the *Rocky*? Old Polly Pry at the *Post* was an O'Bryan, for Pete's sake."

Now, the sound of Liam's wheelchair in the hallway, rolling along linoleum, pulled Maggie from her memory. "Daddy's coming," she said.

At once, Alice Colleen gathered up her logs and put them in a cigar box. "Let me have those, Declan," she ordered, snatching the two pieces from him. He objected with a wail, but Maggie hissed, "Shush!"

By the time Liam's wheelchair appeared in the doorway, all three children were sitting quietly at the table with their hands folded, ready for morning prayer. Maggie went over to help Liam across the uneven threshold between the parlor and kitchen. He was no longer the strapping young fellow she had married. His hair was dull and grayish, and his complexion was the color of oats. His strong arms were frail wings now, and his legs bulged with varicose veins from being manacled to the bars of his cells with only the tips of his toes touching the floor.

"Good morning," he said.

"Good morning, Daddy," Alice Colleen said, while Declan and Frankie sat in obedient silence.

"I heard you singing."

"I'm sorry," Maggie said. "Did we wake you?"

"No, I was awake."

Maggie picked up a pan from the back of the stove. Every morning, she served Liam Cream of Wheat with a pat of butter, sprinkle of cinnamon, and lump of brown sugar. Having been starved for the two years he was in prison, he could only eat soft, bland foods.

"Can you read some pages for me today?" he asked.

"Sure. Watch the kids while I take breakfast to Ma and Pa."

She loaded a tray with eggs, bacon, and toast and carried it to the back of the apartments. Tapping with the toe of her shoe on the door, she called cheerily, "Breakfast."

"Come in."

Maggie stepped into darkness that smelled of fermented rose water and half-rotted meat. No matter how many times she laundered the sheets or drew baths for her parents, the smell lingered, as if it had soaked into the wallboards through the years. Ma sat up in bed, while Pa smoked as he sat in a chair near the window. She set the tray on the round table in the corner, then went to the windows to open the curtains.

As she pushed open a window to let in fresh air, her mother fretted, "It won't get too hot, will it?"

"If it does, call me, and I'll come and close it."

"I'll do it."

Her father's rumbled offer was more than she had heard him speak in days. Sometimes, it seemed he seemed that he had nearly disappeared.

"Thanks, Pa," Maggie said gamely.

She knelt by her mother's bed so that the three of them could say grace together. After, she kissed her mother's forehead. Ma looked more like Auntie Eileen every day. Her skin pulled tightly across her face, flattening lips that were once generous and naturally curved up in a smile. If she would only walk outside, Maggie thought, if she would only go to Mass or talk with some of the neighbors. If she'd only take the time to look at the little border of zinnias that Maggie had planted along the south side of the store, or read the newspapers with the zeal that she'd possessed during the war. But she laid in bed day after day, her only bright spots the few minutes that Seaney stopped by before he went out on his beat, and the few minutes per week that Kathleen could spare for her from being the Grand Lady of all Grand Ladies.

When Maggie came back to the kitchen, she found Liam and the children eating in silence. As she started to gather up the plates to wash them, she heard Kieran crying in the bedroom, awake and hungry for his first meal of the day.

Late that night, Maggie sits in the back yard, overlooking the tangled and unkempt Liberty garden, which has been pecked at by starlings and mowed down by rabbits until nothing much grows there but weeds. The night has cooled with a breeze from the east, where heat lightning dazzles the sky over the Eastern Plains. She lights a cigarette and takes a slow, languid drag from it. The fresh air, the quiet rumble of distant thunder, the whistle of a train far to the north remind her of when she was a girl, playing with Seaney in the back lot until Ma threatened their hides, or in the pastures of Redlands with Seaney and Kathleen, where they could run wild without fear of reprisal. Before they were married, she and Liam would walk the neighborhood on a night as lovely as this one and end up in the shadows beneath the outdoor steps of the apartments, all hands and lips and desire.

But those days have long since passed. Maggie and Liam had had only ten months together before he became a prisoner of the military. Some of those months had been taken up by his trial and time at the Denver County jail, the rest by an anxiety that gnawed away at her soul at the same time that Alice Colleen thrived in her belly. And now, her duties and chores take up everything—her energy, her ability to think, her patience.

In her lap are the pages that Liam has given her to edit. On the top sheet, he has written: *"Some ask me why I would be willing to cause suffering to my wife and child by clinging to an abstract principle and refusing to enlist. To that I must reply that there is no proof that I caused either my wife or my daughter, who was born after I was jailed, suffering. But had I gone to war, I most definitely would have caused them grief. Even if I had come home unharmed and whole, the fact that I would have killed and injured other men for the benefit of an abstract principle put forward by a distant and detached leader such as President Wilson would have caused them—and me—great suffering. A man cannot harm his fellow men without the laws of justice and fairness catching up with him at some later time in his life."*

Does Liam truly believe that? His absence from Alice Colleen's first years, the blankness in Maggie's life that left her straddled between survival and defeat, the silent nights when she longed for his touch—wasn't that also suffering of a sort?

And is it any better now?

As ashamed as she is to admit it, Liam's touch repels her now. Making love to him has gotten mixed up in her mind with the torture he endured. How can her fingers bring a stronger sensation to the flesh on his back than the thud of a blackjack? How can her kiss heal lips that were repeatedly cracked open by blows? She worries that his body is invisibly tainted and defiled, as if the cruelty that he absorbed in his flesh might pass into hers, like a germ or the influenza.

Sometime in the short months between the twins' and Kieran's birth, Maggie had recognized the raw truth: Liam would never be the brilliant wit she married; he would never work in Denver or Colorado again; Sullivan's Grocery would never thrive again; she and the children would be pariahs in Denver, doomed to live haunted lives because their name was Keohane. They would never walk home from church as a proper family of mother, father, and children, or attend school picnics, or musical evenings, or circuses, or enjoy the amusements at White City or Elitch Gardens. They would never, as a family, sit on the stoop in front of the store while the kids draw hopscotch squares with chalk, or play kickball in the back lot, or walk to the lake and back as the sun set behind them.

They would never be the family that Maggie has her heart set on, the one that the characters in her stories, Evelyn and George, possess.

# FOUR

The offices of Graves Industries were housed in one of the most elegant buildings on 17<sup>th</sup> Street. Jim's office, located on the top floor, was equally rich and spacious, with wood-paneled walls, mahogany furniture, and bookcases filled with bound-leather tomes. It was not only the place where he managed his business pursuits, but where his political career had taken root as well. The State Capitol, a few blocks away, was overcrowded, and state legislators from the Denver area were asked to maintain their own offices outside the building. Joel Spratt, his longtime secretary, now shared the ante-room to this office with Nathaniel Thorndike, Jim's legislative assistant.

Now Nathaniel knocked on his door. "Colonel Van Cise is here."

"Show him in, please," Jim said.

Only a few years older than Jim, Denver District Attorney Philip Van Cise was a legend in Colorado. The previous summer, Van Cise had rounded up the Bunco Gang that had been robbing visitors to Denver for years. During Colorado's peak tourist season, confidence men flooded in from Arkansas and Florida. They set up false stock exchange offices, where they lured unsuspecting tourists into investing in stocks through promises that stock prices would rise within the hour. Banking on the average man's ignorance of the workings of the stock market, the gang was able to make thousands in a day.

For years, the Denver Police had overlooked the activity, and the administration of Denver Mayor Dewey Bailey was firmly in the grasp of the criminals. So D.A. Van Cise had recruited Colorado Rangers, whose job it was to patrol Colorado's roads, to serve as enforcers and jailers. Finances were another problem for the underfunded District Attorney's office. Van Cise had contacted thirty prominent businessmen in the city for donations. When the D.A. told Jim that fellow oilman Verner Zevola Reed's widow, Mary, had given $1,500 to the cause, Jim had donated $2,000. At last, the District Attorney's men had raided the hotels and offices of the Bunco Gang. Because he could not use the Denver jail, the District Attorney had converted the First Universalist Church on Colfax into a temporary prison.

Just now, D.A. Van Cise was riding high after the trials of the Bunco Gang, which had resulted in twenty professional criminals landing in the penitentiary in Canon City.

Jim shook the District Attorney's hand. "Congratulations, Phil, on an outstanding success. Please, sit down."

"Thank you. I couldn't have done it without the financial help of you and others who contributed to the cause."

"It was money well spent." Jim offered Phil lemon water from the bar. "I heard that the trials were nearly as thrilling as the arrests themselves. I stopped by one day and couldn't get anywhere near the court room."

Phil accepted the glass. "It was a packed house every day with reporters and spectators who wanted to catch a glimpse of the famous Lou Blonger. Women came to swoon over Jackie French and his mustache." He waited for Jim's laugh. "But they're all in stripes and irons now."

"And at the end of it all, you were hailed as a hero," Jim noted. "For what—the third or fourth time? After the Ludlow Massacre, after your service in the war, after the Tramway Strike, and now this. The newspapers want you to run for Mayor. The *Fort Collins Courier* even suggested governor."

"Bah," Phil huffed. "The next thing I do, they'll be calling for my head."

"That's the way of politics."

"That's what I've come to talk about, Jim. I'm sure you've been following the flap over the Klan meeting at the Denver Auditorium. I know that Ben Stapleton has been a friend of your family's for many years."

"He is," Jim acknowledged. "I'm disappointed that he allowed the meeting, but it's a fine line between freedom of speech and suppression of ideas."

"It was quite a gathering," Phil said. "Nine hundred people attended, about half of them women. The lecturer for the evening was a Klansman by the name of G.K. Minor from Texas. He announced at the beginning that he would not speak against any race or creed, but as a law-abiding citizen. Then he promised that if even one objection was raised, he wouldn't speak at all. And someone did, and many others followed."

"Is it true that three Catholic priests started it?"

"That's right."

One of which was Father Brendan Keohane, the priest at Blessed Savior. Kathleen's connection with Brendan and, more importantly, with Liam Keohane was something Jim had learned about after he and Kathleen had married. When Jim expressed indignation that Kathleen hadn't told him ahead of their wedding, she said that she had never expected Liam to be released from Ft. Leavenworth. She wasn't close to her cousin, Maggie, she claimed, although Jim had noticed that Sean Sullivan graced the Graves' home fairly often. At last, Jim decided it would be best for everyone if Kathleen's family's messy history was kept quiet.

Phil continued. "The Klansmen began to hoot and holler at the three priests and the others, and Mr. Minor thought there might be a riot. He asked the police to escort him out of there. That's when Rice Means, the Director of Safety, closed down the whole shebang."

"It sounds as if it was a terrible lapse in judgment on Ben's part to allow it," Jim agreed.

"A lapse of judgment or a sign of loyalty. Some have said that the meeting was set up with no intention of it ever happening. It was a ruse to allow the Klan to earn public sympathy by claiming that it wasn't allowed free speech."

"Is that what you think?"

"Seems far-fetched to me. I think Mr. Minor gambled and lost when he vowed not to speak in the face of objections. Who would have thought that members of the Catholic clergy would have infiltrated a Klan meeting?"

"I think we've been moving toward something like the Klan for some time," Jim said. "The America First movement during the war seemed to inflame passions against German-Americans, and with the Red Scare so close on its heels, it seems we've returned to the days of the Know-Nothings and the American Protective Association."

Phil took a sip of water. "But weren't you part of the America First movement during the war?"

"Yes," Jim acknowledged. "But I saw it become vindictive, punitive, almost. If someone was not born in this country, they became a suspect."

"You were hailed as the man who put a German spy in prison."

Phil referred to an incident on the eastern plains of Colorado. Jim had witnessed—and been able to stop—the near lynching of an Austrian lightning rod salesman named Emil Reutter.

"I don't believe he was a spy, just a fool."

"He paid for it by being on bread and water in the Denver Jail until his sentencing. But don't be complacent. John Galen Locke is smarter than he appears."

Jim sipped from his lemon water. Dr. Locke, the Grand Dragon of Colorado's Ku Klux Klan, had attracted thousands of members to the organization in just two years.

"Locke is interested in power," Phil continued. "And he'll get it and hold onto it however he can. He has stated that he will not run for office himself, but he will make sure that Klan followers vote for the 'right' men. As we've seen, Mayor Stapleton is one of them."

"And what about you, Phil?" Jim asked. "Are you going to respond to the calls in the newspapers to run for mayor or governor?"

"I have no plans to do so. But I am wondering if you shouldn't throw your hat in the ring as an old-line Republican, a logical choice to counter our current 'parlor Soviet' in chief."

Jim laughed. Governor William Sweet, a wealthy broker with no government experience, had been a Democratic candidate, but it was widely known that his sympathy with the socialist Farmer-Labor party. Talk of Bolshevism had echoed through the state when Sweet took office.

"You're closely allied with Harding, too," Phil continued. "Didn't I see you at Fitzsimons?"

"Yes, you did."

In mid-June, President Harding had stayed in Denver for more than twenty-four hours, the longest stop during his odyssey across America. He had visited the soldiers at Fitzsimmons Army Hospital to reassure them of the government's dedication to the wounded and needy, while Mrs. Harding handed out flowers to each patient. Afterward, U.S. Senator Lawrence Phipps had driven the Hardings around Denver and into the foothills, with an entourage of lesser political figures, wealthy friends and socialites following in a caravan of vehicles. That evening, Jim and Kathleen had attended a reception for the Hardings at the Phipps home.

"I don't think much will change in a year," Phil said. "The country seems to like lower taxes, less regulation of business, and strict immigration rules. It's been a welcome relief from the Wilson Administration's interference."

"Being in the oil business is certainly easier now," Jim conceded. "But I've only started my term as State Senator, and I'm not up for re-election until '26. The people of Colorado deserve a governor with more political experience than I have."

"Think about it, Jim." Phil rose from his chair. As he and Jim walked to the waiting elevator, he said, "I read in the newspaper that you have a new baby in the house."

"A daughter, Susanna, who is already eight months old."

"Time goes quickly when they're that age, even if you wish it wouldn't." Phil shook Jim's hand and boarded the elevator. "My congratulations to you and Mrs. Graves. It's a fine thing to have a daughter to dote on."

It was true, Jim thought as he walked back to his office. Susanna, who had just started to crawl, gave him so much pleasure. Her drooly smiles grew wide when he walked into the room, and when he held her, she cooed happily. He considered Stephen his pride, but Susanna was his joy.

His marriage to Kathleen had turned out well—a surprise, perhaps, for both of them. After a brief ceremony before a Justice of the Peace, their wedding night had been spent in Jim's permanent residential suite at the Brown Palace, which had been specially arranged for the occasion, with canapes and champagne on the sideboard. A Chinese vase teemed with roses, and the satin coverlet on the bed reflected light from the chandelier. The comforts that Jim kept there—his smoking jackets and slippers, the day's newspapers, his brandy and cigarettes—were carefully laid out for him by Harris, who had long since retreated.

When he came from washing up in the bathroom, Kathleen had not yet changed into the satin and lace finery that her maid had laid out for her on the bed. She stood before a trifold mirror, as if admiring herself, but the expression on her face was uncertain.

"What's wrong?" he had asked. "Why haven't you changed?"

"I'm sorry, I—"

"Ssh," he said. "Your modesty is becoming. Let me."

He had stood behind her, his arms around her. As they watched the reflection of themselves, he had taken her hand and removed the tight kid glove, tugging gently on each finger to free it. Raising her hand to his lips, he kissed each of her fingertips, his eyes meeting hers in the mirror. He did the same with her other hand, then kissed her jaw and neck. Her breath grew rapid with desire, and she turned toward him.

"You're beautiful, Mrs. Graves," he said. "So beautiful."

Only after they had made love, and they lay in bed, with her head nestled in the hollow of his shoulder, and her hair spread in wild curls over the pillows, did Jim raise the question of her past. Smoothing back her hair with one hand, he asked, "This isn't the first time for you, is it?"

Silence swelled in the room before she whispered, "No."

"The ambulance driver, then? How did that come about with the strict Red Cross rules?"

"I broke them," she said simply.

"And Eleanora? Wasn't she diligent?"

"Oh, yes, of course, but Hank"—her voice cracked at her dead friend's name—"Hank helped me whenever I asked her to."

"Love does find its way," Jim had mused. "No matter how forbidden or how many barriers are thrown up between lovers."

"How did you know?"

"It's something that a man can tell."

"Does this . . . What does this change?"

"Nothing at all. A bit of disappointment on my part, but I really shouldn't have expected anything different. You became a woman of the world in France."

"Isn't that what you wanted? Someone who is your equal?"

"I don't imagine you made love with him for my benefit, did you?"

He had felt the question ripple through her as if it were a blow. But Kathleen rarely backed down. "No," she said, a painful rasp in her throat. "But I learned . . . what I should do. I learned what I want."

Her confession had reverberated through his body, inflaming his desire. Later that night, however, he had realized that the specter of Paul Reston, buried somewhere in France, would creep along with them throughout their lives.

But, then, so would the memory of Anneka.

When he had offered Anneka a place in his home before he left for France, he had been entirely sincere. He wondered now if he had truly loved her or if he had simply felt compelled to make amends. In his heart, though, he knew that it was more complicated. What he had had with Anneka—and what Kathleen had had with Paul Reston—was indelible. First love, ever fresh and enduring because it was first, and because it had not been sorely tested before it had been lost.

A familiar shadow brushed through his mind. Mina would be twelve now, growing into a woman. By the time he had returned from France, with Kathleen and Ellie safely rescued from influenza and war, Anneka was dead and Mina had disappeared. Jim had hired private detectives to find her, ignoring his mother's palpable relief that Anneka and Mina were gone. After Stephen was born, though, he had quietly abandoned the search. They had all gotten what they wanted: a legitimate heir to the Graves empire.

And now, with Colonel Van Cise's suggestion of the governor's office ringing in his ears, there was no room for Mina's memory in his life.

# FIVE

"Look, the line is moving!" Essie said. "Finally!"

She yanked on Mary Jane's arm, and Mary Jane shuffled a few steps closer to the open flaps of the white circus tent. Essie turned around and pulled on Matt's hand. Ross, Mary Jane's eldest brother, inched forward, too. Avery, her youngest brother, pressed in against him.

A sandwich board in front of the tent announced in sweeping, black letters: HEAR THE REVEREND ALMA WHITE, *World's Only Woman Bishop and Founder of the Pillar of Fire Church. Tonight: 'Women in Politics and Religion.'*

"You are going to love this!" Essie snugged Mary Jane's elbow against her side. "I've been coming to Mrs. White's tent revivals since I was a little girl, and they are so spiritual and holy. Once I nearly fainted from the excitement of it!"

Essie had married Mary Jane's brother, Matt, just six months ago. Mary Jane thought wryly that the vows at their wedding should have been switched: Matt should have promised to love, honor and obey, because that's what he did best. In fact, the entire Grayson family bent to Essie's will, and that was why they were here tonight.

Essie spoke again. "Mrs. White thinks women should vote and work and preach and do all the things that you talk about. She says that women were last at the cross and first at the grave. I bet you'll see some of your ladies' group here."

She referred to the National Woman's Party, which Mary Jane had been involved with during the war. Lately, she had stopped attending meetings. Women were given the vote in 1920, and most of them did as they wanted anyway. Besides, so much had happened to the Grayson family since the end of the war that she had not had time to think about grand causes. Mary Jane had recovered from her bout with the flu in 1918, but her father, Amos, had not. The loss of their patriarch had devastated the family. Mary Jane's mother had wrapped herself so tightly in religion that she could barely speak without quoting the Bible, and Avery and Matt had been left to run the family's quarry together. When Ross came home, he had assumed control of the business. Used to being in charge, Matt had chosen to leave the quarry rather than work as his brother's underling.

Essie jostled Mary Jane forward one more time, and they were inside the tent. Strings of electric light bulbs swayed overhead, and two men fussed over the already red-hot glowing tubes of a Magnavox public address system. More than two hundred wooden chairs squatted in neat rows, nearly half of them already filled. At the front of the tent was a makeshift platform that was large enough for a pump organ and a table topped by a cross and Bible.

An usher in a black robe escorted the Grayson family to a row near the middle of the tent. Mary Jane sat between Ross and Essie, with Avery to Ross' right, and Matt to Essie's left.

When no more chairs could be had, people began to gather along the open sides. Essie trilled, "Oh, look at how many are coming to hear the word of the Lord! Oh, look, look, they're about to start!"

The music of the pump organ resonated through the tent, played by a Negro woman in a flowing blue robe. A man dressed completely in black called out, "We will now sing 'Praise, O, Praise His Name.'"

Mary Jane opened a booklet entitled "Pillar of Fire Praises" that she had been given as they entered the tent. Essie sang in a bright soprano voice, drowning out those around her with her expressions of faith. After four hymns—all with a number of verses—and a lengthy speech by the black-clad man, who introduced himself as Brother Bridwell, a sense of anticipation filled the tent. As people jimmied their chairs and craned their necks, Bishop Alma White came on the stage.

She was grandmotherly and stout. Parted in the middle, her gray hair swept in two wings to a top knot on her head. Her face was pleasantly pudgy, and her eyes behind round, rimless glasses were light and vivid. She moved with a heavy walk, the black of her robe broken only by the thin white band of her clerical collar just below her double chin.

"What a blessing it is to be here tonight!" The microphone screeched, and she backed away from it as the men fiddled more with the glowing box. "What joy I have in talking to you! I started the Pillar of Fire Church right here in Denver about twenty-five years ago, and now it's famous all over the world, thanks to the support of people like you—"

Suddenly, a wave of "ahs" went through the tent. Mary Jane looked over her shoulder toward the back entrance. Avery bounced up on his chair to see, but was quickly hissed at by someone behind him. "Sit down!"

Gliding two by two up the main aisle of the tent were ten men dressed in the ankle-length, white robes of the Ku Klux Klan. As they walked, the robes opened just below their knees, revealing everyday dark-colored trousers and plain leather shoes. Over their hearts was a red insignia with a white "x" inside of it. Their capes billowed behind them, and they wore pointed, white hoods.

Avery's face lit up. "Look at that!"

The Klansmen moved past in silence. At the front of the tent, they split, with half going to one end of the stage and their fellows taking the other end. Bishop White held out her hands to welcome them.

"Bishop White," one of the Klansmen began.

"Speak into the microphone," she said. "Please, over here—"

He stepped toward the microphone but his words were muffled by his hood. "Bishop White, we, the Order of the Knights of the Ku Klux Klan, the Invisible Empire, wish to reverentially offer you a small token of our appreciation for your presence here tonight. With your fine work at the Pillar of Fire Church, you lift up our organization and acknowledge the majesty and supremacy of the Divine Being, and recognize the goodness and providence of exalting Him at all times. Take this donation of fifteen dollars to pay for the rent on the tent and the ground on which it stands and the electricity and other necessities that must be had in order to hold a public gathering to celebrate God's glory."

"Oh, my gratitude knows no bounds." Bishop White accepted the envelope from the Klansman. "Behold," she called to the audience. "You are witnessing an act of charity and kindness by the new Good Samaritans of America, who bring into action the best of man's moral and spiritual fiber."

A second Klansman stepped up to the microphone, his words equally muffled. "I am the Grand and Exalted Gatherer of the Ten Dollar Notes. After the excellent Bishop's talk, I will be outside to speak with anyone who wants to join the mighty army of the Knights of the Ku Klux Klan. To do so, you must be a native, white American, a Gentile and a Protestant, and be of good moral character. The Klan takes only the best people. Please see me after."

"I'll bet he has a grand and exalted dollar sign painted on the back of his robe," Ross whispered in Mary Jane's ear.

She stifled a laugh. She wasn't sure if the Klansmen looked ridiculous or frightening, with their billowing sleeves and capes. But the hoods were daunting. How did they breathe under all that fabric?

Three Klansmen unfurled an American flag as Bishop White intoned: *"'Our Country's Call: Klansmen now are coming; Great and mighty throng, To protect our country Standing 'gainst the wrong. Keep Old Glory waving, Heed the trumpet's call, Klansmen, to our country Be true, one and all, Patriotic heroes count their gold as dross, Standing for their country And the fiery cross!"*

"Amen!" someone called out.

"What do you think?" Essie whispered in Mary Jane's ear. "Have you ever seen anything so thrilling?"

After attaching the flag to a pole, the ten men solemnly marched from the stage. Once they had silently and dramatically exited the tent, Bishop White launched into her speech.

"Two years ago, I spoke on the virtues of the Knights of the Ku Klux and was called a 'mental peewee' by those who cannot tell truth from falsehood. One newspaper reporter even said that it 'was a waste of lather to shave an ass—'"

Essie booed, but Ross laughed.

Mrs. White continued. "There has long been a need in this country for a patriotic organization made up of members who are true Americans and true Christians, and that organization is the Knights of the Ku Klux Klan. But in the same way that Christ was called a law-breaker and trouble maker and was treated no better than a common criminal, the Klansman, who is destined to bring about a mighty revolution in politics and religion, is condemned on a grand scale.

"Do you know what happened just a few days ago at a branch of this church—my church, the Pillar of Fire Church—in Bound Brook, New Jersey? Four hundred faithful and honest men and women were meeting peacefully, when a terrible mob of Catholics, wets, bootleggers, wife-beaters, thieves, and lawbreakers attacked the premises. More than five hundred with evil in their hearts showed up to disrupt the services."

Disgust and disapproval rumbled through the tent.

"At last, the local police showed up to hold the menacing crowd at bay. They were armed and ready to protect those whom God has enlisted to transform America into a righteous and worshipful land under the illuminating rays of the Fiery Cross. That mob had every intention of striking at the very heart of American patriotism and honor. Remember, those sorts are not our friends, even if they are neighbors or fellow workers. They are foes of freedom, they despise American ideals and American fair play, and they want to destroy those who wish to safeguard the liberties of our nation."

"That's right!" Essie jumped up again, dragging Mary Jane with her. As Mary Jane straightened the sleeve over her sore arm, she saw that hundreds had stood up in anger.

"Didn't something like that happen here in Denver only a few weeks ago?" the Bishop shouted over the fervor. "From what I've heard, at a peaceful and legal meeting of the Klan, which was sanctioned by the Mayor of Denver himself, a band of men who follow the Pope would not let those who stand for true Americanism speak their minds freely—"

She held up her hands for calm, and people took their seats. "But let us not become an angry mob ourselves. A Klansman believes wholeheartedly in the Christian faith, the faith that is moral and just, and has the welfare of the most common of people in its heart. The Klansman believes in the eternal separation of Church and State, and in laws that apply equally to all. The Klansman believes in the freedom of speech, a free press, and free public schools. The Klansman believes that the Bible must be in the classroom in order to raise children with morals and firm beliefs in God."

"Yes!" a spectator shouted. "God be praised!"

Bishop White continued. "The Klan is also criticized for its secretive nature, which is said to hide under masks and robes, but how does it differ from the Knights of Columbus, whose secret ceremonies promote the Pope, the Anti-Christ, whose ambition is to rule the world?"

"You tell them, Bishop!"

"It is true that no citizen of foreign birth is eligible for membership, but that is because this is a great American organization for Americans only. No Jew can join, but that is not because the Klan holds any animosity toward the Hebrew, but because Jews refuse to practice Christianity. Roman Catholics are also excluded, because the Catholic Church longs for the commingling of Church and State, and educates its children in its own schools where the truth of the Bible is not taught."

Another round of "boos" followed this statement.

"As for the colored man," Bishop White said, "the Klan is not anti-Negro, as is so often claimed in hysterical articles in the newspapers, but the Negro's friend. In fact, if it weren't for the white man, the Negro would not be in this country, but would still be acting in the most barbaric ways in the savage jungles of Africa, where cannibalism and polygamy and other cruel and barbarous practices run rampant. Remember this, too—it was the white man who liberated colored people from the chains of slavery, which they were brought to by Ham, one of the sons of Noah."

Mary Jane glanced toward the Negro organist. Her face showed no expression—she had undoubtedly heard all this before. The Klan had often been written up in the newspapers as promoting "race hatred," but the organist seemed neither frightened nor upset.

Mrs. White leaned into the microphone. "The Knights of the Ku Klux Klan believe in the protection of our pure womanhood. They champion the cause of woman and protect her rights. Our sisters, our wives, our daughters will no longer be at the mercy of the lawless element. The white-slaver, the home-wrecker, the libertine, the bootlegger have been warned. Sickness, trouble, and death come to the houses of those who are against the Klan. A new day, the day of righteousness and purity, is dawning, and at its horizon is the white cloud and fiery cross of true, one hundred percent American Klansmen!"

The applause continued long after Bishop White said benediction and left the stage. Mary Jane stood on her tiptoes to watch the preacher woman work her way along the first few rows in the audience, blessing those who spoke to her. Several fell at her feet, weeping and praying.

Exiting the tent took as long as entering it had. When the Graysons at last broke out of the crowd into the cool evening air, Mary Jane realized that Avery was missing.

"He'll show up sooner or later," Ross said patiently.

Essie wrapped her arms around Mary Jane. "It's so much fun having another sister. You'll have to come to Fletcher and meet my sister, Judith, and her little boy. You'll love them!"

After Matt kissed Mary Jane's cheek and said goodnight, he and Essie left, bound for Aurora, or Fletcher, as some of the old-timers called it, in their own car. They had moved there after their marriage, and Matt had taken a job with Essie's father at the dairy farm where the Edwards family had lived for three generations. Mary Jane supposed she didn't blame him for leaving, but Matt had been the only one of the siblings who shared their mother's deep religious beliefs. Now, Mary Jane had to listen to it all.

As Ross watched Matt and Essie walk down the street, arm in arm, he asked, "What did you think?"

"Essie nearly pulled my arm off with all that jumping up and down," Mary Jane said. "Bishop White didn't talk much about women, though."

"I think she was so excited by the Klan donation that she forgot what she meant to say," Ross said. "But that was the longest hour I've ever spent."

Mary Jane laughed. Around them, the crowd was rapidly thinning, carrying with it the excitement and energy of the evening. Avery sauntered out from behind the tent.

"Where have you been?" Ross asked.

"I was talking to them. They have another little tent set up in the back. I think I might join."

"I'd go to a meeting first," Ross advised. "See what happens there. If it's the same as what we just heard, what's the point?"

"Oh, it's more than that," Avery said. "They're a law and order organization, and they're helping the police clean up Denver. They've got field men working in every part of the state, and the Klan is growing like a weed here in Colorado, so the bootleggers and criminals don't stand a chance. But they don't allow anyone at their meetings unless they've joined. It's that tight of an organization."

Mary Jane opened the door of Ross' car, while Avery hopped into the back. "Did you see their faces?" she asked. "Did they take off their hoods?"

"No, but wasn't it fine when they gave that money to Mrs. White? That's the kind of thing they do, give money to churches that deserve it."

"We do that every Sunday, and we don't need to wear masks," Ross grumbled.

He guided the car onto the street, headed toward the Graysons' home in Littleton. Avery leaned forward from the back, so close that Mary Jane could feel his hot breath on her shoulder.

"You heard Mrs. White," he said. "The Klan has been talked down since it started by the wets and fish eaters—"

Mary Jane laughed. "What are those?"

"Catholics," Avery said. "You know, they have to eat fish on Friday—"

"Did you just learn that from the Klansmen?" Ross asked.

"Sure, but you heard Mrs. White talk about what happened in New Jersey, and how the Pope wants everyone in America to be a Catholic so he can get more money—"

"And Bishop White wants everyone in America to be a Protestant so she can get more money," Ross said. "What's the difference?"

"Well, because she's right. You don't see Protestants drinking wine by the gallon even though there's Prohibition that everybody else has to follow. Did you know the Catholics own all the stills in Denver? All those Italian bootleggers are Catholics, and the Pope gets a share of whatever they sell. You know, just a couple of months ago, some priest was arrested for selling $20,000 of bootleg whiskey."

Mary Jane had no argument. She had read in the newspapers that the Italians in North Denver sold liquor and drugs along with the produce they grew in their fields. It had never occurred to her that the Catholic Church reaped a reward from it.

"They worship the bones of old saints and burial clothes and beads and stuff," Avery said. "It's hocus pocus."

"You certainly got an education tonight," Ross commented. "Too bad you didn't listen this well when you were in school."

Avery's pouty face disappeared into the blackness of the back seat.

"When I was in France," Mary Jane said, "I was with Kathleen—you know, the one who married Jim Graves. She used to read the Bible with the rest of us, but she went to Mass when we were in New York while we went to the Presbyterian Church." She remembered how jealous she, Hank, and Helen had been because Mr. Graves went with Kathleen to St. Patrick's. "She counted her beads as she prayed, but I never heard her say anything about the Pope."

"Maybe if you'd stayed longer, you would have."

Mary Jane looked out the car window. Her family, especially her mother, had never forgotten that she had been too afraid to stay in France and help with the wounded during the war. Chosen for the Graves Family Foundation Relief Society, she had quickly proven that she was unworthy of the honor.

"I never thought that I was better than Kathleen," she mused. "Although I am a better typist, but just about anybody would have been. She was terrible. But we were equal in the Relief Society."

"And now look at her," Avery said from the back. "She married your boss. Is he Catholic? Don't you have to become one to marry one?"

"I don't know," Mary Jane said. "I don't think they married in a church."

"Your boss isn't a true, 100% American or a Christian as long as he's tangled up with the Catholics. And those kids are illegitimate if their parents didn't marry in the church."

"I was there the day they met."

She remembered the Preparedness Rally, held the week before America declared war on Germany. As Mr. Graves had passed through the crowd—younger then and more handsome—he had asked Kathleen to show him her sketchbook. And then, Kathleen had sent all those sketches to him from France and he had followed her to France like a puppy and its master. Their romance was right out of a dime novel.

With a pang, Mary Jane thought of Anneka, left behind, without anyone to help her, without anyone to see to Mina. What had happened to that little girl? By the time Mary Jane was well, her father was dead, and there was so much that needed tending at home that she never returned to Anneka's smart cottage on Corona Street to ask about Mina. She hoped that Mina had found a family to love her and care for her as Anneka had, as if she were the most precious thing in the world.

She glanced toward Ross. He had not said a word about either Anneka or Mina since his return from the Army. Mary Jane thought of the letter she had written to him revealing the identity of Mina's father. She had not been allowed to send it because the postal worker feared—rightly—that she was ill. After she had recovered, she had torn it up and thrown it in the grate. By then, it was all too late.

"Do you think Essie believes all of this?" she asked him.

"She sure was pie-eyed over it tonight," he said. "I worry about Matt. He follows her like a lost lamb. He'll do whatever she tells him to."

"I bet he's joined," Avery said. "I bet he's a true American, not like your boss, M.J." Lowering his voice, he added, "Or mine."

Ross snapped. "That's enough, both of you. Mom will still be up when we get home, and I don't want her hearing any of this." He threw a glance over his shoulder. "If the Catholic Church practices 'hocus pocus,' what does the Klan do in their fancy get-ups? And Jim Graves and what's-her-name—?"

"Kathleen," Mary Jane supplied.

"—his wife are legally married, whether or not it was in a church, and their children aren't bastards. And ten dollars to join the Klan is more than you make in two weeks, Avery. So think twice about how you want to spend it."

The words echoed through the car. Ross rarely lost his temper. In the back seat, Avery said nothing.

The silence lasted long after the Graysons' neat homestead, with its yellow porch light, came into view.

*******

The next day, as Mary Jane rubs the bar of soap over her palms after lunch in the Ladies' Employee Washroom at Graves Industries, she glances into the round mirror that hangs over the sink. Raynelle stands in her customary place near the door.

Mary Jane thinks about how Mrs. White said that Negroes should appreciate that the Civil War was fought by white men who wanted to free them from slavery. But wasn't it white men who had first put them in slavery?

Raynelle catches the reflection of Mary Jane's eyes in the mirror.

"Hello," Mary Jane says.

Raynelle lets a few seconds tick by before she answers. "You've never spoken to me before."

Mary Jane flushes. "I guess, well, I didn't know, or—"

"I've been standing in the same place for ten years, now."

The scolding stings, but Mary Jane presses on. "What do you do all day? When you're not cleaning for us?"

Raynelle's eyes flick. "I do my job," she says. "Just like you do."

Mary Jane opens her mouth, but nothing comes from it.

"You're gonna be late, Miss Grayson, if you don't hurry."

# SIX

"You can see why we have approached this project with such enthusiasm."

Miss Anne Evans, one of the founding members of the Denver Art Association, spoke. She wore a lace shawl around her neck, and her whitish hair was pulled back severely from her face. She was known throughout the city as an unstoppable force, a patron of opera houses, the Carnegie libraries, and the Greek temple amphitheater built in 1919 in the newly-named Civic Center Park. Today, her audience consisted of a number of artists, including Kathleen, who had gathered for a tour of the Chappell House on 13th and Logan Streets.

"Let's start on the third floor."

Miss Evans stepped up a dark-stained, oak staircase that seemed to hang on its own in the air. The Chappell House was a red sandstone mansion built in the 1880s. Denver's Capitol Hill was rife with homes constructed by gold and silver barons, each one exquisite—the forty-room Kountze house; the Fletcher House, which boasted a roller skating rink on the third floor; Maggie Brown's house with its watchful lions perched on the porch; and, of course, this great house that had recently been bequeathed to the Denver Art Association.

The third floor opened onto a grand ballroom. Miss Evans waited until all the artists were assembled before she continued. "We envision this room not as a gallery, but as a place of teaching. The Chappell School of Art will employ our finest artists—John Thompson, Robert Graham, and David Spivak."

David Spivak, whose father, Charles, was the driving force behind the Jewish Consumptives' Relief Society, nodded his head.

"The school will include a research library, and the smaller rooms that open off of this area will be redesigned as studios for our artists."

Another round of applause echoed in the forty-foot room.

Miss Evans continued. "There is one further announcement I would like to make. As you know, the Denver Artists Club was founded in 1893 by myself, Miss Elisabeth Spaulding, Mr. Henry Reed, and seven others. We became the Art Association after the Great War to acknowledge the professionalism of the growing regionalist art movement in Denver. I would like to announce a further change of name. The Denver Art Association will now be known as the Denver Art Museum. Welcome, founding members."

Mr. Spivak shook Kathleen's hand. "Congratulations, Mrs. Graves, on being a founding member of the Denver Art Museum."

"Thank you," Kathleen said. "The same to you."

"Refreshments will be served in the Gold Room downstairs," Miss Evans called. "Please make your way there if you like, or take your time and enjoy the art in the downstairs galleries."

The Gold Room, named for its décor, could be found on the first floor of the house. Tables with punch and hors d'oeuvre graced the corners. At the far end of the room, white marble steps led to a glass-domed conservatory, where exotic palms and orchids clustered around marble fountains. Captivated by the smell of wet, fresh soil and the spice of exotic plants, Kathleen walked the length of the room, to where a mirrored wall effectively doubled the grandeur of the garden. To think that this existed in Denver, where the soil was so dry that dust swirled through the air.

"While you're here, you must see the tower." Mr. Spivak had followed her. "A previous owner had his child's face sculpted into the stonework around one of the windows. It's a bit of a shock when you first see it, for it seems ghostly, but you'll soon grow fond of the little tyke."

"I'd like to see that."

"May I show you then?"

They returned to the Gold Room, where Miss Evans was announcing, "We will keep this room as it is, for lectures and musical events and such. It is a comfortable venue for entertaining." She spied Kathleen. "Oh, Mrs. Graves, may I speak to you? You don't mind, do you, David?"

"Of course I do. I'm rarely in the presence of such lovely company." He bowed politely. "Another time, then, Mrs. Graves, Miss Evans."

Kathleen joined Miss Evans and her sister-in-law, Cornelia Lunt Gray Evans, by the punch table. Cornelia had retained her dark, sultry looks even as she approached sixty.

"I wanted to speak with you alone," Miss Evans began. "We are planning an exhibition as soon as we have done repairs and rearranging of some of the rooms, and we would love to have one of your works—"

"The sketches that you did in France were so endearing," Cornelia added. "We looked forward to seeing them in the newspapers."

"Thank you," Kathleen said, delighted. "Oh, thank you—"

Miss Evans continued. "But there is something more we would like to ask of you."

"Of course."

"As you know, Denver has a number of excellent artists," Cornelia said. "Why, just look around you—nearly fifty of them are here right now. And most of them are regionalist, painting Colorado scenes and the Indian—"

"But there is one artist in Denver who is internationally-known," Cornelia said. "Her name is Julia Reston. I don't know if you have heard of her—"

"I have." Kathleen spoke in a barely audible voice.

"Then you probably know that she was in Paris at the height of the Impressionist period—"

Something echoed in Kathleen's head: Paul, saying, "It was *la Belle Époque*, you know."

"But she is somewhat of a recluse," Cornelia continued. "And somewhat . . . odd."

Miss Evans resumed. "We would dearly love to have one or more of her works in the collection, if we can possibly manage it. So I have contacted her, and she has agreed to speak to us. I thought it would be nice to take along some of our youngest members to impress upon her the future of this organization. We've asked Elsie Haddon Haynes, and she has agreed to bring one of her landscapes, but we would also like you to accompany us—"

"I can't imagine why you would ask me." Kathleen reached for the back of a chair to steady herself. "With the children, I haven't painted nearly as much as I'd like to, and surely Miss Reston would better respect an artist of her own caliber. Mr. Thompson or Mr. Graham or—"

"Mrs. Graves, are you all right?" Cornelia touched her elbow.

"Mr. Graham and Mr. Thompson are too busy," Miss Evans said flatly. "Besides, you share something else with Miss Reston. Her nephew was killed in the war—"

Kathleen fought to breathe evenly. Surely, they couldn't know that she had loved Paul. Surely, no one knew outside of those who had been in France with her. And, of course, Jim.

"Since you were in France, you might be of some comfort to her. Mrs. Haynes was also in France serving with the YMCA in one of their 'huts.' That is where she met her husband—"

"I'm, I'm very honored," Kathleen stuttered. "I am . . . yes."

"That is good news," Miss Evans said. "The meeting is tomorrow at Miss Reston's home in Park Hill. Shall I pick you up in my car?"

"Yes, thank you."

Taking Cornelia's arm, Miss Evans said, "We will see you tomorrow, Mrs. Graves. Now, we must hurry off to a luncheon of the Library Commission."

Julia Reston's house was a lovely red brick Georgian home in Park Hill. The recessed front door was shaded by a flat door pediment with two white columns. On the top of the pediment, a balcony with railing extended out from the second floor. Directly above the balcony, a gable perched on the roof. On either side of the house, Colorado spruce trees towered, full and bushy, the tips of their branches blue with new growth.

Paul had never been here, and yet Kathleen could almost feel him—

"We're to go around to the back," Miss Evans said apologetically to Kathleen, Cornelia, and Elsie Haynes, a middle-aged woman with soft brown eyes and a gentle expression. Miss Evans' chauffeur followed behind them, canvases in his arms. "It is a peculiar request, but Miss Reston is a peculiar type."

The gate at the side of the house led into a garden that brimmed with lush, blooming plants. The display was as beautiful as that in the conservatory at the Chappell House, but this was outside, amid Colorado's dry heat and unpredictable hail and sparse rain.

"Perhaps this is why she asked us to come in this way," Miss Evans suggested. "This is a work of art in itself."

Cornelia whispered in Kathleen's ear. "Anne is so determined to have an original Julia Reston in the Denver Art Museum that she's willing to enter through the servants' entrance."

Kathleen stifled a laugh.

The back door opened, and Julia greeted them. Kathleen's heart sank at the sight of Julia's eyes. Cool gray-green, shaped like almonds, filled with something more than light—spirit, heart, intellect—they were exactly as Paul's had been. Julia was dressed as Kathleen remembered from the first time she had seen her, at a patriotic rally. She wore a jacket over a man's shirt and a pair of trousers. Her hair was still cropped short and combed back from her forehead.

"Miss Reston," Miss Evans said. "How kind of you to see us. You know Mrs. William Evans, of course"—she indicated Cornelia—"and this is Mrs. William Haynes, one of our talented artists at the Denver Art Museum, and Mrs. James Graves, who is new to our organization. Ladies, this is Miss Julia Reston, whose works of art have been hailed throughout the country and abroad."

Without smiling, Julia shook the hands of each. When she came to Kathleen, Kathleen could not hold her gaze. What did Julia know? Had Paul sent her a photograph of the two of them in France? When she glanced up again, Julia's curious eyes met hers.

"Thank you for coming in this way." Julia ushered them inside. "I wanted you to see my studio first."

The room, which was also the kitchen, smelled of linseed oil and turpentine. Oilcloths spread across the floor beneath a heavy wooden table, and two easels stood in the southwest corner, where the sunlight shone most of the day. Around the walls, half-finished paintings waited for Julia's attention.

"These are lovely!" Kathleen said.

"Thank you, Mrs. Graves."

Miss Evans took command. "As I said, we brought along two of our most talented. If we could just borrow an easel or two"—Miss Evans waved toward the easels in the corner—"we could show you their works."

The chauffeur set Elsie's and Kathleen's pictures on the easels. Elsie's work was of Pikes Peak, painted *plein air* and from a distant perch on another mountain. The colors of the mountains, woods, and field below were soft, pastel, and feminine. Kathleen's work was of the farmyard at Redlands, painted in rich reds and bold blues and greens from the top of the rocky ridge behind the house, where she loved to ride Napoli.

"Where did you study, Mrs. Haynes?" Julia asked.

"At the Herkomer Art School in Hertfordshire," Elsie said. "And in Belgium and Paris."

"Before the war, I assume?"

"Yes, well before the war."

"And you, Mrs. Graves?"

"I'm self-taught." Kathleen realized that her painting looked amateurish and dull next to Elsie's work. "I have no formal training. It's a hobby."

"And how have you signed it?" Julia squinted toward the signature in a corner of the canvas. "K.O'D.Graves?"

"It stands for Kathleen O'Doherty Graves."

Julia's eyebrows lifted, and Kathleen knew that Julia had recognized her. Paul must have sent his beloved aunt her name at some point during the war.

"When I was your age," Julia said, "women weren't welcomed in art schools, even in France, where I lived. The prestigious Académie Julian, where the greatest had learned to paint, charged women twice the tuition for half the instruction. I went there to beg admittance, but the door closed in my face. And still, I painted. There is nothing wrong with being self-taught. And there is nothing wrong with calling art a vocation, not a hobby."

Miss Evans spoke. "As I explained to you on the telephone, Miss Reston, we are here on behalf of the Denver Art Museum to talk about an exhibition that we hope to mount next year at our new Chappell House galleries."

"I assume that you intend for it to be more successful than the Armory Show of 1919," Julia said dryly.

Cornelia snorted, but Miss Evans said in a brittle tone, "Yes, we believe it will be."

"What happened at the show in 1919?" Elsie asked.

"There were . . . problems," Miss Evans said. "Some of it was because of the arrangement—we only had the hallways at the Denver Public Library—and classical art was mixed with Modernist, such as Mr. Thompson's works, and the spectators were seemingly confused—"

"Didn't The Rocky Mountain News call one of Mr. Thompson's paintings a 'downright idiocy'?" Julia asked.

Kathleen raised her gloved hand to her mouth to stifle her laugh. "I'm sorry, I didn't mean to—"

"But that will not happen again," Miss Evans declared. "We have plenty of rooms to create individual showcases for each type of painting, and we will have an opening reception to introduce the artists—"

"I recall thinking then that I would never go to another of those events," Julia said. "Artists are truly hellish people, vainglorious and shallow. I often wished I had never known any of them."

No one dared to snicker, or, it seemed, even to breathe.

Words came unbidden from Kathleen's mouth. "Did you know Manet?"

"No," Julia said, as the others exhaled. "Manet was . . . I believe he died shortly after I arrived in Paris. Why do you ask?"

Because Paul once compared my body to a painting of Manet's, Kathleen answered silently.

"I have always been interested in his work," she lied.

"I believe that it made a stir," Julia said. "He included nudity in his paintings, regardless of the subject matter." Scandalized, the women made no reply, and Julia continued, "If we are finished here, we can move to the parlor, a spot that is—I'm wholly aware—more proper to entertain guests than the kitchen. Rosa will serve tea in a few minutes."

A Mexican woman smiled from near the stove. Kathleen followed Julia, Cornelia, Miss Evans and Elsie through to the parlor.

A grand piano took up most of the space in the long, narrow room, and the walls teemed with paintings—everything from a butterfly resting on a rose, which probably had been painted in the garden of this home, to a street scene in Paris. Kathleen's eyes skimmed from one to another. She wanted to lose herself in them in the way a poor man would cradle gold in his hands.

"Please sit, ladies," Julia said.

Kathleen turned around. A larger-than-life portrait of Paul hung over the fireplace. Paul, in the uniform of a Harjes ambulance driver, Paul with his beautiful eyes, warm smile, strong chin. Grief shuddered through her, moving from her breastbone down into the pit of her stomach.

"Mrs. Graves?" Miss Evans asked from the settee.

She looked around—every eye was on her. "I'm sorry." She took a seat on the sofa next to Elsie. "That portrait is so . . ."

The words hung in the room.

"That is my nephew, Paul," Julia said.

"We are sorry for your loss," Miss Evans said. "He was killed quite late in the war, wasn't he?"

Julia studied the portrait. "That's the odd thing. He actually wasn't killed, although I didn't learn that fact for nearly a full year after the Armistice."

"I beg your pardon," Miss Evans said. "I'm mistaken—"

Kathleen could not breathe. Paul could not be alive. Latour, Paul's liaison from the French Army, had come to her, while she was ill in Paris, with the news. He had given her many of Paul's possessions—

"Yes, it was quite the mistake," Julia said. "The plane in which Paul was flying went down behind German lines. The pilot was killed immediately, but Paul was still alive when he was found by a French farmer in German territory."

"That's extraordinary!" Cornelia said. "How did it come about?"

"It's a long story—some might say a comedy of errors—but Paul was identified as the pilot, and the pilot as Paul. But yes, he is alive and well and living with his wife in Paris. They are—"

Kathleen stood up. "Where is the powder room?"

The women stared at her, shocked by her lack of manners.

"Down the hall and to the left," Julia said.

In the bathroom, Kathleen closed the door and leaned against it. Slowly, she slid to the floor, so that she perched on her heels, her body curled, her hands close to her breast, and her knees brought up to her chin. She tucked her face into the darkness.

It couldn't be, it couldn't be, because if it were, her entire life was misdirection, lost opportunity, a sham. Nothing was real, nothing had value—it was all some sort of cruel ruse.

She heard whispering outside the door.

"Mrs. Graves, are you all right?"

She recognized Elsie's clipped British accent.

She had to stand up, she had to walk back out there, to pretend to be interested, to drink tea and talk about art. But she couldn't. She lifted her head. "I believe I've taken ill," she said. "Will you please call my house to have my car brought over?"

"Would you like me to call Mr. Graves as well?"

"No!" Kathleen reacted. Then, "Thank you, I don't wish to worry him."

More whispering.

"Do you want to stay in there?" Elsie asked. "Rosa says you are free to wait in the kitchen. She has tea for you, if it will make you feel better."

"I'll wait in here. Please, give my apologies to Miss and Mrs. Evans and Miss Reston."

She heard Elsie move away from the door. She wanted to rush out after them, furious and vengeful, to run into the parlor and pull down the portrait of Paul, to scratch and tear at it. Why, oh, God, why had he deceived her this way?

After some time, a tap sounded on the door. Someone with a heavy accent—Rosa—spoke. "Mrs. Graves, your car is here."

"Thank you."

Kathleen rose and walked down the hall, ignoring Rosa's wide-eyed worry.

In the kitchen, Elsie took Kathleen's hand. "I hope this is nothing serious. I hope to see you soon."

"Thank you. Good bye."

As Blount opened the car door for her, she thought, I never want to see any of them again, especially Julia Reston.

# SEVEN

The next morning, Kathleen receives a hand-delivered note: "Dear Mrs. Graves, I hope you feel better today. You left your painting here. I would gladly have it delivered to you or, if you like, you may pick it up at my house this afternoon. Sincerely, Julia Reston."

Kathleen reads it again and again, tears blurring the words. She knows she will go. She knows that Julia knows she will not be able to stay away.

She has known that she would return to Julia's since she had left her house.

Kathleen had slept in her own bedroom last night, left to the privacy of her own thoughts—none of which were, or ever could be, comforting. Why had Paul abandoned her? Why had he changed his mind, decided against her? Had it happened when he met the woman who was now his wife? Or was there a darker reason? Kathleen had often expressed that she didn't believe she could love a man who was as damaged as Henri, whose face was mutilated. Perhaps—oh, God, it was too horrible to think!—Paul's injuries were so severe that he believed she would no longer love him.

When Jim had come into the room, after arriving home late from work, she had feigned sleep. Fortunately, the night was hot, and round fans oscillated in all the rooms of the Graves' home, sending out an electric whirr. He could not have heard her sobs.

She drives her car, a bright blue Nash that Jim bought for her simply because he was enthralled by the color, to Julia's house. She goes to the back door, as she and the others had done yesterday, rather than ringing at the front. Julia opens the door before she knocks.

"Please come in, Mrs. Graves," Julia says. "I'm happy to see you again."

"Thank you," Kathleen manages.

Her painting of Redlands still sits on the easel in the kitchen, although Elsie's painting of Pikes Peak is gone. She looks away almost at once from her work. It seems so plain, the work of a simpleton.

Julia speaks. "I suspect that you wonder if you were included in the prestigious group of artists who are founding the Denver Art Museum because of your own artistic merit or because of your husband's money."

Kathleen inhales in surprise, shocked by Julia's tactlessness.

"I saw your expression yesterday when you looked at Mrs. Haynes' painting," Julia says. "You thought it was better than yours, didn't you?"

"It was," Kathleen admits.

"Yes, it was. Her Colorado landscapes are elegant and masterful."

Kathleen does not venture an opinion.

"But all artists—whether truly good or simply well-trained—can paint landscapes," Julia continues. "*Plein air* artists nearly outnumber the wild places left in Colorado. But art should be an interpretation of reality, a translation of the mountain or field from the artist's unique experience or perspective. Consider this—how can a static, painted landscape compare with what is actually outside our front door?"

"You don't think that a faithful rendering is true art?"

"I think it is easy art."

"Art is never easy. Realizing her rudeness, Kathleen asks, "How were your paintings received at the 1919 show?"

"I had only one." Julia lifts a painting onto the easel where Elsie's work had been yesterday. "I painted it after my beloved, Francine, died of tuberculosis. What do you think?"

Two solid blue figures—women, with Egyptian-like, cylindrical headdress and featureless, silhouetted heads and shoulders—face one another across the width of the canvas. The woman in the left-hand corner floats beyond the other, her outstretched arm on another plane, too high to be grasped. The woman on the right-hand side of the canvas moves directly ahead, on a path clearly defined for her, which her companion seemingly cannot see or travel. Painted in thick, unforgiving strokes, the background is a field of yellow, golden in some places, jaundiced in others.

"It's lovely," Kathleen says.

"Is it?"

Kathleen realizes that Julia expects an answer, not further compliments. "In a way," she admits. "But it's also harsh and disturbing. What does each one want? Why can't they see each other? How can they be so close and yet so far apart? There's so much longing—it makes me sad, it makes me hurt."

Julia smiles. "I believe this painting was referred to as an 'outrage cluttering the walls of the public library.'"

"I'm so sorry."

"But you see, this is what art is. Expression, thought, feeling. It makes no difference what others say—let them disparage it—as long as it is truthful. Do you think your painting is truthful?"

Kathleen studies her painting of Redlands. "It was at one time. That view is from my favorite place to sit on my father's—on my—ranch."

"But it isn't truthful now?"

"I don't believe I am that . . . No."

"Then I would say this to you. Your art must come from deep within, from your most elemental feelings, from the very root of your thoughts. For you, it must come from your enduring passion for a man you have thought was dead for the past five years."

Kathleen's intake of breath comes as a sob.

Julia offers no comfort. "There can be only one woman by the name of Kathleen O'Doherty in Denver with extraordinary artistic talent who would lock herself in my powder room at the mention of my nephew."

Kathleen's voice sounds small, desperate. "We were so in love—"

"He wrote that he intended to marry you as soon as the two of you were free of your obligations after the war ended. And now you believe that Paul betrayed you."

"Jean Latour—Paul's aide in the French Army—told me that he was dead. If I had known he was alive, I would have stayed in Paris, I would have refused to come home, I would have done anything—!"

"I cannot offer any solace to you there," Julia says. "But I would ask you to believe that it was the time, the circumstances, the inanity of whole thing that betrayed the two of you. Paul did not betray you any more than you betrayed him by marrying Mr. Graves."

Kathleen winces. "It was more than a year after the Armistice, and I had been home for—"

"From what I've seen in the newspapers, you married an honorable and decent man."

"Tell me what happened to Paul."

"Let's sit," Julia suggests. "I believe Rosa has left us tea and scones, and I suspect that, unlike the Evans ladies and Mrs. Haynes, you have no objection to taking tea in the kitchen."

Kathleen follows Julia to the kitchen table. She wipes away tears as Julia pours the tea. Julia offers her a scone, but Kathleen declines, certain that she will vomit if she tries to eat.

Julia spoons jam onto her plate. "After the French farmer found him, he took Paul back to his house. Because the Armistice was imminent, the good man didn't want to turn Paul over to the Germans, so he decided to hope instead for the quick arrival of the Americans or British. The farmer's wife took as good of care of Paul as was possible, but you saw the state of farmhouses in France—no running water, open sewage, dirt floors, the animals indoors for warmth. Paul's wounds were far too severe to be treated by anyone but a doctor."

"But why . . . how was it reported that he was dead?"

"This is where it becomes confusing," Julia says. "The farmer had plundered the valuables from both Paul and Kenny, as was the custom, I believe. When the Germans found Paul, which they did, only hours before the Armistice, the farmer handed over the pilot's insignia and papers for some reason. Perhaps he didn't actually know whether Paul was the pilot or observer, or perhaps he thought Paul would be treated better if the Germans thought he was a pilot—they had greatly honored Quentin Roosevelt when he was killed. Paul was taken to the prisoner of war camp at Trier, across German lines, where it was believed that he was Kenny."

Kathleen covers her face with her hands.

"In December, 1918," Julia continues, "he was delivered back to the French in an exchange of prisoners. By then, he had contracted something called brain fever. Because he was so ill, with a terrible loss of memory, he could not identify himself. It was another four months before the mistake was corrected."

"But I was still . . . I wasn't married yet in April. He could have contacted me—!"

"He could barely state his own name, much less write a letter. He was far from well, although he was lucky—or so I'm told. The plane broke apart on impact. The front half plowed into the mud of the field, nearly burying Kenny and the fuselage. The tail section bounced, and Paul was thrown free of it. His left arm and some of his ribs shattered in the impact, and there were open wounds as well. But the days that he lay untended in the farmhouse and the German prison took a terrible toll."

"How is that?"

"His left arm was not properly set, so it does not function well. The scars up and down his left side are ill-healed and painful."

"And his face?"

Julia studies her before replying. "I don't believe it was affected. In truth, I don't know."

Kathleen breathes out. "But you said he married. Who is his wife?"

"Ah, yes, Mélisande," Julia says. "She was Kenny's lover in Paris. After Paul was released from the hospital in Paris, near the end of August, 1919, he found her again to tell her that Kenny had died. He discovered that she had had a child, a little boy, whose name is Alex. You remember, don't you, that Kenny's name was actually Alexander McKenzie?"

"I remember."

"Mélisande had no money, and Kenny's family in New York had refused to acknowledge her claim that Alex was his son. She had no word of the fate of her own family. Their estate in Belgium, which I believe was quite large, had been bombed repeatedly during the war, reducing the buildings to rubble and destroying the fields. It was worthless. She was living as she could, so Paul moved in with her to care for her and the child. In return, she nursed him back to health."

"So they aren't married?"

Julia shrugs. "They act as man and wife, and they are raising the child as their own. In a world where nearly everything was torn apart, does it truly matter?"

Kathleen crosses her arms over her breasts and folds her shoulders inward for comfort. "So he had the mental and physical strength to take up with her, but not to write to me? Why didn't he come home? We would have married, we would have children by now, it would have been—"

"Paul contacted me in January of 1920. I believe you were married by that time."

"For one month! If only he had written you one month earlier—"

"Take care, Mrs. Graves." Julia speaks so softly that Kathleen barely hears it. "You must keep in mind your own children when you wish for the past to be different."

"I can't—" She stops, unable to determine what she wants to say. "How does Paul make his living? Is he a lawyer?"

"He is still with the American Expeditionary Force."

"What? How is that?"

"Do you recall the argument in Congress over whether the bodies of American soldiers should be returned home?"

"I do, I think, I—"

"Well, in late 1920, France finally gave in, although not happily. Since Paul was still in Paris, he was asked to oversee the exhumation of those buried on the battlefields and to manage the repatriation of those left behind in American cemeteries throughout France. It all took tremendous time and effort. He was made a Colonel for his efforts."

"Oh, God! Why would he choose that life? To dig up what was left— the wounds were so terrible even when they were alive . . . to relive that horror—"

"Paul has always been a man of bravery and honor. I never envisioned that he might exercise it in such brutal circumstances."

"I don't understand any of this!" Kathleen cries. "How could he have forgotten all we meant to each other?"

"I doubt he has." Julia pushes a folded sheet of paper across the table. "You will want to read this when you're home. I found it in a book that was sent to me when it was believed that Paul was dead. I am sure that he would not mind if I pass it on to you now."

"Thank you." Kathleen clutches the letter against her breast.

"You may go at any time," Julia says. "You needn't worry about proper etiquette with me."

As Kathleen reaches the door, Julia asks, "Why Manet?"

Kathleen turns to face her. "Paul once compared me to Olympia."

"Ah," Julia says. "Yes, I can see that."

Kathleen reads the letter in her studio, a cottage built on the back edge of the property, which is her refuge, away from the needs of the children and her duties to the household staff.

*November 6, 1918*

*My darling Kathleen,*

*I think of you often. You are my solace and my hope. When I see the sky, when it is not bursting with rockets or hazed by acrid smoke but is blue and clear, I recall your eyes, your hair, your lips and skin. I love you with a certainty I've never felt before. I don't pretend to understand it. How is it that love came so quickly to me, and in a moment, at that? For twenty-five years, I've lived alone, always self-sufficient and cool toward any woman who looked my way. I've never thought of marriage, never thought of family or home or children. But since I met you, I dream as I never have before, I feel with such intensity, I think with such brightness. Every bit of me is twice as alive and filled with desire and strength and determination. All because of you.*

*But it's all so dangerous here, and I don't know if I will live through it. Every day, we wake to the probability of death, and every evening when we sleep, it's with the weight of those lost on our hearts. But as this burden of horror grows within me, so does my desire to live. I want to rip off this uniform and run to where you are. I want to hear you talk about anything that has to do with living. I want to hold you, knowing that you can heal me. I want to see the beauty of living again through your eyes and your drawings. It's so easy to forget about life here, so easy to think that it's futile.*

*I just want to love you and never be parted again. God help me to make it back to you.*

*PAUL*

Two days after the letter was written, on November 8, Paul's plane had crashed, and the long comedy of errors, as Julia had called it, had begun.

It can't be, it just cannot be, she thinks. Her tears have dried—or been depleted—and another emotion is rising in her. Mistaken messages, mixed identities—she has heard of other soldiers who have returned after being reported dead, victims of the chaos and devastation of the battlefield. And others—dead, but cruelly reported as alive or, worse, missing, their fates never to be known.

But it cannot have happened to her, to Paul, to the two of them. It is impossible.

"Mommy! Mommy!" Stephen gallops into the studio, his white-blond hair shining in the afternoon sun, his blue eyes crinkled with a smile. "It's a soo-pwize!"

Kathleen slips the letter into a book on Renaissance painting. She swipes at her eyes to brush away the tears on her lashes. "What is the surprise?"

"Come on!"

Taking her hand, Stephen hurries her out of the studio and onto the graveled path that leads up to the pond.

Jim walks down the path, Susanna in his arms, settled contentedly on one of his hips. She reaches out a slobbered-on hand to Kathleen, who kisses it.

"What are you doing down here so late?" Jim asks. "It's almost time for dinner."

"I'm sorry," Kathleen says. "I lost track of time—"

He touches her face. "Have you been crying?"

"No, just . . . it's dusty today."

He glances out into the perfectly still evening. "I told Mrs. Denny that we would take dinner in the gazebo. They're setting it up now. I thought we could enjoy this beautiful evening together."

"Soo-pwize, Mommy!" Stephen shouts. "Soo-pwize!"

Kathleen looks toward the pond. The house is mirrored in the calm water exactly as Jim had planned. Reeds and cattails grow around the banks, and birds sing, hidden in the verdant growth. Now and then, the water ripples as a Japanese goldfish nips at the surface. At the gazebo, the staff bustles around. One of the maids sweeps up leaves from the gazebo floor; another lights tins of citronella oil to ward off the mosquitoes; and a third strings a garland of flowers along the railings. Two gardeners carry in tables and chairs, while another tests the electric lighting. In the midst of it all, the kitchen staff is in a frenzy of figuring out how to deliver the food so it is hot and fresh. So many people in such a bustle to serve one man, one woman, a child who will only peck at the excellently-seasoned food, and a baby who will eat mashed peas and gravy while her nurse stands by to whisk her away in case of tantrum or spill.

*When I see the sky, when it is not bursting with rockets or hazed by acrid smoke but is blue and clear, I recall your eyes, your hair, your lips and skin. I love you with a certainty I've never felt before.*

"Tell them to stop," she says.

Jim turns toward her. "Why? Are you ill?"

"We eat out-sye," Stephen insists, while Susanna sucks happily on three fingers.

Julia's words run through Kathleen's head: *You must keep in mind your own children when you wish for the past to be different.*

Would she trade Stephen or Susanna, these two beautiful lives, for a life with Paul?

Forget, she thinks, you must forget him.

"Out-sye," Stephen says again. "Daddy says we eat out-sye."

"Of course we can eat outside," Kathleen says. "Of course we can."

After the meal, Jim and Kathleen sit at the table in the gazebo, while Stephen and Susanna play on the lawn. Stephen's newest fascination is with standing on his head, although he has yet to succeed. Upside down, his short legs waggle in the air until he tips over.

"Mommy, look at me!" he calls. "Daddy, look!"

"Bravo," Jim calls, while Kathleen applauds his efforts. "Try again. You're almost there."

Susanna, who has just learned to crawl, is on all fours on a blanket. She drops her head to the ground in imitation of her brother, then rolls onto her side, happily kicking her legs and babbling. The children's nurses, Miss Brown and Miss Davis, hover protectively nearby.

Jim lights a cigarette, a glass of his favorite brandy in front of him. "It looks as if the Moffat oil field will be as productive as promised."

The sunlight strikes his face, highlighting the scar that runs from his temple to his chin. Kathleen thinks of Henri's tragedy, of Paul's wounds. How many scars we carry through our lives, both visible and invisible.

Forget, she thinks. You must forget.

"One well has already proved a high grade of oil," Jim continues. "And just about every oil company in the west has scouts in the area now."

"Including yours?"

"Of course. We've leased almost all the rights in the Iles dome, as well as a good number in the Hamilton and Moffat domes."

"Where are they?"

"Near the town of Craig. The problem is transportation. Too bad David Moffat ran out of money before he finished his railroad tunnel."

"I thought the legislature solved that in the last session."

"It did, in a way." He exhales smoke. "When Pueblo flooded last year, Governor Shoup refused to provide relief money for the town unless the representatives from Pueblo and Colorado Springs promised to vote for money for the Moffat Tunnel in return. They'd been holding out, thinking that if travel over the mountains became easier, it would affect them economically. It was a political con game."

"Con game?" she teases. "Have you been talking to Colonel Van Cise again?"

He laughs. "With the money, Rollins Pass will at last be tamed, along with Monarch and Cumbres. One day, going from Denver to Grand Junction by train will be as easy as going from here to Colorado Springs. They were right to be worried."

"One day?"

"The tunnel won't be done for years. The consensus is that the oil wells sunk in the Moffat Field will be capped until there's transportation to Denver or Salt Lake by pipeline or train. It could be some time before anything comes of it."

"Have you started drilling there?"

"Not yet," he says. "I have three geological parties over there, and a few engineers, as well as my land and lease scouts. Early reports say that the sands are deep, below four thousand feet. A test well at that depth costs over seventy-thousand dollars to drill, so I'm not rushing into it."

"Oh, I hope not," Kathleen breathes.

"Don't worry. I'll bide my time before I ship in equipment. But I'd like to see it. They say that Craig has tripled its population in a month. Perhaps I'll go next spring. Do some hunting while I'm there."

There is so much to admire about him—his energy, his determination, his enjoyment of the challenge. She hears Julia's words: *You married an honorable and decent man.*

"You love the chase, don't you?" she asks.

"You should know that. I chased after you for longer than I care to remember."

She laughs, a single breath that hurts as much as it releases.

"There, you're smiling now."

He reaches across the table for her hand, raises it, and kisses her wrist. As the children teeter and roll on the lawn, she thinks, Let me forget, please, make me forget.

# EIGHT

Sean tensed his muscles outside the Jorgenssen pool hall in the hot July evening. His partner, Joe Flannery, pressed his ear against the wall.

"They're drinkin' lively in there," Flannery whispered. "You can hear the clink of glasses."

Sean, Flannery, and six other Denver police officers crouched in the shadows a tumbling-down warehouse that had once served as a livery. Two more patrolmen were stationed at the back of the building to seal off the alley.

A whistle sounded, and Sean forced his way through the door.

"Police! Stay where you are! Hands up!"

Chaos ensued—drinks spilled, chips and playing cards scattered from the gambling tables, and women hid their faces in shame. On the stage, a trio of Negro musicians ended their version of "Bugle Call Rag" on a sour, screeching note. Sean glimpsed a head of flaming red hair and a face freckled brown by years in the brilliant Colorado sun, rushing for the back door, crowding out with the others.

What was Uncle Irish doing here? This was one of the dirtiest places near the rail yards.

"Stay where you are!" he shouted. "Stay where you are!"

While the other patrolmen ripped open the doors of closed rooms, startling men with girls sitting on their knees and high-rolling gamblers, Sean circulated through the crowd, tapping the shoulders of those who threatened to bolt with his club, keeping a wary eye on the ones in the back. "Line up!" he barked. "Line up, single file, hands visible!"

He searched through the low-hanging smoke and confusion for the patrolmen from the back, but he could not spot them.

The owner, Thorge Jorgenssen, shouted, "I have done nuh-sing wrong. Nuh-sing, never."

"Shut up," Sean ordered.

The paddy wagons arrived, their singsong sirens audible from inside the building. People still flooded out the back door, which should have been sealed. Sean headed back to see what had happened to the other patrolmen. As he pushed his way through the crowd, the patrons shrank back against him in a crushing wave. Three robed and hooded knights of the Invisible Empire blocked his path to the back door.

"This is a police raid." Sean forced his way through. "Leave."

"We're here to assist."

"We're the authority here." He could see only glimmering eyes under the hoods. "Who are you? What are your names?"

Behind him, someone oinked like a pig.

"Quiet!" Sean commanded.

"We prefer to remain anonymous in our service to the community," the Klansman said.

"I tell you again, we don't need your help."

"Our help was requested."

He whirled around at a crash behind him. Five more knights charged through the front door of the speakeasy. Armed with axes and clubs, they attacked the bar, smashing glasses and bottles.

"Stop!" Sean shrilled his whistle. "Stop it!"

Two of the Klansmen wrestled Jorgenssen down and pinned his arms behind his back.

"We'll escort this man to jail," one of them said.

"No, you won't. You're violating the law—"

"We are here to help the law." Addressing the crowd, the Klansman announced, "At any time of the day or night, the Knights of the Ku Klux Klan are ready to help with upholding American values and cleaning up vice from our beloved state. We can respond within three minutes to any spot in this city, so lawbreakers beware!"

"De Klan!" Jorgenssen shouted. "De Klan and de god-damned preachers! I have been persecuted since I come to dis town!"

He spat, and one of the Knights gave him a sharp kick. Sean blew his whistle again, and the patrolmen rushed in from the back door. Now, now that the Klan had completed its drama . . .

Who had asked for the Klan's help? The raid had been devised in secret, but it was evident that the knights had known the entire plan. The Klan was sometimes asked to help undermanned sheriffs and police chiefs in small towns, but not the Denver Police. Passing by Patrolman Wells, who had been assigned to the back, Sean asked, "Where were you? Did you know they were coming?"

"Get back to your job," Wells said.

Sean retreated. He caught a ride to the jail by hanging onto the back of one of the paddy wagons. The scene at the police station was nearly as frenetic as the pool hall had been, except that the Klansmen—whoever they had been—had disappeared.

So had Uncle Irish.

After he finished his shift—hours of turning revelers over to the jailers, booking the known drunks and gamblers, and ferreting out false names and addresses—Sean left the station. Driving through Denver, he went not to Mrs. Potter's boarding house, but to his parents' home. He let himself into the store and climbed the indoor stairs that led to the kitchen, avoiding the squeaks and creaks of the old wood as ably as he had when he was young and sneaking out at night.

No one was in the kitchen, and the tea kettle wasn't on to boil. He could hear the tap-tap of Liam's typewriter in the back room—his old bedroom—but he had no desire to see Liam today. Hearing voices, Sean peeked through the door that led to the parlor. Ma sat on the couch, Declan on one side, Frankie on the other, while Kieran slept in his bassinet. Alice Colleen sat on the floor by the coffee table. Her attention—as well as the boys'—was drawn to a tin of buttons that Ma had set before them.

"And you see this button," Ma was saying. "It's got the Irish knot on it. It came all the way from Ireland, it did, on a mighty ship, with my sister Eileen and me and our—"

Alice Colleen smiled up at him, but he winked and held a finger to his lips. Well practiced in keeping silent, she went back to raking her hand through the buttons in the tin.

He found Maggie at the clothesline, fishing newly-washed diapers from a bucket and hanging them on rigid wires that stretched between t-shaped steel poles. Wooden clothespins dangled here and there. Maggie clipped a corner of a diaper to the wire. Her face—so young, still—was etched with exhaustion.

"Give me that." Sean took the other corner of the diaper and pinned it on the line.

"What are you doing here?" she asked. "Why aren't you sleeping?"

"I had a wild night." He fetched another diaper from the pail and fastened it to the line beside the first, so that the two corners of cloth shared one clothespin. "I didn't feel like going home."

"You mean to your room," she reminded him. "So what happened?"

He told her about the raid on the pool hall and the appearance of the Klansmen at the last minute.

"I didn't think the Denver Police bothered to raid pool halls anymore," she said. "I thought the whole city had gone to the dogs. At least, that's what the newspapers say."

"The newspapers and D.A. Van Cise," he said. "No, I figure that Jorgenssen must have been late on his payments to Chief Williams. To top it all off, we'd hired spotters, you know, to go in there and pretend to be customers, so we'd have eyewitness accounts. Anyway, do you think the spotters would give evidence? No, they refused."

"There's no honor among thieves, I guess."

"Don't quote the Bible at me this early in the morning."

"It isn't early, me brother." She hung the last diaper, picked up the bucket, and dumped the water that had collected in it onto the grass. "You've just forgotten what day looks like. Do you have a cigarette on you?"

"Sure."

He lit one for her, then one for himself.

"I saw Uncle Irish there," he said.

She laughed. "Uncle Irish? Gambling and drinking? Well, that *is* a surprise. I hope you didn't arrest him."

"No, there was a slip-up, and he got away. I didn't see him again."

"Well, good. We won't have to hang our heads in shame."

She was teasing, but he, too, was relieved that Irish had escaped. How did that man manage to have money to gamble?

"You don't think he's up to anything else, do you?" he asked.

"Besides bedding his landlady?"

"Mother of God, Mag, watch your mouth."

"Why? The kids aren't around." She shrugged. "I doubt that Uncle Irish has enough ambition to be a true criminal. Since the mighty He-and-She Graves kicked him off Redlands, his worst sin is probably spending more than Jim shells out to him."

It was true that Uncle Irish no longer lived or worked at Redlands, but Sean had the sense that Irish had made the choice himself. He had taken up residence in a boarding house east of Denver, where he seemed to live easily enough, although he never worked. Maggie was right—Jim Graves must pay him something so he wouldn't come calling on them.

"She married Jim just to save Redlands, you know," Maggie said.

"Why do you say that?"

"Redlands isn't just the little farm that Uncle Irish and Auntie Eileen used to own. Kathleen has been buying up all her neighbors. Another eight-hundred acres just last week, which makes Redlands around eighteen thousand acres."

Sean whistled at the figure. "Who told you that?"

"I've seen the public records at the newspaper office. Our little Kathleen is a major landowner."

"She sure isn't the same girl we used to know."

"Not since she became Her Majesty, the Honorable Mrs. James A. Graves."

Sean laughed. "I'd forgotten we used to call him that."

"It wasn't just the two of us. She used to call him that before he gave her the house that Teapot Dome built."

"You don't think he had anything to do with that, do you?"

"Oh, I think they're all crooked in one respect or another. The whole thing is going to blow up in someone's face, and it might as well be Jim Graves."

"That's a bitter thing to say."

"Well, thank heavens Kathleen's not still living here and working at Graves Oil or someone would have to sleep in the old wheat bin."

Sean snickered, but he missed Kathleen—the old Kathleen, the girl from Redlands who didn't care much about anything except her horse and her sketching. Kathleen's time in France had changed her into a glamorous, sophisticated woman. But to marry Jim Graves, that peacock of a man! Sean hated the way Jim strutted about in his house that had so many rooms they couldn't even be counted, and flaunted his elected position as State Senator, and made no secret of his seemingly endless money. Kathleen had grown narrower, less vivid since she married him five years ago. In becoming a grand lady, she had faded away, like colored cloth that had been left in the sun for too long.

"She must love him a little at least," he said.

Maggie laughed. "With all that money, I imagine she does."

"You wouldn't tell your advice seekers to marry for money, Mrs. James," he teased. "You'd tell them to marry for love."

"Yes, I would," Maggie agreed. "But I would warn them to have a good plan in place—a job at the livery stables or the local fish monger's before they married. Then, someday, they too could have a house with a bathroom and a bedroom for each day of the week, just like the Graves." She ground out her cigarette. "So what about you? Why don't you have a girl yet?"

He laughed, but the question stung. He was twenty-four and without a single prospect. "I'm afraid I'm not much of a catch."

"Let's see, what would Mrs. James say to that?" Maggie pondered. "She'd say, 'Dear Not Much of a Catch, You say that you can't find a woman to share your life. Yet you are a grown man who has a good job. You own a car that is not a rattletrap'"—she cleared her throat to indicate that she thought otherwise of his Model T—"'and you visit your mother often enough to be a good son, but not enough so that her apron strings are wound around your neck.' Right?"

"If you say so."

"If *you* say so." She continued. "'Perhaps you aren't a great whale in the sea of life. But without a trout, you cod be a fine catch for an eager young fisherwoman. So if you see a worm dangling before your eyes, *bite*.'"

Sean laughed. He'd forgotten how fun Mag could be. She'd always been quicker than he was with words and humor.

"I'd better go see where the kids are," she said.

"When I looked in, Ma had them all corralled in the parlor."

"So Ma's out of bed? Saints be praised!"

He said nothing. Maggie blamed their mother's illness—whether feigned or real—on him. It had started after he had enlisted in the American Expeditionary Force and shipped out to France.

"I should go say hello before I go home," he said.

"Let's walk around and go in the front. It takes longer."

They made their way around the far side of the store, passing by the idled delivery truck. A copy of the morning edition of the *Denver City Daily News* lay at the foot of the wrought iron steps that ascended from the outside to the Sullivans' apartments.

Maggie picked it up and unfolded it. "Well look at this."

The headline read: KLAN GRAB NETS BIG GAMBLERS.

She skimmed the article. "There's only one mention of the Denver Police. Are you sure you were really there?"

Sean had just rolled out of bed on Tuesday afternoon, when a knock sounded at the door of his room in Mrs. Potter's boarding house. He pulled on a pair of trousers and buttoned up a plain blue shirt over his undershirt. It was his day off—he didn't have to patrol the silent streets of Berkeley Park tonight. Opening the door, he came face to face with Tony Necchi.

"Holy mother of Mary!" Sean shook Tony's hand. "I never expected to see you again."

"Yeah, well, nobody did after that day at St. Mihiel."

"How are you? Come in."

"So this is where you live?" Tony's Italian accent—shaded by Brooklyn's tenements—was as heavy as it had been five years ago. "Not much better than the trench."

"The rats are smaller."

"Your landlady said you were still in bed. Why are you sleeping now?"

Sean searched through his drawer for a clean collar. "I work at night. I'm with the Denver Police."

"The police!" Tony snorted. "That don't seem right."

"Right or not, that's what I do." Sean attached the collar. "Let me finish up here, and we'll go to the diner across the street. They don't mind if I order breakfast at three in the afternoon."

Tony followed him down the stairs. On the street, Sean noticed that Tony walked with a lop-sided gait, a result of being shot in the leg in the war. The bone had broken, and Tony had spent months in traction. Sean glanced toward Tony's wrist. Although it was hidden by Tony's jacket sleeve, there must be a scar where barbed wire had torn open a long gash. At the diner, Sean waited until they'd been served coffee to ask, "So why are you here?"

Tony dropped sugar cubes into his coffee. "Well, you know, before I went to France, I was working for the telephone company in Brooklyn and living with my brothers, Guarino and Pietro."

"I remember that. You planned to go back to work there. What happened?"

"I did. I been working there, but everybody has a phone now in Brooklyn. But they say lots of people here don't have phones, so I come here to work some more. I'm gonna work for the Mountain States Telephone and Telegraph Company now."

"You can't still be climbing up and down telephone poles with your leg, are you?"

"Sure," he said. "I can't walk so fast or straight, but I can still string wire. Hey, I don't see no Indians or buffaloes out there. Where are they?"

"You're about forty years too late for that. They're all gone."

The waitress brought their plates—both of which were filled with breakfast food—and poured more coffee for them. Sean thanked her, while Tony gave her a look that seared. Sean shook his head as she fluttered away.

"Still after the women?" he said.

"Why not?" Tony said. "I thought you'd be married with six kids by now."

"Not for lack of trying," Sean grumbled. "Why aren't you?"

"Too busy."

Sean chuckled. "Where are you living?"

"I live over in Highlands, just east of here."

"Little Italy, huh?"

"Guarino, he knows a good family up there that used to be in New York, with a room to rent." Tony glanced out the window. "Everybody's a farmer up there. They leave Italy, where everybody's a farmer, and they come here and become farmers. Not me. I done enough of that when I was a kid."

"There are plenty of bootleggers in Highlands."

Tony shrugged. "Say, do you know anything about this Ku Klux Klan? Everybody hates them up there. Somebody told me they come and shoot out our windows, then say it's us who are doing it and that we should be arrested."

"Are you sure it isn't the Roma family saying the Klan did it?"

"Naw," Tony said. "So maybe the Roma boys make some wine or something for the Church, but they're just trying to make a living like everybody else."

"They're trying to make a better living than everyone else, you mean," Sean corrected. "And it's the whiskey and gin that gets them in trouble, not the wine, along with the trail of bodies they leave behind. Is everyone over there involved in some kind of underworld fight?"

"It's just like the Church—you go to Mass hoping the priests are right, so that when you're dead, you end up in heaven. Here, you choose which family you like and hope you don't end up dead."

Sean laughed. "Well, in my neighborhood, Berkeley Park, we've got the Jews to the west of us with their bootlegging and the Italians to the east with their heroin."

"Yeah, and the Irish in the middle buy it all up."

Sean laughed. "I would have beaten the tar out of you for that five years ago."

"Naw, you never would have beaten the tar out of me, 'cuz I would have beat the tar out of you first. I'm not . . . . what was his name?"

"Danhour."

"Right," Tony said. "You and him, the heroes from Company C."

Sean shrugged. "Do you ever think about what we did in France?"

"Naw," Tony said. "I did what I had to do, just like you did, just like all of them did, even the Germans. I got to be an American citizen for it, too."

Sean felt a flash of envy at Tony's apparent peace of mind. "I'll take you over to meet my mother. I've told her about you."

"She won't care if I'm a wop?"

"As long as you're Catholic," Sean said. "It's pretty crowded over there, so don't expect too much. My sister Maggie's husband and kids live with Ma and Pa, all of them on top of each other."

"So send the kids to sleep in the barn," Tony said. "That's what my Mamma did."

"It doesn't work that way in America."

"So make the barn into a house."

"That's not a bad idea," Sean acknowledged. "Come over around six. You can stay for dinner. Mag always makes plenty of food."

# NINE

With Frankie settled on her hip, Maggie sprinkled water onto the surface of the black stove to see if it was hot enough to cook. If the stove wasn't, the sidewalk outside would probably be. It would be warm in the shed tonight, and she had a full load of letters to write.

She plopped a chunk of meat into the cast iron frying pan as Frankie started to caterwaul again. "Now, now," she said. "I've told you, the sooner we get this done, the sooner we can eat."

Sitting at the kitchen table, Declan imitated his brother, their cries ringing in tandem. "What's wrong, Declan?" she asked. "Shh, you'll bring the whole house out to see what we're up to."

The whole house. Actually, she wouldn't mind if Ma came out—she could use a hand with the boys. It was Liam that she didn't want to disturb. Whenever he was roused out of Sean's room, where he worked during the day, he gave the kids and Maggie a sound talking-to, which, although never in a loud voice, made Maggie feel as if she had failed him.

"Alice Colleen," she said. "Give him a cookie and see if he'll stop."

Alice Colleen dutifully leaped from her chair, where she had been drawing on a sheet of old butcher's paper ripped from Pa's supply downstairs. Pulling the chair over to the cupboard, she fished in the cookie tin and handed Declan a crumbly cookie.

He put it in his slobbery mouth, then dropped it and wailed again.

"He doesn't want it," Alice Colleen said.

"Well, then—"

Maggie stopped. Someone was knocking on the front door, which led to the outside landing. She expected Seaney for dinner—he always came over on his nights off—but he usually didn't knock.

"Go see who that is." She directed Alice Colleen over the cries of both boys. "It's probably Uncle Seaney."

"Uncle Seaney!" Alice Colleen skipped out of the kitchen.

Maggie turned back to the frying pan. "Frankie, settle down." She shifted him on her hip. "Let Mommy finish dinner."

The kitchen door opened, and a dark-complexioned man strode into the room, Alice Colleen on his heels. Before Maggie could turn from the stove, he said, "Here, give him to me," and lifted Frankie out of her arms. He walked out of the kitchen, leaving the door swinging on its hinges. Alice Colleen gave her mother a puzzled look before she trotted along after the man.

"Alice Colleen, come back right now!" Maggie shouted.

She grabbed a frayed kitchen towel and pulled the frying pan from the heat. One of her fingers touched the handle, and she brought it to her mouth, sucking at the burn. Shaking off the pain, she scooped up Declan and ran toward the parlor.

The man stood in front of a collection of family photos. In his arms, Frankie was stunned and silent. "Look, there's your uncle Sean when he was a soldier." The man wore a suit, as if he were going to church. His slicked-back black hair smelled of pomade. He pointed at a portrait of Ma and Pa on their wedding day. "Who's this?" he asked Frankie. "Is that your *nonna*? Your Grandmama?"

"What are you doing?" Maggie demanded.

He gazed at her with nearly black eyes. "You looked like you needed help."

Maggie's hackles rose. He had a swagger to him, as if he always thought he was right.

"Who are you?" she asked.

"I'm Tony. Didn't Sean tell you I was—?"

"Tony."

Seaney stepped through the front door, wiping his boots on the mat. Frankie held out his arms to his uncle, and Seaney took him from Tony. At once, Frankie whipped around to stare at Tony, still dismayed. Alice Colleen gave Seaney a military salute, which he had taught to her.

"At ease, Private Alice." He returned the salute. "Give Sergeant Necchi a salute, why don't you? He was in the war, too."

Tony saluted smartly. "Sergeant Antonio Michael Necchi, at your service."

Alice Colleen giggled. The name, spoken with a flourish, sounded almost musical.

"Would you like to introduce me?" Maggie asked hotly.

"Sorry," Seaney said. "This is my sister, Maggie Ke—"

"I'm Margaret James." She had no desire for this irksome man—a veteran—to know that she was married to Liam. "I'm Mrs. James," she repeated, adding, "I write The Thinking Woman column for the newspaper."

Tony skewered Maggie with his dark gaze. "What do you think about?"

"Seaney, is that you?" The call came from the back bedroom. Ma was awake.

"I'll be right back." Seaney set Frankie on the floor. "I need to say hello to Ma."

Frankie took refuge in Maggie's skirt, hiding behind her knees and peeking out at Tony, who grinned at him. The burn on Maggie's finger stung—she needed to run some cold water on it and dress it with iodine and gauze. Just then, Kieran woke with a wail.

Maggie set Declan on the floor and picked up the baby from the bassinet. Holding him against her shoulder, she rocked him back and forth. All this fuss, all this noise—she was worried that Liam would find it too much for his nerves.

Seaney came back into the parlor. "I invited Tony to dinner. Ma's coming out for it. We'll be outside until it's ready."

Maggie flashed him a blazing look. "I'll set an extra plate, then. Come on, Alice Colleen—"

"Can I go with them?"

"No," Maggie snapped. "You need to help me set the table."

In the kitchen, Maggie fed the twins crackers to stave off another dual tantrum. Kieran lay on a blanket in the corner, a pacifier in his mouth until she had time to heat up milk for him. Maggie fried another piece of meat that she'd cut off the side of beef hanging in the cold storage downstairs. Seaney could have telephoned, at least, so she wouldn't have been so alarmed by Tony's arrival. Her heart still hadn't returned to its normal rhythm. She wouldn't have looked such a fright either—she couldn't even remember if she'd combed her hair that morning, and her dress was a stained calico rag that had lost its color, shape, and fashion during the war.

Alice Colleen jabbered on as she carefully positioned the plates and silverware on the table. "Do you know Sergeant Neck-ey, Mommy? He's so tall! Do you think he likes carrots?"

"I need to take dinner to your father," Maggie said. "Watch the boys."

Liam was reading in the chair in the corner of his study. "Who's here?" he asked. "I heard a man's voice."

"A friend of Seaney's." Maggie set the tray in front of him. "They were in the war together."

"I wonder how he feels about it now. Have you talked to him?"

"He just got here," Maggie protested. "He and Seaney went outside."

In the kitchen again, Alice Colleen asked, "Can I sit next to Sergeant Neck-ey?"

"Why do you want to do that?" Maggie asked. "You usually sit next to Uncle Seaney."

"I like him."

"If you want." Maggie turned back to cooking.

Tony lingered after dinner, entertaining them with stories about Seaney's and his adventures in France—sleeping with chickens roosted on their backs or pigs snorting next to their heads in the barns of French farmers; staying at boarding houses with six to a bed; seeing the great cathedrals of France; and playing baseball or cheering on the American military bands during regimental competitions with the French. Maggie had read most of the stories in the letters that Seaney had written home, but Ma, who Tony called "Bella Signora Sullivan," acted as if each were new and fresh.

"What happened to your leg?" Ma asked.

"I got shot at St. Mihiel. Me and Sean was running up a hill that most of them got killed on before they got to the top, and I got stuck on barbed wire and shot in the leg. Sean went on to get a medal while I went off to get my leg stitched back together. But they didn't take the bullet out. So I got my medal from France, too. It's just in my leg."

As Ma laughed in a young, flirty way, Tony winked at Alice Colleen, who was listening wide-eyed to the story. Alice Colleen's face turned as red as Kathleen's used to when she was a little girl. Maggie guessed it was his smile that stirred up so much excitement. He smiled with his mouth closed, curving his lips upward on only the left side so that a dimple formed in his cheek. It was the smile of a man who knew how handsome he was.

He was still at the Sullivans when Maggie took her spot in the shed where she typed her letters. As usual, she had put Alice Colleen in charge of listening for Frankie, Declan, and Kieran, but tonight, she had also left the windows in the apartments open with the hope that a breeze might cool the stuffy rooms. She would be able to hear if anyone stirred.

Tony and Seaney were somewhere on the back of the lot, talking in low voices. Maggie couldn't catch their words, but every once in a while, cigarette smoke wafted in her direction. She knew that they were passing a bottle of alcohol back and forth.

In her shed, Maggie focused on the letter in front of her: *Dear Mrs. James, Try as I might, I have not met any ladies who might be suitable partners for me. I am well-employed and have read a goodly number of books—*

Tony came into the shed behind her. "Sean says I can find a shovel in here."

Maggie kept typing, but pointed with her chin. "In the back."

"Why are you working out here? Why do you work at night?"

Instead of answering, she parried. "Do I need to go inside and count my children to see if you've snatched any away lately?"

Tony gave a snort. "I thought your little boy might burn himself if he kicked too hard. I thought you might burn yourself."

Maggie curled her hands over the typewriter keys to hide the bandage on her finger. "I am perfectly capable of doing my jobs. He wasn't in danger."

"Maybe not, but you just don't know."

His accent added a physical weight to his words: *You chust a-doh-noe.*

Without waiting for her reply, he added, "I got eleven kids in my family. I'm number three. We all take care of each other because Mamma don't have time to do nothing but pray that she don't have no more babies. I know what I'm doing."

Maggie's dislike of him flared again. "The shovel is back there."

She went back to typing, pecking away at the stiff keys as Tony dug around in the junk in the back of the shed. She didn't hear him come out again—he must move silently—but she could sense him standing just behind her, and she could smell his pomade.

She had a choice. She could ignore him or she could confront him.

"Are you two burying a body back there?" she asked.

He was standing with his left foot turned slightly outward to relieve the pressure on his leg, his weight centered over the right leg. "Sean wants to see how tough it is to dig. He's thinking of building a house."

"A house?" Maggie glanced toward the door. "For himself?"

"Naw, for your parents, so they aren't crowding in on your kids." He put both hands on the handle of the shovel. "So, you never answered me. What do you think about?"

"I write an advice column." He looked confused, so Maggie explained, "What they sometimes call a sob sister here, or an agony aunt in Britain."

"I never been there, only to France."

"People write to me about their problems, and I offer solutions for them."

"You tell them what to do?"

"Well, no, yes"—she herself was confused—"I suggest the actions they might take to fix the problem. They can do it if they want to or they can ask someone else. They don't have to do it."

"Which newspaper is this?" Tony asked. "I don't read nothing but *La Frusta*."

"What?"

"*La Frusta*, the Italian newspaper—"

"Well, I certainly don't write in Italian. I write for the *Denver City Daily News*."

"Never heard of it." He nodded toward the typewriter. "How do you know what to say?"

"I beg your pardon?"

"How do you know what to say to somebody about their problem?"

"It's mostly common sense."

"But you don't know these people," Tony objected. "You don't know what they're really like or what they're thinking."

"They tell me what they're thinking."

"What they're really thinking? Or just what they'd tell their mammas or their priests?"

"I have to trust them," she said. "Besides, why would they lie when they write a letter asking for help? It defeats the purpose."

Tony eyed the letter beside the typewriter. "So what's that one say? What did you say?"

She started to hand it to him, but asked, "Can you read English?"

"Not as good as I talk it."

Maggie snickered. "This gentleman says he can't find anyone to marry. I told him to start attending church and concerts and the opera—"

"The opera?" Tony snorted. "Who'd go to that?"

"An Italian, I'd think."

"So, what if there's something this man don't tell you?"

"Such as?"

"You said he's a gentleman. How do you know? Maybe he's mean or drunk. Or maybe he can't find a wife 'cuz he's ugly or 'cuz he was in the war and don't have no leg or something. You're telling him to go to the opera when everybody else would say, that's too bad. You're ugly and you don't have no leg."

"Well, even if he is ugly, shouldn't he have hope?" The smell of pomade was overpowering in the dead air of the shed. "He might be a very nice man that someone could love."

"I think if he's too ugly, you should say to him, you're too ugly. You should tell him the truth."

"Next time, I'll ask for a photograph and a doctor's report to make sure he has all his limbs." She turned back to her typewriter. "I need to get back to work."

But that night, after Sean and Tony had left, and Maggie had checked on Alice Colleen—assuring her that she could go to sleep now—and on the boys, she stood next to the window in Liam's and her bedroom and looked out over the back lot.

*You're telling him to go to the opera when everyone else would say, that's too bad.*

Tony was right. Maybe she didn't know what she was doing. After all, she had spent the last six years pretending mightily to be what she was not—a woman of the world, sophisticated and educated enough to give others sound advice. She hadn't told the truth, so why should she expect others to?

In the bed behind her, Liam rustled, disturbed by her movements. "What's wrong?" he asked. "Are the children asleep?"

"Everything's fine."

She lay down beside him, and he drew her to him, kissing her. He slipped his hand inside her nightgown to cup her breast.

*Mamma don't have time to do nothing but pray that she don't have no more babies.*

"I'm so tired," she said. "Could we . . . not right now."

Liam's hand froze. "All right."

He rolled away, and Maggie took refuge on her side, facing away from him. She felt ashamed—she rarely refused him. It was her duty, it was her purpose. But she could not stop thinking: I cannot have another baby, I cannot get pregnant again. I just can't.

# TEN

On August 2, 1923, President Harding died.

As the funeral train made its way across the country, the nation mourned. On August 10, the day that the president was buried in Marion, Ohio, Coloradans flocked to the grounds of the State Capitol for a twenty-one gun salute. A few hours later, thousands of men in uniform paraded through the streets before an artillery caisson that bore an empty casket draped with the nation's flag. At the Denver Auditorium, the casket was carried inside by an honor guard for the memorial service. The organist played Chopin's "Funeral March," and  Bishop Tihen of the Catholic Church gave the opening prayer. Former U.S. Senator Charles Thomas gave the address, speaking of President Harding's high ideals and devotion to service to his country.

Jim's shock lingered for days after the memorial service. He could scarcely believe that only two months earlier, he and Kathleen had listened to President Harding, dressed in white summer trousers with a generous jacket buttoned over his paunch, speak from the verandah outside Fitzsimons Army Hospital. In the hot sun beyond, veterans, some in army uniform and a few even in helmets, listened for reassurance that they had not been forgotten.

A knock on the door of his office at Graves Industries interrupted his reverie. Nathaniel opened the door from the anteroom and announced breathlessly, "There's a gentleman here to see you."

Nathaniel's fluster alarmed Jim. "Who is it?"

"Dr. John Galen Locke."

"Dr. Locke?"

Nathaniel nodded. "Should I show him in?"

"Of course."

As Jim stepped forward, the Grand Dragon of the Ku Klux Klan entered the room with a pompous swagger. He was small and overweight, with glittering eyes and a pointed goatee. So this was the man who supposedly had been expelled from every legitimate medical fraternity and widely branded as a quack. It was said that he had botched more than one abortion in his downtown office.

"Good afternoon, Senator Graves," Dr. Locke said. "Thank you for seeing me. It's a pleasure to meet you."

Jim shook hands. "The pleasure's all mine." He motioned toward the plush furniture in the corner of the office. "Please take a seat. Would you care for lemon water?"

"Please." Dr. Locke spread his girth across the sofa. "And how are your lovely children? A boy and a girl, isn't it? Your wife—such a beautiful woman—is well?"

"Yes, thank you." Jim felt a frisson of discomfort at the familiarity in Dr. Locke's voice. "How can I help you?"

"I'm sure you, like the rest of the nation, are mourning President Harding."

"Yes, I am," Jim said, still wary.

"Such a shame that he died before he could be exonerated—if he was to be—in the Teapot Dome scandal. Seems Secretary Fall will take the fall alone." The doctor laughed at his own humor. "You're lucky you've escaped notice from the investigation in Washington."

"I have no connection with Teapot Dome."

"But there are those whose leases abut Teapot Dome and who benefit from the presence of such a large deposit. Are any of those leases yours?"

"I couldn't say without looking at a map."

"You've never had any connection with the Continental Trading Company, have you?"

"If I have, it would have been completely above board."

Dr. Locke leaned forward, his beady eyes bright. "Secretary Fall bought a ranch in New Mexico and redid all the buildings so they look brand new. It looks bad when an oilman buys up all his wife's neighbors' farms or builds a house the size of Buckingham Palace."

"Those are my wife's and my private affairs." Obviously, Dr. Locke intended to keep Jim off balance. He asked again, "What can I help you with today?"

Dr. Locke smiled. "The legislation you introduced last session gave a generous amount of money for oil shale studies and experimental stations. Was it just to give a boost to the University of Colorado, where, I believe, your old friend George Norlin is now President? Or was it a boost to Graves Industries?"

During the war, Professor Norlin had led Governor Gunter's Committee to Americanize Colorado, of which Jim had been a member. Professor Norlin had become the President of the university in 1918. Jim had liked the professor, although they hadn't always agreed. Still, Jim had pressed hard to see the Bureau of Mines' program awarded to the university and fully funded and supported by state money.

"Extraction of oil shale is still in the early stages," he said. "Since I'm on the Industrial Relations Committee, I'm hoping that the studies done by the Bureau of Mines will put Colorado ahead of the game."

"Who do you think has more oil, Colorado or Wyoming?"

"It really doesn't matter because we need all we can get. America's domestic production of petroleum doesn't match our consumption—we're about 100 million barrels short. That means that, a few years from now, we'll be dependent on foreign countries, such as Mexico, for our petroleum and oil needs."

"Is Mexico that far ahead of us?"

"Possibly," Jim said. "America needs to become self-sufficient. Buying oil from another country puts us in a dangerous position should there be another war such as the one we just lived through. Remember the fear and confusion caused by the Zimmerman Telegram?"

"Ah, the war," Dr. Locke said. "Wilson's administration sure was different from Harding's, wasn't it? Wilson set about to put everything under government control, like the Bolsheviks, while Harding never gave up on the idea that if business owners increased their wealth, then it would increase the wealth of the entire nation." His voice took on an edge. "But what happened was that the rich kept it all for themselves and let the workers starve."

"Isn't it somewhat early to be judging the legacy of a man who has just been buried?"

"President Coolidge is in charge now," Dr. Locke reminded him. "And he is not as free-wheeling as his predecessor. He's moral and scrupulous— some might say overly so—and prone to conservatism. And just now, any oilman who was mixed up with Harding smells of scandal."

"All of this is a matter of opinion, not fact."

Dr. Locke waved away Jim's words. "Times aren't the same as they were after the war. It's the day of the common man, the man who doesn't live in a mansion and drive a fancy car, but who faces the work-a-day grind. These men served in France and came back thinking they were heroes. But what did they find? The rich had grown richer, and the foreign element had stolen their jobs, without even having to become citizens. Now they're looking for men like themselves to be their leaders."

Jim set down his glass of water. "What do you want?"

"I've heard rumors that you are eyeing the governor's seat next November."

"Those are, as you said, rumors."

"In a year, our organization will have thousands of new members. Nearly seventy thousand American men are joining each day." After a pause, Dr. Locke added, "That isn't a rumor, but a fact."

"What are you suggesting?"

"The members of our organization are one-hundred percent Americans who only ask for an honest leader to represent their interests for the next four years. I'm not in politics myself, but I feel it's my duty to see that men who will enforce the laws of this country are elected to office."

Philip Van Cise's warning rang in Jim's ears: *John Galen Locke is smarter than he appears.* "Are you asking me to throw in my lot with the Ku Klux Klan?" he asked.

"We'd be honored, Senator Graves."

"No thank you."

"I see." Locke rose, and Jim followed. "Perhaps in a few months. It's early yet. You know, we have a governor now who was a wealthy businessman without much political experience, and before him, we had a governor who loved the oil companies. I don't think that the common man has much trust left in either one of those types of fellows." Dr. Locke ambled toward the door, then turned. "Does your wife still attend Blessed Savior? It must be difficult for her, unable to take communion and the other sacraments because she married outside the Church."

"My wife's beliefs are no one's business but her own."

"My apologies," Dr. Locke said. "It must be another one of those pesky rumors."

"Good day, sir."

Locke smiled. "Good day, Senator."

After Locke left the office, Jim sought the drawer where he kept a bottle of brandy. As he drank it, he looked down over the street below.

Being governor in Colorado was, at best, a tricky business—which might be why a new one was elected every two years. Governor Sweet had been sorely criticized for having a limited vision of the average man's plight because of his inherited wealth. Governor Oliver Shoup, who had left office in January, had earned the nickname "Oillie" for favoring the demands of oil companies while in office.

Dr. Locke had come to convey a pointed message: Jim had the connections with wealth and oil that had soured the people of Colorado on their previous and current governors, but he had a third strike as well: a wife who was Catholic.

That night, the entire Graves house was filled with guests. Jim did not remember inviting anyone to the house. It was most likely Eleanora's doing— God knew that Kathleen had no desire or flare for entertaining. He poured himself a brandy and went outside onto the expansive patio. Guests roamed the estate, admiring Kathleen's horses in the stables, which were well-guarded by stable boys, or fawning over Jim's collection of cars in the garage, which were protected by Blount and the assistant chauffeur. Others tossed Corn Flakes into the pond, laughing hysterically as the greedy Japanese goldfish fought over them. Another group of guests took turns on the plank swing that hung from an ancient cottonwood at the back of the property that Jim had insisted remain when the outbuildings were erected. Everyone, it seemed, had a cocktail of some kind, whether shrimp, fruit, or alcohol.

He walked down to Kathleen's studio, which nestled in a secretive corner of the property. The door was slightly open. He went inside to look at her works, haphazardly stacked against the walls or propped on easels. Her paintings were different from the sweet sketches she had done during the war—darker, perhaps, or starker, as if painted by a more forceful and knowledgeable hand. Yet, despite the bold colors and broad strokes, there was something tender about them, something that bespoke of a full heart, a gentle soul.

"Hello?"

Behind him, Ellie glided into the studio. Her blonde hair, cropped now in the latest fashion, curled in delicate waves around her face. She wore an elaborately beaded peacock feathered dress, with glittering silver straps and matching headband. The color in her face was high, and Jim suspected she had been drinking most of the afternoon.

"Are you going to come out?" She handed him a drink. "It's rather rude to stay hidden away."

He sniffed the concoction before he tasted it. "I doubt anyone will care as long as they don't run out of booze."

"Well, I care. Why are you moping in here?"

Jim wasn't sure what had brought him to such a dark mood—Dr. Locke's visit, certainly—but something more weighed on him, something that lurked just beyond his conscious thoughts.

Ellie made a second attempt. "You really must come out. Evan and Perry—who is falling over himself over Evan—have cornered poor Kathleen and are singing every lugubrious Irish song imaginable to her. They're on at least the third chorus of 'I'll Take You Home Again, Kathleen,' complete with staging worthy of Al Jolson. Poor thing, her face is scarlet."

"She'll take care of herself," Jim said. "She's quite good at claiming that she needs to check on the children and making her escape."

"That's not the answer I was hoping for." Ellie gave a silvery laugh. "Now, come, confess. What dark thoughts have you trapped in here?"

He took a drink. "You met Kathleen's lover, didn't you?"

Ellie started in surprise. "Yes, I did. Once."

"Evidently Miss Mills helped them out quite a bit, even to the point where Kathleen spent the better part of two days with him in Chaumont."

"She did?" Ellie laughed again. "Ah, Hank. She was so many things, but above all, a loyal friend."

"Who helped Kathleen break just about every rule of the Relief Society and the Red Cross."

"Kathleen had already broken most of those rules before she left Denver," Ellie said wryly. "And she broke them with your help. So don't insinuate that I failed to do my job." A shadow crossed her face. "Rules didn't matter anyway—my God, there was no rhyme or reason to anything that happened. It was just survive or die, and no one cared how you did either one." Out of breath, she took a sip of her drink. "What is this really about?"

He said nothing, still attempting to fully gather his thoughts. At last, he admitted, "I would have married Anneka, had she lived. I promised her that I would take care of her when I returned from France. And had Kathleen's beau lived, she would still be with him."

"I wish you wouldn't bring this up. It's all such a long time ago."

"Mina, wherever she might be, is twelve, now."

"Whatever you do, don't mention this to Mother," Ellie warned. "She is in a fairly passive mood tonight."

Jim made no reply. When he had returned from France, he had accosted his mother about her failure to take care of Anneka and Mina.

"I have told you how difficult that time was, Jim," she had replied. "With all the sickness in Denver, and worrying about Eleanora—"

"You lost two children, Mother." The fury in him had erupted. "And you watched as the other two nearly died. How could you have let Mina—your own granddaughter—go?"

But there was no—there would never be a satisfactory answer.

Ellie laid her hand on his. "And what regrets would you have had if you had married Anneka? How would you have explained Mina? Would you have kept up the ruse that Anneka once had an ill-fated husband who died from whatever it was you and Mother cooked up? You would never have had a political career with a Swedish maid and a foundling child who highly resembled you at your side."

Jim's eyes went back to Kathleen's paintings. When he had married Kathleen, his father, Arthur, had commented that Jim had thrown away a significant part of his future. His father considered Kathleen no more suitable than Anneka.

"She wouldn't have been Irish Catholic," he said.

"What brought this up?"

"I'm afraid my political career will go nowhere because of her."

"Kathleen is not at all like Anneka," Ellie said heatedly. "She earned respect and admiration in France; she became a dignified and upstanding woman. Mrs. Vanderbilt called the women volunteers of the Red Cross the new débutantes of America."

He swallowed the rest of his drink.

"Oh, for God's sake," Ellie snapped. "It doesn't matter who you married. Someone's going to find fault with her. If she'd been wealthy, they'd say you married for money. If she'd been the daughter of a political figure, they'd say you married for power. Women are such easy scapegoats. 'Behind every great man is a woman' should be amended to say, 'Behind every great man is a woman who is thrown to the lions, dragged through the mud, and crucified on the cross because she is a woman.'"

"The suffragist declaims again."

"If women had more power, there would never have been a war. What woman bears children just to kill them? Men, on the other hand, seem to have no hesitation in that area."

"Are you speaking of Thomas' son, young Leftenant Lloyd-Elliot?"

She waved her hand. "I'm speaking for all of them. Now, come up to the house. Without you, the whole situation has become chaos."

Jim conceded. As he and Ellie entered the parlor, Kathleen broke away from Evan and Perry, who crooned "Oh, Danny Boy" to her. Her face was, as Ellie had said, scarlet. Evan grabbed her hand and begged, "Oh, stay! They have two governesses and ten lords-a-leaping to keep them safe! They're fine!"

Perry added, "And lions to guard the entrance to their bedrooms—"

"And Heavy Dragoons—"

Evan's suggestion produced a joyous bark from Perry, who pounded out a sloppy rendition of Gilbert and Sullivan's "Recipe for a Dragoon" on the piano. Evan joined in until they collapsed into each other's arms beneath the mush of words. As they laughed themselves into drunken tears, Kathleen hurried out of the parlor.

"See?" Jim whispered in Ellie's ear. "She doesn't need anyone to rescue her."

# ELEVEN

When Mary Jane arrived home from Graves Industries, she heard Avery and Ross arguing. She set down her bag and kicked off her shoes before she went into the living room. Her mother sat on the couch, her Bible next to her and a number of religious magazines piled before her. Nearly every wall was decorated with a picture of Jesus or a cross. The heated voices came from the kitchen.

"What's going on?" Mary Jane asked.

"I don't know," her mother said. "But it's giving me a headache."

"Why don't you lie down? I'll start dinner."

The moment Mary Jane walked through the kitchen door, Avery roared, "This is secret. Go away."

"If it's about the quarry, part of it is mine, too—"

"It isn't about the quarry," Ross said calmly. "There's nothing to worry about."

"Well, you're giving Mom a headache, and I need to start dinner."

"In a few minutes."

She left the room, but once she was upstairs, she sulked. If they wouldn't let her into the kitchen, then she would do her other chores. Changing into an old skirt, she went to the garden to water the tomatoes. The garden was just beyond the kitchen window, a perfect place to hear what went on in the kitchen. If she stood in the middle of the row of pumpkins, she could see Ross and Avery as well.

"Please, Ross," Avery said. "You have to listen to me."

"I have been listening to you, and not a word of it makes sense."

"It would be so good for the quarry. Everybody's doing it, and it's helping them with their businesses, because people know it's okay. And the Klan uses a secret code, so that you can tell whether you can trust someone or not."

"A secret code?"

"You know, special words and stuff. I can't tell you more because only members are allowed to know—"

"I don't want to know more. I don't need a secret code to know who to trust."

"Look, you're supposed to follow something called Klannishness—it's in this pamphlet." Avery read from a small book: "*Trading, dealing with and patronizing Klansmen in preference to all others. Employing Klansmen in preference to others whenever possible. Boosting each other's business interests or professional ability; honorably doing any and all things that will assist a Klansman to earn an honest dollar'—*"

"Or a dishonest dollar. Where did the ten dollars that you paid go?"

"Oh, they're completely straight about that. Four dollars goes to Mr. Burns, who is the Kleagle who sponsored me. That's what I want to be—the more people you recruit, the more money you make. One dollar goes to the King Kleagle, whoever recruited Mr. Burns. Then five dollars to the Imperial Fund, which pays the Grand Dragon two dollars—"

"That's Dr. Locke, right?"

"Right."

"So, the entire ten dollars goes to men who are getting rich off other men. Where does the money for your charity work come from?"

"I don't know. Maybe from the robes, they're six-fifty each."

"That's quite a price for a bed sheet."

"You wouldn't be so hard on it if you knew more! It's almost like church. The meeting always opens with a prayer and a Bible verse from the twelfth chapter in Romans—"

"Which says what, exactly?"

"A whole bunch of stuff about loving your neighbor and all that."

"Well, let's just find out."

Ross rose, and Mary Jane stepped out of his line of vision.

"Here's Romans 12:3." Ross read from the Bible. "*For by the grace given to me, I bid every one among you not to think of himself more highly than he ought to think, but to think with sober judgment, each according to the measure of faith which God has assigned him.'*" He paused. "Isn't calling yourself better than a Catholic 'thinking more highly' than you ought?"

"No, because Catholics aren't Christians—"

Ross read from the Bible again. "*Let love be genuine; hate what is evil, hold fast to what is good; love one another with brotherly affection;*

*outdo one another in showing honor'*—none of this sounds like what you're describing."

"Come with me to the Ice Cream Social tonight," Avery pleaded. "It's not fair for you to judge it before you've seen it."

"Can Mary Jane come, too?" Ross asked. "She's been out in the North Forty listening to us all this time."

Mary Jane started. She might have known that Ross would see her. With a chuckle, she went inside.

Avery gave her a scathing look. "Sure, it's for families," he said. "And you'll both see that the Klan is about honor and loyalty, about keeping this country in the hands of the white men who started it and run it now. And protecting things like free speech, and keeping the public schools free from religion, and bringing the Bible back into the schools to teach morals—"

"Isn't having the Bible in school the same as having religion in the school?" Ross asked.

"What?" Avery asked. "No, it's the Bible, not some Catholic or Jew book—"

Afraid Avery might rescind the invitation if Ross kept on, Mary Jane said, "We'll keep an open mind tonight, just as we did at the Pillar of Fire. Right, Ross?"

He grimaced in response.

The ice cream social was held at Cotton Mills, a long-abandoned textile factory along the Platte River near Santa Fe Drive. The brick building, which had once housed the mill's executives, served as offices for the Klan, while the empty warehouse had been transformed into a meeting area with grandstands.

As Avery entered the building, he was greeted by two men, who wore neither hoods nor robes. "AYAK?"

"AKIA," Avery replied proudly. "And these are my guests."

"Welcome," one of the men said. "Enjoy your evening."

"See," Avery said as they had passed out of earshot. "That's the secret code I told you about. You have to join to find out what it means."

Ross rolled his eyes at Mary Jane.

Inside, carnival games had been set up on what was once the factory floor. A kiddie-sized train creaked away on an oval track at the far end of the building. The place bustled with energy and laughter, as mothers and children played the games and helped themselves to free ice cream served by men in white shirts and black trousers.

Ross bought tickets for himself and Mary Jane to play the games. Moving around the floor, they tested themselves at throwing a baseball into a milk can; tossing a ring over a set of Coke bottles; and knocking down targets that were stuffed with beans and slyly weighted at the bottom. Ross won a teddy bear at cornhole and handed it to Mary Jane.

Taking a break from the noise and the children who crowded around the games, they sat at an ornate wrought-iron table in soda fountain chairs to eat free ice cream. As Mary Jane's cone dripped in the overheated shell of the factory, she asked Ross, "What do you think?"

"It could be a church fair, for all the evidence I see of the Klan here."

A gray-haired woman approached them, a bundle of pamphlets in her hands. "Here's a list of KIGY businesses where you should shop. Look for the sign in the window—"

"K-I-G-Y?" Ross asked. "What's that?"

"You aren't a Klansman?"

"No, I'm a guest of one."

"You'll be one soon enough," she said confidently. "It's hard to resist such a welcoming organization. K-I-G-Y means 'Klansman I Greet You.' It tells you that the store you're shopping at is owned by a 100% American. Any other stores, you're sending your money to the Pope or the Jews." She addressed Mary Jane. "So no more Sears or Montgomery Ward, young lady."

"I don't—"

The woman moved on, and Ross pushed the list toward Mary Jane. "Here," he said. "Buy your K-L-O-T-H-E-S here."

Mary Jane laughed.

As if on cue, two men in white shirts and black trousers appeared at the table and sat down without asking for permission. Mary Jane glanced over their heads to where the woman who had just visited the table was watching. Obviously, she had sent them over.

"We hear you're considering joining the Ku Klux Klan," one of the men said.

"No," Ross denied. "I'm not—"

"You're Avery Grayson's brother, aren't you?" The other man said. "I'm Mr. Smith and this is Mr. Herrington." He eyed Mary Jane. "And you are, Miss?"

"This is my sister, Miss Grayson," Ross said.

The men greeted her. "Since you own your own business," Mr. Smith said, "you must be looking for ways to improve your business."

"I am," Ross acknowledged.

"With all the immigrants and others who came in after the war taking what they can, it's hard for the true American to compete." Mr. Herrington continued in the style of a preacher. "But America is for Americans. We need to be on our guard against the alien and the anarchist, who would destroy American principles. Our enemies are many, and it's the place of the Ku Klux Klan to rouse the spirit of the real American to stand guard against these foes, whether they be white, black, or yellow."

Mr. Smith said, "Our hope is to become not just an organization that helps the average businessman along, but one that takes part in the political process so that we elect those who will make strong laws that protect our interests. I'm sure you want to protect your business."

"I do, but—"

"Mrs. Smith, who you just met, says that she's already told you about the KIGY signs that hang in stores. Those signs bring in the kind of customers that you'd want to deal with—people who pay their bills, who aren't bad outside influences, who think and worship as you do. What serious businessman wouldn't want that sort of customer?"

"I own a laundry," Mr. Herrington said. "Since I put that sign in my window, we have been receiving orders from the best families in town. Their clothes are of good quality and still so clean that we almost don't need to do our job." He laughed. "Although we do, mind you. But my workers know that the clothes they are touching haven't been worn by anyone with a lung disease or of a certain skin color or—well, you understand."

Ross looked toward Mary Jane, but at that moment, a loud speaker blared to life. "Please, assemble outside for the night's Grand March. Please, outside, now, for the—"

"Oh, you have to see this," Mr. Smith said. "This will make you join tonight."

They shook hands with Ross and disappeared, as the crowd began to wind down their game-playing and ice cream eating. A few who complained about still having unused tickets were given consolation prizes at the door.

Outside, Klansmen in full regalia directed the spectators to the foot of Ruby Hill, which rose one hundred feet above the Platte River. After the crowd had assembled, a phalanx of silent Klansmen marched from the illuminated stadium to the hill. In three perfectly straight lines, they stood in complete silence, staring out at the crowd.

"Which one's Avery?" Mary Jane whispered to Ross.

"Thirteenth from the left, second row."

Mary Jane stood on tiptoe, straining to count, until she realized that Ross was teasing. "Ha ha," she whispered in his ear.

Atop Ruby Hill, a towering cross burst into flame, the whoosh echoing through the river valley below. The Klansmen covered their hearts with their left hands and placed their right hands on the left shoulders of the Klansmen next to them. To the tune of "Blest Be the Ties that Bind," they sang: *"Blest be the Klansman's tie, Of real fraternal love, That binds us in a fellowship, Akin to that above."*

A Klansman stepped forward. "United in the sacred bond of klannish fidelity we stand," he intoned. "But divided by selfishness and strife we fall; shall we stand, or shall we fall?"

In one voice, the others answered: "We will stand, for our blood is not pledged in vain."

Ross shifted from one foot to another.

"Now we will sing the Kloxology," the Klansman announced.

They joined in the tune to "My Country 'Tis of Thee": *"God of Eternity, Guard, guide our great country, Our homes and store. Keep our great state to Thee, Its people right and free. In us thy glory be, Forevermore."*

"Those aren't the words I learned in school," Mary Jane whispered.

"Or the words we sing at church for the Doxology."

"Anyone who wants to join, please see me now," the leader announced.

The Klansmen marched in silence back toward the mill, leaving the crowd on its own.

"Are you going to join?" Mary Jane asked Ross.

"Good God, no. Let's go home."

"Don't we need to wait for Avery?"

"No, he told me that he has a ride home. I'm suspecting it's our dear, departed brother, Matt."

Mary Jane laughed, but didn't scold.

At work, Miss Crawley asked Mary Jane to stay a few minutes before going to lunch. As the other girls shuffled by, their eyes cast toward the ground, lest the same fate befall them, Mary Jane waited beside Miss Crawley's desk. Once they were gone, Miss Crawley pressed a book into Mary Jane's hands. The title read: *Convent Cruelties OR My Life in a Convent: A Providential Delivery from Rome's Convent Slave Pens* by Helen Jackson.

"You must read this," Miss Crawley said. "It tells the awful truth of the Catholic convents here in America. Mrs. Jackson escaped—thank God—to tell her story. It's as terrifying as Mary Angel's story."

"Who is Mary Angel?"

"She visits the Pillar of Fire Church nearly every year with her tale of being forced to become a nun and all the awful abuse she endured from the priests. The next time she's here, I'll take you."

Mary Jane nodded, unwilling to admit that she didn't want to return to Bishop Alma White's church.

"Oh, and Mary Jane," Miss Crawley said. "Feel free to share the book with your mother. She is such a godly woman."

Mary Jane took the book with her to lunch. Since the other girls had scattered, making the most of their time outside their basement confines, she sat on a park bench on 17th Street and flipped through the illustrations. Poor Helen Jackson had suffered mightily at the hands of the nuns; she had been tied up and left alone in a room for three days, dunked in a cold water bath, forced to drink soup made of dirty water, and had had her hands burned with red-hot pokers. When she escaped from the convent, she weighed only eighty-six pounds.

After work, Mary Jane went into the Employee Ladies' Washroom before catching the streetcar for home. As she was washing her hands, Raynelle held up the book.

"You left this in here at lunchtime, Miss Grayson."

"Oh, I'm sorry." Mary Jane sorted through her bag, certain that she had dropped the book into it. "Did you read any of it?"

Raynelle gave her a stony glare. "I looked at it."

"What do you think? Do you think that something like this really happened in America?"

"I don't know."

Mary Jane turned the book over in her hands. "Have you ever had any trouble with the Klan?"

Raynelle's eyes went dead, as if a light had been turned off. "I need to clean up for tonight."

Mary Jane returned to the sink and wiped it down with the towel that she had used to dry her hands. As she threw it in the basket, she said, "There, it's done."

"I have to get home. If you could leave so I can—"

"Are you married?"

"Why do you want to know all this?"

"I don't know. I'm curious, that's all."

"I have a husband and two boys." Raynelle gathered up the basket of dirty linen. "I need to go home."

"I'll see you tomorrow."

As Mary Jane opened the heavy door of the lounge, Raynelle called, "Miss Grayson, I think that book is real, and I think it could happen in America. Terrible things happen here. Haven't you ever heard of lynching?"

# TWELVE

"Mommy, Sergeant Neck-ey is here!" Alice Colleen bounded through the swinging door of the kitchen.

Maggie stood at the table, kneading dough for biscuits. Liam could eat them if they were fresh and soft, and if the butter on them was completely melted.

Tony sauntered in, no longer dressed in suit and tie, but in work clothes. He wore a white shirt under a drab-colored jacket, which was belted at the waist. His matching trousers were tucked into high, laced-up leather boots. Buckled leather straps encircled the mid-front and the heel of the boots. In his hands, he wadded a flat, brimmed cap, the kind that newsboys wore.

He had taken to joining the Sullivans and Keohanes nearly every Tuesday evening for dinner. After they ate, he and Seaney retreated to the back yard, where they were making doubtful progress on the house for the elder Sullivans. From what Maggie saw from her shed, they mostly smoked and drank.

"Good afternoon." Tony greeted Maggie, then made the rounds of the children. "Hey, Miss Alice, hey—which one are you?"

"Frankie," Alice Colleen said happily.

"Frankie, Declan"—pronounced *Dee-clawn*—"Where's the little one?"

"He's sleeping," Alice Colleen volunteered.

Maggie wiped her floury hands on a towel. "Good afternoon, Sergeant Necchi."

"Hey, Mrs. James, I got a problem."

She brought out the rolling pin and coated it with flour. "What is it?"

"My wife, she don't like me no more."

Maggie paused, rolling pin in midair. Seaney had said nothing about Tony's family, and there had been no indication in any of the conversations with Tony over the dinner table that he was married. What did the poor girl do on Tuesdays when Tony was here?

"I'm so sorry," Maggie said. "Why does she feel that way?"

"I'm sorry," Alice Colleen parroted, and the boys both added, "Sah-wee."

"She says she's going home to her Mamma in Italia," Tony said.

"Is she just homesick? If so, you can—"

"Take her to the opera, I know. Nah, she just don't want me no more."

"Has she been able to make friends in America?" Maggie asked. "Maybe if she had more friends or went out more—she goes to Mass, doesn't she?"

"Oh, yeah, she goes to Mass," he said. "Is Sean in the back?"

"I don't think he's here yet."

"I'll wait for him out there." Tony clicked his tongue at the children, who giggled as if it were the funniest thing they'd ever heard. At once, they started imitating it.

He swooshed through the swinging door and rattled down the wrought iron steps outside as Maggie fretted. She should have thought of something sage and prudent. The conversation had seemed oddly abbreviated, and she worried it was because of her pallid advice. As she cut the dough into biscuits with a jam jar, she chided herself: Mrs. James had failed to do her job.

The following Tuesday, Seaney arrived before Tony did. When he came into the kitchen from the inside staircase, she said, "Oh, I'm glad you're here first."

"First?" He grabbed at a pile of carrots that she was slicing into cubes. "Before Tony, you mean?"

"Yes," she said. "Has his wife left for Italy yet? If she hasn't, ask him to bring her over for dinner. He spends so much time away—"

"Tony's not married. Where'd you get that idea?"

"He told me his wife is thinking about leaving him."

"He's just pulling your leg. He thinks it's funny that you give out advice." He snatched another carrot. "Is Ma in the parlor?"

"Yes."

Awaiting the arrival of the marvelous Tony Necchi, she added silently. He had certainly charmed them all—Ma was up and dressed by four o'clock on the afternoons that he came to dinner. Alice Colleen was so smitten that she not only washed her hands and face before he came, but changed her dolls and herself into clean dresses. Frankie and Declan followed his every move with their eyes, and even Kieran—only six months old—smiled delightedly for him.

How dare he mock her. Well, if he thought that Mrs. James was funny, she would show him otherwise.

When Tony arrived, she was ready for him. After he had walked into the kitchen and greeted her and the children, she asked, "How is your wife?"

"Oh, she left me," he said. "She went home to Italia."

"That's too bad," Maggie said. "Perhaps, in the future, you should change your socks more often."

After a stunned silence, Alice Colleen giggled, her hands over her mouth, and the boys brayed with laughter.

"What?" Tony challenged. "You think that too, Miss Alice? I tell you what, my best pair of socks got a hole where the big toe goes through. I still got four toes inside the sock. That's good enough, huh?" He appealed to Frankie and Declan. "That's most of them, huh?"

As the boys nodded, Alice Colleen suggested, "You should sew up the hole."

"I don't sew."

"You should have Mommy do it. She sews up all our clothes."

"Alice Colleen!" Maggie turned from the oven. "That's enough."

Tony's dark eyes glinted at her. Shifting his gaze to Alice Colleen, he asked, "Do you sew?"

"Not as good as Mommy—"

"Not as well as Mommy," Maggie corrected her.

"I can thread the needle," Alice Colleen said.

"Then when you get good"—he emphasized the word with a smug glance at Maggie—"you can sew up the hole. Promise me you'll do that, huh?"

"Can I, Mommy?" Alice Colleen asked.

Maggie turned back to the stove. "I think Sergeant Necchi would be better off buying new socks. Now, go wash your hands for dinner."

She felt the heat of the stove on her face. Or maybe it was Tony—she was so . . . aware of him, like a blast furnace. He was just waiting for the next challenge from her to let the flame roar, but she wasn't about to give him the satisfaction. She kept her face turned away, attending to the cooking so that he wouldn't see her smile.

That evening, he came to the shed as she was typing her daily letters. He hulked in the doorway, his shoulders nearly touching both sides of the narrow frame, his weight on his right leg.

"So you think my socks stink, huh?"

"I'm only telling you the truth, Sergeant Necchi." She nodded toward the straps on his boots. "Why do you have those?"

"I put the gaffs on them."

"The what?"

"The gaffs," he said. "Big hook things with sharp metal points that go into the wood so I can climb the pole. They go out sort of like this"—he indicates an angle—"so they stick good."

"That's what you do all day? Climb poles?"

"And string wires. Yeah, that's what I done since I was seventeen and come to America."

"Is it dangerous?"

"Not so much as France was." He nodded toward the typewriter. "What are you saying now? You're not telling nobody to go to the opera, are you?"

"No, I'm trying to help this young woman, whose young man only takes her to dinner at the penny cafeterias. She wants to know if she should keep stepping out with him or if she should find a more generous beau."

"Why? Isn't the food good?"

"What do you mean?"

"Well, if the food's good, she shouldn't complain. Her stomach's full, and that's what's important."

"So what would you tell her?"

"I'd say, you got fed. That's good enough."

She laughed. "What about this one? '*I have been seeing a young man that I met at work for three weeks now. Last weekend, he took me to dinner, then the theater, and then, we ended up dancing for an hour at a fine hall. When he delivered me home, he asked if he could kiss me. I said no, but he complained that he had taken me so many places that he deserved a kiss for his efforts. Should I have said yes?*'" She deferred to Tony. "Your call, Sergeant Necchi."

"So he takes her to dinner—and not at the penny place, right?"

"As far as I know, not at the penny place."

"And then, he takes her to the theater to see . . . what, a play?"

"Or an opera," Maggie taunted.

Tony grunted. "Then, he takes her dancing, right? He's good at it, right? He don't step on her toes?"

"Not enough to break them, anyway."

"Then she should kiss him."

"Why's that?"

"Because he just did all that stuff so she would. No guy wants to see a play or go dancing. He just wants the kiss."

"Surely, he wants to eat well and be well-entertained—"

"Naw, he just wants the kiss. He don't care about the rest of it." Tony leaned against the door jamb. "Don't you believe me?"

"I have no doubt of your experience, Sergeant Necchi."

Maggie wiped at the heat in her face. She shouldn't be talking to Tony Necchi about kissing. It was wrong, it was improper, sinful. But Maggie's heart felt lighter—by years. She wished she were kissing Liam beneath the outside steps after an evening walk around the neighborhood. She wanted to feel his hot, restless breath on her neck and the fullness of his shoulders beneath her hands. How she missed those days.

"So what are you gonna tell them?" Tony asked.

She straightened up. "To Miss Penny Cafeteria, I'll say that she should offer to improve the young man's taste"—she paused, but Tony didn't acknowledge the pun—"in restaurants by taking him to one she enjoys—"

"Only if she pays."

"What?"

"Girls work in America," he said. "So why shouldn't she pay? Maybe she makes more than him."

"If she pays once, he might expect her to pay every time."

"No wonder he goes to the penny place." Tony pointed with his chin. "And the other one?"

"I'll tell her that she does not owe the young man a kiss, and that he's wrong if he expects one in return for taking her out for a lovely evening. Her company should be enough for him. But it might be nice to offer him a peck on the cheek just to show her appreciation and seal their friendship."

"And if she does that, he is going to tell her to drop dead."

Maggie's laughter rang through the shed and out into the night. She immediately shushed herself—the windows of the apartments were open. "Well, if he does, she won't have to worry about kissing him."

The word, "kissing," lingered on her lips, as if it were some kind of sweetness.

"American girls are crazy and free," Tony complained. "That's all we hear about, that American girls don't need nobody to tell them what to do.

That they can do what they want. They can drink and smoke and they can stay out all night and dance. Why don't you tell them just to do what they want to do?"

"I'm supposed to give moral guidance," she countered. "I'm not about to tell them to run wild. That would be wrong."

"This is all too hard for me," Tony said. "I'm goin' back to digging a hole."

The next time he comes to the Sullivans' apartments, Maggie is waiting for him. In fact, they are all waiting for him—Alice Colleen, Frankie, Declan, and Kieran. He's barely through the kitchen door when he says, "Hey, Mrs. James, I got a problem."

Alice Colleen covers her mouth in giggly anticipation. The boys stop banging and babbling and scrapping, bright eyes fixed on him.

"What is it, Sergeant Necchi?" Maggie asks.

"Now that my wife is gone, I don't have nobody to talk to. Should I go to the opera?"

Maggie pretends to ponder, aware of the kids' bated breath. "No, I don't think so," she says at last. "But if you're lonely, you could get a dog."

"Naw, I had one in Italy. It just run away."

"Perhaps a three-legged dog," she says. "Then you could catch it when it ran."

Alice Colleen laughs gleefully, as do the boys. Tony winks slyly at them, then turns the full heat of his gaze on Maggie.

# THIRTEEN

On the fifth anniversary of Armistice Day, Margaret Sanger came to Denver to speak at the Open Forum of Grace Methodist Episcopal Church at 13th and Bannock. Braving the cold November evening, Jim and Kathleen managed to find a seat in the church along with hundreds of spectators, who shivered in the drafty 1880s stone building.

Mrs. Sanger was introduced by Judge Benjamin Barr Lindsey, known throughout the country for creating the juvenile justice system in Denver. A balding man in his fifties, he sported a bushy mustache that nearly brushed up against the circular microphone.

"As it is now," he said, "our world is threatened with the possibility of overpopulation, with wars over territory and resources becoming more common and deadly. That is why we must have legal dissemination of scientific birth control information and methods. Birth control enables parents to carefully plan their families and lifts the moral, social, and intellectual standards of our population. I often hear of women who have been maimed or have died because they had to resort to illegal operations to prevent pregnancy. I estimate nearly one-thousand of these operations happen in Denver each month." He waited until the murmur of shock subsided. "But you have not come here tonight to hear me speak. You have come to hear one of the saintliest, most cultured and useful women in this world: Mrs. Margaret Sanger."

An attractive dark-haired woman with wide-set, compassionate eyes and a firm mouth stepped up to the microphone. The sanctuary erupted in applause, and she was unable to speak for several minutes.

"Thank you, Judge Lindsey," she said at last. "And thank you for that lovely reception. I love coming to Denver. It is such an enlightened city. The women here are the most beautiful in the world, so fresh and charming, and they are also some of the most intelligent, for they have used the vote effectively. In most cities, I speak to the wives of peddlers and railroad and dock workers. In Denver, I know I am speaking to the wives of doctors, lawyers, politicians, and the members of prestigious clubs. And, of course, the National Woman's Party."

A group of women stood, proudly wearing tricolor sashes of purple, white and gold. Hearty applause echoed through the vaulted church. Looking over her shoulder, Kathleen saw Julia Reston standing among the representatives. She quickly turned toward the front.

Mrs. Sanger continued. "As Judge Lindsey said, reckless procreation is threatening to grow beyond the earth's ability to manage it. Every year, there are more who fall into poverty, who can't support their offspring. The Catholic Church, followed by millions, keeps women poorly educated and economically chained to housekeeping and childrearing. It poses the biggest threat to the health and well-being of women worldwide."

Kathleen shifted uncomfortably. Jim laid a hand on her arm.

"We at the American Birth Control League, have three principles that must be met before a woman has children," Mrs. Sanger said. "First, children should be conceived in love. Second, a child should be born of the mother's conscious desire, and third, a child should be begotten only in conditions of health and self-directed means that allow for the responsible upbringing of that child. That is why every woman must possess the power and freedom to prevent conception by using birth control without shame or guilt."

The church hall erupted in cheers People jumped to their feet, clapping and nodding. Mrs. Sanger and Judge Lindsey stepped away from the podium to mingle with the crowd. At the same time, the members of the National Woman's Party surged forward, gathering around Mrs. Sanger.

"Are you going to join that fray?" Jim asked.

Kathleen saw Julia filing toward the exit. Julia tossed a look over her shoulder, aimed directly at Kathleen.

"No, I think I'll wait for a few minutes."

"I want to speak with Ben." Jim took Kathleen's arm. "Do you want to go ahead?"

"I'll wait for you in the vestibule."

Julia stood near the door.

"Mrs. Graves," she said. "I'm surprised to see you at this gathering."

"I'm here with my husband, who is speaking with Judge Lindsey."

"Ah, of course, the politician, and the politician's wife, to whom Mrs. Sanger referred," she said. "Were you offended by her speech? Surely it is contrary to your beliefs."

"I'm not offended, although I learned that such a thing—"

"It's called birth control," Julia supplied.

"—interferes with God's will. If a woman has a child, it is His doing."

"More likely, it is her husband's." When Kathleen did not reply, she continued. "I know nothing of the Catholic Church, but so often, regardless of religious belief, the woman is not a true equal in the relationship, and too often, the man is lord and master, and a brute at that. It is for that woman that Mrs. Sanger speaks, not for you or most of the women here tonight. She speaks for the ones who have no voice or choice or safe haven in their lives, and we must speak for them as well."

Kathleen thought of Maggie, whose three boys were so close to one another in age. Maggie spent her entire day tending to someone—if it wasn't one of the children, it was Liam or Aunt Maury or Uncle Seamus. But Maggie had a voice, and certainly she was neither downtrodden nor lacking in education. She had always been Liam's equal—just as smart, just as witty, just as intellectually inclined. Her beliefs hadn't held her back.

Julia spoke again. "I've written to tell Paul that we've met. I sent the letter some time ago, but I've heard nothing back from him."

Kathleen struggled to stay composed—to keep her face neutral, to restrain herself from rushing again to the powder room to sink into despair. She glanced behind her, where Jim inched his way down the aisle of the church. As he approached, a charming smile on his face, Kathleen said, "Miss Reston, may I introduce my husband, Jim Graves? Jim, this is Miss Julia Reston."

Jim shook Julia's hand. "I'm pleased to meet you."

"You have a very talented wife, Senator Graves."

"Thank you," Kathleen said the words at the same time as Jim.

Without any further conversation, he added, "Please excuse us. We like to see the children to bed in the evenings."

"Of course," Julia said.

As Kathleen and Jim waited in the blistering cold for Blount to pull up in the Silver Ghost, Jim asked, "How did you meet Julia Reston?"

"Through Anne Evans," Kathleen said quietly. "Miss Evans is hoping Miss Reston will donate a piece of art to the museum."

"I didn't think her art was palatable to many outside of her own circle."

"She has a more modern style than some are used to."

"You do know that she is a lesbian?"

"Yes, I know. She was . . . widowed, or whatever you would call it, several years ago."

"I would call it degenerate."

"You've never said that about Evan and Perry's relationship, which they carry on under your own roof."

"Are you objecting to that? If so, it would be inconsistent, at the least."

"I'm not objecting to either," she said hotly. "It's just that Evan and Perry should be considered equals with Julia and Francine—"

"Francine?" Jim interrupted. "Did you make Julia—as you are evidently comfortable calling her—aware of your relationship with her nephew?"

Her heart caved in her breast. Surely Jim didn't know that Paul was alive—how could he?

"I didn't tell her," she said. "But she recognized my name, my maiden name." At his silence, she explained, "I sign my works K.O'D.Graves. The initials gave it away."

The Silver Ghost arrived, and Blount came around to open the car door. As the car traveled toward the Denver Country Club, Kathleen stayed silent, unwilling to discuss Julia when the truth was so volatile. Jim stared out the window, sitting far from her on the leather seat. As the Capitol building on Lincoln Street came into sight, a bright glow wavered near the steps. People ran along the sidewalks, shouting and heaving buckets of water.

"What is that?" Kathleen asked.

"I don't know. It looks as if the State House might be on fire. Park the car," Jim ordered Blount.

He stepped from the car as soon as it was still. Kathleen followed.

On the grayish steps that led to the main entrance of the Capitol building, a blazing cross towered some twenty feet into the sky. The flames emitted the greasy black smoke of gasoline fumes. Someone threw water on the cross, and the flames flared upward.

"Good Lord!" Jim pulled Kathleen against him, so that her face was protected by his arm and chest. Still, the heat grazed her cheek. She coughed into the wool of his coat.

"Let's move back," she suggested.

"Go back there with Blount," Jim ordered. To the chauffeur, he said, "Stay with Mrs. Graves. Do not allow her out of your sight."

Kathleen grabbed his arm. "Where are you going? Jim, don't—"

"I want to find out what I can."

He disappeared. Kathleen squinted into the darkness, trying to trace his path, but the brilliant flame and the acrid smoke obscured her ability to see the entrance to the Capitol and the lawns to either side.

"We have to have more water!" someone shouted. "A little bit will just make it spread!"

"Where's the Fire Department?"

"Who knows? There are crosses burning all over the city. At Washington Park and Cheesman—"

"At City Park—"

"Where are the police?"

"Right there! Wearing their other uniforms!"

On the Capitol steps, well behind the cross, about fifty Klansmen stood in a shadowy line. They made no effort to stop those who tried to extinguish the cross, but remained unmoving and silent.

Kathleen turned to Blount. "Go back to the car."

"Mr. Graves said I was to stay with you, ma'am."

"I'm not in danger," she said. "You are. Go back to the car. Drive home and send Drake back with the touring car."

"Yes, ma'am."

Kathleen turned toward the burning hulk. My God, to burn a cross on the very steps of the government. Was the message that the government was behind them or that the government was the enemy?

Behind her, someone shouted for everyone to clear the way. A Ford truck reversed up the slope of the lawns until the back tires jounced against the concrete of the Capitol steps. Two men leaped from the truck and wrestled a logging chain up the steps. Joined by others, they tied the ends of the chain to ropes, and the ropes to the fender of the truck.

"Everyone out of the way!" the men shouted. "Get out of the way!"

The crowd scrambled to safety. With a roar of engine, the truck surged forward, and the ropes dragged the heavy chain around the base of the cross. The cross swayed, and someone screamed. As the truck growled forward, the cross toppled in a violent flare of embers and smoke. Some covered their faces and shied away from it, but others rushed forward, tossing bucket after bucket of water on it.

As the flames fizzled, the crowd chanted, "No Klan! No Klan!"

From out of the darkness, Jim reappeared. Kathleen ran to him, and he put his arm around her.

"Where's Blount?" he asked.

"I sent him home. Drake is coming back with the Lincoln."

"And you stood here alone? My God, didn't you see them in front of the Capitol?"

"I know, but I'm in no danger—"

"You're a Catholic. Didn't you think of that?"

"No," she said, shocked. "No, I just thought of Blount, of a black man . . . What is this all about? What did you find out?"

"Your guess is as good as mine," he said bitterly. "Governor Sweet is busy denouncing it for the newspapers—which I will do tomorrow—but he doesn't know anything more than I do. Perhaps it's for Armistice Day, or perhaps it's just a show of power. John Galen Locke is one for spectacle and drama."

"Mr. Graves, sir, the car is here."

Drake stood just behind them.

Jim turned toward him. "I'll drive."

With Drake in the back of the touring car, they made their way to the Country Club. As they turned onto Circle Drive, Kathleen spotted a glow directly to the south.

"Is that another one?" she asked.

"Yes, Mrs. Graves, it's on the golf course," Drake offered.

"Stephen might see it and be afraid!"

Jim sped into the driveway. Kathleen tumbled from the car without waiting for either man to open the door for her. Upstairs, she rushed to the nurseries. Miss Brown and Miss Davis, the nurses, stood at the end of the hallway, looking out the windows toward the golf course.

"They're all right," Miss Brown said. "They didn't wake up."

"Thank you," Kathleen said, as if the women had been responsible for Stephen's and Susanna's ability to sleep through the upset. "Thank you."

"Do you know what's going on?" Miss Davis asked.

"I'm afraid not. Evidently, this is happening all over the city."

"It's a warning to the immoral and the lawbreakers in this town, the ones that the police haven't done anything about," Miss Brown added.

Kathleen made no comment, but said goodnight and started toward her bedroom. As she passed by the staircase that led back into the magnificent foyer, she encountered Beryl, her lady's maid, standing nervously on the landing beneath the stained glass window.

"You can take care of things tomorrow," Kathleen said. "It's too late—"

Beryl shook her head. "That isn't why . . . I wanted to thank you, Mrs. Graves, for letting my brother come home rather than wait with you at the Capitol."

"I didn't know Blount was your brother."

"Yes, ma'am, he is."

"I'm sorry he had to see that," Kathleen said. "I wish things were different in Denver right now. The Klan is wrong, as far as I'm concerned."

"Thank you for thinking that."


In her bedroom, Kathleen changes into her nightgown, which Beryl has laid on the bed, but she is too restless to sleep. The evening has been filled with too many threads, from Mrs. Sanger's speech to the burning crosses, all soured by her nonsensical disagreement with Jim over Julia. She lies in bed and pretends to read.

So, Julia has written to Paul—and has heard nothing in return. That simple fact should harden her heart against him, make her forget him as completely as he has evidently forgotten her, but it hasn't worked that way. Instead, she finds herself pining again—for France, for her work with the Red Cross, for modest *hôtel* in Montdidier, for the elegant chateau in Amiens, for him.

Near midnight, Jim comes into her room through the door that connects his bedroom to hers. He wears his clothes from earlier in the evening. He smells of gasoline fumes, and his face is marbled by soot. He sits dejectedly in an armchair next to the dark fireplace.

"Are you all right?" she asks.

"They let the one at the golf course burn out. Like the others, it was wood wrapped in gasoline-soaked burlap."

"Why would they burn one here?"

"I don't think they like the privileged any better than the poorest immigrant. Or they are sending a message to those who oppose them."

"You think it was to frighten you?"

"I believe that's exactly what it was." He leans forward. "Kathleen, you aren't necessarily protected by who you are, by who I am. You shouldn't have been on your own tonight."

"I know, but Blount—"

He interrupts her. "Dr. Locke came to my office."

"When?" she asks, confused. "Tonight? Is that where you went?"

"No, a couple of months ago, after President Harding died." He lights a cigarette and waves out the match. "He insinuated that I have some weaknesses that could jeopardize my political career."

"Such as? You've done nothing—"

"Teapot Dome, which has cast a shadow over anyone who has oil interests in Wyoming, and . . ."

She waits, but nothing else comes. "Oh," she says, in sudden realization. "And me. Of course. That is why you were so . . . But I've never made a secret of my faith—everyone knows, they've always known—and it made no difference when you were elected to the state Senate."

"But my constituency as governor would reach far beyond this neighborhood, where most of us think alike. It would include the entire state."

"There are Catholics living in every county of Colorado—"

"True, but I think that discretion is required of both of us, given that the Klan is so dogged about finding fault."

He speaks of Julia, of course. She opens her mouth to reply—she has the right to choose her own acquaintances, and Julia can teach her so much about painting. And Julia's peculiarities and her past with Francine hurt no one. But it is Julia's personal connection to Kathleen that makes the relationship questionable. She wonders whether she would go to Julia's home to paint or to hear news of Paul.

"Why didn't you tell me about Locke before now?" she asks.

"You've kept your own secrets." He exhales smoke. "Were Stephen and Susanna still sleeping when you came in?"

"They didn't wake up at all."

"The untroubled slumber of youth. For them, tomorrow will be the same as today."

"You need to rest." She pats the mattress. "Why don't you come in here? Wash up while I—"

"No, I'm going downstairs for a while," he says. "I'll see you in the morning."

# FOURTEEN

The fifth anniversary of the Armistice Day fell on Sunday, November 11, 1923. Sean attended a commemoration service at the glorious Cathedral of the Immaculate Conception, where Father Charles McDonnell spoke of the sacrifice American Catholics had made in "sunny France," a phrase which evoked raucous laughter and applause. After he left the service, Sean drove toward Berkeley Park. As he neared Sullivan's Grocery, a glow appeared in the sky. It was too close, too low in elevation, to be one of the crosses on Table Mountain. Panicked, he careened around the corner. On the well-kept lawn of Blessed Savior burned a cross that was twice his height. He slammed on the brakes, killing the idle of the car almost immediately. Leaving it catty-corner across the street, he ran to where ten or so men stood idly by with pails and buckets.

"Put it out!" Sean shouted. "Start a bucket brigade!"

"No!" About twenty feet from the cross, Father Keohane knelt, his Roman collar reflecting in the light of the flame. "We're letting it burn. If we put it out, it shows that we are afraid. If we let it burn without making any action toward it, it says we're not intimidated."

"But we can't let them think we're too frightened to do it, either."

A few of the men nearby mumbled in agreement, and Danny MacMahon voiced an open protest. "Exactly what I say."

"You can put out this one, Sean, but what about the one over on West Colfax? Or in Five Points, in the Negro quarter?"

"There are others?"

"According to the radio, at least eleven." Brendan rose from his knees. "The symbol of Jesus' sacrifice and love for us is being used as a weapon of hatred, intolerance, and persecution."

Father Devlin shuffled from the shadows beyond the church.

"Thank God you've come, Seaney," he said. "I called the police and do you know what the man on the telephone told me? 'Watch your trash fires, old man, you might burn down your sanctuary.' I told him 'twasn't a trash fire here. I don't burn outside t'incinerator, I said, and hardly in the night —"

"Who told you that?" Sean asked. "Which patrolman?"

"His name was Wells, I think, Patrolman Wells."

Walt Wells. The same one who had muddled the raid on Jorgenssen's gambling hall.

"Did he say he would file a report?"

"He told me there's nothin' to be done," Father Devlin said. "I told him you'd not say that! Your word's sterlin', I told him, and everyone knows it. I've known you since the day you came into this world, I said—"

"I'll make sure one is filed."

"This can't be happenin' to us, Seaney. This church has been here fifty years, now, almost since Denver was settled. I've been here thirty of those. Some of the best families attend Mass in this sanctuary."

Sean placed his hand on Father Devlin's sagging shoulder. "Go inside and rest. We'll clean this up."

Father Devlin tottered away, his hands clasped before him, his head bowed.

Once Father Devlin had returned to the rectory, Brendan spoke again, a cloud of steam encircling his head in the bitter cold. "We must consider ourselves as soldiers, standing for peace and tolerance. You heard what happened to Patrick Walker, didn't you?"

"I heard," Sean said.

Patrick Walker, a member of the Knights of Columbus, had been abducted as he was walking home from the theater around midnight a couple of weeks ago. Five Klansmen forced him into a car and drove him to a cabin north of Riverside Cemetery, where he was beaten with the butts of revolvers until he lost consciousness. When the police had inspected the cabin a few days later, they found the floor boards stained by Walker's blood.

"And to do this on Armistice Day, too," Danny said. "It's a slap to anyone who was in the war, or who lost their sons in the war."

The flames of the cross wavered in the evening breeze. Everyone took a step backward, as the gasoline soaked rags twisted away and fell to the ground.

"Should we put it out now?" Danny called.

Brendan made no objection, and Sean said, "Go ahead."

Danny threw a bucket of water on it, followed by others. Slowly, the rags hissed into blackness.

"Go inside, Brendan," Sean said. "I'll finish this."

Brendan nodded. "I'll check on Father Devlin."

With the others, Sean shoveled the ashes into the buckets and carried them to the incinerator until the cross was just a dark stain on the lawn.

When Sean reported for duty at the Police Department, he sought out his supervisor, Sergeant Denton, and told him of the burning cross.

"Wells investigated it," Sergeant Denton said. "No evidence of crime."

"Wells didn't even visit the site," Sean said.

"He felt no need to." The sergeant called across the crowded room. "Patrolman Wells! Come over here."

Patrolman Wells lumbered across the room. He was heavy-set, with a wide face and black eyes. He had several inches on Sean, and his girth swayed as he walked.

"Why didn't you go over to Blessed Savior?" Sergeant Denton asked.

Wells glanced coolly at Sean. "Why, the old man was drunk as a skunk. He was slurring his words and I couldn't understand his dialect. It was too foreign."

Sean took the bait. "He's not foreign! He's as American as—"

"As you are?" Wells imitated an Irish brogue. "He kept goin' on about a lad named Seaney. 'Twouldn't be you, would it?"

Sean tossed him a sour look. "The Klan is responsible for this, and yet no one has the spine to stand up to them."

"Especially not the priest who knelt on the ground while it burned. His spine was bent over his counting beads—"

Sean jabbed at Wells, who sidestepped it. The punch landed on air.

"That's enough!" Sergeant Denton ordered. "I'm going to reassign you, Patrolman Sullivan. A new beat might help you to sort out your biases from your sworn duty—"

"But, sir, I grew up in Berkeley Park. It's my home—"

"It's time for a change, then, don't you think? Sloan's Lake is a good match for you. Patrolman Berger can take over Berkeley Park tonight."

"Please, I've a duty to see to—"

"You've a duty to do what I tell you to do."

Gloating, Wells turned on his heel and left, but he and two other police officers, Patrolmen Able and Peters, were waiting for Sean in the lounge. Sean opened his locker, wedging the door between him and Wells.

"So, Seaney," Wells said. "You're going over to Jewtown."

Sean gathered his baton and badge from his locker.

"They're all foreign or stupid over there in the ghetto," Able offered. "Nobody speaks English, and they can't eat human meats like pork and fish, so they eat dogs."

"But you'd know all about eating fish," Peters said. "Maybe you should offer them some."

Wells and Able laughed.

"You know, Judge Lindsey's been setting them free for years through his Juvenile Court," Peters said. "They break the law, and come to him and say, 'I'm poor, and I don't have a mother or father, because they died of the spitting cough, and I got it, too.'" Peters gagged a couple of times in imitation. "And old Judge Lindsey says, 'Poor little tyke. Go home and take care of yourself, and next time you kill somebody, come to me, and I'll let you go again because you have such a bad deal at home.' Then, they just go back to their old ways, but even worse because they know they'll get off."

"Shut up." Sean slammed his locker and elbowed his way out of the room, leaving Wells and the other two laughing at him.

That night, he walked along the darkened, silent streets of Little Jerusalem, near Sloan's Lake. The lake spread motionless in the cold, calm evening, and the brick bungalows were shuttered, nearly hidden, except for the lamps on the doors. Along Colfax Avenue, store fronts extended for blocks, many of them in squat brick buildings with floor-to-ceiling glass windows on either side of the main door. Some of the store signs bore a foreign script of thick, wavering lines, but the businesses were the usual type: grocery, meats, clothing, shoes and such. Sean peered into a drug store that looked like any other.

As he turned, two teen-aged boys approached, black beanies on their heads. They wore black trousers and jackets over white shirts, and their hair and eyes were dark, black as the windows around him.

"Good evening," he said, but the boys passed in silence.

Bitterness blossomed in Sean. To be reassigned here—among these heathens, with their indecipherable language, and their refusal to believe in the Son of God. It would take him years, his whole lifetime and half of eternity, to know them—even if he wanted to.

As it happened, his initial encounter came on the first Friday night he patrolled the West Side. He walked his beat, bored already by the quiet, by his isolation, his displacement. The legendary gangs of criminal boys turned loose by Ben Lindsey had yet to materialize, although there were plenty who didn't speak English. He hated being spied on by the men and shunned by the women, who would not meet his eye, but who hurried their children out of his sight. What did they think he was—a degenerate who would lure the children into the alley with candy?

He was a couple of blocks north of West Colfax when a roar echoed through the cold, brittle air. Motors revved and tires squealed, horns honked, and voices hooted in unintelligible catcalls. Sean sprinted toward the cacophony, cutting through alleys and across lawns. He burst onto a side street littered with the multi-colored remains of bottles and mounds of rotten food. Everything was silent, although the smell of automobile exhaust lingered in the air.

"What in God's name?"

The steps of the brick building were covered with trash. A precisely-lettered sign with a six-sided star emblazoned on the building read, "Congregation Beth-el Israel." Glass crunched beneath Sean's feet as he bounded up the steps to the door, but it was locked. Confused, he hurried past the dark, quiet businesses on Colfax Avenue. At a single-story shop, the long glass window had been smashed into jagged shards.

He knocked on the door. "Hello? Police here! Is everything all right?"

No one responded, yet he could hear whispering. Sean reached through the broken window, unlocked the door, and let himself inside. The store was half the size of Sullivan's Grocery, and not a single light shone from any part of it. He clicked on his flashlight. Glass display cases stretched about three-quarters of the way on either side of the store, leaving the center of the store open. Shirts and trousers hung from racks above his head. In the back, hat boxes towered to the ceiling in neat stacks.

"Hello?" he called. "Who's here?"

After more whispering, a dark-haired woman emerged from the shadows. "Good evening," she said. "A window has broken."

"Someone's broken it, you mean. Was anyone hurt? Should I call for a doctor?"

"No, it's all right now."

Another woman spoke rapidly from the shadows in a language Sean could not comprehend. Stepping into the light, she tugged at the first woman's sleeve, trying to pull her back behind the hat boxes.

"I'm sorry," Sean said. "You'll have to speak English. I don't understand . . ."

His voice trailed off. He had no idea what language it might be. Before he could speak again, the first woman said, "My brother's wife says we shouldn't trust you. You might be one of them."

"Who?"

"Who?" she mocked. "The Klansmen, of course. They come on Fridays, on our Sabbath. They honk and shout. They throw trash on our streets and defile our services. What, you didn't see them, Officer, at the door of our synagogue, wearing their peaked hats and burning their torches?"

"No, I didn't—"

"Are you blind?" The anger in her voice rolled over him, a crushing wave. "This is nothing but another pogrom."

"A what?"

"A pogrom. The persecution of the Jews. It happened in the old country. Don't you read history?"

"I am not a Klansman," Sean assured her. "I'm an officer of the law. Now, please, I need to see what's happened."

He switched on the electric overhead light.

"Have you no respect?" The woman immediately switched the light off, casting the store into darkness once more, while the other woman called, "No, don't do that!"

"What's wrong?" Sean asked, befuddled.

"We don't use the electricity on our Sabbath, and to turn it on or off is against our laws."

"Your laws? I'm sorry."

Sean assessed the damage as well as he could by flashlight. Picking through the shard-strewn shirts and ties, he discovered a large, gray stone. "Here it is. It's a rock, not a brick."

"What difference does that make?" the woman snapped. "Put it over there. I shouldn't take it from you."

He laid the rock on the display case. "Are there any men here?"

"Not now. My brother is observant."

"Pardon?"

"He's at the synagogue tonight."

"The synagogue"—the word caught on his tongue—"was locked."

"They do that for protection. So that they can pray in peace."

The light of the flashlight caught her full in the face. Her complexion was smooth and even, with liquid eyes and a wide, soft mouth. She showed no fear, except for a slight tremble of her lips. "What's your name?" he asked, foregoing more business-like questions.

From the back, the other woman spoke in English. "You must wait until Max returns! It isn't right to talk to him—"

The woman ignored her. "Chava Rosen."

It was a declaration, raw and strong, filled with pride and determination. She spoke the name as a challenge, a gauntlet. Without thinking, he smiled at her.

"Do you find our troubles funny?" she asked.

"No," Sean denied. "No, I was only . . . Who's Max?"

"Max is my brother and Rachael's husband."

Sean noticed that the other woman was pregnant. "And you all live here?"

"Not here. We live near the lake."

"What are you doing here, then?"

"We heard the sounds and came out to see what had happened."

"It's not safe out there. Especially if this is the work of the Klan—"

"Who else would do such a thing?"

Sean picked up the rock from the display case. "I probably won't catch the culprits, but I'll be through every night but Monday and Tuesday. I can keep an eye on the store for you."

"What, you're not going to look for them?"

"There's not much I can do. They're long gone."

"Then, how are you any different from them, if you won't help us?"

Sean had reached the end of his patience. "Listen here, Miss. Just a week ago, a cross burned on the lawn of the Catholic Church I attend. That's how I came to be here, because I reported it."

"You shouldn't be here?"

"I've always worked my own neighborhood, with my own kind—"

"Which neighborhood is that?"

"I'm from Berkeley Park."

"And what is your own kind?"

"Irish Catholic."

"An Irish Catholic from Berkeley Park," she mused. "Forced to protect those who don't believe in Christ. Or perhaps you won't protect us, because we're not your own kind?"

Sean sputtered. "That's not it, not at all. I have a duty to uphold the law, and I'll do my best to see nothing like this happens again. Now, at least let me walk the two of you home. You need to go somewhere safer than this."

Rachael spoke again to Chava in the foreign language, and the two went back and forth, their voices rising, until Chava conceded, "Fine, all right. My sister-in-law is already worried at the things we've done that we shouldn't have. She and my brother are more observant of the laws than I am. You can help us so that we don't break any more."

Sean had no idea what she might be talking about, but she had more salt to add to the wound. "That is, if your precious Irish Catholic sensibilities will allow you to help us."

"I have told you that you can trust me," Sean snapped. "But if you want, you can wait here for the Klan to come back for a second pass—"

"Please," Miss Rosen interrupted. "We want your help."

She instructed him to lock the door of the store and close it behind him. Outside, the two women linked arms—for protection against him, he supposed—and led the way up the street. He followed at a respectful distance.

Two blocks up, directly across from the shore of Sloan's Lake, they came to a darkened brick bungalow. Miss Rosen asked Sean to unlock the door and open it, then to hang the key on a peg. As he did, he caught a glimpse of the interior of the house, where a table was laid with dinner plates and lit by candlelight. It reminded him of a sanctuary.

As he stepped out into the frosty air of the evening, Miss Rosen followed. He stopped on the top step of the porch.

"Thank you," she said.

"You must have a beautiful view of the lake from here."

She pointed. "And of the mountains."

He glanced to the west. The gasoline-powered crosses on Table Mountain blazed in the darkness. At once, he realized that she would not forgive him for what he was—a Catholic in a Jewish neighborhood, an outsider, as much a stranger to her as she was to him—and that he could not expect anyone here to befriend or help him.

He tipped his hat toward her. "Goodnight."

Without waiting for a reply, he walked into the darkness.

# FIFTEEN

It wasn't easy to clean up the store. As Chava swept the floor, shards of broken glass as fine as snowflakes slipped through the bristles of the broom and lodged in the crevices between the floorboards. Max took on the task of boarding up the window. Joining them was Judah Rapp, who had long been Chava's best friend, graduating with her from Denver's North High School. Wearing leather gloves, he lugged large chunks of glass to a wagon outside.

The loss of the plate glass window made the store dark and cheerless. Chava stopped sweeping as Rachael picked through the shirts in the display case, shaking glass fragments from them.

"They'll have to be thrown out," Chava said.

"But if we launder and iron them—"

"They won't look as fresh as they should."

"If I'm careful—"

"Chava is right," Max called from the window. "It's better to let them go to the rag picker than have our customers angry with us."

"But—"

"You can't argue with both of them, Rachael," Judah warned. "*Gey shlog dayn kop in vant.*"

Rachael lay the shirts aside, and Judah winked at Chava. The Yiddish proverb translated as "Go bang your head against the wall." It was often used when children wanted what they couldn't have. But in this case, it was true—one Rosen might be prevailed upon, but two of them became a formidable opponent.

The blame—or the credit, depending on how one saw it—went back to their father. When Chava was young, Herschel Rosen declared that his daughter had more wits about her than any of her older brothers and set out to educate her as thoroughly as he did Max, Samuel, Aaron and David. Little Chava tagged along with her father and the boys to the great libraries and museums of New York. After her mother died, Chava became both the matriarch and the adored pet of the family, lighting the candles at Sabbath only hours after she had outdone her brothers at lessons in arithmetic and language.

When Chava was fourteen, Herschel fell ill with tuberculosis, leading to the inevitable move to Colorado to "chase the cure." Max had accompanied his father and sister west, while the other boys stayed in Manhattan to finish their schooling. Within months of their arrival in Denver, Herschel succumbed to the disease at the Jewish Consumptives' Relief Society. Chava finished her secondary education, then studied Childhood Development at Hunter College in New York. After she graduated, she had returned to Denver, where Max had fallen head over heels for lovely Rachael Bronstein. Chava had taken a job at the Jewish Sheltering Home for children of those who—like herself—had lost parents to tuberculosis.

On Sunday evening, Max and several of the West Side's leaders met in the living room of the Rosens' house. Judah was there, of course, as well as handsome Charles Ginsberg and curly-haired Phillip Hornbein, young lawyers who were already well-known in Denver; and Rabbi Linderman from Beth-el Israel. After coffee and cake had been served, Rachael excused herself, claiming fatigue, but Chava stayed in the room, sitting next to Judah.

"We have to stand up for ourselves," Charles said. "Last month, Ben Laska was abducted at gunpoint and beaten with blackjacks by Klansmen, and now Max's store has been attacked."

"I agree," Phillip said. "Rabbi Wise has called on Hebrew men, as 'freemen and free citizens,' to fight against racial discrimination and religious bigotry in our midst."

"It isn't our place to fight religious intolerance that is not within our own people," Rabbi Linderman countered. "Klansmen are mostly Protestants, and it's the duty of the Protestant ministers to take up the burden of the battle."

"And let what happened to Joseph Zuckerman happen again?"

"What was that?" Chava asked.

Charles eyed her. "Mr. Zuckerman was shot in the back because he refused to serve William Clawson on our Sabbath. When the case came to trial, Clawson's attorney, Foster Cline, argued that it was not murder because a Jewish life is worth nothing. And Judge Hersey told the jury— from which Jewish men had been excluded—that murder was too strong of a charge for Clawson. Clawson was acquitted of all charges."

Chava felt the spark of thousands of years of persecution. Jews were accused of making money that should belong to "real" Americans. She had never understood that sentiment—what stopped those who considered themselves "real" Americans from doing the same?

"Charles fought against Judge Hersey," Phillip said. "When Rabbi Friedman of Temple Emmanuel refused to condemn the judge, Charles went to Immaculate Conception and asked Father McMenamin for help. It is shameful that the Hebrew men of Denver must count on Catholic priests to aid their causes."

"And, now, with Ben Stapleton as mayor, we'll see more Klan judges seated on the bench," Charles said. "In fact, when Judge Hersey retires this year, a Klansman by the name of Clarence Morley will take his place."

Judah spoke. "I believe that Bishop Tihen and Father McMenamin are wholly embroiled in their own fight against the Klan, and I know from my friend and fellow member of the People's Council, Father Brendan Keohane, that Father Matthew Smith intends on speaking out against the Klan in the *Catholic Register* newspaper. The Catholics aren't hiding away."

"I cannot let any harm come to Rachael or our child or Chava by speaking out against the Klan," Max said heatedly. "What will they do next week? Another rock through the window? Or will it be a brick wrapped in flaming burlap? Or a stick of dynamite—which they are fond of using in Five Points?"

"I met the new policeman," Chava offered.

Silence met her, and she took a sip of coffee.

"I'm sorry," Charles said. "The new policeman?"

"My sister and my wife took it upon themselves to walk down to the store and see what the commotion was about on Friday night," Max said sourly. "Evidently Patrolman Berger is gone, and a new man is on the beat."

"That was foolish!" Charles said. "And to leave the house on the Sabbath—"

"We've been told all of that by my brother," Chava said. "But I did it out of the fear that there were looters or vandals in the store."

"And what would you have done if there were, Chava?" Max asked. "The policeman is most likely a Klansman, too."

"No, he isn't," Judah said firmly. "His name is Sean Sullivan."

Chava started in surprise. Judah had said nothing about knowing Patrolman Sullivan this morning.

"How do you know him?" Max asked.

Judah continued. "He's the brother of Maggie Keohane, whose husband is Liam Keohane, the Conscientious Objector whom I represented during the war, and he is a devout Catholic. The last time I was there, Mrs. Keohane asked me if I thought he would be all right. She wanted to reassure their mother that he would be safe while patrolling the wicked streets of the West Side."

A chuckle rounded the room.

"He was a hero of some kind during the war," Judah added. "I can tell you that his mother is kind, and that Maggie and Liam and their children are delightful. I see Patrolman Sullivan's presence here as a chance to reach out to our Catholic neighbors."

"Bishop Tihen has always offered the proverbial olive branch," Charles argued. "And if we can form a concerted front of resistance against the Klan—"

"The Klan is protected by the Mayor's office," Phillip said. "As such, it can't be assailed by any other means than political. What we must do is to recall Ben Stapleton and elect a mayor who is not a member of the Ku Klux Klan."

"Who would that be?"

"The most likely Republican candidate is former Mayor Bailey."

"Dewey Bailey!" Judah exploded. "He was elected on the promise that he would lower costs on the tram—which he did at the expense of the workers, whose salaries were lowered. Bailey is responsible for the Tramway Strike, and for the deaths of a dozen workers and women and children in the violence that followed—"

"He is currently our only choice," Phillip said calmly. "Colonel Van Cise has once more refused to run—I've spoken with him again. I believe he intends to leave politics altogether and retire to private practice for the sake of his wife and children."

"What about Jim Graves?" Charles asked. "There's a good Protestant who could take on Stapleton and the Klan."

"Jim Graves is a friend of Stapleton's, so I doubt he would run against him. Besides, he has his eye on another office this fall."

"Governor?"

Phillip nodded. "And if he doesn't become a casualty of Teapot Dome, we must do everything we can to put him there. But there is good news. There is a new Assistant District Attorney in the Denver D.A.'s office. Colonel Van Cise has assured me that he's an honorable and honest man, and I believe he could be a strong ally for us. Here is his card—"

Sensing that the meeting was at an end, Chava gathered up coffee cups and plates of half-eaten cake. Once in the kitchen, she stepped outside the back door and went to the side of the house. A bone-chilling breeze blew from Sloan's Lake. As she leaned back against the house, Judah joined her.

"Did you come to cool down?" she asked.

Judah laughed. "Aren't you glad your world is filled with children and singing and dancing?"

"I can speak out as well as the next man."

"We all know that."

"I'm afraid I might have spoiled any goodwill that the new policeman, that Patrolman Sullivan, might show us," she confessed.

Judah laughed. "So he isn't safe on our wicked streets after all?"

"I made sure that he knew I didn't like him and that he wasn't welcome in our part of town."

"Ah, you are a force to be reckoned with," Judah said. "But, Chava, next time you decide to go on a crusade to save us from the Klan, don't do it on the Sabbath. I think that they"—he nodded toward the house—"are more upset over that than over anything else."


On Monday morning, Chava took the streetcar to the Denver Jewish Sheltering Home on 19th and Lowell. Established in 1908 by Mrs. Fannie Lorber, the Home had started with eleven students in one clapboard house, but now nearly fifty children resided there. Only recently, the sterile dormitories had been razed, and cottages built to house the children in true homes.

Chava entered the kitchen of the preschool cottage and shed her coat and hat. The room was cozy, yet utilitarian. As live-in matron, Sadie Bergman kept a clean, healthy home.

"I'm here, Mrs. Bergman," Chava called.

Sadie appeared in the doorway. "I'm off to the market. Then I'm going for morning tea with the ladies of the Benevolent Society. I'll be back to fix lunch."

Chava wished her well and went to the living room, where the children were gathered. The boys played on the floor with blocks or metal cars, while the girls played with their dolls. "Miss Chava!" the cry sounded, and Chava knelt to take her charges into her arms—ornery David, sweet Levi, beautiful Leah, so many others.

"Oh, I've missed you!" she said. "Is everyone here well? No sniffles? No coughs?"

For the past two years, she had been teaching the youngest in the Home the basics in Hebrew and English—colors, numbers, shapes, simple objects. The children filled her heart and gave her a purpose beyond Max's store or Rachael's spotlessly kept house.

"You would bring every one of them home, if you could," Rachael often teased her.

"Yes, I would," Chava replied. "I love them."

"Marry Judah and have your own, then."

"Judah!" Chava laughed. "We're friends, that's all."

"Oh, that's *meshugaas*. He can't keep his eyes from you. And, you're nearly twenty-six, almost an old maid."

"*Fun an alte moid vert a getraye vayb.*"

It was an old Yiddish proverb: From an old maid comes a faithful wife.

Rachael laughed. "But you aren't an old maid because you're ugly or poor. You choose to be one. So marry Judah and make him—and us—happy."

Now, at the Sheltering Home, Chava said to her charges, "All right, let's say our morning blessing. Quickly now, yes, that's right." After the children settled in a circle, she said, "Let's say the Hebrew together. *Modeh ani lifanecha, melech chai vikayam, she-he-chezarta bi nishmati be-chemla—raba emunatecha!*"

"Now, the English," Chava instructed. "I thank You, living and eternal King, Who has returned my soul into me with compassion—great is Your faithfulness!"

That night, after she finishes cleaning up in the kitchen for Rachael, Chava slips outside and makes her way through the alley behind their home to the store. Letting herself in the back, she settles into a dark corner near the still-intact window that provides a clear view of the street. Huddling in her coat for warmth, she watches the deserted street until she hears footsteps moving steadily up the street. Patrolman Sullivan appears and pauses, as Chava has hoped, beneath the single outdoor light above the store's entrance.

He wears his uniform, of course—a thigh-length dark jacket with wide lapel, gold-colored buttons down the front, and utilitarian pockets over both chest and hip. His hat is cocked jauntily on his head. She catches in the yellowish cast of the lamp, the clear, light color of his eyes. His chin is well-formed and his mouth sensitive. Sean, she thinks. It's a strong name.

Patrolman Sullivan taps the plywood sheet that covers the broken window, and Chava draws back into her corner, afraid he might spot her. What would she say if he noticed her? How would she explain herself if he found her—again—skulking in the darkened store? The absurdity of it makes her laugh, and she covers her mouth with one hand, as if she is a silly schoolgirl. But seemingly satisfied that the wood is sturdy, Patrolman Sullivan moves on, disappearing from her sight.

She waits until she is certain that he has turned the corner at the end of the block before she stands and presses one palm against the glass, as if she might somehow touch him, as if she might somehow know him.

# SIXTEEN

On Christmas afternoon, Maggie and the children made their annual visit to the Graves' home. Seaney drove, with Ma in the front seat of the car, wearing her best church dress and a flamboyant hat that had long gone out of style. Alice Colleen sat between Ma and Seaney on the bench seat, while Maggie wrestled with the three boys in the back, trying to keep them from dirtying their church suits, but giving up on keeping her own skirt from getting wrinkled. Tony Necchi followed behind them in his own car, blissfully alone.

Expensive automobiles already lined the half-mile drive at the Graves' home. Seaney was directed to drop his guests at the door and to leave his car with a valet who would park it.

"You don't think he'll sell it or something, do you?" Tony asked Maggie as the valet drove away in Tony's modest Model T.

"I have no doubt he will," Maggie said. "And I'm sure it will fetch a better price than, say, that Pierce Arrow over there or that Packard—both of which he's left behind."

Tony snorted. Taking Ma's arm, he crooned, "Let me, Bella Signora Sullivan." He escorted her up the lengthy pathway to the front door, past well-tended gardens that had been turned into a winter wonderland, with miniature scenes of tiny skaters, sledding children, and sleighs. The others followed behind.

"There's Jesus!" Alice Colleen pointed to a nearly life-sized nativity scene near a young spruce tree. "And the three kings!"

Frankie bowled through the snow toward the manger, but Seaney caught him around the middle. "Oh, no, you don't," Seaney said. "Let's go inside."

Kathleen and Jim greeted their guests beside a Christmas tree that towered in the center of the massive foyer. Jim was in tuxedo and tails, and Kathleen wore an ankle-length midnight blue satin dress with a ruff of silver fox fur around the hem and the bottoms of the bell sleeves. In her hair, Kathleen wore a comb that sparkled, as if made of diamonds.

"Maggie, Seaney, Aunt Maury, I'm so glad to see you." She kissed Ma on the cheek. Bending at the waist, she greeted the children. "Alice Colleen, you are prettier each time I see you." Alice Colleen speechlessly eyed her, awed by her splendor and beauty. "Frankie, Declan, what big boys you've become." Straightening, she took one of Kieran's baby hands. "Oh, you have grown, too, sir. I wouldn't have recognized you without your sister and brothers."

Maggie felt a twinge of guilt. Kathleen seemed happy enough to see them, even though their dresses were of taffeta and the boys' suits of gabardine. For his part, Jim greeted them warmly.

Kathleen stepped away. "Corporal Necchi! Oh, it's so nice to see you again. Jim, this is Tony Necchi. We met in Chaumont during the war—"

"It's Sergeant," Seaney corrected her.

"Sergeant Necchi, then." She waved toward the interior of the house. "Do you remember Mrs. Brently, our director? She's here with her new husband, and I'm sure she'd love to see you. That evening in Chaumont was so much fun—"

Maggie's envy flickered into full-blown jealousy. So Kathleen had known Tony as well.

"Any of the other girls here?" Tony asked. "What about the one that laughed all the time?"

Kathleen's smile faltered. "Oh, Hank, oh, yes, she caught flu, and—"

"Madame." Someone whispered in Maggie's ear. "If you'd follow me, I will escort your children to the children's celebration."

Maggie followed the footman through rooms overflowing with holiday cheer: enough evergreen garland to make Maggie suspect that, somewhere, an entire forest was now just a maze of stumps; countless silver and gold stars twined into the garlands so that the light caught them and made the entire house sparkle; a Christmas tree around every corner; and enough knick-knacks and decorations to fill the Daniels & Fisher Department Store.

In the second dining room, a life-sized Christmas Town had been constructed for the children to play in.

Maggie examined the houses. "These are Lincoln Logs!"

"Yes, ma'am, Mr. Graves ordered them specially so that the children could have this village. It's very clever."

And very expensive.

Two girls held tea in one Victorian cottage, while a boy hammered at a horseshoe at the blacksmith's shop. Susanna, a year old and barely toddling, sat on a child-sized chair, eating a piece of cake. She wore a less elaborate copy of her mother's dress—midnight blue velvet with satin sash and white Peter Pan collar and cuffs. A nursemaid quickly tucked a bib around her, but there was already a chocolate stain on one cuff.

A model train chugged around Christmas Town on a shelf that was built two or three feet from the ceiling, out of reach of the children. Scenes from the Colorado mountains had been painted along the wall, so the train traveled from the eastern to the western slope. At one point, the never-built Moffat Tunnel swallowed the choo choo for a bit—wishful thinking on Jim Graves' part. Dressed in a green and red plaid vest, black bow tie, and black trousers, Stephen stood beside the unfortunate footman who had been put in charge of running the train.

"Make it go back!" Stephen ordered, definitely his father's son. "The udder way! Udder way!"

Silently wishing the beleaguered man luck in keeping Frankie and Declan from dismantling the village, Maggie went back to the parlor. She found Tony and Ma standing next to yet another decorated Christmas tree while Seaney was off finding punch.

"This is something." Tony looked around. "What did this Jim guy do during the war? Sell Belgium to the Germans?"

"With Edith Cavell and Mata Hari thrown in," Maggie said. "No, it's one simple little word: oil."

"Maybe if Sean and I keep digging around in your backyard, we'll find some, and then we can build a house like this for your parents."

"If you build a house like this, we get it, not Ma and Pa."

"Okay, I promise," Tony agreed. "Where's your husband today? Why didn't he come?"

Maggie wished she had a cigarette. "He wasn't well enough to go out today."

"What happened to him? Where did he fight during the war? Sean never says nothing about it."

"It's a long story."

Liam had not wanted her to come today. As she had dressed for the party, he objected to Maggie taking the children to the Graves' home.

"I wonder if Jim Graves ever loses sleep over the fact that he made millions of dollars from the deaths of innocent men."

"I can't imagine Jim Graves losing sleep over anything."

"He isn't someone I want our children looking up to—"

"We'll see him when we walk in. Then he won't speak to us again. Kathleen might, if she remembers we're there. If not, we'll just eat and come home."

"But I don't want the boys to think that it's all right to exploit and oppress others in order to have such riches and personal gain. I wish I could go along and explain to them—-"

"They aren't old enough to think all that," Maggie snapped. "Besides, Stephen and Susanna are the only cousins they have right now. I'd hate to think that we live less than an hour from them and don't know them." Unable to let it go, she added, "I think you'd be happy they have family and aren't growing up in an orphanage like you and Brendan did."

Liam had met that with stony silence. Wheeling himself to Seaney's room, he had closed the door behind him.

Uncle Irish sauntered through the crowd, joining Tony and Maggie just as Seaney returned with punch for his mother. After Seaney introduced Tony, Uncle Irish turned to Maggie. She kissed his cheek in greeting.

"Muffin, where are those little ones of yours?" he asked.

"In Christmas Town with the others. They'd love to see you."

"I'll stop by," Uncle Irish promised. "It's stuffy in here. Do you want to walk outside?"

Maggie laughed at the double meaning. Retrieving their coats from the butlers, they went out the back of the grand foyer to the great stone patio that stretched the entire length of the house. Darkness was already falling, and the temperature had dropped, but some of the hardier guests were admiring the snowy vignettes secreted throughout the estate. Uncle Irish lit cigarettes for Maggie and himself as they walked along the gravel path, which had been cleared of snow, to the frozen pond.

Two gardeners struggled to push tiny tins filled with oil and burning wick onto the ice with long sticks. Maggie glanced over her shoulder as Tony and Seaney came to stand beside Uncle Irish.

"Why don't you just walk out there and set the cans on the ice?" Tony asked one of the gardeners.

"Mr. Graves has requested that we not step on the ice."

"They might leave a boot print," Sean grumbled.

"He should have been in the army," Tony said. "He woulda been a great general. Tell your men to do something, then tell them they can't do it in the only way it can be done."

The four of them laughed—even Seaney, who was still pouting over being assigned to the West Side of Denver. Here they were, the poor relatives, just one step above the gardeners and footmen, standing out here in the frigid air while inside, the guests marveled at their luck in being invited to one of the Graves' extravaganzas.

A tuxedo-clad waiter approached them. "Mr. Graves has asked me to tell the guests that the traditional Christmas toast will take place in five minutes."

"Well, we wouldn't want to miss that," Maggie said.

Trooping inside, Tony and Seaney gathered fresh cups of punch for everyone while Uncle Irish joined Maggie's mother on a loveseat in front of the fire. Maggie took up a place just behind them.

Jim and Kathleen stood in front of the massive fireplace.

"Thank you to all the friends and family who have joined us here today," Jim said. "We look forward to this afternoon throughout the year"—beside him, Kathleen beamed—"because we see so many who are beloved and precious to us. This is to you"—he lifted his cup of punch—"and to 1924. May it be a happy, blessed, and prosperous year for all of us."

"Hear, hear." The murmur filled the room.

"Will we have a new governor by next Christmas?" someone called.

Jim laughed. "Since there is an election in November, the answer is yes. I will not speculate on who it might be."

As the guests applauded, the children were led from the second dining room and positioned in front of the Christmas tree. Stephen was at the head of the parade. The younger children, such as Kieran and Susanna, were carried by maids. Alice Colleen and Frankie obediently took their spots, but Declan spied Maggie and ran to her.

She picked him up and put him on her hip. "Don't you want to stay up there with Frankie and your sister?"

He shook his head violently.

"Let's start with 'Jingle Bells.'" A pianist seated himself at the Steinway. "*Dashing through the snow—*"

Tony sang along, his baritone full and rich in Maggie's ear. Perhaps it was the heady smell of cinnamon and spruce, or the sparkling glamor around her, or the hour that she had been free of children that made her turn to him and drawl, "Why, Sergeant Necchi, if you had sung to your wife—or your dog—this way, you might still have both of them. In fact, I believe you're good enough to sing opera."

"Naw, I just sing to make you smile. Your smile is so pretty."

Maggie turned away, but she could feel him standing right behind her, almost touching her. She hoisted Declan on her hip and stepped closer to the back of the loveseat. Ma looked contentedly over her shoulder and reached up to pat Declan's knee. Maggie focused on Alice Colleen and Frankie, who were mouthing the words they knew. Her heart beat wildly in her breast.

After the carols, the children were invited to open their presents. Maggie set Declan down, and he joined the others. Alice Colleen received a foot-tall, china-faced doll with blond hair and blue eyes while the boys were given brightly-painted metal cars with steering wheels that turned. The cars could be wound with keys so that they ran on their own.

Maggie pocketed the keys. "Better give those to me before they're lost."

Kieran received a stuffed teddy bear. As the maid handed him back to Maggie, he rubbed at his eyes. His bedtime was fast approaching.

"We should go home." She nodded at Seaney, who stood behind Tony. Leaning down, she said, "Ma, if you want to stay, I'll ask Tony if he can bring you home."

"I'll do it," Uncle Irish said.

Maggie breathed a sigh of relief that she wouldn't have to speak with Tony again. His words—*Your smile is so pretty*—echoed in her head, causing her palms and the skin on her neck just below her ears to feel hot. As she guided her children through the carol-singing crowd, she fought the urge to turn and look at him—maybe even to cast one more smile at him— before she left.

At home, she takes the children into the store and up the steps to the kitchen, while Seaney brings up their presents and other belongings. On the inside landing, she captures galoshes and coats and mittens and hats as the boys run through the swinging door of the kitchen and into the parlor, eager to reunite with the gifts they'd received that morning.

After Maggie bids Seaney goodnight, she joins the children in the parlor. Liam waits for them, seated in his chair, the woolen lap robe that Maggie had sewn for him for Christmas over his legs. Around him are a number of packages wrapped in blue and white printed paper.

"What's this?" Maggie asks. "We opened all our presents this morning."

Liam smiles. "Not all our presents."

He gives each one of the children a bag of chocolate malted balls, then hands Maggie a small, wrapped box. Inside, a locket nestles in a velvet bed. Opening the locket, she finds a picture of Frankie on the left side and Declan on the right.

"Liam," she says. "Oh, thank you, this is lovely."

She brushes her hair aside so that he can fasten it around her neck. Alice Colleen studies it, a serious expression on her face. "Why didn't you put my picture in it, Daddy?"

"Because you're too beautiful to fit in a tiny little heart," he says. "You need to be in a big one, like this one." He lays her hand on his chest. "And Kieran's too young to be in one. But those two"—he nods his chin toward the twins—"are too rascally to sit still, so Mommy needs the locket to remind her what they look like."

Maggie wraps her hand around the locket, her eyes filling with tears. Alice Colleen pops a chocolate ball in her mouth, seemingly satisfied with the explanation.

"Now, who wants to sing Christmas songs?" Liam asks.

"We did that at Cousin Kathleen's house," Alice Colleen says.

"But we can sing again," Maggie corrects her. "I'll make cocoa."

In the kitchen, she stirs the milk on the stove and heats up Kieran's last bottle for the day, listening to Liam and Alice Colleen sing.

*I just sing to make you smile. Your smile is so pretty.*

She shouldn't have praised Tony's voice in such a coy and flirtatious way. She had known it was wrong, even sinful, when she said it. But being away from the house, being out of sight of the kids for the first time since Kieran was born, smoking beside the lake with Seaney and Tony and Uncle Irish—she had felt grown up and savvy, a clever and attractive woman. She had been, for one moment, Mrs. James.

After cocoa, singing, and prayers, the boys go down easily, exhausted by so much excitement. Liam promises Alice Colleen that she can eat a malted milk ball before breakfast tomorrow morning if she goes to bed right away. Maggie settles Kieran in the crib in Liam's and her bedroom.

She unclasps the locket and lays it in its velvet bed. "It's so precious," she says. "How did you manage it? Where did it come from?"

"Judah did it all for me," Liam says. "He brought over the gifts this afternoon while you were at Kathleen's. How was the party?"

She does not answer right away. All she can think of is her exchange with Tony.

"Oh, you know," she says lightly. "There was more to look at than the eye can take in, and more to eat than any number of guests could possibly want, and more for the kids to play with than a three-ring circus. That house would be beautiful if it was half the size—and it would still fit ten families—but it's just monstrous as it is now."

"I've always liked Kathleen, though."

She lies down beside him. "I'm sorry about this morning, Liam."

"I am as well. You're right. Alice Colleen and the boys should know their cousins. There were many days when Brendan and I wished we had cousins or an aunt or uncle or two."

She kisses him, and his arms enfold her. For a while, she forgets that his arms are thin and his legs are wasted. She only remembers how much she has always loved him.

# SEVENTEEN

In January, Jim and Kathleen held a reception at the Brown Palace in honor of the National Western Stock Show. As specially-chartered train cars of prospective buyers from Chicago and the east pulled into Union Station, Denver's population soared with local visitors—Colorado ranchers, cattlemen, horse breeders, and other livestock managers from the eastern plains and from beyond Continental Divide.

The guests at the party were the usual, as well as a slew of invitees from the State House and from Stock Show itself. Legislators from Denver mingled with cattlemen from Wyoming, while women from the Denver Art Museum talked with Montana ranchers' wives. The dress at the party was traditional western: a melange of fringed leather jackets and skirts; heavy fur coats; silver conch belts and buckles; elaborately tailored and embroidered shirts; turquoise bolo ties; and a collection of hats, from the oversized Stetson to the everyday felt cowboy hat. Nearly all of the boots were hand-crafted, but as usual, Jim's boots topped them all. Rising to the knees, the beige leather was embossed with a series of traditional Indian symbols, including feathered leaves and sunbursts. The cocoa-colored box of the boot sported a heel of plated silver.

As the night wore on, the crowd narrowed to just the regulars. Evan and Perry were drinking near the piano, although no one was drunk enough to play yet. Once that started, the party would get—as it usually did—out of hand.

"This city and its cows," Marie pouted. "Why is there so much fuss about it?"

"First of all, they're cattle, not cows," Jim said. "And for Kathleen and me"—he smiled in her direction—"the fuss is to raise the better bloodline of purebred Herefords. My stock comes from my ranch in Durango, and hers from Redlands."

"Who's winning?" Samuel asked.

"My lovely wife," Jim said. "Last year, she took reserve champion breeding stock with a corral full of heifers from Redlands, losing only to Ken Caryl Ranch's famous stock. My poor beasts came in fourth."

"Fourth is nothing to sneeze at," Mrs. Crawford commented.

"Ah, but it isn't the blue ribbon," Jim said. "My wife is far better than I am at recognizing excellent stock."

"I suppose you regret going back to the Legislature after so much fanfare," Mr. Crawford said.

"Oh, it isn't that different from herding pens full of cattle that will eventually end up at the slaughter house," Jim said flippantly.

The guests laughed, but Samuel, known for spoiling the mood, asked, "How will the Klan affect the election in the fall?"

"Oh, Lord," Marie groaned. "The election isn't until . . . whenever it is. Do we have to talk about it now?"

Samuel insisted. "The Klan is already planning—"

Arthur cleared his throat. "I hear there is a new man in the Denver District Attorney's office who is looking into the Klan's activities."

"Well, if Colonel Van Cise deals with the Klan the way he did the Bunco Gang, the church basement will be full of robes and hoods," Mr. Crawford said.

Laughter rounded the room. Colonel Van Cise had created an indelible image when he incarcerated the Bunco Gang in the Kindergarten room at the First Universalist Church. Stories abounded of hardened confidence men being interrogated while seated in red, child-sized chairs.

Arthur continued. "The new man is a war hero. He is as decorated, I'm told, as Colonel Van Cise." Arthur looked directly at Kathleen. "It is Colonel Paul Reston, Julia Reston's nephew."

Kathleen's hands and heart drained of blood. Every nerve in her body flamed, every muscle turned to stone.

"That's impossible!" Ellie reacted. "He was killed in the war. We had firsthand knowledge of it."

"His plane was shot down over German lines just days before the Armistice," Thomas added.

Jim said nothing, but his hands shook as he lit a cigarette.

"Well, obviously, that information is mistaken," Arthur said. "He joined Colonel Van Cise in the D.A.'s office just after the first of the year, for whatever good it will do."

"Kathleen, dear," Victoria said in her acid-sweet voice. "You meet with his aunt to discuss the Museum, don't you? Surely she's said something about it."

Everyone—Jim, Ellie, Thomas, Victoria, Marie—looked at her. She swallowed, once, twice, before she was able to force herself to speak. "She told me it was a case of mistaken identity. The plane carrying her nephew and an American pilot crashed behind German lines. The pilot was killed, but somehow the names were confused, and it was reported that Miss Reston's nephew had been killed and the pilot had lived."

With a lurch, Jim went to look out the window. Ellie leaned back in her chair, her expression crossing from disbelief into anger, while Thomas stared in surprise at Kathleen.

"What an extraordinary story!" Victoria said. "I'm surprised it wasn't reported in the newspapers when the mistake was discovered. What a terrible thing for the pilot's family—to expect a son to come home from war only to find that he died without anyone recognizing or honoring him."

Eyes fell again on Kathleen. "I don't know," she said.

"From what I've heard, the Reston family is very well-connected in New England," Arthur said. "It's in lumber and has been for decades. I'm surprised Colonel Reston didn't stay in the east and take some role in the family business. What has he been doing since the war?"

How did Arthur know all this? Again Kathleen was caught—did she explain where Paul had been, or did she pretend ignorance and commit something close to a lie?

"Do you know, Kathleen?" Victoria prompted.

"I think he's been living in Paris," she said.

"He went to Yale Law School," Thomas offered. "Perhaps he's practicing law."

"I was unaware that the family had breeding," Victoria said. "You would never know it from the way his aunt dresses—"

"For God's sake, Mother," Jim snapped.

"I wonder what brought an eastern lumber tycoon cum Yalie cum army flyer cum military colonel cum Parisian lawyer to our dusty, prairie cowtown," Marie inserted slyly. "We have no trees to speak of. What do you think, Jim?"

"A woman." He turned from the window. "It's always a woman."

"Oh, Jim, you tease!" Marie laughed. "The story would be too incredible if Colonel Reston had come to Denver looking for a long lost love. It sounds like something Eleanor Glyn might write."

Kathleen stood abruptly. "Excuse me."

With as much dignity as she could muster, she left the room.

She went into the bedroom that she and Jim shared in the suite. Sitting at the vanity, she looked at her face in the mirror. What was Paul doing now, only a couple of miles from her, so close that she could walk to him? Was he standing at a window in Julia's house, thinking of her, knowing that he would not sleep or eat or behave rationally until he saw her again? Was every nerve in his body alight, with hope, sorrow, anger, grief—every emotion, it seemed, that existed?

A knock sounded on the door, and Kathleen picked up a hairbrush and ran it through her hair. "Come in," she called.

Ellie entered the room, furious. "How long have you known this? Why did he come back to Denver? Was it for you?"

Kathleen laid down the hairbrush. "I've known . . . Julia . . . Miss Reston told me—told us that he was alive when I went to her house with Anne and Cornelia Evans and Elsie Haynes."

"So you've known for some time? Did you write to him? Did you ask him to come back?"

"No," Kathleen said. "I've had no communication with him."

"Why did he come here, then?"

"I don't know," she admitted. "He married in Paris and has a son—a stepson, that is—who is actually the son of . . . I'm sure he brought them with him."

Ellie paced the room. "You must remember, Kathleen, that, as much affection as I have for you, I will always be my brother's strongest ally. I will not allow him to be hurt in love again."

Again? Kathleen wondered. Aloud, she said, "I have no intention of doing anything that will hurt him."

"What about your own self-interest?" Ellie asked. "I saw you with Paul in France. You loved him with a passion that you have never shown toward Jim. You broke whatever rules you had to in order to be with him. You cannot, you absolutely cannot, do that to Jim. You cannot destroy him."

Kathleen opened her mouth, but no words sounded. She could not imagine Jim as capable of being destroyed—the man who had the world in his hand, who took whatever he wanted, who gave just as easily to whomever he favored. She did not possess that kind of power over him.

"This is a surprise to me," she said. "I had no knowledge of it until your father spoke."

Ellie opened her mouth as if to challenge the statement, but asked instead, "Are you coming out again? It doesn't look good for you to be hiding away in here when so many know about your past."

"Would you—just this time—would you make my excuses to the guests? Please, would you say I'm not feeling well?"

After a moment of disdain, Ellie said, "I will, but think carefully on this. You may think my mother is the Valkyrie in this family, but I am her daughter."

Jim came into the bedroom after the party had grown loud and careless, with voices echoing from the high ceilings of the suite. He closed the bedroom door behind him and leaned against it. Kathleen could smell brandy.

"So," he said, "Paul Reston has been miraculously resurrected." Mocking her accent, he added, "Saints, preserve us."

"I had no idea that he had come back to Denver."

"You should have told me from the moment you heard he was alive," Jim lashed. "Did you tell our guests everything that you know or is there more?"

Kathleen repeated the story that Julia had told her, including the tale of Paul's wife, Mélisande, and their child, Alex. "I had no reason to think that any of this would matter," she said. "Julia gave me no indication that Paul might come to Denver."

"And you haven't seen her recently?"

"Not since Thanksgiving. I've been so busy painting for the exhibition—"

"Yes, that's all we've heard about," he said dryly. "What do you intend to do now?"

"I have no plans to do anything."

"I have never known you to be without a plan, especially if there is something that you want." He lit a cigarette. "Be careful, Kathleen. If a man is not positioned wisely when an oil well blows, the force of the gusher can carry him sky-high. You, my sweet, are looking down the well."

He left with a slam of the door—which did nothing to disturb the partygoers. The next morning, when Kathleen went into the main room of the suite, the room was silent, tomblike, the remains of the party already swept away by the maids. In the second bedroom, which served as a guest bedroom, Kathleen found Harris, Jim's valet, hanging clothes in the closet.

"Where is Mr. Graves?" she asked.

"Mr. Graves is at the State House."

So he had fled, run away from his anger and thrown himself into work. Given the armful of clothing that Harris was hanging in the closet, she assumed that Jim had decided to take up permanent residence in the suite.

Within an hour, she had dressed and packed. Instead of going home, she drove south, toward Louviers. At the farmhouse at Redlands, Napoli waited for her. As the groomsman who tended the horses on the ranch saddled him, she went into the house and changed into riding pants and a flannel shirt of her father's. Despite the snow on the ground, Napoli took on the challenge of climbing the ridge to the west of the farmhouse, picking his sure-footed way up the icy rocks.

As they reached the ridge, Kathleen patted his neck. "Good boy, good horse." Although the sun shone warm on her face, she could see her breath.

Dismounting, she sat on a boulder that overlooked the barnyard and the track that led into Redlands from the county road. At Jim's insistence, the farmhouse where she had been raised had been redone with plumbing and electricity so that the children could accompany her. The outbuildings were meticulously maintained—another condition of Jim's. He swore he would not have his wife and children playing at being paupers.

Below, a rusted Ford truck inched its way from the main road to the farmhouse. Her father climbed from it, a miniature figure from this far away. He shaded his eyes against the sun and looked toward at the ridge. Kathleen waved her arm back and forth. She mounted Napoli and rode down the ridge to the house.

"Caitlyn, me love," Her father caught Napoli by the reins.

She dismounted and kissed his cheek. "I'm so glad you came."

"Aren't you supposed to be at Stock Show today? The morning newspapers were all fluttering about the party you had at the Brown Palace last night and wondering whose stock you were going to buy this year."

"Oh, that . . . Can we walk to the stream?"

"Sure." He patted Napoli's neck affectionately. "Are you bringing this old nag along?"

As they strolled, she told him of Paul's unexpected return to Denver.

"I'm not sure I understand this," he said. "This man has been alive all along, and no one knew?"

"His aunt did," Kathleen said. "She told me last fall."

"Seems like something of a miracle, if you ask me."

Kathleen winced, remembering Jim's term, "miraculously resurrected."

"What should I do, Papa? I can't ignore him—I can't pretend he isn't here. We'll run into each other eventually. How do I act? What do I say? How do I keep everyone from watching me with suspicion?"

Her voice echoed from the banks of snow along the creek. Napoli neighed, unsettled by his mistress' distress. She wiped at the tears that stung her eyes in the cold of the morning.

"Whoa," her father said. "You're asking too many questions. Let's start over. Why would you even think about Paul Reston again? Why would you want to see him?"

Kathleen stopped beside the creek, allowing Napoli to wade forward for a drink of the icy water. "I know it's wrong, but—"

"I'm not worried about right or wrong," he said. "Why does he even matter now? You're a married woman. You have two beautiful children— Stephen is a pip and Susanna is a living doll. And your situation is as close to perfect as—"

"It isn't about the money," she said hastily.

"Don't be a fool. If you didn't have Jim, you'd be living in a two-bedroom house in Berkeley Park, taking care of a raft of children, just like Maggie. You need to realize that his money has given you opportunities that most women can't even dream of."

She bridled at the harsh words. Once, during their time in the Relief Society, Helen had pointed out to Kathleen that the subject of money would come up if the man Kathleen married were poor, so why was it *outré* to talk about marrying one of the wealthiest men in Denver? Papa—and Helen— were right. The money mattered.

"But how can I go forward now that he's here?"

"How can you go back? Tell me, Caitlyn, what kind of husband is Jim? Does he drink too much? Does he gamble away his fortune? He's too high and mighty to beat his wife—"

"Of course he doesn't do that!"

"So, tell me, what are his faults? Where has he failed you?"

She did not answer right away. To expose him seemed unfair—after all, this was about Paul. "He's vain," she said at last. "He can be selfish and petty and vindictive—"

"As just about any man can be—"

"And sometimes, he hides away in his study—for days, sometimes—in a dark mood—"

"What man doesn't have dark moods or bad days?"

"He uses money to make a show—"

"As do you," her father scolded. "A single dress of yours costs more than your mother ever spent on clothes in her lifetime. You drive a bright blue car that everyone recognizes, and you throw parties that are written about in the newspapers."

When she did not answer, he said, "Regardless of what you think now, you and Jim have a strong and successful union. You have six years of marriage under your belts—and you're still speaking to each other, which is more than your mother and I or Maureen and Seamus had. You've witnessed Maggie and Liam's mess—you know that happiness in love doesn't come that easily. And I believe Jim loves you, and he loves your children. The few times I've seen him with them, he's been affectionate and patient."

"Yes, he loves us. But I have to find out why Paul didn't make an effort to find me. Why didn't he contact Julia and have her—?"

"Caitlyn, me love, stop. That is exactly the kind of thinking that will drag you deeper and deeper into a dark cave. I've had thoughts just like that throughout my entire life. What if this, what if that."

Of course, he had agonized over his unhappy marriage to Mama, his one child—a girl—despite a desire for more, and the struggle to make Redlands a profitable enterprise.

She tried again. "But if I know the answers—"

"I can see you're going to visit him, regardless," he said. "But I doubt the answers will make you feel any better than you do now. Take someone with you so that you're not tempted by him. A friend, or—"

"Julia will be there." Her eyes clouded again as she spoke the next words. "And his wife will be there."

"Good," her father said firmly. "Maybe then you'll see what a pipe dream this is."

# EIGHTEEN

Paul Reston had arrived at Denver's Union Station a week before Christmas, 1923. Stiff from the bone-wearying trip from New York, he favored his left side as he swung down the steps of the train to the platform. The peculiarities in his movements were habit now, but he was aware of the curious and, at times, impatient glances he received in crowded train stations or streets.

Union Station overflowed with noise and energy. Men wrapped in voluminous fur overcoats and women in open-toed sandals with sparkling jewels on their wrists commanded Negro porters to haul their trunks and cases. A wild-haired, red-eyed preacher shouted prophecies of doom, while a woman with a sagging basket of half-rotted fruit begged for money. Near the entrance, a Salvation Army band played Christmas carols, its sergeant swinging a bucket for donations. Paul had nearly reached the recessed doorways when a child dashed in front of him, thrusting a flyer at him. "KKK celebration on New Year's Eve!" the boy shouted. "Don't miss it!"

Paul stuffed the flyer into the pocket of his woolen coat. Outside, on Wynkoop Street, he hailed a taxi. As the car crawled along an ice-laden street jammed with horse-drawn milk wagons, delivery bicycles, streetcars, and Christmas shoppers, Paul studied the elegant, neoclassical architecture of Denver's booming business district. On 17th Street, the stone façade of Graves Industries appeared, graced by a colorful banner over the main entrance wishing MERRY CHRISTMAS AND PEACE ON EARTH, FROM MR. AND MRS. JAMES A. GRAVES AND FAMILY. Paul looked away. To the west, the immense, snow-capped mountains rose majestically against the azure sky, and the snowy foothills seemed only a quick walk away. He could not help but think the word, "Home," although he had never seen this state, this city, before.

Letting himself into Julia's house in Park Hill, he called, "Hello?"

Julia appeared from a door to his left. Her snowy hair lay in a practical bob around her face, and she wore a loose smock that was smudged with paint. The smell of oil paints and canvas permeated the foyer. Again, the word "home" went through Paul's head.

"Merry Christmas," he said.

"Good Lord! Paul! Oh, come here! Oh, you don't know how I've missed you!" Julia embraced him, and he kissed the top of her silky head. "Let me look at you." She stepped back. "I see no sign of your wounds. Did you recover completely?"

"As well as could be expected." He straightened his spine. His left shoulder now sagged below his right, the result of being slammed against the earth. A series of ugly, purplish welts ran along his ribcage, and his two broken ribs had not healed well, leaving unsightly bulges near his armpit. Fortunately, the severity of his wounds could be hidden by a combination of good posture and elegant tailoring.

"And still as handsome as ever." Julia touched his cheek. "Come into the parlor. When did you get here?"

"This morning."

"And you let me know nothing about this. How French of you."

Laughing, Paul took a seat in an armchair, and Julia sat on the sofa. His portrait hung above the fireplace. Julia had painted it years ago—when he was still whole and healthy and looking forward to a bright future. He wore the uniform of a Norton-Harjes ambulance driver, the one he had worn in October of 1918, when he had met a scared-to-the-bone Kathleen at the train station at Montdidier. She had been so determined not to fail the French soldiers or the Red Cross. How could he not have loved her from that moment forward?

Julia rang the bell, and a dark-skinned woman came from the kitchen. Julia introduced her as Rosa, acknowledging that she was more a friend than a household worker. Paul shook Rosa's hand.

"Pleased to meet you, Colonel," Rosa said.

"Call me Paul."

"Bring us whatever you have in the kitchen that's edible," Julia said. "And whatever we have that's appropriate to celebrate with at this hour of the morning."

Rosa nodded and left the room.

"I've been desperately lonely without you," Julia said. "Where is your wife?"

"It's a long story."

"I have the rest of my life."

Rosa returned, setting the tea service in front of Julia. She'd included scones, jam, clotted cream, and a bottle of sherry on the tray.

"Excellent choice, Rosa," Julia said. "Now, tell me all."

As Julia poured the tea, Paul said, "You know that, after I got well, I continued to work for the AEF. I thought it would be fulfilling work, helping to sort it all out. But—"

The excavation of battlefields, the exhumation of graves that had moldered for five or more years, the search through the rubble of villages, tunnels and fortifications for bodies—it had all been unbelievably horrifying. The men under his command, nearly all Negro, had made jokes to bear it: The German bodies rotted quicker than the others, coming out of the ground as nothing but mush, and the drunkards kept the freshest, preserved in the sauce they'd consumed. The war remained so present yet: miles of unexploded ordnance, broken rifles, battered tanks. Soldiers looted bodies, and the officers overlooked it. Girls—twelve, fourteen, sixteen but with the appearance of women in their thirties—gathered near the fields, no longer kept away by Pershing's orders or the legal French brothels. They sold themselves to the grave diggers for pennies.

The fields of flowers were the worst. The poppies of Flanders Field had long gotten their due, but these flowers—bell-shaped foxgloves, heady chicory, heavy-headed thistles, St. John's wort—weren't the flowers on which the heroic had fallen; these brilliantly-colored blossoms grew lush from feeding on decomposing human remains.

"But as bad as it was for me, it was far worse for others," Paul said. "Families would arrive in France, having spent their life's earnings to travel there in search of their loved ones. I met young wives with babies, and parents whose faces were old beyond their years. If I had any news for them, it was usually bad. More often, I had no news at all of their son or husband or father."

Julia made a sound, a pained and broken, "Oh."

"And it weighed on me." He studied the portrait of himself. "I had a breakdown early in 1922. For three months, I was prescribed bed rest and calm. The Army quietly discharged me with a couple of medals and full military honors. It overwhelmed Mélisande. She went to join her sister and parents, who are living in the south of France. She took Alex with her. She made it clear that I was not to follow her."

"I'm so sorry. I had no idea."

"She has her own ghosts to deal with. She's a refugee from Belgium, and she walked with thousands of other Belgians to reach Paris, suffering whatever happened along the way. Her brother died, and her sister was taken away by the Germans as . . ."

"Are you in love with her?"

"She's lovely and bright, and she can be warm and gentle—when she wants to be. She's also highly damaged, as so many of the Belgian and French are. We loved one another as two very desperate people might. At times, we were happy and affectionate; others, she threw plates at me. We stayed together because it was better than being apart."

"That's the basis for most marriages, I suspect."

Paul sipped from his tea. He missed Mélisande's dark intellect and bitter wit, but it was the loss of Alex that nagged at him most. After the war, Paul had written to Kenny's parents on Mélisande's and Alex's behalf, but he had received a polite letter from them that dismissed Mélisande's claim. Yet anyone who had known Kenny would have no doubt of Alex's paternity. Alex had inherited all of the traits that had made Kenny so successful and popular at Yale: good humor, good looks, and crackling intelligence.

"I can't blame her," he said. "Since the brain fever, I'm not as sharp as I was, and the breakdown revealed how weak I am. Anyway, our relationship was mostly for Alex."

Julia mulled over his words as she poured glasses of sherry. "And now you've come back for Kathleen, haven't you?"

"Yes."

"I'm afraid it's a mistake. She will never leave her husband."

Paul's throat closed against the question that had haunted him for years, but he forced himself to speak. "Does she love him?"

"Perhaps," Julia said. "I don't know. I've met him, and he is quite the man about town. Handsome, dignified, the perfect politician. And she seems to relish her role as a society woman who attends countless charity events and manages her husband's donations—which are fantastically generous. One or both of them are written up in the newspapers at least once a week. But all that doesn't matter. They have a son and a daughter, and she is a practicing Catholic. With all her fine jewels, she still wears a rosary."

"She has always worn one." Paul smiled as he remembered how she had carefully removed the rosary, kissed the figure of Jesus, and laid it on the nightstand before they made love in Chaumont. Even as she was about to sin, according to the Church, she believed in forgiveness and hope.

"What did you expect, Paul?" Julia asked. "What did you want?"

"Since you wrote to me, I've awakened every morning thinking of her." The words burned in his chest, both hopeful and despairing. "I've gone to bed every night thinking of her. I couldn't keep living that way, so lost, so pointless. I had to come back and reconcile with it."

"I hope you can. I hope she can, too. I've grown rather fond of her, despite her money."

Paul laughed half-heartedly, and Julia asked, "When will you see her?"

"I'll let her come to me. She'll know soon enough that I'm back."

"Are you testing her?"

"I wouldn't do that. But I want her to come to me—if she wants to—on her own terms." He swallowed back his doubts. "Now, tell me about Denver. Where have I brought myself to?"

Julia waved a hand in dismissal. "A troubled and unpleasant place, I'm afraid. The Ku Klux Klan seems to have taken over just about everything."

"The Ku Klux Klan? I thought that was a southern organization, some remnant of the Civil War. Wasn't the movie, *The Birth of a Nation*, about it?"

"I suppose it was. But the Klan came to Denver a couple of years ago with the force of a hurricane. The knights—as they call themselves—say they are for law and order, but they seem to stir up a great deal of religious and race hatred. They burn crosses at the homes of anyone who offends them and barge into the worship services of the Catholics and Jewish peoples. I believe the Negroes have been all but chased out of town."

"I had no idea," he said. "Surely it isn't welcome in this state. Wasn't Colorado part of the Union?"

"Evidently it has a powerful draw."

"What's being done about it?"

"Not much of anything, I don't believe. The police are useless—or part of it—and our government officials seem stymied. Governor Sweet yammers on about them, and the Mayor of Denver is one of them. The only one who has stood up to them so far is the Denver District Attorney."

"What's the D.A.'s name?"

"Another noble cause, Paul?"

He laughed. "I'll need employment if I'm to live here, Julia, and, as far as I know, I'm still a lawyer."

"There will be no stopping you, I suppose." She reconsidered. "The two of you might have something more in common. He, too, was a Colonel during the war. His name is Philip Van Cise. But, please, no more about this now. Tell me about France. I miss it so."

The job at the District Attorney's office came easily to Paul; he and Colonel Van Cise instinctively appreciated each other's straightforward mannerisms, and their shared war experiences supplied an immediate bond. Colonel Van Cise had served as an observer from reconnaissance posts and hot air balloons.

"My off-the-ground experience wasn't nearly as heroic as yours," he remarked.

"Nor as deadly," Paul reminded him.

"Perhaps." He shrugged. "But, to the matter at hand, have you heard of Ward Gash?"

"I'm afraid not."

"He was working as a janitor in Denver when he received this letter."

The Colonel slid a one-page letter across the desk. The letterhead identified it as from the "Imperial Palace, Invisible Empire, Knights of the Ku Klux Klan." Beneath the type, which was in all capitals, was a drawing of a Klansman on horseback waving a torch. Addressed to "Janitor Ward," the letter included the charges of "abusive language" and "intimate relations with white women." The letter closed with the sentiment: "NIGGER DO NOT LOOK LIGHTLY UPON THIS. YOUR HIDE IS WORTH LESS TO US THAN IT IS TO YOU."

Paul pushed the sheet away from him. "What was done about this?"

"I convened a grand jury to look into it, but it failed to find enough evidence to charge anyone," Colonel Van Cise said. "Ward—who's a good boy—left town, and I was left with nothing. So I chose five trustworthy men to infiltrate the Klan. They attend Klan meetings, note who's there, and report weekly on the Klan's activities. I need someone to follow up on their information."

"I'd be honored, sir, if you asked me," Paul said.

"It's more dangerous than you'd think," the Colonel said. "I want Locke and his ilk to know that I haven't forgotten them, and I want you to be the public face of that opposition. You'll be as much of a target as I am."

"Well, we've both been targets before, haven't we?"

And so, within a week, Paul was sorting through the spy reports, investigating any potential wrongdoing, and reporting directly to D.A. Van Cise. Out of a sense of obligation, he wrote to Mélisande:

*I've arrived in Denver, in Colorado, where I'm staying with my Aunt Julia. I've also secured a job at the District Attorney's office as an investigative prosecutor—you would call me a* procureur. *Please keep me informed of your address if you move, so I can send money for Alex's and your living expenses.*

The letter struck him as cold and formal, but he and Mélisande had parted on bitter terms. Even though they had lived together for nearly three years, they had never found in each other what they had each lost in their first loves.

He offered an olive branch: *Please tell Alex to write to me whenever he wants. Tell him that Papa Paul will always love him, no matter how far apart we are. Let me know how you are faring as well. I will help as I can.*

Kathleen comes to him on a gray, misty evening near the end of February. When Julia shows her into the parlor, Paul's heart beats in violent anticipation. How lovely she is—dressed in a gold bodice that drapes in elegant lines to a chocolate-colored skirt, a simple brown cloche hat with a bow, and brown gloves. Paul takes in the richness of her clothing, happy to see that her old imperfection—curls that escape onto her neck—still exists. She sits stiffly on the divan, while Paul takes the nearby armchair.

Julia stays with them for a short while, carrying on a mostly one-sided conversation about the Denver Art Museum exhibition. Kathleen answers in polite snippets. Her eyes dart here, there, looking to the hallway that leads to the stairs or toward the kitchen. She looks everywhere but at Paul.

"I must excuse myself," Julia says. "I must paint with great fervor if I'm to keep up with the talented Mrs. Haynes and with you."

Kathleen's attention comes to Julia. "Oh, not me—"

With a wave of her hand, Julia slips away, leaving them alone. Kathleen's watery eyes meet Paul's, her lips trembling.

"Kathleen, it's so good to see you," he says.

"I still can't believe you're alive," she whispers. "When I heard you were dead, I felt as if I had died, too, as if I couldn't possibly still live—"

"I know." He leans forward and brushes a curl from her cheek. "I know—"

"Please, I'd like to meet your wife and son."

"They're in France."

His words destroy her self-control. She sobs, then puts a hand over her mouth. "Tell me, tell me now, before I say anything more—did you choose her over me?"

"No, never," Paul vows. "You have to believe I never left you. It was a cruel twist of fate. Our plane went down only hours before the Armistice was called. We all knew it was coming, but Kenny wanted one more shot at glory—"

"Glory! Oh, God, if only —"

"I've thought that a million times. And a million times, I've wished that we'd run away that day that we were trapped in the *abri* outside of Amiens. Or during our time in Chaumont."

"Chaumont."

She whispers the word as if it is sacred. Chaumont—where they had made love for the first time, and for the last, during three days of leave that Paul had secured. He remembers it still as if he were looking at a painting of the scene: the simple trappings of the room, the way the sun fell across the floor, and Kathleen, with her pale skin and her hair a tangle of copper and gold. She had allowed him to explore her body, to taste her skin, to breathe in her scent, to become one with her in a way that transcended the earthly.

"Those were the happiest days of my life," she weeps. "We were so young, and everything was so sweet." The words that follow come in a rush. "Oh, why didn't you find me? Latour did. He came to the hotel where we were staying and told me you were dead. If I'd known you were alive, I would never have come back to America. I would have stayed in France. I would have begged for bread on the streets to survive—anything!—until I found you or you found me again."

"I lost track of you. I was flying so much by then that I barely had time to eat or sleep, and the mail only came now and then. Where were you on Armistice Day?"

"In Paris." Painfully, she recounts, "After Chaumont, we were moving so fast and so often that I couldn't keep up, either. We'd barely set up in a town when we were ordered to go somewhere else. It was chaotic, as if the entire system had collapsed. Finally, we arrived in Récicourt, which was so close to the Front that we were ordered to leave by the military. But we stayed until . . ."

"What happened?"

"Hank caught the flu, and then Ellie—Mrs. Brently—did, too. I tried to take care of both of them, but I caught it, too. So we were moved to Paris, but Hank—oh, God, Paul, she died!"

He moves to the divan and gathers her against him. Her warmth, the same scent of rosewater that she wore in Chaumont, the way her hair tickles his chin and cheeks—this is the woman he should have been holding and loving for the last five years. Her arms come around him, undeterred by the abnormalities of his left side.

"I'm so sorry," he says. "Dear Hank—she was such a good friend to us. So you were in Paris when Latour found you?"

"Yes, but why didn't you send him back to me to tell me you were alive? He found me easily enough the first time, why couldn't he—?"

"Poor Latour, he survived four years of war only to be hit by a drunken taxi driver in Brussels three days after the Armistice."

"He died?"

"Yes, and I couldn't have contacted him to let him know I was alive even if I'd been able to," Paul said. "I was a prisoner in Germany until nearly mid-December, under the name of Alexander McKenzie. By the time I reached the French hospital in Bellegarde, I had brain fever. Every time I woke up, I had to go through a list of questions—Where was I? How had I come to be there? Why was I there? I had no idea I'd been mistaken for Kenny—I heard his name over and over, but I thought it was in my dreams. They'd given me morphine for the pain in my ribs, and I couldn't tell what was real from what I'd imagined."

"But you must have known I'd come home, to Denver, to Redlands. You could have found me so easily!"

"By the time I was healthy enough to sit up and write a coherent letter, it was 1920. I knew I was too late. I knew you would have married by then."

She begins. "Only because—"

Her words end in a sob. Tears drip from her chin, staining her bodice. Paul's heart and throat pulse with pain, and he draws her closer, kissing the top of her head. Nothing can undo the pain and sorrow they have suffered for each other.

"How did you come to be married?" she asks.

"When I went to tell Mélisande that Kenny was dead, she was nearly crazed with grief. I had no idea that she had a son. Taking care of them seemed the right thing to do."

"Did you—do you—love her?"

"We were both haunted by what we had lost. Loneliness, grief, an inability to manage in the world—those things kept us together in a way that love alone never could have. And I grew to love Alex as much as a father loves his son."

"Why didn't you stay in Paris, then?"

"When Mélisande left me, I had nothing more to keep me there."

"She left you? Why?"

"A number of reasons," Paul says.

He doesn't tell her that Mélisande had found the letter that Julia had sent him, in which related that she had seen Kathleen. The row they had had because of the letter had left them both exhausted. With wild and raw grief, Mélisande had beaten her fists against his chest, crying, "You can go back to her, but I can never see Kenny again!" Ironically, it had been those words—*you can go back to her*—that had made Paul reread Julia's letter again and again, until his desires grew unbearable, until he had to return to America and see Kathleen again.

As if she has intuited his thoughts, she asks, "Why did you come here?"

"I came here because, even if I can't have you, my life is with you, my girl of the Wild West."

She lets go of his hand and stands, and he rises as well. "Oh, Paul, oh, it's impossible now! I know it is! I have a husband, a family—children who are as precious to me as Alex is to you."

"We promised one another to keep the faith of our love alive—"

"I did! You don't know how—you didn't see how I wept, how I lay in bed, even after I was married, even when I was with . . . I would close my eyes and wish that . . . I would open them hoping to find it was you with me. Oh, my God, it was so sinful, but I couldn't stop myself!"

Tears stream down her cheeks, and she sweeps them aside with an impatient hand. "I promised God anything—my soul, Jim's soul, the souls of everyone I'd ever loved—if I could just go back and save you. Even my children, my babies—I was willing to sacrifice them for my own selfish needs. But I had to let it go, finally, I had to make a choice to live in the present. I'm sorry, I'm so sorry!"

In an instant, she is gone.

Shattered, Paul retreated to his study at the back of Julia's house. Elbows on his desk, he put his fingers to his temples. Mistake after mistake after mistake: joining the U.S. Air Service, which not only separated him from Kathleen, but placed him in mortal peril; becoming involved with Mélisande out of pity and shame that he had lived and Kenny hadn't; and now, coming to Denver, where Kathleen had moved on so gracefully and completely. Perhaps volunteering to go to France in the first place—so long ago in 1916—had been his first mistake.

A tap sounded at the door, and Julia entered, carrying a decanter of Scotch and two glasses. "If I recall correctly, this is to your taste."

As she poured two fingers in a glass, Paul admitted, "I don't drink much anymore. Mélisande drank enough for both of us."

Julia handed a glass to him. "I'm assuming your reunion with Kathleen went as predicted."

When Paul didn't answer, she advised gently, "Perhaps it's time to put the past to rest. You've seen her, you've explained yourself so that she no longer thinks she was abandoned. But you're a young man, Paul, smart and handsome, with a future. For my sake, don't let it slip away."

Paul downed the Scotch, wincing at the burn in his throat, chest, and gut. Did he still know how to connect with the living? He had spent so long in the miasma of war and death that he felt unprepared for living. The world favored men such as Jim Graves, who glittered with wealth, health, and success, not those whose bodies and hearts and minds had been damaged by war.

Julia rose. "I'll say goodnight. Don't stay up too late."

"Goodnight."

Once she left, he drank a second glass of Scotch. Kathleen's words—*I had to let it go, finally, I had to make a choice to live in the present*—echoed in his head. Hadn't he grieved long enough? For Kathleen, for Kenny, and in some ways, for himself and the part of his life that had been lost when he had been mistaken for Kenny. His grief had driven Mélisande away, and with her, Alex. Julia was right—he needed to rebuild his own life in a meaningful and productive way. The question was how.

# NINETEEN

In his suite at the Brown Palace Hotel, Jim read the morning papers in disbelief. John Galen Locke had been wrong when he had predicted that Interior Secretary Albert Fall would take the fall alone. The guilty were spilling like dominoes across a floor: Harry Daugherty, who was Attorney General under President Harding; William McAdoo, who was Secretary of the Treasury under Wilson and his son-in-law; Josephus Daniels, the Secretary of the Navy during the war; and both Roosevelt boys, Archie and Theodore, Jr., war heroes whom Jim had once met when he trained at Plattsburg in 1916.

There were local scandals as well. Both Frederick Bonfils of the *Denver Post* and John Shaffer of the *Rocky Mountain News* had allegedly received stock payments in order to keep the scandal from flooding the newspapers. George Creel, who had once lived in Denver, had dirt on his hands as well.

And now, in an act of hubris, oilman Harry Sinclair, whose stock value had increased thirty million dollars in just three days, had refused to testify before the Public Lands Committee in Washington.

A knock sounded at the door of the suite, and Jim took a sip of brandy. Even though it was too early to drink, brandy was the only solace for the dark mood that he had been suffering from for the past several days. Harris answered the door, then stepped aside. "Please, come in, sir," he said.

Jim folded the newspaper and set down his glass of brandy, steeling himself as Arthur Graves came into the room, his habitual frown leading the way.

"Good morning, Father."

After nodding in greeting, his father said, "Your mother is worried about you. She said that you're living here more or less permanently."

As always, Jim's mother had her ways of knowing where he was and what he was doing. "It's more restful," he said. "I'm able to work in the evenings."

"Has something happened between you and your wife?"

The bald question echoed from the elegant cornices and fixtures in the room. "Nothing has happened between us," Jim replied. "I'm caught up here, and she is painting for the exhibition at the Denver Art Museum."

The explanation must have sounded as weak in his father's ears as in his own, for his father's grayish face shriveled in disdain.

"She is also visiting her former lover at his aunt's home. You know she went over there again a couple of days ago. Your mother heard it from one of her acquaintances."

Jim winced. Damn, Ellie must have shared Kathleen's history with Paul with his mother. He hoped that Marie or Evan would not catch wind of it.

When Jim did not reply, his father resumed. "To see you married to a woman who was never worthy of you. To watch as she makes a fool of you—"

"If this is what you've come to say, Father, you can save your breath. Your opinion of Kathleen has never been a secret."

His father thrust a newspaper toward him. "Look at this."

The headline teased, "WHO IS BOILING IN THE TEAPOT TODAY?" The article began with the sentence, "What a mess our nation is in!" and continued on about J. Leo Stack, a little-known nominee for Congress from Denver whom oilman Edward Doheny had paid to secure a lease on land in Wyoming. Jim skimmed the column until he read: "Our own state's oilmen are lying low. Colorado's favorite, Jim Graves, has given up one palace for another, abandoning the lofty grandeur of his home in the Denver Country Club for a suite of rooms at the Brown Palace Hotel. Some speculate that he is hoping that Senator Walsh and his Teapot Dome subpoena crew won't think to look for him there, while others suggest that he and other old-line Republicans are hiding from the Grand Dragon under the fanciest sheets in town. We at this newspaper wouldn't mind if he were busy redecorating his rooms into campaign headquarters. So put the kettle on, Senator Graves, and let's hope your 'Teapot' doesn't boil over!"

"You need to go home, Jim," his father said. "You need to resume your normal routine and you need to pay attention to your political career. You need to see to it that your wife is under control."

His father stood, and Jim rose as well. As he reached the door, his father flung one more admonishment in Jim's direction. "You need to go today."

After his father departed, Jim finished his brandy, trying to overcome his anger and anxiety. What did his father know of his home life or his relationship with Kathleen? His father had never addressed Kathleen directly, had never held a conversation with her or attempted to get to know her. He wouldn't even call her by name. Then again, how well did Jim know her? Would she be the same woman now that she'd seen Paul? Whatever words had already passed between them would surely color her decisions now. After a long while, he called Harris and gave him a long list of instructions. The last was to pack up Jim's belongings and call Blount to bring down the Silver Ghost from the house.

Outside the Brown Palace, reporters waited for him, as if they had been camped for days. "Senator Graves," one called. "Did you see the headlines? Are you connected in any way with the men who've been indicted or subpoenaed?"

"Senator Graves, what interests does Graves Industries have in the Teapot Dome area? Do you have leases there?"

"Senator Graves, according to my sources, you have leases in Alcova and Bar Nunn. Can you say for certain that they aren't part of the Naval Reserve lands? And since some of your oil fields border the Naval Reserve, can you assure us that you aren't taking oil from the Reserve?"

Jim spied the Silver Ghost at the curb about twenty feet away. Blount stepped from the car and hastily loaded the baggage.

"Excuse me," Jim said. "My car is here."

"Senator Graves, are you running for—?"

He climbed into the back seat, and Blount closed the door, silencing the questions. Harris sat in the front seat. Looking over his shoulder at Jim, he reported, "Everything that you requested will be waiting for you when we arrive."

"Good man, Harris."

At home, Jim discovered that Kathleen wasn't in the house. He found Stephen and Susanna playing in the nursery playroom. Both children jumped up and ran to hug his legs.

"Did you bring us presents?" Stephen asked.

"I haven't been out of town." He laughed. "And I swear that you have every toy in Denver right here in this room." He glanced up at Susanna's nurse, Miss Davis. "Where is Mrs. Graves?"

"She's painting until noon. Then, she'll join us for lunch."

"Not today." He smiled down at the children. "Mommy and I are going to lunch together today." When Susanna objected, he said, "We'll have a good dinner all together. Miss Davis will speak to Mrs. Bains for us and tell her to fix whatever you and Stephen want." He glanced at the nurse. "Will you do that for me, Miss Davis?"

"Of course, Mr. Graves."

Jim found Kathleen in her studio at the far end of the snowy lawn. He tapped at the door, then entered without waiting for a reply.

She sat before an easel, a paintbrush in her hand, a blue smock over her clothes.

"Stephen and Susanna have been asking for you," she said without greeting him.

He caught the reproach in her voice. "I stopped by the nursery to see them."

He glanced at the painting, which was in an entirely new style. She no longer painted in realistic, carefully detailed lines, but in broad strokes that gave only the impression of the painting's subject. Seemingly overnight, she had assumed a unique and—Jim had to admit—intriguing style.

"Are these for the museum?" he asked.

"Yes," she said nervously. "I'm hoping they'll choose at least one."

"Well, put away your paints," he said. "We're going out today."

"I'm hardly dressed," she protested. "I have an old blouse on under—"

"It doesn't matter."

The Lincoln waited for them in the driveway. It was the heaviest of his cars—barring the Silver Ghost—and the most likely to travel through snow. After Kathleen had donned her heavy seal fur coat and hat and gloves, she asked, "Where are we going?"

"It's a surprise."

He drove the car up the winding, mud-slicked roads of Turkey Creek Canyon. At the gated entrance to the Graves' property, he climbed from the car and peered through the unlocked gate at the track beyond. It had been cleared by a heavy dray, leaving a snow-packed tunnel through which they could enter.

As they bumped and spun over the snow, the moss-covered rock exterior of the Graves' castle in the mountains appeared. It jutted upward from the granite rock on which it was built, reminding Jim of the castle in Edinburgh, Scotland. Stone chimneys graced the various rooftops, and a portico built of the moss rock protected the heavy wooden front door.

"This must be Inglesfield," Kathleen said. "I didn't think you ever wanted to come back here."

"I've been back a few times."

The front door was unlocked, and a fire burned in the stone fireplace. Deep-cushioned sofas, with heraldic emblems emblazoned on the armrests, sat on either side of the fireplace. A massive grizzly bear hide spread across the floor between the sofas. The room blazed with color, from the rose-beige shine of the burnished pine floor to the golden latches on the doors and windows. Above, the soaring vault of the Great Room reached upward nearly three stories.

"I didn't expect it to be so large," Kathleen said.

Jim set a picnic basket near the fire. "My grandfather never tired of building another wing here or an extra turret there. There's plenty of granite to be had out there."

"Where did he get the money?"

"In his day, it wasn't so much money as determination. He'd had a bit of luck in a silver strike—nothing like Tabor or some of the others—but enough to buy a mountain where there was no gold or silver. He put the castle together one rock at a time, I think. In his spare time, he founded Graves Fuel and Coal."

"When did he die?"

"When I first went to college. I must have been eighteen or so."

"And he lived here?"

"He never made it his home. Just a summer place or hunting lodge. We rarely saw him, anyway. He wasn't keen on belonging to the 'Seventeenth Street Crowd' that my mother and father were in at the time. I don't think he and Father agreed on much."

"That seems to run in the family." Kathleen ran a hand over the uneven rock of the fireplace. "Who built the fire?"

"The caretakers, Mr. and Mrs. Holden. They live about a mile away. They keep the drive open and maintain the place."

Kathleen moved to the south side of the Great Hall, where deep bay windows reached from floor to ceiling. The sunshine caught in her hair, sparking it with copper.

"This is lovely," she said. "I'm sorry it carries such sad memories. Where is the lake?"

He joined her. "Down there, hidden by the trees. You can see just a bit of shoreline in summer, when the water is blue."

"When were you last here?"

Jim looked up to the balcony that ran along three sides of the Great Hall. At one time, he had chased Anneka along it—up the main staircase, along the balustrade, out onto the roof terrace, then back inside and through a maze of rooms that led to the turret. She could run down the spiraling steps of the turret in a flash. Jim was much clumsier in his boots.

"Come with me," he said. "I'll show you the rest."

He led Kathleen up the grand staircase to the landing, which looked down into the Great Hall. The closed bedroom doors were swollen with winter and humidity, and Jim leaned heavily against the first to open it. "This was my room."

The narrow bed was obviously a child's, with its quilted coverlet and teddy bear near the pillows. The rest of the room was filled with toys—a hobby horse, its reins forever tugging at the bit in its mouth; a hand-carved German train that chugged around on its own little wooden track; a ship in a bottle.

"How old were you when . . . ?"

She didn't finish the question, and Jim said, "I was eight when Stephen and Elizabeth drowned. More than twenty-five years ago."

Her voice welled with emotion. "How terrible to lose a child."

"Enough of this," Jim said briskly. "It's not why we came here. Let's go downstairs and eat. If I remember correctly, the only warm spot in this behemoth is directly in front of the fire."

In the Great Hall, he spread the heavy blankets that had been packed in the car on the bear rug. "This was one of the largest grizzlies known to roam Colorado. My grandfather shot it himself. Here, sit down. This bear's been dead for forty-some years. It won't mind." He nodded toward the picnic basket. "What did they send for us?"

As she unpacked the basket, Jim shed his raccoon coat and jacket. It was too cold to roll up the sleeves of his shirt, but he undid the collar. As they ate, their talk was of safe and tried subjects: of the children; of the continuing cold streak; of the gossip in their circle of friends. When the conversation waned, Kathleen asked, "Why did you bring me here?"

Jim lit a cigarette before answering. "You went to see him, didn't you?"

She ran a hand over the fur of the bear. "Yes."

"So, what should I do now? Pack a larger suitcase? Rent an entire floor at the Brown Palace?"

"You needn't do anything. In fact, you can stop hiding out there, unless you have some reason to. Is Marie staying there just now?"

"Perhaps, but on a tawdrier floor," he said. "You needn't worry about what I've been doing. I've been waiting for you to make your decision."

"My decision?"

"About what you will do about Paul Reston. I doubt your love for him has waned that much."

She looked down at her plate. "Please, let's not talk about it."

"I'm not owed an explanation? I know what he was to you, and it's only fair that you tell me what he still means to you."

She rose and went to the fireplace. With a poker, she aimlessly jabbed at the logs. A memory of Anneka standing in that spot, the same poker in her hand, ready to knight him, came into Jim's head. *You are my queen,* he had said, but that was so long ago, and now Kathleen actually held that role. Today, he saw that as a bitter pill.

"I never wanted this," she said. "I never wanted him to come here—I never dreamed he would come here. I thought he was dead, and I'd long since left it behind. And there's you, and Stephen and Susanna . . . I told him he had come to Denver with false hopes."

"What do you mean, 'false hopes'? Isn't he married?"

"His wife stayed in France. Evidently, the marriage didn't work."

How brazen of Paul to waltz into Denver after six years and ask a married woman to give up her husband and children for him. He must have tremendous faith in her love for him.

"So he comes here thinking he has the right to disrupt our marriage?" Jim's fury erupted. "Why would a decent man do that? Did you give him the idea?"

Her reply was steely. "You've forgotten who and what I am."

"No, I have not. You profess to be pure and without temptation, but you are deceptively good at getting what you want."

"I have never called myself pure!" She swallowed to calm herself. "I just want to be who I was. I thought we were happy—"

"But now, you're not?"

"I don't know. Everything's all . . . I'm confused."

Jim tried to calm himself. "You need to know," he managed. "I need to know. I'm going to run for governor, and I need to announce it soon. It's only six months to the primaries, and the newspapers—"

"I've seen them."

He joined her at the fireplace, tossing his cigarette into the flames. She tortured the logs again with the poker, watching the embers flare up and fly away.

"With all this mess around Teapot Dome, and the Klan tailing me, I can't risk a personal scandal," he said.

She flared as quickly as the embers. "Is that what you're worried about? Not that you could lose me? Not that I might love someone else, or that Susanna and Stephen could be hurt? Well, rest assured, I won't cause a scandal."

"You've put yourself in this position, by neglecting to tell me that Paul was alive, by acting coy and secretive when he came to Denver." The accusation echoed through the Great Hall. He rarely raised his voice—he had long ago learned it did little good—and he had never before shouted at a woman. Feigning calm, he added, "My mother knew you'd visited him before I did. My father told me."

"Of course, she did," Kathleen blasted. "Perhaps I'm not the right one to be at your side when you run for governor, anyway. I will never be a Bonfils or an Evans. I will never belong to Louise Hill's Sacred 36." Her tone turned bitter. "I will never be like your mother."

"I wouldn't want you to be like any of them or—God forbid—like my mother. But those whose wealth grew with the war are considered dishonest or untrustworthy. They're seen as mired in blood and profiteering. We can't have any gossip about our marriage."

"Again, you're more worried about your reputation than about your marriage. God forbid your parents or their narrow-minded friends think ill of you!"

He chose to ignore her. "There are others things, as well."

"There couldn't possibly be."

"Liam Keohane. If Locke ever got wind of that—"

"I can't do anything about my relatives!"

Her complaint echoed throughout the Great Hall.

"If you want to see Sean, meet him somewhere and avoid their home until the election is over."

"Seaney doesn't live there, but Aunt Maury does. Since my mother died, she's the closest that I have—"

"Do it quietly, then. And I know you go to Mass."

Her frustration overflowed. "What does it matter? Dr. Locke already knows about my faith."

"But there's no sense in baiting the bull. So, please, don't make a show of it."

"I don't make a show of going to Mass. That would be sinful." Turning, she added, "You seem to have thought of all these conditions for me, but you haven't even asked me yet if I want to be the governor's wife."

"You've always known that was part of our marriage agreement."

"I didn't realize I had entered a 'marriage agreement.'"

"You knew exactly who I am and what I want when you married me. And you've played your role with a fair amount of gusto so far. The only difference is that the stakes are higher now." His patience waned. "I don't think you take me seriously enough, Kathleen. My love is just as precious as Paul Reston's. Think twice before you throw it away."

She jabbed at the embers. "I have no intention of doing that, but I won't give up my own life, either, and become just a puppet or a doll. Isn't there anything on your side? There were rumors in the typing pool—"

He thought of Mina, but the little girl had faded so far into memory that he could not imagine she still existed. Most likely, Mina had forgotten Jim and the house on Corona Street as well.

"There are always rumors. A few minutes ago, you insinuated—without grounds, I might add—that I've been seeing Marie at the Brown. It seems you're just as willing to believe the rumors as the girls of the typing pool were."

She winced, obviously offended by the comparison.

"My life has always been public record," he said. "And, yes, I sowed wild oats, as they say, in college—as you well know from Evan's stories. But since the war, I have been an exemplary husband and father. I have been faithful to you since the day we married. I've done nothing I should be ashamed of."

"I haven't done anything, either," Kathleen said hotly. "Loving someone else before I married isn't shameful. Speaking with him again isn't shameful. Attending Mass isn't shameful. What Liam did—standing up for what he thought was right—isn't shameful either."

"I misspoke. I didn't mean to imply shame. So, will you be with me during my run for governor?"

She hesitated, but replied, "I will be with my children and husband, as I promised long ago."

Suddenly, the day felt worn out, all life wrung from it. Jim had the sense that he and Kathleen had just become partners, not husband and wife, not lovers—and certainly not free or easy with one another, but guarded and distant.

"Let me douse the fire," he said. "And we'll be on our way."

# TWENTY

Sean parked his car in front of Sullivan's Grocery and lit a cigarette. For a month, he had walked the streets of Little Jerusalem, and nothing had improved. No one greeted him as he passed, no one spoke with him, and—either thankfully or disappointingly—no crimes had occurred. His job had become purposeless, boring, and it would continue that way. When he had reported the trash on the streets and the broken glass to his superior officer, Sergeant Denton, he had been told to ignore it.

"It was probably a wedding," Sergeant Denton said. "They stomp on glasses to celebrate. That's probably the trash you saw in the street."

"Someone threw a rock through a storefront window."

"Why didn't the owner report it?"

"They don't trust the police over there."

Sergeant Denton smirked. "When the owner steps forward, I'll send a detective over to look into it. But from now on, whatever you see or hear on Friday night, you can consider part of their religious celebrations."

As he left Sergeant Denton's office, Sean sensed Wells and the others laughing. Oh, what a joke it was—the good Catholic altar boy was now banished to Jewtown.

So, why did the West Siders make him so angry? Why did it bother him so that they shunned him? He had fought for France without knowing a single Frenchman, and he'd never resented it. Yet these Jews and their lack of even the smallest sign of courtesy infuriated him. Let the Ku Klux Klan ruin their streets and defile their synagogue—what did he care?

Maggie came from the store, wearing a stylish jacket and skirt. She started to open the door of the delivery truck, but came over when she saw him sitting in his car.

Leaning into the passenger's window, she asked, "Is this a private pout or can I join?"

"I'm not pouting."

"Oh, yes you are. You look like last week's custard left out in the sun."
She climbed into the car. "Drive me downtown. I have to return tomorrow's
letters to Mr. Ledbetter."

As she settled into the passenger seat of his Model T, she asked, "So
how are the sneaky and rotten denizens of Jewtown treating you?"

"About the same as my sneaky and rotten superior at the station."

"You know that Liam's best friend, Judah, lives over on the West Side.
He was Liam's lawyer."

"I thought Frankie MacMahon was his best friend," Sean said sourly.
"This Judah fellow seems like a poor replacement."

"Now, see, Seaney, that's just the attitude that will get you into trouble,"
she scolded. "Judah helped us—he helped me quite a bit. He's polite and
well-meaning, although a little too Bolshy for me. He got me my job at the
newspaper. And Frankie's no good now, is he? He's dead."

"Better dead than one of them," Sean grumbled. "I met one."

She gave him a sidelong glance. "Heavens, they're not Martians."

"Are you sure?" He told her about the incident in the Rosens'
Haberdashery. "I did everything wrong. She asked me if I'd ever read
history, for Pete's sake."

"And have you?"

"What do you mean?"

"Well, just like we have our own history—Christ and the Roman
gladiators and the popes and all—they have theirs. It's pretty Old Testament,
the one we never read."

"Old Testament," he mused. "I'm pretty sure she wouldn't mind having
not just an eye for an eye, but both my eyes."

"Better learn to squint, then. Park over there."

He edged the Model T into the curb, and they both went into the
newspaper office. When she entered, Maggie was hailed by a number of
reporters: "Hello, Mrs. James." "How are you, Mrs. James?"

She waved back at them. A disheveled, graying man in an ill-fitting
suit stepped from a private office. "Running it a little close, aren't we, Mrs.
James?"

"As usual, Mr. Ledbetter," Maggie called frivolously.

Sean stood near the outer door. Around him, reporters shouted into
telephones or squabbled over typewriters. Loose sheets of paper floated
from desks onto the floor, but no one stopped to scoop them up. The noise

of the presses, which were in a back room, was deafening, even through thick walls. Maggie leaned over a desk, talking with a prim woman who held a red pencil in her hand. She touched the woman's shoulder as they shared some joke, and Sean felt a pang of jealousy. Maggie was different here—not his little sister, or the mother of four, or a housewife. She was free, easy, confident—a woman who garnered respect and popularity. Wasn't there anywhere he belonged? He wasn't at home in his childhood house, or at the police station, or in Kathleen's bombastic world, and definitely not on the West Side.

Maggie returned with a box overflowing with letters. "Ready to go?"

As they made their way to the door, Mr. Ledbetter called from his office, "Three o'clock tomorrow, Mrs. James. Early press time."

"I'll be here."

When they left the office, Maggie asked if she could drive. "Usually I have a baby on my lap when I drive. This will be heavenly. We might even take a detour. In fact, maybe we'll lose our way for a day or two."

Sean took the passenger's seat, the box of letters on his lap. "You answer all these in one night?"

"Not all," she said. "I choose the best eight or ten to be printed in the newspaper and answer those in depth right away. I make notes on the rest, and give them to my assistant, Thalia—you saw her—who types up letters based on my notes. Then I look them over, and if I like them, sign them. They're mailed out with advertisements for local businesses, who've paid for the honor. So everyone gets an answer from Mrs. James—even if their letter doesn't appear in the newspaper. Mr. Ledbetter may look like the cat dragged him in, but I'd fear for any cat that tried it."

Rather than turning on Federal, she kept going on Colfax, taking Sean through the blocks of stores that he patrolled. In the daylight, the sidewalks teemed with makeshift markets and tents where vendors sold wares.

"Where are we going?" he asked. "I don't want to see any more of this part of town than I have to."

"Be patient." She continued to the west, to where a sign stretched over the road that read: "He who saves one life is considered as if he preserved the whole world" above the words, "The Sanatorium of the Jewish Consumptives' Relief Society."

She parked the car on the dirt road outside the gates. "This is where people with tuberculosis come to die. It's free for them, and their families are cared for as well. The big hospital near downtown wants to cure them—and it wants them to pay—and so it won't take the saddest cases. For a long time, they just died in the streets, until a Russian immigrant named Dr. Spivak came up with this place."

Sean studied the quiet, bucolic buildings in the distance. Dairy cattle grazed in the pastures, rows of fruit trees flourished in the orchard, and crops grew in the fields beyond the buildings. It would be a peaceful place to die.

"How do you know about it?" he asked.

"After Liam went to prison, I was so desperate," Maggie said. "I couldn't keep the store going on my own, and we needed money so badly. Judah brought me here so we could pick up a typewriter—the one Liam uses now—so I could work. He told me about something that the Jews do called *tzedekah*—"

"*Tze* . . . what?"

"It's like charity, but it's not. He explained it as giving what you can and how you can—so it isn't like Jim Graves being photographed for the newspaper every time a silver cuff link falls off his sleeve and is caught by a starving urchin, whom he graciously allows to keep it. It's more of a way of living, making sure every action is the best you can do for others."

"Haven't we always done that?"

"Yes and no. We give at the church, we go to the orphanage raffle and that kind of thing, but this is, well, it seems more generous to me, because it's personal, and it doesn't make a fuss of itself." She nodded toward the hospital. "Judah helps the people here with their wills and such. He doesn't charge them for it."

"They can't be more generous than the Catholics. Think what John Mullen has done for Denver—"

"I know what he's done," she said shortly. "And I know what Kathleen and her golden goose have done for Blessed Savior. All those new altar cloths—'the gift of Mrs. James A. Graves.' And that's what I mean—Kathleen got recognition for her donation."

"I don't see anything wrong with that. She did a good thing—"

"I think of my work as *tzedekah*. I don't have money or power, I don't have any worldly goods that anyone would want—unless you count the delivery truck, and they're free to take it—and so I give them"—she knocked her knuckles against her head—"what's up here."

"You get paid for it, though."

"Yes, but I take even the stupidest problems, even the most boring or crazy things, as seriously as I take the tragic ones."

"Why are you telling me this?"

"Because if you think about doing what you can for the folks on West Colfax instead of thinking about how different they are, you might make some friends over there. And we all know that you aren't very good at making friends."

"Neither is she."

Maggie smirked. "Why does this woman bother you so much?"

"I was trying to help, and she just . . . well, she wouldn't even let me speak, she was so angry and vicious—"

"The two of you sound like peas in a pod to me." She put the car in gear. "I better get home and see what kind of mess Ma has let the kids make. Thanks for coming with me."

The sun had nearly set that evening when Sean saw Chava walking near the lake. She wore a brown woolen coat and a reddish-brown cloche. The sun on her dark hair, which curled gently around her chin, brought out the auburn in it. Below her left eye, he noticed a small, teardrop mole, where her cheekbone joined her temple. Her eyes were light brown, with flecks of amber, like tiger's eye jewels.

His heart beat so hard that he hunched his shoulders to puff out his heavy woolen coat. He couldn't let her see his nerves or it would be another disaster for him. Maggie was right—he needed to take charge of the situation.

"Miss Rosen." He tipped his hat to her.

"Patrolman Sullivan," she acknowledged. "You're watching over us tonight?"

"Yes."

"Beware of the boys from the yeshiva. They can be quite argumentative after a full day of the Torah and the Talmud."

"I'll be vigilant," he promised. "As I always am when I'm on duty."

She laughed. "You have no idea what I said, do you? The yeshiva is the school, and the Torah is the same as your Old Testament. The Talmud is a book of laws. I am teasing you—the boys are quiet and have good manners." She bit her bottom lip. "I'm sorry. I shouldn't do that. Someone has told me I should be nicer to you."

"Who told you that?"

"Someone I consider to be a very good judge of character."

"Well, he's wrong—whoever he is. When I reported what happened on Friday night, I was told it was all part of your religious services."

"What? Breaking windows? Honking horns and racing motors outside the synagogue? Who told you this? The Sabbath is about prayer and reflection."

"As I said, there's not much I can do for you."

She opened her mouth as if she would berate him, but said, "Thank you for reporting it."

"Where are you going?"

"To the Community Center. I teach a class in the new building—you should know where it is, if you are to patrol here. Walk with me, it's just a few blocks."

"So, it's where you work?"

"Oh, no, this is something I do on my own. I teach immigrants how to speak English and how to understand American customs—like money, or buying things in a store, or paying for the streetcar—"

"They don't know how to do that?"

"Some of them come from very poor places. They've never seen an automobile or skyscraper before. Everything in America is new and frightening for them, and they've had a long journey to come here. Some of them are just exhausted and sick."

"Where do they come from?"

"Mostly Russia. There aren't as many now—the new laws have made it so our people can't come to America as easily as they once did."

"So this is your *tzedekah*?" Sean hoped he wouldn't earn her contempt by pronouncing it incorrectly.

She laughed, delighted. "Where did you hear that word?"

"I have my secret source."

"Yes, this is *tzedekah*. I am a teacher, and so I teach. The German Jews who live near the big hospital think we're barbarians over here. It's sort of how you think of us—"

"I didn't say that!"

"Some things don't need to be said. So we work very hard to Americanize our new people. We teach them English, and to keep a house as an American would, and to dress as an American. The sooner they have learned our customs, the less likely they are to be bothered by those who hate us."

Sean thought of the men he had seen all dressed in black, with bushy beards and curls in their dark hair. Obviously, the people of the West Side had a different opinion of what an American looked like.

Chava's amber eyes flashed. "Come with me to my class. My students, they come from places where the police attack their homes and burn their things. Come with me and show them what an American policeman is like—"

"Oh, I don't think that's a good . . . I just told you, there's nothing I can do for you—"

"What, you can't promise them that you won't beat them? Or burn their furniture in the street and kick them out of their homes? "

"Of course I won't do that!" Sean lowered his voice. "But I don't understand any of this—"

"Well, I don't understand you either if you can't promise to be kind."

She wheeled away, heading down the street ahead of him.

"Chava!"

She turned. "You said my name wrong. It is Chava"—she made a guttural sound in her throat—"not Hava."

"I'm sorry." Why was he always apologizing to this woman? "I've never been good at foreign languages. When I was in France, I was a fool at it."

"Yes, I can see that," she said. "Just come along with me, Sean Sullivan"—she perfectly enunciated his name—"and I will do the talking."

She was, as he should have expected, true to her word. She spoke in Yiddish or Russian or both—he wasn't sure—while men in ill-fitting black suits, and women with their hair hidden beneath tatty scarves, and kids in mismatched, hand-me-down clothes who looked as if they hadn't seen sun in years listened intently. Every time Chava gestured toward him, he smiled like an idiot.

Chava spoke in English. "So, now we say, 'Welcome, Patrolman Sullivan.' Yes, all of you."

"Velcome, Patrolen Sool-ee-vahn."

"Thank you," Sean said.

"And when you are scared or see something wrong"—she inserted a foreign word—"you say, 'Help me, Patrolman Sullivan.'"

They repeated it with varying degrees of success. Chava turned a brilliant smile on Sean. "That's it. Unless you want to hear a lecture in Yiddish on what a bank is and why you should put your money in it."

"I need to go back to work."

Chava walked him to the hallway. "Class ends at 8:30."

She closed the door in his face.

But he was back at 8:30, after prowling the silent streets with his thoughts firmly centered on the Louise Guldman Community Center. She smiled when she saw him loitering outside the door of the classroom. As he helped her into her coat, she said, "Now, you have met some of our people, and it wasn't so terrible. And they think you're a good man now."

"As far as I know, you could have been telling them that I was the giant squid from *20,000 Leagues under the Sea*."

"You're so funny!" Chava said. "Tell me what you did during the war to become a hero, now that I know it wasn't for speaking French. I heard that you won a medal."

"Where did you hear that?"

"I have my secret source."

In the cold air, his laughter came out in a puff of steam. "I didn't do anything more than any other American soldier—or British or French—did."

"They didn't all win medals."

"It isn't something I like to talk about."

"Why?" Her gaze skewered him. "Because it makes you sad? Or angry? I know many who say that."

"I don't know. I just . . . it was long ago, I'd rather just forget it happened."

"Then we'll forget it."

They came to the Rosens' house on Osceola Street. Chava took a key from her bag. As she started to unlock the door, Sean asked, "Do you need me to do that?"

"Not tonight." She tossed him a smile that sent warmth down his spine. "But thank you for asking. But, oh, one more thing. Will you sign my petition? If you haven't already done so somewhere else."

She took a sheaf of papers attached to a clipboard from her bag.

"What's it for?"

"It's to set up an election to recall the Mayor."

"Mayor Stapleton?"

"He said he wouldn't be for the Klan, so we voted for him, but then he let them meet at the Auditorium. He's not a good man."

Sean signed the page by the light of the porch. When he handed it back to her, she read, "Sean Murphy Sullivan. I must be the only one in this neighborhood to have a Catholic on my list. It's quite a prize." She sobered. "Oh, but now you mustn't sign any others, because your name can only appear once."

"I won't," Sean promised. "It was nice to meet your students."

"You haven't met my students."

"What?"

"Those are the people I help. My students are at the Sheltering Home. And yes, you must come and meet them. You must meet my little ones."

# TWENTY-ONE

"Hey, Mrs. James, I got a problem."

Tony leaned against the jamb of the door that led from the kitchen to the parlor. He wore his telephone company uniform of tan jacket and trousers and his leather boots. He held his hat in his hands.

Maggie stood at the kitchen table, kneading bread dough. Alice Colleen sat at the table, printing on a sheet of lined paper. Since she had learned to write the alphabet, she had taken to pretending that she was Mrs. James. Maggie invented problems for Alice Colleen to solve—my kitten is lost, I can't tie my shoes by myself, I don't like carrots but my mother says I have to eat them—and Alice Colleen wrote and "posted" the letters in an old cigar box of Pa's. She couldn't spell many words, but she filled the pages with neat letters, and then "read" her replies to Maggie. On the floor, the twins built towers of wooden blocks with Kieran, who had just started to toddle around on his own.

At Tony's words, Alice Colleen dropped her pencil, her face lit with adoration, and the boys quieted to listen.

"Why, Sergeant Necchi," Maggie said sweetly. "You do seem to have more than your fair share of problems. What is it now?"

"My three-legged dog, he got fleas."

The boys and Alice Colleen laughed out loud.

"Are you sure it's the dog that has fleas?" Maggie asked.

Tony rubbed at his arm, then at his neck—tilting his head to one side and screwing up his mouth as he scratched. The children guffawed. "Yeah, I'm sure."

"Sheep dip," Maggie said.

"What?"

"Douse him in sheep dip."

"You think that'll work?" Tony deferred to Alice Colleen, who blushed and giggled. "What about you, Frankie? You think I should do it? Declan? Um—"

"Kieran," Alice Colleen supplied.

"You, too, Kieran?"

The twins nodded their heads. "Sheep dip," Frankie said.

"Da-da," Kieran agreed.

"Well, then, okay, I'll get some sheep dip." Tony winked at Alice Colleen, who nearly swooned. "I gotta go say hi to your *nonna* and then go help your uncle Sean."

With a wave, he left the kitchen, but Alice Colleen and the boys jabbered on about it, wondering about the color of the dog and how big it was. Maggie smiled. They truly believed that Tony owned a three-legged dog with fleas, that all of this was not just a game.

"Do you think it will work, Mommy?" Alice Colleen asked. "I feel sorry for his dog."

"I think the dog will be fine."

"I wonder what his name is."

"You'll have to ask Sergeant Necchi the next time he's here." Maggie shaped an oval of dough in a pan and covered it with cheesecloth to rise. "But right now, pick up your toys and things so we can eat. I have to take Daddy's dinner back to him."

The next time Tony arrived at the Sullivans' apartments, Alice Colleen headed the pack of tumbling children that met him at the front door. Maggie followed from the kitchen, wiping her hands on a towel.

"How's your dog?" Alice Colleen demanded. "What's his name?"

"Pershing," Tony said, without a moment's hesitation. "I did what you said and now he don't know whether he's a sheep or a dog. He don't bark no more, he baas."

"Oh, no!" Horrified, Alice Colleen turned to Maggie. "Mommy, will he be all right?"

"I think Sergeant Necchi is teasing us," Maggie said.

"Me? I'm not teasing. He kinda growls in his throat and then he baa-aa-arks."

The boys imitated the sound, jumping and running, while Alice Colleen's laughter peeled through the room. "Baa-aa-ark! Baa-aa-ark!" In the midst of it all, Kieran began to whimper, not yet old enough to keep up.

Maggie picked up Kieran. "They're just being silly."

"Hey, Mrs. James," Tony said. "I like it when you smile."

"Baa-aa-ark! Baa-aa-ark!"

Beneath the laughter, Maggie heard the roll of Liam's chair. "Alice Colleen, Frankie, Declan!" she snapped. "Quiet now! You've disturbed Daddy! Shhh!"

Liam appeared from the hallway that led to the bedrooms. "What's going on out here?"

Maggie hoisted Kieran higher on her hip. "Liam, this is Tony Necchi. He's the one who's helping Seaney build the house for Ma and Pa. Tony, this is my husband, Liam."

Tony offered his hand, and Liam shook it. And even though it made Maggie ashamed of herself, she couldn't help but notice the difference between the two hands: Tony's, with its dark skin and strong fingers, and Liam's, pale and bony.

"Nice to meet you," Tony said.

"You were in the war?" Liam asked.

Maggie's breath caught in her throat. "I'm sorry the kids got so loud," she said quickly. "I'll make sure they don't do it again."

Alice Colleen volunteered. "Tony was a soldier with Uncle Seaney."

She saluted as Seaney had taught her, and Frankie and Declan clapped the palms of their right hands to their foreheads.

"Don't do that, Alice Colleen," Liam warned. "I've told you before, do not salute in this house. Boys, stop."

Tony cast a puzzled glance toward Maggie. "I gotta go find Sean," he said. "Good evening, Mrs. James, Mr. James."

He went out the front, closing the door behind him. Frankie and Declan kept making baaing or barking noises, their voices hushed. Alice Colleen sat down on the sofa and crossed her arms, pouting at being scolded by her father.

"What was all this about?" Liam asked Maggie. "What were you doing?"

"He was teasing us, that's all." Maggie put Kieran down on the floor, and he crawled over to where Frankie and Declan sat. "That's why the kids were laughing."

"You were laughing, too."

"It doesn't hurt anyone to laugh a little."

"You looked at him like—"

Liam said no more, but Maggie knew. She looked at Tony in the same way that she used to look at him when he devised limericks as they walked around the lake, or kissed her beneath the outside steps, or read to her from a book of poetry or philosophy. She looked at Tony in the same way that she had when she anticipated of the next witty thing that might come from Liam's lips.

"Why don't you all go out in the kitchen," Maggie said to the children. "Alice Colleen, you need to finish your letters, and boys, you need to pick up your toys."

Obediently the kids went into the kitchen, and Maggie closed the door behind them. She sat down on the sofa while Liam wheeled to his spot near the home altar.

"Let's go up into the mountains this weekend," she said. "The snow should be melted and maybe the wildflowers will be in bloom. We'll take an early train, and we'll take a picnic lunch, and—"

"I have no intention of parading through Union Station to board a train."

"The kids never get outside," Maggie protested. "I don't even have time to take them to the lake, and it's four blocks away—"

"What do you think would happen if I were recognized in Union Station or at the lake? People would stare, they'd be hateful and rude—"

"We'd ignore them. We have so far—"

"Ignore them? You've made it clear that you're ashamed to be married to me—Sean's friend just called me Mr. James and you didn't even try to correct him."

"He's Italian, he's confused enough as it is. And why does he matter? He's just here to help Seaney build the house, and he just comes in to say hi to Ma and the kids—"

"It sounded like far more than that."

She took in a breath, fully expecting to deny it, but instead snapped, "I laugh because the kids laugh. There's nothing sinful about that."

Liam began to wheel across the room.

She stepped in front of the chair. "You were never afraid when you were in prison," she rasped. "All that time, all they did to you, you were brave. You stood your ground. Why can't you be as brave now? Go to Mass with us. Go for a walk around the lake with us. Say to people, I did what I did. I wasn't afraid then, and I'm not afraid now."

"I'm not afraid now," Liam said. "I have never been afraid. But I'm not willing to allow Alice Colleen and the boys to witness the abominations and slurs that are used against me in public."

"But we're prisoners here! We never go anywhere. The kids don't know how to play outside, because there's no one to watch them or to teach them to—"

"Don't!" He struggled to calm himself. "Don't ever call yourself a prisoner again. You have no idea what it's like to be in prison or to be at the mercy of cruel and sadistic men."

The bitterness in his voice shocked her. In the reams of pages that he had written about his experience, his tone was always even-tempered and logical. He never wrote with any kind of unbridled emotion.

"I'm sorry." She knelt down in front of him, so that her face was level with his. "When you were gone, I used to try to imagine it. I used to lie in bed with my wrists crossed over my head, trying to imagine what it would be like to be manacled to bars so far up that my feet didn't touch the ground. I couldn't—and I didn't know whether to feel guilty that I couldn't or to be relieved—"

"I'm relieved you couldn't." He gestured toward his wasted body. "If we were called out in public or someone accosted us, how would I protect you or the boys?"

"I withstood the nasty comments for three years, Liam. I learned to ignore them. I was strong, I was able to fend them off. Let me be your protection now. I can take care of you, and I can keep us safe as well."

"Yet you're so afraid that someone will find out your name isn't Margaret James," he said sourly. "Maybe the 'prison' you're in is the one you've built by lying about who you are."

He wheeled forward, and Maggie jumped up and out of the way so that her toes weren't crushed.

"Liam!" she called, but Alice Colleen came from the kitchen.

"Mommy, can we have some cookies?" she asked. "We're hungry."

"Yes," Maggie said. "And play with the boys. I need to go outside for a few minutes."

"I don't want to play with them."

"Then take them back to Grandma. Let her watch them."

She ran outside and trundled noisily down the wrought iron steps to the street below. Whipping around, she stood in the shadows beneath the stairs. She had done everything for Liam—kept him in food and a home and raised his children, and he gave nothing back.

She put her hands over her face. What a mess. Tony and his stupid games—she never should have encouraged them. And why was he always here, anyway? The house for Ma and Pa, which Seaney and Tony had been so eager to start last fall, was progressing at a snail's pace. It was nothing more than a ruse to drink and talk about the war. They should just forget it and find somewhere else to walk down Memory Lane.

She heard Seaney's car pull up in front of the store and stepped out of the shadows. He whistled a tune as he rounded the corner of the store. "What are you doing down here?"

"I need you to do something for me," she said.

"Sure, what is it?"

"Please, would you start getting here before Tony? And would you make sure he doesn't come upstairs?"

"Why? What's he done?"

"He upsets the kids."

"I've only seen them laugh when he's around."

"That's the problem. He gets them so stirred up—"

Seaney's eyes darted upward toward the apartments. "It's Liam, isn't it? He doesn't like it. Well, Tony's my friend, and Ma likes him—"

"I have a lot to take care of, Seaney, since you decided you couldn't be bothered with running the store or helping out with Ma and Pa."

"Don't start that again," he said. "I give Ma and Pa as much as I can from my salary. And I'm not making a king's ransom, either. Why can't Liam help out? Tell him to get out of that bedroom and find a job. He's a bookkeeper, he could do that from a wheelchair—"

"He isn't strong enough anymore—"

"Well, he's strong enough to write that stupid book—"

"He was tortured by his own government, by our government!"

"He chose to fling mud in the government's face," Sean lashed. "Tony and I chose to fight for our country, and he chose to go to Fort Leavenworth. So don't be saying anything against Tony. He's a veteran and a patriot."

"Just keep him outside," Maggie said. "That's all I ask."

"I'll keep myself outside, then, too. You can explain to Ma why I don't come to see her anymore."

"Fine, both of you. I don't care."

Above them, the door to the upstairs landing opened. Alice Colleen wandered outside, looking over the railing for her mother. "Mommy," she called. "Declan spilled the milk."

# TWENTY-TWO

In May, Jim Graves announced his candidacy for governor. Packed into the lobby of Graves Industries with the other employees, Mary Jane stood on her tiptoes to gain a clear view.

The whole thing was as grandiose and staged as a P.T. Barnum circus. Standing at Mr. Graves' side, Kathleen wore a dress of cobalt blue, with a sash around her hips that tied in a rosette on the left side, its diaphanous tails streaming in the colors of the flag of Colorado—gold, red, and white. Mr. Graves' apparel was not so subtle. He had complimented his dark pin-striped suit with a tie that perfectly matched Kathleen's dress, and his cowboy boots were emblazoned with the emblematic red C and golden circle of the flag stitched amid a twining pattern of white and blue. Behind them, Mr. Graves' family appeared proud and untouchable. Mrs. Brently— or Mrs. Lloyd-Elliot—stood with Susanna's hand in hers. Beside her, Colonel Lloyd-Elliott wore his British uniform, his hands on Stephen's shoulders. The elder Mr. and Mrs. Graves sat to the left of Kathleen.

While Mr. Graves outlined his plans for Colorado—completing the Moffat Tunnel; broadening economic opportunities for the people of the Western Slope; continuing experimentation in extracting oil from shale; funding various highway ventures, as well as the state's land grant universities and other institutions—photographers snapped pictures, leaving the air with the frazzled smell of lightning.

When asked about the Klan, Mr. Graves stated, "I have no obligations to or connections with the Ku Klux Klan in Denver or in the state of Colorado. I stand here as a man whose business and political dealings are conducted in broad daylight without the need to hide my identity or purpose beneath shrouds of white or behind flaming crosses."

Most of the employees burst into applause and shouts of approval. Mary Jane searched the crowd for Raynelle. Their friendship—if that's what it was—had forged itself in minutes and half-finished conversations in the washroom. Mary Jane had learned enough about Raynelle to know that she lived in the part of town called Whittier, and that her sons, George and Harry, were twelve and nine. Her husband, Aaron, worked as a mailman in the Five Points and Whittier neighborhoods. She also knew that Raynelle read the *Denver Star*, the newspaper published for Denver's black community, just as fervently as Avery read the *Protestant Herald*, the Klan's paper.

Mary Jane lowered herself from her toes, and edged her way through the crowd of employees to the steps that led to the typing pool and the Employee Ladies' Washroom.

Raynelle sat on a stool, smoking and reading her newspaper. At the sound of the door, she jumped to her feet, scuffed out the cigarette beneath her foot, and wadded the newspaper and stuffed it into the laundry bin.

"I'm sorry," Mary Jane said. "I didn't mean to surprise you."

She shifted her foot to cover up more of the ashy stain on the tile floor. "I thought everyone was upstairs."

"They are. Why are you here?"

"Someone might want to use the toilet, and so, we ladies were told to stay at our posts. And see, someone does."

"I don't, really. I just couldn't find you. But you should have been there. He says he's against the Klan."

The word, spoken so bluntly, echoed around the tile walls and floor of the bathroom. Raynelle's face hardened, and the light left her eyes. Mary Jane turned toward the sink. She splashed water on her face, mostly to hide her embarrassment. Why had she brought up the Klan to a Negro woman?

"I'm sorry," Mary Jane said. "I shouldn't have—"

"Saying and doing are two different things."

"So you don't believe him?"

Raynelle clicked her tongue, as if she were deciding whether or not to speak. "Do you think we really didn't want to come today—me and the other lady custodians and janitors? We were told by Mr. Spratt to stay at our posts. No one wants to see black faces in the photos in the newspapers, Miss Grayson."

"I'm sorry." Without thinking, Mary Jane blurted, "My brother has joined the Klan."

Raynelle turned away. "Maybe you better go back upstairs."

"Avery—my brother—says it's a good organization, that it helps keep law and order, but Ross, my other brother, doesn't see it that way. He says they're ninnies in nightgowns."

Raynelle folded clean towels that she pulled from a wicker basket, making an effort to match the edges exactly.

"Please," Mary Jane pleaded. "I just want to understand it all."

At last, Raynelle said, "We have to close our drapes at sundown, so we won't get a bottle of flaming rags and gasoline through our window. Cars race up and down the alleys behind our houses, hitting everything in sight—the incinerator or the fence or a dog digging in trash. They don't even stop to see if they've killed it."

The bitterness in Raynelle's voice silenced Mary Jane.

"Aaron starts his shift early, so that he can be done when school gets out," Raynelle continued. "George and Harry go to Whittier Elementary, which is just up the street from our house, but we can't let them walk home alone. We don't let the boys play in the front yard anymore, either. We're near prisoners in our own house, where we've lived since we married."

She stopped, out of breath. Upstairs, applause filled the lobby. Mr. Graves' announcement celebration must have ended. A roar of voices echoed down the stairwell and into the washroom—a hundred discussions of Mr. Graves' candidacy or his boots or his words.

"Denver was a fine place to live until the Klan came." Raynelle rushed onward. "Some say it was the best city for the Negro to live in. We have our own restaurants and the Cosmopolitan Club in Five Points, where everybody's welcome—and lots of people come there who can't go anywhere else. The Jews and the Japanese and some of the others. But the Klan threatened to kill Dr. Clarence Holmes, the president of the NAACP, and burned a cross at his house. He got a letter—Aaron saw it—that said they'd kill him if he didn't leave town. He's a dentist—has been for years—and a fine, God-fearing man."

All Mary Jane could offer was a weak, "I'm sorry."

"The Klan isn't ninnies in nightgowns at all, Miss Grayson. It's evil, and it preaches that it's all right for people to hate each other."

Voices rang out in the hallway beyond the washroom, and Mary Jane slipped into a stall. After the other women left, she washed her hands and paid Raynelle the nickel fee. "I'm so sorry about this," she said. "I don't know what to do."

"Whatever you can, Miss Grayson. Do whatever you can."

On Friday, Mary Jane joined Essie and her sister, Judith Dercum, for a trip to their home in Aurora. Seated between them on the seat of a Model T

Ford, Mary Jane found herself bombarded from both sides. Essie, the driver, chattered in her left ear, while Judith, no less gregarious, monopolized her right ear. Their voices alternated, one picking up where the other left off.

"They say we'll have our own organization by the end of the year," Essie said. "A chapter of the Ku Klux Klan just for women—"

"Some of the best women in town are leading it" Judith continued. "The Imperial Commander is Mrs. Gano Senter. Her husband owns the Kool Kozy Kafe on Curtis Street, where you have to know the Klan password to get in—"

"And Dr. Minnie Love, who started the Children's Hospital, will be the Excellent Commander. She's a State Representative, too, and she has a whole list of laws she wants to—"

"And it will cost the same as the men's, ten dollars. I wonder if we'll wear robes and hoods—"

"Oh, no hoods!" Essie protested. "Why would I go to all the trouble to marcel my hair if I'm going to hide it under a hood? Doesn't it look wonderful, M.J.?"

Before Mary Jane could answer, Judith said, "Oh, look, here we are!"

The Edwards Dairy sprawled across the prairie east of Denver. Black and white Holstein cattle grazed in the fields, and a picture-perfect barn dominated the flat ground at the bottom of a rolling hill, with the main farmhouse nearby. Matt and Essie's cottage and Judith and her husband, Andy's, modest home were set off from the farmhouse by a few hundred feet.

"I'm so excited for you to meet Clyde," Judith said. "He's the best in the world. You'll meet Minnie, too, but well, just don't pay her any mind."

"Who's Minnie?" Mary Jane asked.

Essie explained. "Judith and Andy took in Minnie out of the goodness of their hearts. She was an orphan after the war, and they felt it was their Christian duty to help her. But she's turned out to be—"

"She is so slow, and she is, well, such a sad sack," Judith supplied. "You'll see, she rarely talks, and she's just a Gloomy Gus all the time. I don't think there's one spark of personality in that child. But she's one of God's children, so we help her as we can."

Judith led Mary Jane and Essie into the house. "Minnie, we're home," she called. "Get the tea ready. Where's Clyde?"

Mary Jane heard a muffled reply from the kitchen, and a little boy of about eight ran into the living room. He was missing a front tooth, and his skin was freckled. His hair was brownish and fine.

"Oh, there's my Clyde." Judith rubbed his head, and he pulled away from her hand. "This is your aunt—are you his aunt? Well, anyway, that's what we'll call you—Aunt Mary Jane."

"Hello, Clyde." Mary Jane offered her hand, but Clyde just sniffed.

"Shake Aunt Mary Jane's hand," Judith instructed.

Clyde shook Mary Jane's hand, then ran off to play.

"Oh, he's such a pip!" Essie laughed. "Never still for a minute."

"Minnie, where's the tea?" Judith called. "Hurry up with it." She addressed Essie and Mary Jane. "I'm afraid it will be dinner time before she gets here. She's not very quick at things."

The door to the kitchen opened. Mary Jane expected to see a dark, deformed or twisted child, but the girl who carried in the tea tray had honey-colored hair and pale skin.

Mary Jane leaped out of her chair. "Mina!"

The tray wavered in Mina's hands, and Judith growled, "Don't spill it, Minnie. Mind yourself."

Mina set the tray on the table, and Mary Jane opened her arms to her. Mina ran into them. "Oh, Mina, Mina, I looked and looked for you after . . . and you've been here all this time?"

"Miss Mary Jane," she said. "Oh, do you know—?"

"Minnie," Judith commanded. "Please go into the kitchen and start dinner. We'll want it at six o'clock when the men come in."

"Yes, Miss Judith."

Mina dropped her arms from around Mary Jane's waist. She wore a plain blue dress, and her hair was drawn back in a braid. The dress, too small by at least a size, pulled around her neck and left her wrists dangling.

Once the kitchen door closed behind Mina, Judith cautioned, "You need to watch what you say in front of her. She's still confused by what happened to her during the war."

Mary Jane whirled around. "No wonder! Her name is not Minnie. It's Mina, it's Swedish, and she isn't slow. She's reserved, that's all—"

"Mary Jane!" Essie scolded. "Sit down! You're being rude!"

Mary Jane sat down, but shock left her light-headed. She could not speak for fear that she would shout. A thousand unhappy memories—of the war, of the flu, of her father's death—rushed through her head.

Essie spoke. "Without Judith and Andy, Minnie would have been left on the streets—"

"No, I was looking for her after I recovered from the flu—"

"You know her mother died?" Judith asked.

"I was at the funeral. She was there with Miss Edwards, the nurse—"

"Miss Edwards is our sister, Jenny," Judith said. "But Jenny isn't a nurse. She's a school teacher, and she had to go back to work at the Denver schools. She had nowhere to put . . . Mina. She tried to take her to a neighbor—"

"Mrs. Stroop—"

"But that neighbor had died, too. So, she asked me to watch her. Clyde was two at the time, so Andy and I took her in." She paused. "We changed her name to Minnie to help her adjust to being with us. She was so confused, so upset and despairing. Poor thing, she kept talking about a man who was going to come and take them to his house—"

"The father, probably," Essie said. "Who by then was most likely six states away and loving up another girl."

"She wouldn't believe that her mother was dead," Judith said sadly. "I don't know why. The funeral evidently didn't convince her—"

Mary Jane remembered the funeral: held outside in the bitter cold, with the coffin on the horse-drawn hearse, and no semblance of a church service. Mina had been only seven, and everything had happened so quickly.

"So we told her that her mother had gone away and would come back for her soon," Judith concluded.

"She thinks Anneka is still alive?" Mary Jane asked.

"Anneka—that's right. I knew it wasn't an American name."

"Oh, she should know her mother would never leave her!"

Judith shrugged. "We've done the best for her that we could."

"How did you know her mother?" Essie asked.

"Ross was going to marry her."

"Ross!" Essie exclaimed. "Matt told me that Ross has never been serious about a girl."

"He was about Anneka. He asked me to look after her while he was away with the Army." Mary Jane considered. "What happened to the house? To her things? They were expensive and beautiful. And Anneka's clothes—"

"We took them," Judith said. "We sold most of the things—you're right, they brought a good price—and then we moved to Arkansas. Andy took up farming there, but it didn't work out. We went to Indiana, then to

184 • LAURIE MARR WASMUND

Iowa, but those were no good either, so we came back here, and he went to work for Daddy."

"She seems so sad," Mary Jane said. "She was never like that before Anneka died, and she was ahead of her grade in school—"

"I suppose you know that her mother was a maid," Judith said. "She says that's what she wants to be when she grows up. That's why we let her do the cooking and cleaning around here."

"It's a kindness that Judith is training her for a good job." Essie leaned forward and spoke in a sweet, sad voice. "It's all she'll ever be."

"I want to talk with her," Mary Jane said. "Alone."

Essie shot her a scathing look, but Judith said, "All right, but please don't mention that her mother died. Don't bring that sorrow into her life."

Mary Jane went into the kitchen, where Mina peeled potatoes into a pan. At twelve, Mina stood nearly as tall as Mary Jane. Her figure was beginning to fill out, with rounding breasts and hips. Her face, despite its chronic solemnity, was as lovely as Anneka's.

"Mina, I'm so glad I found you," Mary Jane said.

"Did my mother go to Mr. Yeem's house when she left me?" she asked. "Is she there now?"

"No, oh, no! She would never have left you—" She stopped, remembering her promise to Judith. "She didn't go to his house. I . . . I don't know where she is."

Mina carved the potatoes, her gaze downward.

"Where is your doll? Do you still have her? What was her name?"

"Marta. I still have her."

"Can I see her? She was so pretty."

Mina set aside the potatoes and led Mary Jane through the living room—while Judith and Essie glared—to her room. Marta sat in one corner of the room. Her china face was cracked and chipped, with one eye entirely missing. Her human hair straggled in clumps. She wore a dirty, yellow taffeta dress that Mary Jane remembered as part of the matching set that fit both Mina and Marta. She wondered what had happened to the other dresses for the doll; obviously, the girl had outgrown them.

"What happened to her face?" Mary Jane asked. "It was so lovely."

"Clyde swung her against the chimney."

"That wasn't very nice, was it?" There was almost nothing else in the room—no books, no toys, no puzzles or amusements. "You're in school, aren't you?"

"I go to the Coal Creek School."

"Where are your books? Shouldn't you be doing your schoolwork?"

Judith called from the living room, "Minnie, are you watching the dinner?"

"I have to go," she said.

After she left, Mary Jane sat on Mina's bed. The last time she had felt this helpless was when Anneka was dying of flu, and her house was quarantined to visitors. And then, Mary Jane herself had gotten sick, and she had lost—no, Mina had lost everything.

During grace and dinner, Mary Jane tries to act as if nothing is wrong. Mina eats with the family during the meal, but she never speaks. On the other hand, Clyde—the sweet little boy—reaches across the table or demands what he can't take for himself from his mother, without a single please or thank you.

Andy, who is thin and reedy, with dark hair and narrow eyes, likes to tease. "Minnie, here, is about as talkative as that old scarecrow up in the cornfield. Or maybe he's more talkative. What do you think, Minnie, who talks more? Him or you?"

Forced to join the conversation, Mina lifts her gaze from her plate. "I do."

"Two words! She knows two words! It's a miracle, isn't it, Judith?"

"Oh, Andy, quit." Judith and Essie laugh.

"You know any more words?" Andy winks at Mary Jane. "Two more words. Just two more."

Mina eyes him coldly, and Mary Jane sees Anneka's strength and stubbornness in her gaze.

Andy leans closer to her. "Say your name," he taunts. "Surely you know that. Tell our guest your name. Come on, chicken, you can do it."

"Chicken," Clyde supplies.

Her lower lip trembling, Mina says, "Minnie Mary Dercum."

"Good job, frogmouth," Andy said. "Gosh, you are a quick one, aren't you?"

"Frogmouth," Clyde echoes.

Mary Jane catches the bitter bite of Mina's glare. Her lips move as if she might protest, but she looks down into her plate, taking tiny forkfuls of food.

"Mina has always read quite well," Mary Jane says. "I'm sure she knows more words than almost everyone else at this table."

Andy's jowl clenches.

"Her name is Minnie," Judith reminds Mary Jane, while Essie lets out an indignant sigh.

Clyde stands and reaches for the potatoes at the far end of the table. Matt absentmindedly helps him to move them as he stares at his sister.

After dinner, Mary Jane knows she cannot stay in this house another minute. She catches Matt as he goes for a smoke out on the front porch.

"Will you take me home?" she asks. "I don't feel well."

"Tonight?" Matt complains. "It's an hour away—"

"You don't want me to be here if I'm sick. What if Essie catches it?"

At last, Matt grudgingly agrees. Mary Jane goes to Mina's room to tell her goodbye. "I promise, I will come back to visit," she says. "I promise."

But Mina has experienced a lifetime of broken promises. "Goodbye," she says, her voice void of emotion.

On the way home, Mary Jane feels as if someone has knocked her off her feet or punched her in the stomach. How could life have treated such an innocent so harshly? As Matt pulls into the driveway of the Graysons' home, Mary Jane asks, "Do they hit Mina—I mean, Minnie?"

"What?" Matt asks.

"Andy and Judith, do they beat the little girl?"

"I don't think so," he said. "They're good people. They go to church every Sunday, and they take Minnie and Clyde with them."

"If they hit her, would you tell me?"

Matt turns toward her. "What is wrong with you? Essie told me that you knew this little girl's mother, and thought she was the greatest, but that doesn't mean you can just charge in there and make trouble. Minnie has a good situation with Andy and Judith, especially considering who she is—no mother and her father is anybody's guess. And no, I won't tell you if they hit her, because that's their business, and not yours or mine."

Mary Jane's mother waits for her just inside the front door. Ross stands behind her. He nods at Matt, who declines his mother's offer to come inside. "I'll call you, Mom," Matt says, and goes to his car. He pulls out of the drive a moment later.

"What is going on?" Mary Jane's mother demands. "Essie called and said your behavior was disgusting. After she and Judith were nice enough to invite you for dinner, she said you got into a fight with Judith over her daughter. What was that all about? Essie is one of the most Christian of women I have ever met. I'm sure her sister is, too."

Mary Jane runs up the stairs to her bedroom. Sitting on her bed, she covers her face with her hands. Poor Mina, oh, poor Mina! How did she end up with such mean-spirited people? And there's nothing Mary Jane can do to help—she's afraid that the more she defends Mina, the worse they will treat her.

A knock sounds on her door. Ross opens it and says, "Come and sit with me for a while."

Mary Jane dries her eyes and follows Ross down the stairs. Outside, the evening is still warm, with a breeze from the south. They sit side by side on the porch swing, and Ross gives it a push with his foot, sending it to and fro.

"What's going on, M.J.?" he asks. "You're usually pretty chipper, but Essie said you were out of sorts the entire evening."

"Oh, Ross!" Mary Jane turns to face him. "It isn't just me. This has to do with you, too. It's about Anneka."

"Anneka?" He shifts in surprise. "I haven't thought of her in years."

Mary Jane tells him of Mina's situation with Judith and Andy. "They treat her like a servant, and then tease her because she resents it."

"I still don't see what this has to do with me."

"You were going to marry Anneka. You were going to be Mina's father."

Ross kicks off the porch, and the swing resumes its motion. "I fell in love with Anneka the first time I saw her—I think because she was just so darned pretty. I knew I would be called up by the Army any minute, and I didn't want to leave without having something to come back for. I doubt it would have lasted long after I came home. I really didn't know her that well." He shrugs. "You know I didn't even know about her death until I was home again, and by then, it was all so far in the past . . ."

Mary Jane takes in a breath. She has always assumed that Ross was heartbroken over Anneka's death, that he had lost his great love. But, in the end, Mary Jane had actually spent more time with Anneka and Mina than Ross had. She is the one who loved them so deeply.

"We have to do something for Mina," she says. "We have to bring her here to live."

"What are we going to do?" Ross asks. "Take her from their house like she's a lost terrier? Matt barely speaks to me as it is. I'm not going to pick a fight with his in-laws, and I suggest that you let it go as well."

"But someone needs to help her!"

"Well, then, if this little girl means so much to you, help her. Instead of going over there and getting everybody so riled up that they call Mom—and believe me, I heard about it for an hour before you got home—keep still and do what you can for her."

"I doubt I'll be invited back."

"Sure you will. Just apologize. As Mom says, they're good Christians. They'll forgive you. You're sure Anneka and Mina had no other family in Denver?"

Mary Jane hesitates, but answers, "I'm sure."

"Then, you're it, I guess." He stands. "Come on, get some sleep. But before you do, you'd better apologize to Mom."

"In a minute."

Ross goes in through the screen door, and Mary Jane hears him call goodnight to their mother. She remembers Raynelle's words: *Do whatever you can.* Ross is right—the only way to help Mina is to pretend to be Essie's and Judith's friend. It isn't enough, though; it will never be enough.

# TWENTY-THREE

On a warm afternoon in July, Sean caught the trolley to the Denver Sheltering Home at 19th and Julian. The Home bustled with activity—builders sawed and pounded; women in aprons weeded the gardens; and children played with balls, or tended to the animals that lived in the barn. A troupe of tap dancers practiced on a wooden stage that had apparently been erected for some sort of outdoor concert. He found Chava on the porch of a neat cottage, reading to her students. When she spotted Sean, she smiled warmly. "We have a special guest today," she said. "A friend of mine, Patrolman Sullivan. He keeps our streets safe at night."

Sean blushed, but not because of the unwarranted praise. How beautiful she was. Her love for her charges blossomed in her smile. Her eyes glowed as she asked each child to say his or her name for him. The boys bowed, the girls curtsied, well coached by their teacher. Most of the children had dark eyes and hair, with richly complexioned faces. The few blonds and redheads had a delicate paleness, their skin even fairer than Kathleen's. "Now," Chava instructed. "Spend a few minutes at play, and then we'll go inside."

"All their parents are sick?" Sean asked after the children had bounded to the swings and merry-go-round.

"Not all," she said. "Many are orphans."

"Orphans?" He thought of Liam and Brendan, those feisty orphans from Mount St. Vincent's, who had come to dinner at the Sullivans' house in tan overalls and cardboard shoes. Chava's students wore no uniforms, but dressed in clothing any child would wear.

"Some of them will go home when their parents are well," Chava said. "Others will be here until they're old enough to work."

"Don't you worry that you might come down with tuberculosis?"

She pushed back a lock of dark hair. "It's a worry, I suppose. But I would still come here. Mrs. Lorber—who is a great, great woman—and

Superintendent Gilman believe in scientific charity, which I studied in college. I want to see how it works in real life."

"What's that?"

"It's the belief that simply handing out money to the needy creates poverty, because they are unable to escape their situations. But teaching them to live and work in the world prevents poverty and despair." She lifted her chin. "Superintendent Gilman hires only qualified college-educated professionals as teachers here. When my children go to Cheltenham Elementary for school, they know much more than the students from the neighborhood."

Sean smiled at her confidence and pride. How did someone become so sure of themselves?

One of the girls, a pixie with tight ringlets and a clean, white pinafore, dashed up to Chava and tugged her skirt. Chava bent forward as the child whispered in her ear. "I'll ask him," she told the girl. "You go and play." She turned to Sean. "Leah has asked me if the 'handsome gentleman' will dance with us."

"Dance?" Sean protested. "Oh, I'm no good at that! We learned to dance when the girls' classes came in once a month for lessons, and I was always paired with my sister, Maggie—"

"It's not the tango." She called to another teacher on the grounds. "Will you watch them for me?"

The other teacher nodded, and Chava led Sean inside the classroom. It was newly painted, with a hodgepodge of child-sized tables and chairs. A brightly-colored rag rug carved out a large space in the middle of the room. A rolling chalkboard posed in one corner, the English alphabet written in dusty white across it. Another wall was pasted over with sepia-toned photographs and colorful drawings.

Sean moved toward the wall of illustrations. "Who are these?"

"Family. Some real and some only in the mind of the child."

He studied the drawings, stick figures mostly, and counted the faces. Mother, father, a few grandparents, a few siblings, a dog here and there. Chava's voice sounded at his shoulder. "I ask them to remember those they can and to imagine those they can't, and to honor them in a family portrait."

"My family annoys me to tears," Sean admitted. "But at least I don't have to imagine them."

"That happens in most families, I think," Chava said. "Sometimes Rachael makes me want to run away from home, but I love her."

Sean turned toward her. "Run away? To where?"

"That's the problem. I don't know."

Sean snorted. "I ran away once—to France—and ended up right back where I started."

She laughed and took a spot on the rug. "Now the dance. It's nothing hard. Although it's properly done with hands on one another's shoulders, that's too hard for the children. So we simply hold hands"—she reached out to him—"in a circle."

Sean took her hand. He felt sweat on his forehead—the embarrassment of so many years of being told by the nuns that he had the grace of a bull.

"Now, step right." She moved easily. "And your left foot crosses behind. Yes, that's good. Then, step right again, and swing your left foot forward. Now, step on your left foot and swing your right."

Sean plodded his way through the steps. "It's not even," he complained. "The left foot does less than the right."

"But that way, the circle moves around the room. See?" Her light feet, clad in low-heeled, strapped pumps, did a quick gambol on the rug. "Try it with me."

Sean stepped, his feet heavy and slow, his mind equally so. He forgot to cross his left foot behind his right; he took an extra step to the left. Feet askew, he faltered, and she grabbed his arm.

"You can't stop!" She laughed. "It's a train wreck if you do! Just remember—right, cross, right, swing, left, swing."

"You can't expect me to remember all that!"

"What, you can't keep up with a group of five-year-olds?" Standing directly in front of him, she took both his hands in hers. "Here, follow me."

But he could not think. With her head bent so she could watch his feet, and her warm hands cupping his, the dance steps escaped him entirely. She smelled not of his mother's rose water or heavy French perfume, but of a world where clothes were starched and cheeks were scrubbed into rosy bloom by women who cared for orphans as if they were their own. With just a slip of his hands around her waist, he could gather her in and hold her against him . . .

She looked up at him, eyes moist, lips parted, as if the same thought had occurred to her.

"Miss Chava!" Voices rang out as the children filed through the door. Sean dropped his hands and stepped away from her. His neck and ears burned.

"Come in and make a circle," Chava instructed. "Hold hands. Boys, here, girls—yes, that's right."

Sean found himself gathered into the circle, little Leah and a string of girls to his left, and the boys on his right. Leah clung to his hand, laying her cheek against it. Gently, Chava said, "Straighten up, now, Leah, so we can dance."

She cranked up the cumbersome phonograph in the corner, and the strangest music that Sean had ever heard filled the room. It was an eerie blend of instruments—piano, violin, accordion—that sounded distinctly like wailing.

Sean focused on his feet, trying to recall exactly what they were to do and when. Chava ably directed the children, who seemed to have far less difficulty with the steps than he did. "Cross behind when you move to the right, David, not in front," she urged. "Step to the left now, Sarah."

Giving up, he allowed his feet to go at will, and discovered Chava's curious eyes on him. She didn't smile, and he resigned himself—she knew by now that he would never be a ballroom sensation. But her look was far from disappointed. It was appraising, tender, inviting.

The music accelerated, as if trying to cheer itself up, and Sean's feet demanded his attention. Instead of merely stepping to the left, the children were now hopping. Fearing that he might stomp on tiny feet if he attempted anything but the most basic of shuffles, he moved only enough to stay out of their way.

The music ended, and the tight circle dissolved into a mass of bodies. The girls crowded around Sean's legs, asking questions that he tried his best to answer. Where did he live? Was his house nice? Did he have any brothers or sisters? Was his sister pretty? Some of the boys joined the curious group. Sean asked them whether they played baseball.

"Poor Patrolman Sullivan!" Chava winked at him. "You'll make him want to run away from us!"

"I'd love to stay," Sean said apologetically. "But I'm on duty tonight—"

"I'll walk you out," she said. "Say good-bye to Patrolman Sullivan."

Once again, children clustered around his legs. He promised to visit again. Freeing himself from the mob, he walked with Chava to the door.

"Thank you for coming," Chava said.

"I'll never get my feet untangled, you know."

Chava laughed. "We'll see about that."

As he left the Sheltering Home, the music whirled in his head, and he found himself whistling the tune—even though it was the most mournful, unmelodious thing he'd ever heard. That evening, he found himself dawdling along the block where the Rosens lived, hoping for a glimpse of her. When he passed the house—for the third time—she stepped out from the alleyway that ran along the side of the property.

"The children loved you today," she said. "You made them laugh."

"For good reason. Did you have their toes examined by a doctor afterward to make sure I didn't break any of them?"

"Leah and Sarah fought over who would hold your hand the next time you visited. You have several admirers there—but only one of them is over three feet tall."

"Which one could that be?"

Inside the house, someone turned up the volume on the radio. An announcer introduced the Paul Whiteman Orchestra, live from New York. Almost immediately, the orchestra launched into "Side by Side."

"It's Rachael's favorite radio show," Chava said. "She turns it up loud enough so the whole neighborhood can enjoy it."

"Chava!" Rachael called from inside. "Are you coming?"

"In a minute," Chava called back.

"I should go," Sean said.

"Oh, not yet! Come with me."

He followed her into darkness, his eyes adjusting slowly. At the back of the house, she stopped near an open window. A sliver of yellow shone through the curtains, which had not been pulled all the way. There was just enough light to see the way around the yard.

A booming male voice announced: "Now, the orchestra will play the new Irving Berlin song, 'What'll I Do?' from the *Music Box Revue*, sung by tonight's guest, Mr. Walter Pidgeon."

Chava touched Sean's arm. "Dance with me."

"I've forgotten how to do it," he admitted.

"Not that dance," she said. "Listen."

The strings in the orchestra swelled up into a gentle waltz, enriched by a sonorous and powerful man's voice. Chava raised her right hand into the air. Nervous, Sean took her hand and put his left hand on her back. They moved across the carpet of grass. Obstacles barred their way—the dips and rises in the uneven ground, a wayward bucket, and a rake that had been leaned against the fence—but they swirled in fairy tale fashion across the width of the tiny back yard. The stars twinkled above them, the light from the window glowed golden, the music played only for them. Chava's gaze never faltered from Sean's, as if she cared for him, as if she were as in love with him as he had just discovered he was with her.

The music ended and the audience applauded as the announcer shouted, "What a voice! Mr. Walter Pidgeon, ladies and gentlemen! And now a word from Lux—"

Chava lifted her hands and put her palms on his cheeks. Standing on tiptoe, she kissed him. "Are your feet untangled yet?"

"I have no idea. I can't feel them any more."

She kissed him again, laughter still on her lips. Her body against his was all warmth, and her lips softness. When he pulled away from her, their foreheads touched, and for a moment, they stood without moving, breathless and silent. This was no fairy tale; this was a woman filled with desire and need. Chava lowered herself from her tiptoes, and Sean wrapped his arms around her, kissing the top of her head as she snuggled into his chest.

"I've wanted to do this since the first time I saw you," he said.

She lifted her face. "Oh, no! I was so ornery to you then."

He kissed her nose. "You still are, forcing me to dance when I'm barely good at walking."

"Wait until I teach you the Hora."

"What's the Hora?"

"It's the dance at all Jewish weddings—"

He dropped his arms from her. "I have to go."

"What happened?" she demanded. "What did I say?"

"I've no business"—he could not bring himself to say "kissing"—"doing such a thing. I've no right. Forgive me."

"No right?" She seemed slow to understand. "That's not true—"

"No. It's wrong for us to . . . wrong for me, that is." He started toward the street. "I'm a policeman here, not a . . . I have a professional duty. I need to do my job."

"Sean, wait," she called. "Wait, please!"

"No, I have to go. I'm sorry."

He strode through the alley to the street. For the rest of the night, he traipsed through his beat so disoriented that he wouldn't have noticed anything amiss, even if it were right under his nose. The next day, as he lay in bed at his lonely room at Mrs. Potter's boarding house, he tossed and turned, unable to sleep. There was too much light, too much noise, too much evidence of people living. Doors slammed, the ancient plumbing creaked and groaned, and a phonograph scratched out murky music for hours.

He put his arm over his eyes.

He could not stop thinking of her, of her hands on his face, of the warmth of her mouth on his. When he held her, her head rested just below his chin in a perfect fit. He wanted to kiss the mole on her temple, to run his finger down her neck to the swell of . . . Sitting up in bed, he put his face in his hands. Oh, God, what was he to do?

Late in the afternoon, still sleepless, he made his way to the church. He found Brendan in his office, reading a newspaper. Tapping on the open door, he asked, "Can I talk to you, Father?"

"Sean!" Brendan said eagerly. "How nice to see you. Please, come in, sit down. I've just been reading an article in the *Catholic Register* about the state of Bavaria. There is tension in that part of the world between those who want the return of the king and those who have started to follow a man named"— he looked over the top of his glasses to read the name—"Adolph Hitler who is sponsoring a nationalist patriotic program similar to our Klan. "

"Let's hope they choose the king. Having the Klan in one country on earth is bad enough."

Brendan laid aside the newspaper. "What brings you here? Is this a professional visit or a personal one?"

"I'm not sure." Sean sat in the chair facing Brendan's desk. "I've fallen in love with a woman I can't have."

Brendan's face registered shock. "Another man's wife?"

"No, oh, no, not that—"

"Then—?" Realization dawned in his face. "You've been patrolling over on the West Side. Have you met someone there?"

"Yes."

"Oh, Sean, what can I say? If anything, Kathleen's sad predicament should have taught you that mixed marriages are never successful—"

"I can't imagine Kathleen's life as a 'sad predicament.'"

"She can't take communion or participate in the rites." Brendan corrected him. "But, at least Mr. Graves is a Christian, albeit a Presbyterian. The Jews—well, they are true infidels. Better a pagan, who has never heard of Christ, than a—"

"Bishop Tihen's been spending a fair amount of time with them."

"He has been helping with the recall of Mayor Stapleton," Brendan said sternly. "The Hebrews are—oddly enough—our allies in these hard times."

"Isn't Judah Rapp one of them?" Sean asked edgily. "Aren't some of your other socialist friends?"

"But that is politics." Brendan shook his head. "What is it you find attractive in this woman?"

"She's funny and smart and pretty." Sean spread his hands. "She's just everything I ever wanted—"

"What are her thoughts on God? Has she spoken any blasphemy toward our Christ? Has she tried to convert you to the ancient ways?"

Sean bit his tongue—what sort of demon did Brendan think Chava was? The look on her face as she danced with the children was angelic. "We haven't discussed it."

"Does her family know? Does yours?"

"No, no one knows."

"That, at least, is a blessing. And the young lady feels the same about you?"

"She was the one who first . . . yes."

"Sean, listen to me," Brendan said. "This is a temptation you must resist. Do you hear? For the young lady's sake, as well as for your own. You need to remove yourself from her as much as possible."

"But I'm policing there now—"

"Take a different route through the neighborhood, then, one that you know won't lead to an encounter. Surely you don't have to pass her way every night. Don't seek her out, and if she approaches you, you must tell her you cannot see her and why. Promise me, Sean—you need to find a woman in our parish who will make you a good wife. Someone who shares your faith, which has always been so strong, and someone who believes in Christ and our Holy Mother."

"Yes, Father."

"You understand, don't you? You understand the peril to your immortal soul? And to hers?"

"Yes, Father."

"Come to Mass tonight. I think you need to spend some time with God."

Yet, even in the Church, Sean's thoughts of Chava would not abate. As he knelt to pray, he felt her hands on his, and her fingertips on his neck, just below the hairline, and the press of her breasts against . . . My God, he had to stop this, whatever it took.

For the next two nights, he followed Brendan's advice, walking past the Rosens' home well after midnight. Brendan was right—they both stood to lose their souls. Yet he had never known such absolute loneliness, such emptiness, such a sense of having nothing that was worth having. Every dark memory he had seemed to come back to haunt him. He tried to fill the hours by praying, but he could not keep his mind on God, on the Church, or even on Brendan's warning.

On the third night, something compelled him to break his routine—and his promise—and pass by the house. It was nearly ten o'clock when he did, late enough that she should have been asleep. The street was deserted, dark, and even though he lingered for a few seconds, no one responded from within the Rosens' house.

Good, then, she had come to her senses. He walked on, trying to convince himself that he was relieved. Yet when he reached the alley, she stepped out from the shadows. He stopped short, reading her accusation in the set of her mouth: he was a coward.

"You said you had no right to kiss me, but I have a right to kiss you," she said so stiffly that he knew she had rehearsed the speech. "I can do what I want—"

"Not when it's foolish—"

"What, you think I am a stupid, little girl who can't judge foolish for herself?"

"I didn't say that!"

"Then what?" Before he could answer, she said, "You run away from me, not even passing by our house! You won't even look me in my eyes!"

"We're from different worlds. It's best if we—"

"Different worlds!" Scorn turned her deep voice to gravel. "So this tree isn't real? And the lake is a mirage?"

"That's not what I mean, and you know it." His temper rose. "You can't ask me to forget who I am, and what I'm doing here. You can't forget why I'm here, not by my own choice, but—"

"That again! So you are just the poor Catholic trapped in a neighborhood of Jews—"

"We would never have even met if I hadn't been reassigned here. It wasn't fate, it wasn't a natural course of things. It was a dirty trick of the Klan."

"Oh, so that's how you feel about us. Still, after you've met my students and my little ones, and I've told them that they can trust you. All we are to you is a dirty trick!"

"You know that's not true!" He softened his tone. "There are men here—there must be—who would love you, who'd want you for a wife. You're beautiful, and you're—"

"Maybe there are. But maybe I prefer your company to theirs."

He said nothing. He was so confused, so torn, between what was right and what he wanted. He should leave now, for both their sakes.

But Chava said stoutly, "I'm a woman, Sean. I'm not foolish or stupid. I can do what I want. I can make my own decisions. I have my own money, and I have a good job. I don't need—and I certainly don't want—to be told what to do!"

Her eyes accosted him, glittering gold in the streetlight. Her jaw was set as hard as granite, and her eyebrows arched in disgust and anger. Her full lips were pushed out in a pout. Her words weighed on his heart. What was she to him? Everything that mattered. Everything that had a name, a place, a purpose in his life.

"I know," he breathed. "Oh, God, Chava, I'm so sorry." He meant it about everything—the dance; the kisses; his decision not to see her; and what he was about to do. Everything, everything. And then, his arms lifted of their own accord, and she was in them, and he was kissing her again.

# TWENTY-FOUR

That summer, Chava fell in love—twice.

The first time was with Hannah Berta Rosen, who was named for Rachael's grandmother and for Max and Chava's mother. Chava arranged for another teacher to take her place at the Sheltering Home so that she could care for Hannah while Rachael, who had had a difficult delivery, napped in the cool darkness of the bedroom. At least twice a day, Max rushed home from the store, delighted by his beautiful, new daughter and anxious about his beloved wife.

The second time Chava fell in love was just as all-consuming and irreversible. Sean stopped by the Rosen home nearly every night that he was on duty. On warm nights, Chava slipped away with him to stroll around Sloan's Lake or to sit beneath one of the sapling trees that had been planted on the shores. Some evenings, he spent only a few minutes with her—long enough to say hello and to kiss her once or twice—but on other nights, time was lost to them.

Everything about him endeared her—his slender hands, the squareness of his jaw, his thick eyebrows, his raven hair, the way he wrestled with himself to form a logical opinion and then spilled all his thoughts at once in a tangled mess. And, oh, what feelings he aroused in her! Chava wondered if Rachael felt such wild, giddy desire for Max. Did Max's kiss make Rachael's legs turn to melted wax? Did she murmur nonsensical syllables when his lips grazed the tender skin near her ears and on her neck? Did she lift to the tips of her toes and press herself against him when they embraced? Before they had married, had she touched herself as she lay alone in bed at night, and wondered how he might feel between her thighs?

On a warm July evening, Chava met Sean in the backyard long after Max and Rachael had fallen, exhausted, into sleep. Sean stood behind her, with his arms around her waist. Above them, the night sky opened out into a brilliant display of stars.

"Look, there's the summer triangle," Chava said. "Altair, Deneb and Cygnus. See the Milky Way? If you find those three stars you can see the whole of our galaxy. And there's Scorpio, and Sagittarius, very near the horizon, and . . . Are you looking up?"

"I've seen stars before."

She turned to face him. "You must look up, it's beautiful."

He lifted his face. In the dim light from inside the house, Chava could see the shadow of his black beard on his chin and cheeks, and a cluster of moles on his neck. She stifled the urge to kiss the skin below his Adam's apple.

"My cousin Kathleen and I used to lie on our backs in her father's hayfield and try to count the stars," he said. "But she always cheated."

"Cheated? How?"

"She'd let me get so far, and then she'd point in some other direction and say, 'Did you get that one?' And, fool that I was, I'd always look and lose my place."

Chava laughed. "I'd like to meet her. She sounds clever."

"Devilish is more like it." Sean lowered his gaze. "Would you really like to meet her? There's some big to-do at the new art museum on Sunday, and she has a painting in it."

On Sunday, Sean picked Chava up from a spot on the edge of the lake. He wore a suit and tie, with his hair neatly clipped and slicked back with pomade. It was the first time that Chava had seen him out of uniform.

"You look very nice," Chava said, as he held the car door open for her.

"As do you."

A large banner on the front lawn of the Chappell House on 13th and Logan announced the grand opening of the new galleries of the Denver Art Museum, with an exhibition of the works of fifty-two local artists, the Evans American Indian collection, and works by world famous artists. Nattily-dressed, well-to-do people already swarmed in the gardens. Chava smoothed down her plain, lavender tea dress, hoping it had not wrinkled too badly during the car ride. The doorman graciously pointed them toward the Gold Room, where refreshments were being served, and to the galleries on the second floor of the house.

"Well, aren't we the bee's knees," Sean whispered in her ear.

Chava laughed as they ascended the staircase to the second floor. The first gallery teemed with paintings of Colorado's scenery. A placard stated that it was the "Plein-Air Gallery."

"Have you ever seen so many pictures of mountains?" Sean asked, as he glanced first to the right, then to the left, without stopping to study any of the works.

"I suppose if you live here, that's what you paint." Chava paused in front of an impressionistic depiction of Long's Peak. "But they're all different. Mr. Graham's work is much less realistic than Mr. Bancroft's."

His mouth turned downward. "Couldn't one of them have gone out to Hugo or somewhere?"

"And paint what? Empty sky?" They moved on to an adjoining room. The paintings were more abstract in this room, bursting with color and vitality. But, Chava had to admit, a number of them still featured mountains.

"Oh, there's Kathleen," Sean said.

Chava recognized Kathleen Graves from the photographs and illustrations that appeared at least once a week in the newspapers. She wore a shimmering golden dress in the new garçonne silhouette. The narrow shoulder straps widened as they led to a bodice overlaid with chiffon patterned with delicate gilt-golden rings. A frothy sash tied around Kathleen's waist in an elaborate bow, its gilt-edged ends floating to her knees, and the gilded hem of the skirt was elegantly staggered in length. Chava was certain that she had seen the dress in one of the fashion magazines that Rachael collected; it was at the very least Parisian and very possibly a Jeanne Lanvin.

"Your cousin is Jim Graves' wife?" Chava asked.

"Didn't I mention that?"

"Seaney!" Kathleen came to greet them. "I'm so glad you came."

"This is Chava Rosen," Sean said. "Chava, this is my cousin, Kathleen."

Kathleen showed no reaction toward Chava—she didn't seem to notice or care that Chava was Jewish, or not well dressed, or entirely out of place in this crowd. She led Sean and Chava to her painting, which was a boldly-imagined red rock landscape done with thick, demanding strokes and dramatic colors. Storm clouds hovered over the scene, in charcoal, black and yellow, but the land below looked equally threatening, as if it would reach up and snatch the moisture that it wanted so badly from the clouds. The painting spoke of uncontrollable, barely restrained passion.

Sean looked it over. "Is that Redlands?"

"Yes." To Chava, she explained, "Redlands is my ranch."

"Is Jim here?" Sean asked.

"Right over there. With his family."

And there, across the room, the black and white photographs from the newspapers came to life: Jim Graves, with the thin, tantalizing scar that ran from his eye to his chin; his perfectly tailored silk suit; and his exotic cowboy boots. A consummate politician, Jim welcomed Chava with as much ease and friendliness as Kathleen had. When someone else commanded his attention, he graciously excused himself by shaking both Chava's and Sean's hands.

"There's someone you must meet, Seaney," Kathleen said. "In the Modernist Gallery."

As they followed Kathleen, Sean whispered in Chava's ear, "What's Modernist?"

"No more mountains," Chava quipped.

The paintings in the room left reality behind. Many were cubist, or Dadaist, or styles that Chava did not recognize. Kathleen stopped before a painting of a pure white dome against a burning turquoise sky that radiated outward in ocean-like waves. The card beside it read: "'Sacre Coeur, Paris, in Sun' by Julia Reston." A woman stood near the painting, her white hair cropped short. She wore trousers and a jacket and tie.

Kathleen introduced her as Julia Reston. She then introduced a good-looking man in his thirties as Julia's nephew, Paul. Paul stood close to Kathleen—perhaps closer than he should, Chava thought—and the expression on her face changed. She resembled her painting—her face filled with emotion that longed to be released, with longing so deep that it was essential for her survival.

"Paul is only newly returned from France," Julia said. "He was with the repatriation services for the past several years, helping to bring home our dead. My second painting was designed with his work in mind."

The painting had been created with a monochromatic palette, much of it in pleasant sepia, startlingly marred by black, gray and white. At the bottom of the canvas—which spread liberally across one wall of the gallery—disconnected shapes jumbled and humped in grotesque piles. It took Chava some time to recognize the ugly mess as the bodies of fallen soldiers in varying states of decay. Some were skeletons, who still wore tin helmets or clutched bayonet-mounted rifles in their hands, while others were heaps of rag and putrid flesh. Miss Reston had depicted some with their mouths open in shrieks or with their hands clawing futilely in an effort to be saved. Faces floated upward from the clump, fading into nothingness in a vicious gray stain at the top of the painting.

"I call it 'The Challenge of the Dead,'" Julia explained. "Paul has told me of the terrible state of the corpses—if I may speak plainly—that he excavated for repatriation. All of those men who stood so proudly, whole and strong—German, British, French, American—now indistinguishable from one another in the grotesquery of death."

"Sometimes it looked very much like this," Paul confirmed.

"Excuse me," Sean said. Without waiting for Chava or Kathleen, he walked away.

Kathleen looked in surprise at Chava. "Do you want me to go talk to him?"

"I will," Chava said.

But Sean had already left the gallery, and he wasn't in any of the exhibition galleries. Chava retraced their steps down the stairs to the entrance hall. She found him at last in the Gold Room, where punch had been ladled into sparkling crystal glassware. Guests mingled in small groups, eating delicate petit fours or wandering through the adjoining observatory to view the rare, tropical plants. Sean sat rigidly on a sofa that had been pushed against the wall. His hands sprawled on the cushion on either side of him.

Chava sat down beside him. "What's the matter? Are you ill?"

"No." He swallowed a couple of times. "I just . . . what Paul Reston said. And that horrible painting. It brought back all kinds of things I don't want to remember."

She laid her hand on his. "I'm so sorry."

He pulled his hand away. "And we're here on a pretense anyway. I didn't bring you here to look at paintings. I wanted to you to be impressed by Kathleen and Jim and . . ." He gestured at the guests in the Gold Room. "I don't know squat about art, but you're so smart that I wanted you to think I was, well, I wanted you to think that I was something other than a country bumpkin."

She laughed, but he did not.

"Do you want to leave?" she asked.

"No one's going to miss me here."

Sean was silent during the drive back to Sloan's Lake. Several times, Chava opened her mouth to speak, then reconsidered. What a mystery he was—funny and ironic one minute, suffering and dark the next. When he parked beneath a towering elm near the shore of the lake, he said, "I'm sorry I ruined your afternoon. It was supposed to be fun."

204 • LAURIE MARR WASMUND

"Will I see you on Tuesday night?" she asked.

"I don't know," he said. "I don't . . . I'll see."

All of Sunday night, and all of Monday and Tuesday, Chava fretted. If Sean didn't return, if he avoided Osceola Street and the Rosen home, if he decided he could not face her—the permutations and possibilities ran through her mind, paralyzing her, stripping from her the joy of caring for Hannah and teaching her students.

On Tuesday evening, she donned a light sweater and settled into the shadows at the side of the house long before the time he usually stopped by. When she heard him approaching on the sidewalk, she stepped out into the street.

"I was afraid you wouldn't come," she said.

"You're right," he said. "I was determined not to."

He did not stop walking, and she joined him.

"Why?" she asked. "What happened the other day to change your mind? Is it because I'm Jewish or that I have no money or position? Your cousin's dress was so beautiful— I think it was edged in real gold leaf—and mine was so ordinary. Was I an embarrassment to you?"

"Mother of God, no!" Lowering his voice, Sean said, "If anyone's an embarrassment, it's me. I'm sorry for acting that way."

"But why? Why did you act that way?" She laid her hand on his arm, and he started, as if she had pinched him. "Yes, that painting was ugly and disturbing, but that was Miss Reston's intention. After all, it was called, 'The Challenge—'"

"If I tell you, you'll think I'm a fool, you'll think I'm a coward—"

"Why would you say such a thing? You came home from war a hero—"

"That's just it. I was no hero. I'm a fraud."

"Come with me," Chava said. "Let's sit by the lake."

They chose a bench that faced Sloan's Lake. Sean kept his body rigid, barely settling on the bench, as if he wanted to flee. Chava swung her knees toward him, so that she could look in his eyes. "Tell me," she whispered. "Trust me."

Still looking toward the lake, he said, "My mother likes to say that I came home from the war without a scratch. She brags about it all the time, even to my friend, Tony, who came home with a bullet in his leg. I get so tired of hearing it because I don't, I can't think, I just don't feel that way. I feel like one of those floating faces in the painting, like I died, too, in some way. Inside my head, I guess, or my heart, maybe. I don't know, it sounds stupid when I say it."

"Not at all. I studied psychology in college. Freud talks about the unconscious mind as being the guardian of all the thoughts and memories that we are afraid to face, such as pain or loss."

"I don't understand a word of that."

"I think it's the same as when you were a child and broke your mother's favorite vase. You hid it so she wouldn't find out. We hide things we don't want to think about in our unconscious mind."

"Then she found it and tanned your hide for it."

"Yes, she did, and the things that we try to ignore usually find their way back to us, too, and they make us feel sad and lonely and without hope."

"Tony was with me almost all the time," he said. "We did the same things, and he just says that he did what he had to do, and it doesn't bother him a bit. But that painting—" He shivered. "What was that Julia woman thinking? Isn't art supposed to be pretty? And why would Paul tell her about it? And to include the Germans after the things they did—"

Chava said nothing. They all ended up dead in the trenches, she thought, and that was what Julia Reston was trying to convey. The pointlessness, the horror, the tragedy for all involved.

"I killed so many Germans," he continued. "Tony and I—we were almost always chosen for night patrol because we . . . and I don't know how many we killed. And I don't know who I killed." He looked at her, stricken. "What were their names? Where did they come from? Who did they leave behind? I was no better than they were—in fact, most of them were probably better men than I was—yet they died and I lived."

"What about your faith? Don't the priests at your church offer any teachings on this?"

"They say I did it for God and country," he said. "But there was another soldier—his name was Danhour—and I hated him. He was stupid and arrogant and a bully, everything I couldn't stand." He swallowed. "But I was just like him."

"What do you mean?"

"He and I, we went on a rampage, and we killed almost an entire trench filled with Germans with our bare hands, and we were called heroes for it." Sean's voice caught in a sob. "Everyone said we were heroes—the Army, my mother, the newspapers, even Tony thought I was. But it was animal craziness, some kind of sick vengeance, and now I have to live with it. Every day, every minute, I have to live with the shame of it."

She reached for him, and he buried his head on her shoulder, his body shuddering. "No, no," she soothed. "Don't think about it, it's over—"

"That painting made me realize my soul was lost, just like those faces in the painting. I'm as dead as they are."

"Sean, listen to me." Chava lifted his face. "Look at me, listen to me. Whatever you did in France, however terrible it was, the life you're leading now is righteous and kind and sane. You can't change the past, but you don't have to relive it. There's a passage in the Talmud: 'Do not be daunted by the enormity of the world's grief. Do justly, now. Love mercy, now. Walk humbly now.' It says 'now' three times, for a reason. You're doing good now, today, in the present. The past—the war—it's gone."

"I don't know how to escape it. And I don't want you to hate me for it, I don't want you to think—"

"I love you."

As the declaration echoed across the silent water, something bubbled up in Chava, something that made her want to laugh, giddy and joyful, reckless and free. This, she thought, this is what I have always wanted. Something both beautiful and agonizing, gracious and wild, powerful and delicate.

Sean reached for her. "Oh, Chava."

Chava covered his face with kisses, until her happiness became his.

# TWENTY-FIVE

Seaney must have warned Tony about coming around the Sullivans' apartments, because for two weeks, neither of them graced the property with their company. Maggie breathed a sigh of relief, but Alice Colleen stood at the front window and watched for their cars almost every evening.

"Doesn't Sergeant Necchi like us anymore, Mommy?" she asked. "Is his dog still sick?"

The boys parroted her questions, and Maggie said, "I think he's just too busy to visit right now. And I'm sure his dog is fine."

"Perching," Alice Colleen said. "That's his dog's name. Perching."

Maggie smiled. She missed Tony as much as Alice Colleen did. When she went down to the shed in the evenings, she listened to the activity in the backyard. She wondered if the house would ever have walls.

Then, one evening, Tony slipped almost silently into the shed behind her. Going to the back, he pawed through the jumble of tools. Clatter, clatter, clatter, bang—he made no attempt to be careful or quiet. Maggie gave up on typing and went out into the cool evening. She sat on the old Liberty Garden rain barrel and lit a cigarette.

When Tony came out, he said, "Hey, Mrs. James, sorry if I wasn't quiet enough for you."

"Did you find what you were looking for?"

"Sure, why not?" he said. "So can I build this house or do I need to be quiet back there, too? You can't hammer without making some noise."

"You don't understand. My husband is very sensitive. Light, loud noises, lots of movement—the kids are too much for him sometimes."

"He's not much of a father if he don't like his kids."

"That isn't what I said!" Maggie snapped. "And you have no right to—"

"He shouldn't be so ashamed."

Maggie's heart leaped—had Seaney told Tony about Liam? "He is not ashamed."

"Then, why don't he come out? There's plenty of them who came back hurt. Why don't he talk to Sean or me? We were there, too."

"The word is doesn't," Maggie said.

"What?"

"Why *doesn't* he come out? Why *doesn't* he talk—?"

"Why don't you wanna answer me, Mrs. James? What happened to him in the war? Sean never says, like it's some big secret."

"Well, we all know what you and Seaney did in the war," she said bitterly. "All your stories of running around France listening to bands and playing baseball and visiting Catholic cathedrals—oh, Ma loves to hear about that. And your phony salutes with the kids—*Sergeant* Necchi. It was so much fun for you, such an adventure, and since Seaney's been back, he hasn't wanted to have anything to do with the store, because it's too boring for him."

She ran out of bile, panting slightly. To mask it, she inhaled again and breathed out a mouthful of smoke.

"You wanna know what we did in the war?" Tony asked. "You really wanna know?"

"If you want to tell me," she said flippantly.

"We played God."

"What?"

"Me and him, we played God, and we were good at it. We were the best. We went out almost every night, and we crawled around through the mud and over the dead bodies and horses, and when we come to the German trenches, we dropped in and killed everybody but one. Only one. And we took him back with us. Most of the time some skinny, stupid looking one so he don't give us no trouble. And we'd kill all the ones that weren't doing nothing to us, but who were just doing what they were told to do."

Maggie put her hand up to her mouth.

"And you know what?" Tony continued. "You can't use a gun when you do that, 'cuz you gotta be quiet. So you know how we done it? With our hands. I come up behind those guys and slit their throats with my bayonet. I never even got blood on my hands, I was so good. Then Sean would step around me and he had a quick pig stick to just below the ribs, just where the heart is, for the next guy, and that way, we'd clean out the trench. And we brought one guy back to our side to be taken somewhere clean and dry and given all sorts of good food so he'd tell us everything he knows. And the others were just dead."

Maggie could not meet his gaze. Seaney, Seaney, who used to cry on slaughtering days because the lambs and the piglets that he'd fed and cared for died violent and ugly deaths. Seaney, who wouldn't shoot blackbirds nibbling in the garden, because he hated to see them flop around in their death throes. God, how easily this world chewed up and spat out men.

"So whatever your husband did, well, it's probably no worse than that," Tony went on. "And yeah, now maybe we laugh too much, or we make your kids too loud by joking and stuff. You want us to talk about what we did in the trenches instead? In front of your Mamma and your *bambinos*? What do you want, Mrs. James?"

He punched the name, as if to wound her.

"I didn't know any of that," she admitted. "The stories Seaney tells—"

"Yeah, you don't know because we don't talk about it to you or your mother or pretty little Alice. We tell you about how much fun we had and we don't ever talk about the bad. So you and every other mother and wife and kids don't have to know what we done."

He left, without the tools he'd gathered from the back of the shed. A minute later, Maggie heard the engine of his car roar to life and the crunch of gravel beneath its tires. He was gone.

She went back to the shed. Picking up a letter, she focused on the handwriting, but she couldn't decipher it because of the tears in her eyes. She thanked God that Liam had not witnessed or done any of what Tony described. Slitting throats, stabbing in the heart, playing God. She remembered the words Liam had written: *A man cannot harm his fellow men without the laws of justice and fairness catching up with him at some later time in his life.*

Thank God Liam had chosen a different path—no matter how difficult it had been.

When Maggie comes up from working in the shed, Liam is still awake. He puts his arm around her, and she rolls into the warmth of his body, her head in the hollow of his shoulder.

"Remember when we lived at the Erwins'?" She whispers so that she doesn't wake Kieran, who sleeps behind a screen in their bedroom, the last available space in the apartments. "I loved that house."

"It was a good place to live. Why were you thinking of it?"

"I used to imagine it was where George and Evelyn lived." She names the characters from the short stories that she once wrote for *Ladies' Home Journal*.

Liam chuckles. "I haven't heard Evelyn's name in a long time. I didn't know she still existed."

"She doesn't, really. I haven't written a story about her in years. Not since Alice Colleen was born."

"That's because we have so many blessings that there's no reason to imagine them anymore."

She wonders: the overcrowded apartment, the defunct store, and the half-built house on the back lot. Her parents live as recluses, and Seaney has deserted them all.

"I wish the war wouldn't have happened," she whispers. "I wish we could go back. We lost so much—Frank and Donnell and so many others. It changed Seaney, and it changed you." She hesitates. "And I changed, too."

She waits for him to ask her to explain, but he doesn't. And how would she, anyway? She doesn't know what she truly wants or how she would live without Liam and her children.

"We're taught that all things work together for good for those who love God, who are called according to his purpose," Liam says. "I was called according to his purpose, and so were you, to be my wife and my dearest love and the mother of our beautiful children."

Does she believe that? It's straight out of the Catechism and the Bible. But she can't reconcile the cruelty of man—Tony and Seaney randomly killing and Liam manacled to the bars of his cell—with things working together for good.

The next evening, she waits at the bottom of the outside stairs for Seaney. When he arrives, his face is dark and brooding even before he sees her. "Come up and see Ma," she says. "She's missed you."

"What about Tony?" he demands. "Is he still banned from your precious household?"

"Bring him along if you want." Maggie grabs the railing and climbs up the steps to the apartments.

Sean comes inside about a half-hour later, bringing Tony with him. Ma comes out to the parlor to talk to them, while Maggie stays in the kitchen. She lets Alice Colleen and the boys go into the parlor. The sound of their laughter brings tears to her eyes. She wishes she could join them, but she is determined to disregard Tony Necchi. It isn't the children that he disturbs too much. It's her.

She peeks through the partially-open kitchen door. Her mother chatters and coos, Kieran on her lap, and Seaney smokes peacefully, sitting in Pa's rocker, while Tony leans back comfortably in one of the dining room chairs. In the corner, Alice Colleen writes her pretend letters—one of which she presents to Tony, saying it's about "Perching"—and the boys play with cars on the floor. Declan and Frankie even share with each other—a rare event these days.

Tony's words come to her: *We tell you about how much fun we had and we don't ever talk about the bad.*

Liam's words come to her, too: *So many blessings that there's no reason to imagine them anymore.*

Tony looks up, his liquid black eyes challenging hers.

He holds her gaze until she closes the kitchen door.

# TWENTY-SIX

Mary Jane took Ross' suggestions to heart. She apologized to Essie and Matt and to Judith and Andy about the way that she had acted at their house. In return, they welcomed her to their home nearly every weekend. On either Friday or Saturday nights, she went to dinner—cooked by Mina—at Judith's house and spent the night at Essie's. On Sunday mornings, she went to the Pillar of Fire Church, where the Klan was openly praised. Bishop Alma White was not often in town—she had a large congregation in Zarephath, New Jersey—but her message was delivered by her subordinates. Mary Jane brought home pamphlets illustrated by Reverend Branford Clarke showing Klan members in hoods and robes at the side of Jesus distributing the five loaves and two fishes and acting the Good Samaritan. There was even a puzzling illustration of robed and hooded Klansmen following behind George Washington as he led his troops during the American Revolution.

Mary Jane delivered books to Mina, but Judith's assessment of the girl carried some truth with it: the bright seven-year-old who could read adult novels had grown into a twelve-year-old who struggled with her studies. She squinted at the words on the page and seemed entirely undone by math problems. Mary Jane wondered if she needed glasses.

On a Friday night in July, the Dercum house was in an uproar when Mary Jane arrived after work. Dressed in their best, both Mina and Clyde were gathering up shoes and sweaters, while Judith and Essie primped in front of the vanity in Judith and Andy's bedroom.

"There's a family dance at Cotton Mills tonight," Judith explained. "There's even a midnight supper—"

"I wish you'd dressed nicer, M.J.," Essie scolded. "You might find yourself a nice husband—"

"Well, we'll fix that." Judith dragged Mary Jane over to the mirror and forced her to sit down by putting her hands on her shoulders. "What do you say, Es?"

"Mascara and lipstick, and definitely rouge. You look like you spend your days in a basement typing."

"That's because I do," Mary Jane managed as Judith dotted her cheeks with rouge.

"And we'll curl your eyelashes, too." Essie picked up something that looked like a surgical tool. "It's called a Kurlash."

"No, thank you," Mary Jane said.

"Close your eyes while I put on mascara," Judith ordered. "You know, when Essie and Jenny and I were in high school, we used to smear soot from the fireplace mixed with Vaseline on our lashes. Thank heavens that Maybelline made this cake stuff."

In the mirror, Mary Jane glimpsed the reflection of Mina standing in the doorway. She opened her mouth to invite her into the room, but Mina stepped out of the doorway and disappeared.

After Judith administered a great puff of powder, Mary Jane eyed herself in the mirror. She looked nothing like she usually did, but she wasn't sure it was an improvement. She thought of the girls in France, who wore circles of rouge on their cheeks and dark kohl liner on their eyes. On the street corners, they begged for cigarettes from the passing soldiers: "*Avez vous une cibiche?*" If a man offered a cigarette, the girl left with him.

Judith surveyed her handiwork. "If you don't have a prospective husband by the end of the dance tonight, Essie and I will start kidnapping men for you."

A knock sounded on the door to the house, and Essie left to answer it. She screamed, and Mary Jane and Judith looked at each other quizzically in the mirror before they ran to the parlor.

Five Klansmen stood before the fireplace, their arms folded across their chests and their hands hidden up their sleeves. "Good evening, ladies," one of them intoned in a solemn voice.

Mina ran to Mary Jane and stood slightly behind her. Mary Jane laid her hand on Mina's shoulder.

"One, two, three," one of the men said, and they pulled up the hoods. Andy, Avery, and Matt stood before them, with two workers from the dairy. Andy let his hood drop back into place over his face. "You didn't recognize us, did you?"

Essie burst into laughter, followed by Judith. "You are scary," she said. "I have to give you that."

Andy spied Mina hiding in Mary Jane's skirts. Lifting his arms, he came toward them. Mina grabbed onto Mary Jane's hand as Andy yelled, "Boo!"

"Don't," Mary Jane said.

"You know who I am, don't you?" Andy said. "I'm your tickle friend, come to tickle you!"

He pulled Mina against him, tickling her with his free hand. Mina flailed. "Don't! Stop!" He kept on, and Mina's complaints turned to sobs. Andy grabbed her beneath the knees, lifted her up in his arms as easily as if she were a cat, and stuck his hooded face into hers. "Are you scared?" he asked through the mouthless hood. "Boo! Boo! Boo!"

Mina screamed, and Mary Jane shouted, "Stop it! She doesn't like that."

Judith said, "Oh, they're just playing. They do it all the time. He thinks it's funny."

"But she doesn't. She's crying."

Annoyed, Judith said, "Let her be, Andy."

Andy lowered her to the ground, and Mina took refuge beside Mary Jane, her young breasts clearly outlined as she gasped for breath, her hair pulled from its pins. Andy whisked off his hood, a sour look on his face. His gaze traveled from Mina's face to her knees and back again, and something—the sheen of sweat on his forehead and chin, or his mussed hair, or the way his upper lip curled—sent a chill through Mary Jane.

She stepped in front of Mina. "Leave her alone."

"We need to go, anyway," he said. "It's an hour to sundown."

"What happens at sundown?"

"Wait and see," Avery answered. "We're taking a little detour tonight."

"As long as we aren't late for the dance," Essie said.

They climbed into two automobiles. Matt and Essie and the two dairy workers crowded into Matt's Model T truck, while Andy, Judith, and Avery took the front seat of Andy's Model T touring car. Mary Jane and the two children piled into the back. Mary Jane sat between Clyde, who sulked, and Mina. She put her hand over Mina's, and Mina clenched it in her fingers.

"Do you know where we're going?" Mary Jane whispered.

Mina shook her head.

The cars barreled along dusty roads until they came to the Colfax viaduct over the Platte River. When they reached a large body of water to the west, Andy shut down the lights on the car. Behind him, Matt followed suit. The two cars idled in the near darkness.

"Where are we?" Mary Jane asked.

"Shhh," Avery said. "Welcome to Little Jerusalem."

A flashlight's beam wavered across the lake, and Andy revved his engine. He sped forward, cutting through side streets until he came to West Colfax. As he passed along the route, he shouted and honked his horn. Following in his car, Matt did the same, as did about four more cars that had roared out of the twilight.

Andy cruised toward open fields to the west, then swung the car around and made his way back to West Colfax, the others following. At the corner of West Colfax and a side street that Mary Jane couldn't identify, he braked and honked.

"Suey! Suey!" he yelled out the window. "Here, pig, here, pig!"

"What are you doing?" Mary Jane asked.

"That's the synagogue." Avery pointed to an unassuming brick building. "Where the Jews worship on Friday nights. Slimy worms, they don't even know that Sunday is God's day."

"It's a church?" Mary Jane asked.

"How can you call a building used by people who don't believe in Jesus a church?" Judith asked. "It's a house of infidels who are lower than snakes. I would spit on them if I ever saw them."

"Spit on them," Clyde echoed. "Pig, pig, pig!"

The two dairy workers sprang from Matt's car, hooded and robed, and ran to the steps of the synagogue. They dumped buckets of black ooze on the steps and in front of the door. The ammoniac smell of manure pierced Mary Jane's nostrils. Running back to their car, the two men jumped in it and honked. At once, Andy sped down West Colfax, away from the synagogue and out of the neighborhood.

"What was in the buckets?" Mary Jane challenged. "What did they dump on the steps?"

"Just a little suggestion," Avery answered her. "We're hoping they'll all leave town. Go back to whatever filthy country they came from."

Mary Jane glanced at Mina in alarm. Neither she nor Clyde had shown any reaction as the dairy workers dumped manure on the steps of a place of worship. Mary Jane had the unsettled suspicion that they had seen this several times before.

"Tonight, let's hear the story of Jonah." Judith turned from the front seat to face the children. "Jonah was told by God to do his duty, but instead, he tried to run away. He stowed away on a ship and was found by the sailors as a terrible storm approached. They knew Jonah had brought the evil storm down on them because he was a Jew. Jonah promised that if they threw him overboard, the storm would cease. So they did, and he was swallowed by a great whale. And for three days, that poor fish tried to digest him in its stomach, but on the third day, it spit him out, because he was indigestible. That's because Jews are unrepentant and traitorous. They crucified Christ, and they refuse to celebrate Christmas and Easter, and now they run businesses that cheat Christians out of their money."

Mary Jane blinked. "I've never heard it told that way."

"That's how Bishop White tells it," Judith said. "But we know that we're saved because we believe in—"

She nodded at the two children in the back seat.

"Jesus Christ our Lord," they said together.

"But—" Mina said.

"What is it, Minnie?" Judith asked impatiently.

"The whale spit Jonah out because he was a Jew and indi—, indigest—"

"Indigestible," Mary Jane supplied.

"But if Jonah had been a Christian, wouldn't he have been digested and died?"

Mary Jane squeezed Mina's hand, proud to see that the Mina who absorbed everything still lived in this quiet, sad girl's body.

"Don't be impertinent, Minnie," Judith snapped. "You shouldn't question the Bible. It's God's word. The point of the story is that Jews are hated everywhere."

"I always learned that the story of Jonah is one of forgiveness," Mary Jane said. "God saves Jonah by having the fish swallow him, and Jonah gets a second chance to serve the Lord. And he does."

"Oh, come on, M.J.," Avery groused. "Don't cause a fight. You're not always right, you know."

Mary Jane sniffed and looked out the window of the car.

Andy turned the car toward downtown, while the other cars veered away in opposite directions. Mary Jane's stomach sank as she realized that they were driving into the narrow streets of Five Points. The closely-packed, two-story brick bungalows sat far off the street, fronted by concrete stoops and patches of grass. Nearly every house on the block was dark.

What had Raynelle said?

*We have to close our drapes at sundown, so we won't get a bottle of flaming rags and gasoline through our window.*

Andy braked the car and dimmed the acetylene headlights. In the front seat, Avery lifted up a long, thin cylinder. "How long's the fuse?" Andy asked.

"Plenty, so we can get away. The blasting cap's well in it."

Mary Jane's heart clambered. "Is that dynamite? Where did you get it? Did you take it from the quarry?"

"It's my quarry, too," Avery said.

Mary Jane grabbed onto the back of the front seat and pulled herself forward. "What are you going to do with it? Are you going to blow up someone's house?"

"There isn't enough here to blow up a house—"

"Just a room or two," Andy snickered.

"We throw it on the street," Avery said. "It leaves a nice hole for them to clean up. Sometimes it breaks a window or two. It doesn't hurt anybody. They're all off the streets by now."

Andy laughed. "And if they aren't, well . . ."

What if little George or Harry were walking home from a friend's house? What if Raynelle's husband, Aaron, was coming home late from his postal rounds?

"Stop!" Mary Jane reached over the high-backed seat and grabbed Avery's shoulder.

"What in the hell are you doing?" Avery whipped around to stare at her, the unlit dynamite still in his hand. "You could blow us all up!"

"Let me out," she said. "I don't want anything to do with this!"

"Don't be stupid," Judith rasped. "We're not going to let you out in this neighborhood. Andy and Avery are trying to protect you from them. They're trying to let them know they better not try anything like that janitor did a while back."

"People live in these houses," Mary Jane cried. "Families, just like yours, like mine. They have husbands and children, and—"

"Oh, to hell with this," Andy said. "Let's go home."

"What about the dance?" Judith and Avery protested together. "Aren't we going to Cotton Mills?"

Andy punched the car into gear and fishtailed down the street. "I'm not in the mood now."

"I want to go home," Mary Jane said. "I want to go to my home."

Without a word, Andy turned the car southward toward Littleton. Mary Jane leaned back against the seat, tears in her eyes. Clyde scooted away from her—as if decency might be contagious, she thought bitterly—but Mina placed her hand on Mary Jane's. Mary Jane flipped her hand palm upward and held Mina's tightly.

When they arrived at the Graysons' home, Judith turned to Mary Jane. "You ruined the night for all of us. I hope you're happy."

"Mommy, I need to go to the bathroom," Clyde said.

"Just get out and go," Andy snapped.

"Where are your manners?" Judith scolded. "This is the Graysons' yard! Do you need to go, too, Minnie?"

"Yes," Mina barely breathed.

They all piled out of the car. While the others went in, Mary Jane sat on front porch. She heard her mother's and Ross' greetings, the questions about what they were doing there, the offer to make tea or coffee. Mary Jane she wrapped her arms around her shoulders for warmth in the cooling night air.

The screen door opened, and Mina came out, carrying a blanket. "Here," she said. "I thought you might need this."

"Thank you." Mary Jane wrapped the blanket halfway around her. "Cuddle in here with me."

Mina glanced warily toward the inside before she sat down. Mary Jane tossed the blanket over Mina's shoulders. Together, they listened to the crickets, and the call of a great horned owl, and the coyotes who skulked through the foothills beyond.

"Why were you so upset over the story of Jonah?" Mina asked.

"I was taught different things, things that seem—I don't know—kinder than what Bishop White teaches. I just wanted you to hear the story the way I learned it."

Mina mulled it over. "Why did you cry over the dynamite?"

"I was scared. I didn't want anyone to be hurt."

"Why not, if they're so bad? Miss Judith told me never to speak to them, especially if it's a man."

"They aren't bad. Their skin is a different color, that's all. A friend of mine lives in that neighborhood, and she is so nice. She has a son who is about your age, and he plays and goes to school and does all the things that you do. It would be awful if he were hurt, don't you think? He's just a little boy."

"Maybe that wasn't his house. Maybe it belonged to a bad one."

"But we didn't know that—"

The screen door of the house creaked open. "Minnie," Judith ordered. "Go get in the car."

Mina unwound herself from the blanket, told Mary Jane goodnight, and went to the car.

Judith loomed over Mary Jane. "You can feel how you want about things, but you are not to encourage Mina to be rude—"

"I don't."

"In the car, you encouraged her to question the Bible. You encouraged her to question me."

"I didn't do that. She asked the question on her own."

"Essie and I ask you along because you're Matt's and Avery's sister, but don't think that we like you. After tonight, I doubt if we can even pretend anymore."

Judith marched toward the car.

After the Dercums left, Ross joined Mary Jane on the front porch. "I thought you were going to keep the peace with them."

"I can't seem to. Or maybe I don't want to. They talk about being Christian, but they don't mean Christian, they mean Klansman." She turned toward him. "You don't think I'm wrong, do you?"

"We all have our reasons for what we do," he said tightly, and she knew that he was thinking of his refusal to help Mina.

Upstairs, as she dressed for bed, Mary Jane caught the reflection of herself in the vanity mirror. She still wore the lipstick, rouge, and mascara that Judith and Essie had applied. As if it were some kind of Klan stain, she scrubbed at it, using water from the basin. As she dried her hands, she saw Mina's flushed and angry face as Andy tickled her. Then, she heard again Mina's heartless statement: *Maybe that wasn't his house.*

She did not know which was worse: Andy's lust for Mina or the vile teachings of Judith and the Pillar of Fire Church.

# TWENTY-SEVEN

On Monday morning, Mary Jane dreaded seeing Raynelle. She felt ashamed that she had taken part in the drive through the West Side and Five Points, ashamed that she even knew people who would do such a thing. Andy and Avery had obviously thrown dynamite into the sleeping, residential streets of Five Points before. Who knew what damage they had caused?

When Mary Jane entered the washroom before work, Raynelle remarked, "You look as if you haven't slept in days."

"Oh, you were right about everything! About Klansmen causing mayhem in the Negro and Jewish part of town—"

"Shhh." Raynelle glanced toward the door before offering Mary Jane her stool. "Here, sit down."

The story poured from Mary Jane's lips, as if she had carried the burden for so long that she might burst from the weight of it. She told Raynelle about finding Mina, about Judith's treatment of her, about Andy's interest in her, about Avery and Andy's rampage on Friday night. By the time she finished the story, her handkerchief was wringing wet with tears, and she was late enough to the typing pool that Miss Crawley would dock her pay.

"The little girl," Raynelle pondered. "There was always talk of Mr. Graves having a child or two without anyone knowing any better. Nobody was surprised by it—I mean, don't all rich men do that? I guess I always figured it had been taken care of."

"Maybe they think it has been," Mary Jane said bitterly.

"You have to do something for her."

Raynelle's words echoed what she had told Mary Jane about the Klan: *Do whatever you can.*

"I can't! I tried to make friends with Judith and Essie so I could spend the weekends there, but I can't get along with them when they do such terrible things. Ross is right. I can't just take her away like she's a lost puppy or something."

"Listen to me." Raynelle stepped forward, and Mary Jane looked up at her. "Do you know why colored women like to work for Mr. Graves?"

"What? Because he pays well?"

"No, because he never does anything to them, he never asks for anything sexual."

Mary Jane gasped at the word, but Raynelle said, "You don't think that happens? It happens to white women, too, but nearly always to black women. It's not often that a black woman finds a place where she's treated as well as a white woman is."

"I never . . . I never thought about that—"

"And Mrs. Graves is the same. Beryl, her lady's maid, is black. She manages all Mrs. Graves' clothes and her hair and her jewelry. She helps her dress and even runs her bath. I could probably count on one hand the number of white women in Denver who would allow black hands to touch their clothes or their jewelry. But as far as I know, Mrs. Graves has never made any fuss about Beryl's skin color."

"Kathleen wouldn't. She just isn't like that."

"They have good hearts, Mr. and Mrs. Graves do. And this little girl is in a situation that Mr. Graves won't let even his Negro employees get into. You have to tell him."

"I'm afraid." Mary Jane accepted a clean handkerchief from Raynelle. "I don't want to do anything that would hurt Kathleen or their children—"

"That's already been done," Raynelle said. "But she's a grown woman, and she knows who she married. Do you think she'd be that surprised?"

Mary Jane thought about the way Mr. Graves had flirted with the girls of the Relief Society. She'd assumed it was for Kathleen's benefit, but perhaps, he was the kind of man who had a penchant for any woman who responded to his overtures. There had always been rumors to that effect in the typing pool.

"Would you come with me if I arranged to speak with him?"

Raynelle stepped back as if from scalding water. "I can't. You must know that. I can't risk my job."

"But if he treats you like anyone else—"

"I'm still a black woman, still at the bottom of the barrel. Anyway, Mr. Spratt wouldn't allow me on the fifth floor." As Mary Jane blew into the handkerchief again, Raynelle suggested, "Ask Miss Crawley. She could get an audience with Mr. Graves."

"Johanna?"

"You're brave to call her by her first name."

Raynelle was right. Mary Jane needed someone who held some sway with Mr. Graves. Johanna had sat on the committee that chose the Relief Society members during the war; she was one of his most trusted employees.

"I wish I could think of another way to protect Mina besides being mixed up with the Klan," Mary Jane said.

"That little girl is lucky she has you."

Raynelle took a clean towel from the pile on the shelf and wiped the tears from Mary Jane's cheeks and chin. With her fingers, she smoothed back the stray hairs from Mary Jane's face.

"You'll be brave, Miss Grayson," Raynelle said. "You'll do what you should. But now, you better get to work before you get fired."

After work, Mary Jane lingered while the other girls straightened their typing stations and rushed out, eager to go home. When everyone had left but Miss Crawley, Mary Jane approached her.

"Why, Mary Jane." Johanna switched from stern taskmaster to friend in her Jekyll and Hyde way. "We haven't talked in so long. But I must ask why you were so late this morning. I had to write up a complaint."

"I understand," Mary Jane said. "But I need to speak with Mr. Graves."

Miss Crawley's face closed. "Do you have a complaint about me?"

"No, no, it's a . . . personal matter."

"I believe he is out of town, visiting the Moffat Oil Field in western Colorado." Her brows furrowed. "Can you tell me why you need to see him?"

"Do you remember Anneka Lindstrom? She was in the National Woman's Party with us during the war."

"Why, of course."

Mary Jane told the story again. Johanna listened with a half-shocked, half-knowing expression. At the end, she said, "I knew that Anneka and he had some sort of connection. It was evident whenever they spoke."

"What should I do?" Mary Jane asked.

"I don't think you should do anything now, before the election. But after—"

"I believe Andy Dercum could hurt Mina."

"Hurt her? In what way? Is there violence in the house?"

"I don't think they beat her. But she's as pretty as Anneka was, and she is growing up. Her body is changing into a woman's, and Mr. Dercum—"

"Ah, I see." Johanna considered. "What about Mrs. Graves?"

"Kathleen?"

"I never particularly liked her, but she might be able to find a home where the girl is safe. The Catholics have a number of orphanages—"

"She's not an orphan!" Mary Jane's words echoed through the empty typing room. "She's his daughter, and she should be living in their big mansion with his other children."

"I'm afraid what you want is impossible. To claim an illegitimate child would ruin him. To bring her into his home would be a mistake."

"So my choices are to leave her in a home where she could be raped or to see her sent to an orphanage?" Mary Jane fumed. "I won't do either."

Johanna glanced toward the door, checking for eavesdroppers. "Surely you realize that this could jeopardize your employment here."

Mary Jane's spirits sank. A typist was easily replaced as a Negro bathroom attendant. "I . . . I don't know—"

"Do you think that Mrs. Graves knows about this child?" Johanna asked. "You've had some dealings with her."

"I haven't talked with her since she married. But I don't think she would allow this to happen to Mina. But she might, well, she might be willing to try to save my job if I spoke to her first, rather than to him."

"Let's visit Mrs. Graves," Johanna decided. "If she already knows and refuses to help, then there's nothing to be done for the child."

"So you'll go with me?"

"Do you really want to do this alone? I would be terrified—I am terrified. But I'll send a note to her asking for a time we can see her."

Kathleen agrees to see them on Tuesday. She sends a car to Graves Industries to pick them up—a sky blue Marmon driven by a Negro chauffeur who opens and closes the doors for them without saying a word. In silence, he drives south of the city, past the rolling lawns of the Denver Country Club to the house on Circle Drive. When he stops the car in front of it, both Mary Jane and Johanna stare.

"I didn't think it would be this big," Johanna whispers.

"Oh, do you think we should do this?"

"It's too late now. We're here."

"Thank you," Mary Jane says as the chauffeur closes the door behind her. He says nothing, but tips his hat to her.

A butler greets them at the front door and leads them to a parlor larger than the Grayson house. Kathleen sits in an oversized armchair, but when she sees Mary Jane, she leaps from it and opens her arms. Mary Jane embraces her.

"I'm happy you're here," Kathleen says. "And Miss Crawley, it's nice to see you after so many years. Sit down, please, and I'll call for tea."

She rings a silver bell, and Mary Jane stifles a laugh—here is the girl who once jumped her way through "I'd Like to Be a Monkey in the Zoo" on the springy bed of a hotel room in New York, a feather-filled pillow in each hand.

A maid arrives with tea and cakes.

"What brings you here today?" Kathleen asks as she pours. "I'm often at the building, but it's for Foundation work. It never takes me to the basement."

Johanna does not deign to reply, so Mary Jane says, "We're still down there. Annabel and Mavis and me, along with two others you don't know."

"You must tell them hello for me. I wish they'd come today, I would have loved to have seen them."

"We're here for a very different purpose, I'm afraid," Johanna says staunchly.

"What is it?"

Johanna nods toward Mary Jane, whose tea cup chatters against the saucer in her hands. She sets it down.

"It's a long and complicated story," she says. "After I came home from France, my brother was called up to go to the Army. Before he left, he fell in love with a woman who was a widow with a young daughter. They planned to marry when they came home, and he was to be the girl's father."

Kathleen smiles politely. "And did they marry?"

"No, Ross—my brother—came home all right, but the woman, her name was Anneka"—Johanna clears her throat, and Mary Jane realizes she's making a mess of the explanation—"she died from the flu." Mary Jane's voice catches. "I'm sorry, even now, it's upsetting for me—"

"I'm sorry, too," Kathleen says. "Your poor brother."

Mary Jane speaks again. "While Ross was away, he asked me to be Anneka's friend. She didn't read or write English as well as she did Swedish, so I would visit her once or twice a week and read Ross' letters to her. We became good friends. She was so nice and so pretty, probably the prettiest woman I've ever seen. Her daughter, Mina, was just like her."

"I see." Kathleen's voice is still polite and distant. "Did Mina have the flu as well?"

"No, she didn't, but Anneka didn't have family in Denver, and after she died, Mina was without a home."

Kathleen's interest perks up. "What happened to her?"

Mary Jane hesitates, and Johanna says, "That's why we're here."

"Kathleen," Mary Jane says. "This is hard for me to say—"

"Go on."

"As I said, Anneka told me she was a widow, and that her husband had died in Sweden before she came to America. But the dates, the times, didn't match up, and I became, well, suspicious. Anneka was too young to have been married and given birth to the baby in Sweden, and Mina herself used to say she was American. One day, it was just before the war ended—"

"It was the day of the last Liberty Loan rally, which was in October," Johanna supplies. "The National Woman's Party had marched in protest, and Anneka was with us—"

"You knew her, too?" Kathleen asks.

"Yes, although not well."

"That's right, it was the day of the rally," Mary Jane says. "I went to see Anneka after work, but she already had a visitor. It was Mr. Graves, and he was talking about how he wished Anneka would not go out because of the flu that was going around at the time. But it was too late, she had already caught it—"

"How did Mr. Graves know her?" Kathleen asks, her voice sharper.

"She worked for his mother, and—"

Realization forms in Kathleen's face. Mary Jane doesn't need to say another word: Kathleen knows. Mary Jane wipes the sweat from her palms on the dainty linen napkin in her hand. "I'm sorry," she says, but the words come out weak and meaningless.

Kathleen sets her tea cup on the table, gently and without spilling it. She swallows a number of times before she asks, "Where is Mina today?"

"That's why we've come," Johanna says. "Through a series of twists and turns, the girl has ended up at the home of Judith and Andy Dercum. They live on the plains east of Denver, near Chambers Road, isn't that correct?"

She defers to Mary Jane.

"They live on a dairy farm out there," Mary Jane says. "But they don't treat Mina well. She's considered a servant, and they don't even call her by her name—they call her Minnie—and she doesn't have anything she needs, and I think she needs glasses—"

She stops. Her words are moving faster than her thoughts.

"How old is she?" Kathleen asks.

"Nearly thirteen," Mary Jane says. "And Mr. Dercum, well, he doesn't treat her as a father would a daughter, but as . . ."

Her words fail entirely. How can she say aloud something so unthinkable? She glances toward Johanna, who stiffens her shoulders and says, "He treats her as a man would treat a young woman in whom he has a romantic interest. I have not seen the child, but Mary Jane tells me she will be as lovely as her mother was. And her mother was only seventeen when she—"

Kathleen stands and walks to the fireplace mantel. She grabs onto it with both hands. Her body sways as she tucks in her chin and looks at her feet as if she is trying to keep from vomiting. Mary Jane glances at Johanna, fearing that Kathleen will fall to the floor.

"I'm so very sorry, Mrs. Graves," Johanna says.

"Mr. Graves took good care of Anneka and Mina," Mary Jane offers, hoping to ease Kathleen's pain. "The house where they lived was beautiful, and they had the loveliest clothes and things. Mina was so smart—she loves to read—but Andy and Judith are teaching her things that aren't right—"

Kathleen whips around suddenly, and Mary Jane starts, afraid that Kathleen will tell them to get out or that they are fired. She is nothing like the girl Mary Jane knew in the Relief Society. She stands straight, her face cold and determined, her hands at her side, poised and unmoving. She's almost as imperious and formidable as her husband.

"I want to see her."

Mary Jane exchanges a look with Johanna. Neither of them speaks, as if the demand is unreasonable or impossible.

Kathleen repeats it in a stronger voice. "I want to meet her. I want to see her for myself. Can you arrange that for me?"

"Yes," Mary Jane says. "Yes, oh, I was hoping you would!"

# TWENTY-EIGHT

After Mary Jane and Miss Crawley left, Kathleen collapsed on the sofa, the three cups of barely-sipped tea in front of her. She buried her face in her hands as bitterness rose up from the pit of her stomach. My God, my God, to have been ambushed and taken unawares in this way! To have known nothing about it, to have had no idea!

She had been lied to by every member of the Graves family: by Jim; by Eleanora, whom she had always emulated and whom she now considered her friend; by Jim's cold and unforgiving father, who thought her beneath his notice, and his snide and overbearing mother. Every one of them must have known, and yet, not one of them had felt obliged to inform her. Just as the deaths of Jim's older brother and sister had been buried in silence, so had Mina's existence.

And why had they put this child into such a terrible situation? Surely Anneka must have had family somewhere—if not in Colorado, then in Sweden. Grandparents, uncles, aunts—Jim could easily have located them through his lawyers, who were the best and most expensive in Denver.

And he had told her he had nothing to hide. Nothing in his past that could damage his political career. She slammed a fist against the coffee table, and the teacups lurched and slopped. Who was Anneka? A naïve girl who fell under the flirtatious spell of a rich and handsome man? A woman who dare not refuse for fear of losing her job? Why hadn't she exposed Jim, claimed her due reward as his lover and mother of his child? Some sort of reckoning, of justice, was due here.

"Mrs. Graves," Miss Brown stood at the door of the parlor. "Is it all right if the children come in? They're done with today's lessons."

Kathleen swallowed. "Of course, send them in."

Stephen strode into the room, confident and busy, followed by Susanna, who bounced along behind him. Miss Brown placed five children's books on the coffee table.

"These are the choices for today," she said.

"Thank you."

Susanna put a book in Kathleen's hands. Stephen settled on the floor by Kathleen's feet with a top that he wound up into a wild spin as Kathleen began to read. Susanna cuddled against her mother, and Kathleen put her arm around the girl's shoulder. She kissed Susanna's head as it rested against her breast.

As Kathleen read the words by rote, a stream of anger coursed up and down her spine. In France, in the time of war, a child might be lost to its parents, but not in the United States, especially when that child came from a family of astonishing wealth and privilege. Mina had been only seven years old, only three years older than Stephen was now, when her mother died and her father disappeared. My God, to go from comfort and stability to living with strangers—how that must have confused and hurt the little girl.

"Mommy, read!" Stephen said, and Kathleen realized that she had stopped.

"Come up here beside me."

Stephen joined his mother on the sofa. She kissed the top of Stephen's head, just as she had Susanna's, and started to read again. How rarely he was still; given to industry, he was forever trying to take things apart or put them together or figure out how they worked. How lucky Stephen and Susanna were. They would never know anything that approached want, and they would never be without adults to protect them from the world.

And all the while, Jim's rightful heir, the firstborn, was neglected and forgotten. If he had taken responsibility for Mina before he married Kathleen, she could have decided whether or not to accept it before she irrevocably tied herself to him. Now, it was an impediment to everything— to his career, to their marriage, to Stephen and Susanna's upbringing. How could she forget? How would she forgive?

She received a note from Mary Jane that Mina would be alone at the Dercums' home on Thursday afternoon. The note explained that Judith Dercum was taking Clyde to a doctor's appointment, and that she and Essie would then take him for an ice cream sundae treat. They would be gone from about two until around five.

Kathleen picked Mary Jane up from the alley near Graves Industries in Seaney's Model T, which she had borrowed for the day. Black Ford cars were commonplace, and far less recognizable than Kathleen's flashy Nash.

As she drove through miles of fields where the stubborn prairie grass had been plowed up to grow wheat and corn, Mary Jane warned her that Mina had been misled by her adopted parents to think that her mother was coming back for her.

"Why didn't they tell her the truth?" Kathleen asked.

"I think they wanted to spare her grief, but instead, she thinks that her mother has abandoned her." Mary Jane gave Kathleen a sidelong glance. "Mina asked me if her mother went to live with Mr. Graves without her."

"Wasn't she with her mother when she died?"

"I don't know. I was sick myself at the time—they even found a hospital bed for me, although the hospitals had been full for weeks. I nearly died. My father did, after he caught it from me."

"I'm so sorry."

"Mina was at Anneka's funeral, but it was held outside, and lasted only a few minutes because of the cold. I don't think she understood what it was all about."

When they reached the Edwards Dairy, Mary Jane instructed Kathleen to park in front of two small cottage-like homes set off from the main part of the barnyard. Climbing from the car, Mary Jane knocked at the door, then opened it and went inside, calling, "Mina, we're here."

The girl came into the light from a corner of the room, and Kathleen's heart stuttered. Any hope that she might have harbored that Mina was not Jim's daughter was dashed. Mina resembled Stephen; in fact, if there had not been an age difference between them, they might have been mistaken for twins. While Mina's hair was darker than Stephen's, her eyes were the brilliant blue that Victoria, Eleanora, Jim, and Stephen shared.

Mary Jane said, "Mina, I'd like you to meet Mrs. Gr—"

"My name is Kathleen."

"I know you." Mina said. "You're married to Mr. Yeem."

"Mr. Yeem?"

"It's a childhood name," Mary Jane explained. To Mina, she said, "You're old enough to know that his name isn't Mr. Yeem. He's Mr. Graves."

"He's running for governor," Mina said.

"That's right." Kathleen had hoped for anonymity, but of course, her photograph was often in the newspapers. "I'm pleased to meet you, Mina."

"They call me Minnie."

"I think Mina is a beautiful name. Do you mind if I call you that?"

Mina shook her head. "No, ma'am, Mrs.—"

"Kathleen."

"Mrs. Kathleen."

"Why don't we sit down?" Mary Jane said. "We can have tea in a few minutes."

Kathleen took an armchair, while Mina and Mary Jane sat next to each other on the sofa. Mary Jane looped an arm around Mina's shoulders.

"Where did you get your name?" Kathleen asked.

"Mother called me Mina. She was Swedish, but it's an American name, because I was born in America."

Kathleen caught the pride in Mina's voice. "That's important to you, isn't it? That you are American?"

"Mother always told me that no one could take that from me."

"She sounds very smart and wise."

Mary Jane rose from her chair. "I'll make the tea while you and Mrs. Kathleen talk, Mina."

At once, the girl was ill-at-ease, wiping her hands on her skirt, her eyes darting toward the kitchen.

"Would you feel better if you went to help Miss Mary Jane?" Kathleen asked. "Please, go ahead."

Mina jumped from the chair and ran toward the kitchen.

While she was gone, Kathleen looked around the living room. The fireplace mantel held an assortment of inexpensive but stylish knickknacks: a set of white ceramic Japanese dolls; figurines of a shepherd and shepherdess; a cast iron circus elephant. On a sideboard, Kathleen found a copy of the Bible, open at Romans 12. Beneath the left-hand cover of the Bible lay a smaller book bound in white that was titled *KLORAN: Knights of the Ku Klux Klan*. Opening it, Kathleen read: "The Kloran is 'THE book' of the Invisible Empire, and is therefore a sacred book . . ."

A sacred book? Did it rival the Bible? Something popped into her mind. In Creil, that overflowing bowl of humanity, she had tended to wounded Arabs who carried with them a book called the Koran. Was this book of the 100% Christians named for the sacred text of the Muslims? She flipped through it. Most of it was nonsensical—unwieldy names had been given to the officers, such as "Kligrapp" or "Klaliff." The sacred rituals appeared tedious and complicated. English words such as character, cavern, or conclave appeared as karacter, klavern, and klonclave.

Hearing movement in the kitchen, she quickly replaced the *Kloran*. In the back of the room, a three-foot tall doll with a cracked face sat in the corner. The lace on the hem of the doll's soiled yellow dress straggled across her legs. Kathleen ran a finger down one of the doll's ruined cheeks.

The kitchen door opened, and Mina carried in the tea tray, which was almost too much for her thin arms. Kathleen returned to her seat in the armchair, while Mary Jane followed Mina. Carefully, Mina poured the tea for the three of them, then inquired about lumps of sugar and milk.

"You're very good at this, Mina," Kathleen said as she took her cup and saucer.

"It's my job."

"Your job?"

"I'm supposed to do the cooking and cleaning," Mina said. "My mother was a maid, and Miss Judith said that I will be one, too."

"I see," Kathleen said. "Do you remember where you and your mother used to live?"

"We lived in a pretty house. It had flowers and a white fence."

"Tell me about your mother."

"She used to sing to me, and I would dance with Marta—"

"That's your doll?" Kathleen gestured toward the ottoman. "Where did you get her?"

"Mr. Yeem"—she glanced at Mary Jane—"Mr. Graves gave her to me. He told me that she was made to be my twin. But she was too pretty to be me. She looked more like Mother."

Kathleen thought of a doll that Jim had bought for Susanna—a red-headed, green-eyed beauty that resembled the little girl. Had Jim employed the toymaker who had created a "twin" for Mina so many years ago to create a likeness of Susanna as well?

"Do you know where my mother is, Mrs. Kathleen?" Mina asked.

Kathleen took in a quick breath. "I'm sorry, I don't."

The light left Mina's eyes. "Why didn't she go to live with Mr. Graves?"

"Sometimes our plans don't work out." Kathleen changed the subject. "Do you go to school now?"

"Yes."

"What grade are you in?"

"Only the sixth, because I am stupid."

Kathleen winced. "Who told you that?"

"Miss Judith says God makes some people smarter than others, and I wasn't one of them."

"What time will Miss Judith be home?" Mary Jane asked.

"Around five."

Mary Jane eyed Kathleen meaningfully, and Kathleen set down her tea cup. "We need to go. Thank you so much for the tea, Mina."

Mina looked at her hands, and Kathleen thought, I cannot leave her like this. As Mina gathered up the cups to carry to the kitchen, Kathleen volunteered, "I'd like to help you."

"No, that's my job," Mina said.

"I'll help, too," Mary Jane offered. "That way, we'll be done lickety-split."

In the kitchen, Mina pumped water into a dishpan and poured some of the left-over tea water into a second pan for rinsing. Without hesitating, she stuck her hands into the wash water.

"Pour some warm water in the wash," Kathleen suggested. "That way, your hands won't get so cold."

"Miss Judith says that's wasteful, and waste is a sin. The hot water is needed for rinsing."

Kathleen looked at Mary Jane, who shrugged. There was nothing Kathleen could do; she didn't dare to contradict Judith Dercum. Picking up a towel, she dried, while Mary Jane, who was more familiar with the kitchen, stacked the cups and saucers in the cupboard.

"I used to serve tea and coffee in France," Kathleen said. "Do you know where that is?"

"Yes, Mrs. Kathleen, it's in Europe."

"That's right. Far across the ocean. We used to make coffee and cocoa in cans that were this big"—Kathleen rounded her arms—"and we'd serve a thousand cups of cocoa in just a few minutes. We were always washing cups for the soldiers who didn't have their own."

"Soldiers?"

"Yes, it was during the great European war. Do you remember it?"

"My mother left me during the war. So did Mr. Graves."

"I, too, lost my mother during the war," Kathleen said quickly. "She had the flu, like your mother."

Kathleen caught Mary Jane's warning shake of the head from the corner of her eye.

"Is your mother coming back one day?" Mina asked.

"My mother died. She was too sick to get better."

Mary Jane put away the last cup. "We should be going. Miss Judith and Clyde will be home soon. Would you mind keeping our visit a secret? I'll tell Miss Judith and Andy when I come over tomorrow. Is that all right?"

Mina nodded. As Kathleen and Mary Jane left, Mina stood at the door, her hands, raw and reddened by the cold water, hanging helplessly at her side.

Just as the car rolled forward, she rushed outside. "Mrs. Kathleen!" she called. "Will you come visit me again?"

Kathleen faltered. No, she would not come again. She could not risk it, not until she had talked to Jim, and even then—

"I will try," she said.

Mina's face clouded over at the meaningless promise, and she went back in the house. She closed the door behind her immediately.

Kathleen kept her foot on the brake, and the Model T idled.

"I want to tell her," she said. "I just want to tell her everything—about her mother, about her father"—her words ratcheted in her throat—"and about the people she lives with. Oh, to tell her she's stupid and has to be a maid when she's grown—who would be that spiteful?"

"We can't tell her anything," Mary Jane reminded her. "Not unless something can be done about it. It would be cruel."

Kathleen's lungs tightened, as if they might explode into a scream or a wail. How could she leave this child here, without any offer of help or hope? How could she drive away, knowing that the girl would be mortified and tormented by the people who were supposed to be her protectors?

"Do you know why I left France?" Mary Jane asked suddenly.

She exhaled. "No, but I've always wondered. Helen and Hank and I always felt so badly about that, as if we'd failed you somehow. That first night was terrible, I know, but we saw much worse later in the war. We made it through by helping each other to stay calm and strong—and we came to love each other. Even Helen—who never thought I was good enough for the Relief Society—even we became good friends. We would have helped you if you'd stayed."

"It was a terrible mistake to leave," Mary Jane admitted. "By the time I was home, I had seen so much in the hospitals and on the streets of Paris that it didn't bother me as much. How different my life might have been if I'd stayed. Like yours—oh, I don't mean I would have married Mr. Graves—"

Kathleen smiled. "I know what you mean."

"But after that first night in France, I just wanted to turn back the clock. I wanted it to be two or three weeks before when I—when we—hadn't yet seen the war. Those days in New York, and seeing the sights in Paris. Oh, it was so wonderful, so much fun. But once we were in Montdidier—"

"We were all shocked—"

"My nerve failed." Mary Jane picked at her gloves. "Then, after Anneka died, I felt the same thing. Please, just let me go back and see if I can keep it from happening. And now this—I just keep thinking, if only I hadn't gotten sick—twice—from the flu. If only I'd mailed that letter to Ross, he might have been willing to help Mina. You'll help her, won't you?"

Kathleen put the car in gear. "I will do everything I can to see that she is where she belongs."

Mary Jane looked out the passenger's window, and Kathleen knew that her words sounded as weak as her promise to Mina had. She herself did not know how she would help Mina. Not yet, anyway.

"What was Anneka like?" she asked. "I only need look at Mina to know she was beautiful, but was she smart or cultured or . . . ?"

Her words trailed away, and Mary Jane answered, "She was perfect."

Kathleen swallowed back her questions—what more was there to be said? As the Model T rolled down the hilly drive toward the road, a black truck swung into the dairy, empty milk cans clattering in its bed.

"Oh, no," Mary Jane said. "Oh, they shouldn't be back from delivering milk yet!"

"Who are they?"

"Andy and Matt, my brother."

As the truck passed, Andy Dercum glared at Mary Jane, then at Kathleen. He spoke to Matt, and Matt leaned forward for a better look.

"Let's go!" Mary Jane said. "Oh, I hope they didn't recognize you."

But Kathleen could feel Andy Dercum's dark, glowering gaze follow her as she drove the car out of the barnyard and onto Chambers Road.

# TWENTY-NINE

At the Denver District Attorney's office, Paul shuffled through a stack of reports. As the Klan's activity had picked up through the summer, the five spies appointed by Colonel Van Cise to infiltrate the Klan delivered more information about what transpired on Kastle—or Table—Mountain. The reports detailed the Klan's political agenda and its lists of "unpatriotic" businesses owned by Catholics, Jews, and those who did not agree with "klannishness."

At the meetings, Grand Dragon John Galen Locke demanded that people be "brought up the hill" to prove their loyalty to him and the Klan. Sometimes politicians were summoned; other times, business owners, such as the publishers of the *Denver Post*, were called before him. Only a week ago, a party of Klansmen had brought a newly-awakened Ben Stapleton up the hill in his nightshirt, where Stapleton groggily vowed to work for the Klan "heart and soul" if he won the recall election in August.

The spy reports illuminated the lies that Locke spread about both Philip Van Cise and Paul: "John Galen Locke called Colonel Van Cise 'the dirtiest and crookedest cur that ever was in Denver.' Says family was forced out of South Dakota because they were crazy. Paul Reston went cuckoo after war and was in insane asylum. Now Colonel Crazy and Colonel Cuckoo run D.A.'s office. Locke says, 'If Ben Stapleton is re-elected, Van Cise will move to California! Imagine being rid of Philip the Great once and for all! Maybe he'll take Poor Paul with him.' Klansmen respond with, 'Cuckoo, cuckoo' like a clock."

Today, something new appeared in the spy reports: "Locke said Jim Graves didn't serve in Army, but wife went to war for him. Also something about Mrs. Graves at a dairy in Aurora."

Paul flipped the page to look at another of the reports. "Locke mentioned that Mrs. J. Graves spotted at dairy in Aurora in Model T car. Joked that Graves must not be doing so well in the Moffat Oil field if that's the best she has to drive."

A third report read: "Rumors in Klan ranks that K. Graves, seen at dairy in Fletcher, has connection to child or children who live there."

That afternoon, Paul drove east to Aurora, which was more or less a one-street affair. Three dusty blocks of Colfax Avenue supported the usual small-town assortment of wares: a drug store, a couple of general merchandise stores, a lumberyard and hardware store, banks, an auto dealer, a few repair shops, and a livery stable.

He drove down the rough dirt of Chambers Road past modest brick homes and barns, and miles of open prairie. The first dairy that he came to, the Edwards Dairy, seemed to be the grandest of the residences in this area. Paul pulled off to the side of the road. Once the dust settled, he stepped out of the car and walked a few feet. Grazing cattle, peaceful barnyard, no children in sight. In fact, nothing seemed unusual about the place.

He climbed back in his car and drove to the Graves' palatial house in the Denver Country Club. He parked his Packard in the smooth, graveled drive and passed through the towering entryway to ring the doorbell.

A butler answered immediately, as if he were standing just inside waiting for visitors.

"May I speak to Mr. or Mrs. Graves?" Paul asked.

"Mr. Graves is out of town," the butler replied. "And Mrs. Graves is at Redlands today."

Redlands. The name struck Paul with a poignant nostalgia. How often Kathleen had talked of the place as if it were mythical and otherworldly.

In his car again, he drove to the tiny town of Louviers and asked directions to Redlands at the livery stable. Driving west from the town, he followed a trail of dusty roads to two stone pillars on either side of a dirt driveway. On one of the pillars, a flat, stone nameplate had been etched: Redlands. On the other: Graves Land and Cattle. Kathleen O'Doherty Graves, Owner.

At the end of the dirt drive was the barnyard: a modest house, an old-fashioned barn, and a windmill that creaked with every turn of its rotor. A chicken house, granary, shed for sheep or goats, and blacksmith shop with anvil lay beyond the house and barn. Out of place in this homely and hard-worked place was Kathleen's bright blue Nash.

She stood in the nearest corral, brushing down a reddish-brown horse. She wore brown riding pants, knee-high boots, and a poorly-fitted flannel shirt that obviously belonged to her father. She stopped when she saw Paul, frozen in surprise. As he climbed from the car, she asked, "What are you doing here? How did you know—?"

"Everyone in your little town of Louviers knew where Redlands is," he said. "I received directions from at least four different locals at the livery stable and the story of how you've acquired most of the county."

She laughed. "That's an exaggeration."

Paul walked to the corral through air that smelled of fresh cut grass and sunlight. "I stopped by your home in Denver. The butler told me you were here. I was actually looking for your husband."

"Oh. This must be an official visit of some kind, then."

"It is. But not so official that I can't take a few minutes to look around. So this is Redlands." Paul gestured to a red rock ridge that rose into the sky beyond the barnyard. "That's in your painting at the art museum."

"I'm glad you recognized it."

His confidence wavered. Her reply was too formal, too closed off. Was she worried about the implications of his visit or did she still harbor uncertainty about their meeting at Julia's? Determined to set things right, Paul stroked the velvet softness of the horse's nose. "This must be Napoli," he said. "Well, sir, I feel as if I've known you for years. Does he still run like the devil?"

"We've both slowed down some," she said. "He has from age, and I have because of responsibility. The children, you know. Although I know I wouldn't fall off and break my neck, Jim isn't as confident."

"Neither was I, until you proved me wrong in Amiens. But Latour never recovered from your refusal to call that horse in Amiens *un diable*. He muttered, Diablo, Diablo, again and again in disgust. I don't think he considered the Spanish language as having any legitimacy."

"I would still call him Diablo today. I'm from the part of the world where Spanish names are as common as English." She hefted herself up on the wooden railings of the corral fence and crawled over the top and down. As she turned toward the house, she stopped short at the sight of his car.

"It's a Packard."

"Do you think I'd drive anything else?" he said. "I drove one of these in every conceivable condition—weather, bombardment, no roads—and it rarely failed me."

"Oh, it brings back memories," she said. "Come inside."

In the kitchen, she took a pitcher of lemon water from the ice box. "I come here to be who I was before I married. Jim grew up being waited on hand and foot, but it makes me feel lazy or presumptuous or something. I come here when I want to brew my own cup of tea."

Paul laughed and took a cool glass of lemon water from her.

"Come into the parlor," she said. "It's my studio away from home."

In the parlor, the apparatus of the artist—easels, blank canvasses, rags, oilcloths—clustered in a sunny corner near a large picture window. Traditional sitting room furniture—a blue velvet fainting couch and deep-seated club chair—consumed the rest of the small space, along with a couple of claw-footed tables. The parlor smelled of linseed and turpentine.

Paul looked over the tubes of paint on an architect's table near the easel. "It's funny. Most people think of freshly-baked cookies or their mother's perfume when they think of their childhood home, but for me, it's the smell of oil paints."

"From Julia's apartment in Paris?"

"Yes, that and the stench of desperation from artists who never sold a single painting and were begging for Julia's patronage."

Kathleen laughed, and Paul noticed that the inner wall of the room had been framed in cork. Tacked to the cork were the sketches that Kathleen had done in France. She had hung them more or less chronologically, so that the drawings traced her journey from Colorado to Bordeaux and beyond.

"Julia gave me this idea," she said. "When I saw all her works hung in her parlor, I decided to do something like it."

"It's amazing they weren't lost in transit. Somewhere in France, there are warehouses of moldy Christmas fruit cakes meant for American soldiers."

She laughed again. "Some of them did go missing, but Jim received most of them. He would show them to his employees and to the newspapers, and then he would give them to my parents." She paused, overcome with emotion. "My mother kept them, even though she didn't approve of my drawing. I found them in her cedar chest."

"Perhaps she recognized your talent after all."

Paul traced their relationship in the sketches: the stroll through the countryside in Montdidier; tea at Mme. de Troyes' *hôtel*; the outing at the tower when he gave Kathleen the colored pencils; the wild horse ride in Amiens; the days together in Chaumont. Many of the drawings were of Helen or Hank or Mrs. Brently and of places that Paul never saw. He followed the progression to Armistice Day in Paris. In one sketch, Jim Graves spoke with a young man with an unnaturally stiff face, who stood next to Helen.

He gestured toward a sketch of a simple rainbow with a multi-colored stick figure beneath it. "Why did you keep that?"

"Because you drew it for me." She laughed. "The day you gave me the colored pencils. Remember?"

"Very well." After giving Kathleen the pencils as a Christmas gift, she had colored the rainbow to test them. Paul added the stick figure portrait of Kathleen, whose hair was a scribble of red. "I have relived every day we had together for years now."

Paul moved on to a page of his own handwriting that was tacked to the wall. It read: "*In driving an ambulance, I have only one duty and that's to save lives. I don't engage in violence or compromise my moral beliefs, as the soldiers have to, in killing others. I'm not caught in No Man's Land either literally or in any other sense. I'm in control of my actions.*" He had signed it, "*Paul Everett Reston, November 4, 1917.*"

His stomach churned. The brutality of the Air Service, where he had had to look into the eyes of those he killed, had forever wounded him.

"I wish I'd kept my promise to myself," he said.

"What do you mean?"

"If I hadn't volunteered for the Air Service, things would be much different." He turned toward her. "I'm sorry our last meeting ended so poorly. I realize now that I was thinking unrealistically, perhaps even pathetically. But I need you to know that I still, that I will always love you. It's the one thing that hasn't changed."

She said nothing.

"Kathleen, I'm a damaged man, a haunted man." He studied the sketches. "In 1922, I was with my aide on the edge of a trench that we'd been clearing for days, one body after another—French, British, American, German—all mixed together. It was one of those places where everyone had had a go at it. I looked up into the sky, which was brilliant and blue that morning, and I noticed a single bird flying over the field, above the bodies and the stench. It was followed by another, and another, and soon, the sky filled with birds, flying toward some saplings in the east. My French liaison, who was from a village a few kilometers away, said, '*Ils reviennents*—'"

"What does that mean? I've forgotten nearly all my French."

"'They're returning.' My liaison told me that the birds had been gone since the shelling began in 1914. But now, the trees in the village were heavy with nests. The flock formed a dark, dense cloud in the sky, but it didn't just fly overhead. The birds twisted and soared, forming different shapes—some of them geometrical—falling and rising again and again. The men in the trenches stopped their work, and everyone watched. And then, the birds passed, and the sky stretched empty once more."

"What a beautiful sight to have seen."

"But I couldn't see the beauty of it. Suddenly, I was unbelievably tired. I couldn't keep my eyes open, and I thought my arms and legs would drag me into the earth. I couldn't think—even the smallest decision was too hard. I didn't recognize anyone, and I couldn't remember names or places. The birds reminded me of flying, of not having solid ground beneath me, and it brought back the panic of my last flight." He swallowed twice to quell the emotion in his voice. "I remembered Kenny. I remembered that I'd lived and he'd died."

She blinked back tears as she surveyed the wall of sketches. "I put this up as a sort of memorial to you, to honor you. I didn't know—is there a marker for you somewhere in France that should be for Kenny? I put it up as a memorial to me, too, to the girl I was. You see, after Hank died, and then you, I lay in bed for days, afraid that the same would—or maybe should—happen to me. After all, Hank lived a blameless life, and I had . . . well, you and I had broken so many rules. Then—"

She stopped, and Paul saw the indecision on her face. "What is it?"

"Then Jim came to Paris," she said quietly. "And he stayed with me day and night. He fed me soup and brought me water, and he washed my face and hands. He could have hired every nurse in the city to do it, but he did it all himself. I remember—or maybe I've imagined it—that he whispered to me, begging me to live, to come back to him. I had to live, simply because he wanted me to so badly."

Paul looked toward the sketches. Were they only history now, a record of a love that could never be again?

"Please don't think I came here frivolously," he said, "to ruin your marriage or to cause conflict for you. I spent days—weeks, even—thinking of the consequences for both of us."

She lifted her chin and straightened her shoulders. "What brought you here today?"

"Let's sit down."

She perched on the fainting couch, her shoulders erect, while he took the armchair.

"One of my jobs for Colonel Van Cise is to monitor the Klan's activities," he said. "Where they meet, who they're talking about, how they're approaching this election. At last Wednesday's regular meeting on Table Mountain, John Galen Locke implied that he has some kind of information about you and a child in Aurora."

She put her hand to her mouth. "Oh, no, we were afraid it would happen."

"You and Jim?"

"No, no," she said. "Oh, it's such a long story. I haven't even talked to Jim about it."

"Where is he?"

"He's in Craig, looking over the new oil field."

"So, did you visit a child in Aurora? Who is it?"

"She's Jim's daughter."

Paul leaned back into the armchair as shock registered through his body. He hadn't expected this. Or perhaps he had. A man who came into staggering wealth at such a young age would most likely believe that everyone and everything catered to him, including any woman he wanted. "Did you know?" he asked.

"I found out just the other day." In measured tones, she told Paul of the visit from two employees of Graves Industries and the trip to the Edwards Dairy to see the girl. "As we were leaving, Mary Jane's brother and Andy Dercum saw us. They're both Klansmen."

"And they passed it on to John Galen Locke's lackeys, I assume. I suppose her brother felt important for a few minutes. Do you know if Jim knows that Locke knows?"

"No, I don't. We've only been in touch by phone, and he's been in places where there are no direct connections, but only operators—"

"Who could be tempted to listen in to a conversation between a famous man and his wife."

She moved to the window. "This will ruin him, won't it?"

Paul joined her. "I don't know, but it will make running for office difficult. Locke will see him—and everyone in his family—humiliated. He says cruel and false things about his enemies—I know, I'm one of them—and his followers don't even bother to question him. If he says Jim is a bad choice, they'll believe it."

"He's been planning to run for governor his entire life, and his parents are so . . . oh, I feel so betrayed!"

Paul drew her against him. She laid her head against his chest, her arms around him.

"For years, I've been part of his family," she said. "And not one of them has said a word to me about this. You remember how much I admired Ellie when we were in France. And yet she's never spoken to me about it"—her voice filled with bitterness—"although she was quick enough to warn me that she would turn against me if I saw you after you came home."

Paul buried his face in the wind-blown smell of her hair—fresh grass, soil, the earth, the scent of the horse, of its warm body and stiff hair. Life, so vibrant and true, so warm and comforting.

Kathleen's words tumbled from her. "Jim told me he had nothing to hide. And I believed him, even though I'd heard talk years ago when I was at Graves Oil. But once this is known, I'll be seen as the one who ruined him because I found Mina. If it were up to his family, they would let her be a maid for those awful people for the rest of her life. They're so ambitious, so concerned about who thinks what—"

"You mustn't do this to yourself—"

She looked up at him. "And this happening at almost the same time that you've come back . . . Regardless of all I've said, of all I tell myself, I'm still so in love with you."

He kissed her on the lips, and she rose up so that her body pressed against his. With every kiss, their desire grew deeper, and he remembered what it had been like to have her in his bed for those three days in Chaumont. Then, they had had plans for a future that would carry them through to their deaths.

"I want to . . . I need to see you again," she said.

"I'm here any time you want me to be, my girl of the Wild West."

Kathleen put a fingertip on his lower lip. "It's your mouth I want to kiss. Your lips that I want against mine. Your hands on my skin, your body warm against mine."

"I'm not the same as I was. I can't hold you as tightly as I want. My ribs—"

"I can feel them. I don't care."

They stood, silent, motionless, their arms around each other.

"I'm sorry," she whispered. "I'm sorry I married and didn't wait—"

"You thought you were waiting for a ghost."

"But if I'd kept the faith, as you said—"

"That was unfair of me," he said. "I shouldn't have been so cruel."

"No, it was understandable." She pulled away from him. "But what am I going to do now? How do I go on? How do I sit at the same table with him, knowing that he's let this child suffer for all these years? What if he's elected? Do I stand next to him and smile when I know that his daughter is living in fear and neglect?"

"What do you want to do about the girl?"

"She needs to live with her father. There's no reason why she hasn't done so for the past six years. It's a sin."

"And if he doesn't agree?"

"I don't know."

"Your children could be compromised by this. If this girl were to grow up under the wrong influences, she could become a threat to Stephen and Susanna and their legitimate inheritance."

"She's certainly under the wrong influence now."

"Ask him to give up the race. If he doesn't, Locke will make sure that Mina's existence is the talk of the town. Jim needs to deal with this quietly, for your sake, for your children's, for his sake as well. There will be other years to run for governor."

She nodded. "I'll send a telegram to him asking him to come home as soon as I'm back in Denver."

"I think that's wise."

"But for now, please, let it just be the two of us. These minutes together are precious, and they might be the only ones we have."

Paul ran a tender hand down her cheek. "Let's go outside, and you can show me Redlands. I've waited seven long years to see it."

# THIRTY

Everyone who was anyone was in Craig, in the northwestern corner of Colorado, for the summer of 1924. The biggest domestic players in the oil game—Mutual Oil, Texas Production, Standard Oil, Midwest, and two worldwide leviathans, Shell and Royal Dutch Company—had laid bets in the Moffat Oil Field, along with hundreds of smaller companies and the usual smattering of wildcatters. The sleepy town's population had soared to over ten-thousand in the past year. Most of the new residents lived in a sprawling tent city on the road south of the town. Everything smelled of money—and it flowed directly from the ground into the pockets of anyone connected with oil. Geological consultants charged one-hundred dollars a day in fees; a crew of four engineers cost three-hundred a day.

Jim arrived on the train on a dusty Friday morning to find the town's streets nearly impassable. Fortunately, Joel Spratt had managed to rent a home while the owners were in California for three weeks. Otherwise, Jim doubted that he and Harris, who had accompanied him, would find a hotel room.

Joel had also arranged for Jim to speak at the Lions Club about the oil business. Despite the disdain for oilmen that inundated the Denver newspapers in the wake of Teapot Dome, they were welcomed as lecturers at banquets, church picnics, and community gatherings in this parched corner of the state.

In the basement of the Christian Church, Jim was introduced by one of the leading citizens of Craig, Mr. Larson. A number of land men from Graves Industries also attended the meeting.

"Today's speaker might not need any introduction in a few months," Mr. Larson announced to scattered applause. "I'll just say he's one of the best oilmen around, and he has multiple crews in this area. His company is rated as Class Triple A1, the highest ranking given by Bradstreet and Dun, and his assets total over $75,000,000. I'd like to introduce State Senator Jim Graves."

Jim took his place at the podium. "I hear you have oil somewhere around here." The room exploded in laughter. "I want to find it, and I want you—the residents of Moffat and Routt counties—to benefit from my findings."

He waited for the applause to end.

"This area has been called a geologist's paradise," he continued. "My own geologists have reported to me that there are a number of unusual folds and formations near here—some unlike anything they've seen before. And because the Moffat Field has so much unique promise, it's important to approach it in a careful and conscientious way. How many of you are landowners?" A dozen or so men raised their hands. "To you, I would give this advice. When signing leases, sign for the entire acreage. We oil men like to stretch our legs"—he waited for the laugh—"when we explore, and if we're hemmed in by leases given to other companies, we aren't as likely to drill a test well or develop the property. Even if you're offered a better price for a partial lease on your land, go with the producer who will lease the full acreage. That way, the producer is confident that he has room to move if a test well comes in. He doesn't have to worry about wildcatters or other companies stepping on his wells."

Jim noted a number of nodding heads. "Also, beware of those companies—and especially wildcatters—that have shoddy equipment or practices. Part of what you have to offer here in the Moffat Field is pristine land and water. If incompetent drillers come on your land, they may bring up impure water with the well that won't only ruin your oil and gas sands, but your supply of water for cattle and other livestock. So, when you lease, check with the Bradstreet and Dun index, as Mr. Larson has so ably done"—more laughter—"and sign with companies that are reliable. There are plenty of them in town. Thank you."

Applause rang through the room, and for an hour after, Jim answered questions, while his land men drew up leases. It was nearly dark before he reached his house in the northern end of town. There, Harris presented him with a warm meal, supplied by a townswoman who cooked for a living.

After the meal, Jim dismissed Harris and retired to the modest living room to read the local evening newspapers. He had barely made himself comfortable with a glass of brandy and a cigarette when a knock sounded on the door.

A man in a chauffeur's uniform stood on the neatly enclosed front porch of the house. In the dusty street, a black Cadillac idled, with a second one just behind it.

"Senator Graves," the man said. "I'm here to ask if you would please join Dr. John Galen Locke this evening for an outing."

Jim's heart tattooed. The Grand Dragon? What the hell was he doing in Craig?

"I'm sorry," he said. "I have other plans—"

"Dr. Locke thinks it's in your best interest to speak with him."

Fury darted through Jim. "You can tell Dr. Locke that I tactfully disagree."

The chauffeur signaled, and two men climbed from the second car. The driver came around the hood and crossed his arms over his chest.

The rear window of the Cadillac lowered slowly. The round, goateed face of the Grand Dragon appeared. "Please join me, Senator Graves," he called. "We have things to discuss. For one, I'd like to know why your wife is cruising around Denver in a beat-up Model T while you're over here tending to business. You're doing all right in the oil fields. So why isn't she being chauffeured around in the Silver Ghost, as a woman befitting her station should be?"

The story was undoubtedly a ruse to lure him into the car—God knew what Kathleen was doing—but as Dr. Locke spoke, the two men from the second car started up the steps of the porch. Obviously, Jim had no choice but to accompany the Grand Dragon.

"Let me get my coat and hat," he said to the chauffeur.

The two men halted, and the chauffeur retreated to open the back door of the car. Jim slid in next to Dr. Locke, who took up a good part of the rear seat. At once, the chauffeur made a tight U-turn, leaving the empty, silent street in a rush of dust. Locke pulled a black curtain down over both rear windows and took a cigar from his pocket. "So glad you could join me, Senator. Do you mind if I smoke?"

"Go ahead," Jim said tightly. "What's this about?"

The Grand Dragon puffed to light the cigar. "Look at this. It's a CYANA cigar."

"I'm familiar with the brand."

"Do you know what some of the citizens of the Invisible Empire think CYANA stands for?" Dr. Locke laughed. "'Catholics, You Are Not Americans.' Pretty clever, isn't it?"

Jim did not reply.

"Your wife has never given up her Catholic roots, has she?"

Dr. Locke's question rubbed at a raw spot. Jim and Kathleen had barely spoken since the day at Inglesfield, although, true to her word, Kathleen had congenially accompanied Jim to social and political functions. Still, the specter of Paul Reston hovered between them.

"I will not discuss her," he said.

"Let's not be hasty," Dr. Locke said. "She gives quite a bit of money to the Catholics, doesn't she, especially to Blessed Savior? Unless I'm mistaken and your wife is an heiress, that's your money she's giving away, Senator. Do you ever wonder where it really goes?"

"I've never concerned myself with it, no."

"Straight to Little Italy, Senator. That's where your money goes."

"Little Italy?" Jim scoffed. "You're definitely mistaken about that. My wife is an Irish-American, and so are the priests and most of the congregation at Blessed Savior."

"Irish-American," Dr. Locke mused. "One of the hyphenated types, eh? Not a true American, but clinging to the old country as if it's better than America."

Too late, Jim realized his mistake. Those who hyphenated their heritage were the subjects of ridicule and contempt throughout the country. Today, everyone wanted to be known as 100% American.

Dr. Locke continued. "The Vatican funnels the money she gives to the Catholics to the Eye-talians so that those bootlegging wops can sell more liquor—to the Irish, that is to the Irish-Americans—and give more to the church. So that the Pope can be richer than God. A vicious circle, you might say."

"I've never seen any proof of that."

"And the priest at Blessed Savior, Father Brendan Keohane? Isn't he somehow related to your wife?"

Jim began to sweat in the close quarters of the car. "Where are you taking me?"

"Liam Keohane, Denver's arch slacker. Married to your wife's sister, I believe."

"My wife has no brothers or sisters."

"That's right. She's a cousin, isn't she?"

Jim did not deign to answer. Dr. Locke's probing was a ploy to unnerve him. He refused to give the Grand Dragon the satisfaction.

"And you are quite generous in paying off your wife's father's gambling debts," Dr. Locke said. "Wish he had better luck at the horse races in Overland Park and the crap shoots in the Bottoms."

Irish O'Doherty and his profligacy. Jim had long ago resigned himself that he would support Kathleen's father for the rest of his life.

"Take me back to my house," he said. "We have nothing to discuss."

"Calm down, Senator. We have a long evening ahead."

Jim stared toward the front windshield of the car until the Cadillac stopped. When the car door opened, the two bodyguards appeared at the window to wait for Jim to climb out. The two cars had driven only as far as the east side of Craig along Victory Way, the main thoroughfare. The Congregational Church was just ahead of them on one side of the street, while the public park spread in barren openness on the other. A plank stage had been erected at one end of the park.

"Come this way, Senator." Dr. Locke climbed from the car. "You're my special guest tonight."

Dr. Locke led him to the back of the stage, where a hooded, robed knight perched atop a horse. When the faceless, featureless guard moved his head, the black holes of his eyes stared without discernible direction. The horse, draped in white hood and blanket as well, stood eerily still in the breeze that blew from the west.

A double phalanx of robed and hooded guards armed with high-powered rifles formed a corridor for Dr. Locke. The Grand Dragon strode confidently through the ranks, jovially greeting some of the men and introducing Jim. Jim cringed each time he heard his name spoken. Word was sure to get around. He tried to lag far behind, but the phalanx closed in behind him. From the corner of his eye, he could see the barrel of a rifle in the hands of a white-robed figure.

"I trade only with Klansmen," one of the guards said. "I can recognize a Jew from a mile away. I can smell a Catholic's fishy breath."

Jim caught only a flash of the Klansman's eyes beneath the hood.

The guard spoke again. "AYAK?"

"What?" Jim asked, shaken.

"We have a coded language, Senator," Dr. Locke volunteered, drawing Jim toward seats in a rainproof shelter to one side of the stage. "We use the first letter of the word. AYAK means 'Are You a Klansman?' AKIA means, 'A Klansman I Am.'"

Such stupidity. "Why did you bring me here?"

Dr. Locke seated himself comfortably in a throne-like wooden chair with arms and a velvet cushion. He gestured for Jim to take a less ostentatious chair beside him. "So you can see for yourself the solid, loving brotherhood we have. Don't condemn too quickly, Senator. Watch and listen. Learn."

On either side of the stage, automobiles had parked in neat lines, their windshields angled toward the stage. No one sat in the drivers' seats, although the view would have been perfect. Between the parallel lines of cars, benches stretched in rows, most of which were already filled with spectators.

"Perhaps you aren't aware that our organization runs with military precision," Dr. Locke said. "We have a 'major' named in each county, who is helped by his 'captain.' Lower ranks—sergeants, corporals—assist in recruiting voters in their county. By November, we will have fully saturated every nook and cranny of Colorado. How many do you think are here tonight?"

It appeared that nearly every resident of Craig had turned out. Husbands guided their wives and children to the seats, and men shouted hearty greetings to one another over the heads of the ever-swelling crowd. Surely, some of the members of the Lyons Club were there, perhaps concealed under robe and hood.

"I'd say there were fifteen hundred or so here," Dr. Locke answered his own question. "And the reporters from the local newspapers are here, too. You never turn down a photo opportunity. What do you say, Senator? Should I invite them up?"

"I am here entirely against my will."

Dr. Locke laughed. "Yet there you sit."

On the stage stood a wooden altar, draped with an American flag. A collection of Klansmen in white, red, and purple robes milled about on it, discussing the night's protocol. A knight in a purple robe stepped forward and spoke into a scratchy broadcasting microphone that was rigged to a gasoline-powered generator. "Attention, please. Attention!"

The crowd quieted as ten hooded knights hefted a fifteen foot cross up with ropes next to the stage. Another knight stepped forward with a torch and touched the bottom of the cross. The flame darted out and upward, engulfing the entire structure in a split second. Black smoke wafted over the assembly, and the initial burst of gasoline-fueled flame emitted a sickening stench. The crowd let out an "ooh" as the flame from the cross reflected in the windshields of the parked cars. The park looked as if it were surrounded by fire.

Two search lights burst on, their beams intersecting in the sky. Once the attention of the spectators had been drawn upward, the search lights fell to the ground, illuminating Victory Way, where more than one hundred robed and hooded Klansmen marched down the street.

The only sound was the crunch of feet on gravel as the Klansmen paraded two by two. In silence, they turned into the park and strode up the aisle to stand in military formation in the green area in front of the stage.

Without preamble, one of the purple-robed knights on the stage launched into a lengthy prayer that ended with an invocation to God to oversee the meeting of fine men dedicated to justice, freedom, and America. Then came the singing of "America, the Beautiful," accompanied by a recording that blared over the public address system.

Two knights removed the flag from the altar, revealing communion vessels, an open Bible, and a sheathed sword. Prayerfully muttering incantations, one of the men removed the sword, then laid it on the altar.

This was the Grand Dragon's cue. He rose, and two knights rushed forward to sheathe his portly body in a beautifully tailored robe of white satin. With his arms stuck out like a fat doll's, he waited patiently as the men tied a purple satin sash around his waist. Moving gracefully, he appeared from out of the shadows behind the lit cross. Jim could see his profile as he stood in front of the microphone.

Surveying his followers with fatherly benevolence, Dr. Locke called, "It warms my heart to see a gathering of so many fine Americans. Your presence here tonight is a tribute to America!" He paused for thunderous applause. "We are the heart and soul of Colorado and its people. We are the proud bearers of morality and righteousness, working for a purer place to live, where our children attend schools free of the influence of Jews and Catholics, a state where white, Christian men and women can live in prosperity and happiness. Come join with me!"

He shouted over the din of applause. "We will keep Colorado a white man's state! The Jews will crawl into the slimy holes in the ground from whence they came! The Catholics will see their false idols fall from their gilded thrones in the Vatican! And the Negro will remember that he is a guest of the white man in this country!"

Jim stood quickly, bumping into the two robed men who had dressed Locke. If he slipped off the back of the stage, he might be able to disappear into the darkness beyond.

"But, let's talk about your town now," Dr. Locke said, and the crowd fell silent. "Craig has changed in the past few months. While the change has brought prosperity, violence and crime have also arrived with the workers in the oil fields. The tent city south of town is a hotbed of gambling, drunkenness, and unspeakable vices." He waited for the boos to subside. "And while your local elected officials might be nice folks they are either too incompetent or too afraid to enforce the law. They leave you and your families helpless and fearful. But the Knights of the Ku Klux Klan are with you in this time of need, and this fall, we intend to help you elect officials who will clean out the undesirable and criminal elements. We will stand with you, and we will stand strong."

Jim edged toward the back of the stage.

"Where are you going, Senator?" one of the guards asked. "The Grand Dragon wants you to stay."

Dr. Locke's voice reached him. "Every day, more of the candidates in this fall's state election are coming to see the way of the light and truth! Denver Mayor Ben Stapleton's become a Christian again. Hallelujah! All it took was a little ride with the Grand Dragon to convince him that thumbing his nose at the Invisible Empire isn't a good idea. He's going to remain Denver's mayor, folks, and he's one of us!"

"Ben! Ben! Ben!" The mantra filled the air.

Dr. Locke's voice rose above it. "At the last meeting we held on Kastle Mountain, Ben promised us that he will clean the Catholics out of Denver! But Colorado will be electing a new governor, too, this fall, too. We know that Judge Clarence Morley, who is a loyal member, has no stain on his record. His work in the West Side court has been stupendous in seeing that criminals are punished, despite the likes of the Denver Police and namby-pamby judges like Judge Ben Lindsey. But it's Jim Graves who is doing so much for this area right now, isn't it? Drilling oil wells, bringing his crews in to spend money on lodging and food—in fact, I've heard that the man himself is currently in town spreading his largesse. Some of you work for him, and you know he's a good man. But is he a Christian like you and me, or does he need to take a ride with the Grand Dragon to be converted?" The crowd roared with delight. "Is he a 100% American, like you and me, or do his relationships entangle him in a web of undesirable sorts?"

Jim froze. If Dr. Locke started in on Kathleen, by God, he would wrest a rifle from one of those hooded jackasses and kill Locke here and now.

"Time will tell." Dr. Locke backed down. "And I will speak more on the matter in a few weeks, when the election is closer—"

Dr. Locke concluded with a promise that Klansmen would be elected to every government office in Colorado. The crowd's response was so loud that the purple-robed Klansman had to shout several times before he could recite: "Our Father, Who art in heaven, Hallowed be thy name . . ." A great roar of a thousand voices joined in.

As the Klansmen marched out of the meeting, the Cadillac pulled up behind the stage. Dr. Locke signaled to Jim to follow him, and the chauffeur held the door for the two men. The car drove only a couple of blocks before it stopped at a hotel. In the lobby, Dr. Locke and Jim were escorted by the concierge to a private meeting room. The chauffeur and the two bodyguards stayed outside.

A bottle of whiskey and a box of CYANA cigars waited for them on a round table in the center of the room. Dr. Locke poured two glasses of whiskey and handed one to Jim.

"So, Senator Graves, what did you think of our little get-together?"

Jim turned the glass of whiskey in his hand without drinking from it, although he longed to toss it back. But Dr. Locke was playing a game of nerves now, and Jim refused to fold so quickly.

"Some of our citizens think that Clarence Morley would be a good governor," Dr. Locke said. "But you have a following throughout the state, too—here, and on the eastern plains, where you drill for shale oil. I would much rather support you in the upcoming election—that is, if we can work out a deal."

"A deal?" Jim's shoulders tensed.

"Our membership is strong in Pueblo and Trinidad, places where you aren't as well-known. In Cañon City, there are so many citizens of the Invisible Empire that we can put multiple candidates up for each office. Just about every white man who lives in the towns south of Denver, in Douglas and Elbert Counties, is a citizen of the empire." Dr. Locke sipped at his whiskey. "Larry Phipps, the Republican candidate for the six-year U.S. Senate term has given us a generous donation in return for our support at the polls. He isn't a member of the Klan and, like you, has no interest in pursuing an association. He simply knows how to succeed. And he is running unopposed in the primary, which you are not."

"I trust the best man will win in the primary."

"Oh, he will," Dr. Locke assured him. "So let's talk about what I've wanted to talk about all evening. What relationship is Minnie Dercum to your wife?"

"I know no one by that name."

Something ticked in Jim's head. He had heard Philip Van Cise talk about the "badger game," which was a con in which a respectable man was called to a hotel—usually the Brown Palace in Denver—on some pretense. A seductive woman—a "frail," as they called her—would lure him into a compromising position. Once they were engaged, two men, one of them pretending to be her husband, would burst into the room. The choice for the "chump" was either ruin or money.

Jim wondered if Minnie Dercum might be in a room upstairs.

"I believe there's some relationship between your wife and Minnie," Dr. Locke said. "Mrs. Graves and one of her friends visited Minnie just the other day."

"Who my wife visits is her business, not mine."

"Oh, pardon me. Perhaps I should call young Minnie Dercum by the name she was born with. Mina Lindstrom."

The whiskey in Jim's glass sloshed from side to side as he started, bringing a knowing smile to Dr. Locke's face. My Lord, Mina, missing for so long. The thought of her battered its way through his head to his heart, pounding in his chest and upper arms, and seizing up his gut.

"My, my, Senator," Dr. Locke drawled. "You've had a snappy response for everything I've said to you this evening until now. Perhaps you can't deny that you recognize that name?"

He was caught. Denial would brand him a liar; acknowledgment would secure Dr. Locke's hold on him. "No, I can't," he said at last. "Nor will I."

Dr. Locke smirked. "Her mother, Anneka Lindstrom, was a maid in your mother's house, and a very pretty one at that, I've heard. I'm sorry she died during the epidemic of '18. What a shame that she left her young daughter behind."

"What do you want?"

"Perhaps you might not be so opposed to the deal I was talking about now. Andy Dercum, who is Minnie's—or rather, Mina's—adopted father, is a loyal Klansman who has been very happy with his promotion to Kleagle in exchange for the information about your wife's visit. But I'm sure he wouldn't mind having a little more passed on to him for his loyalty. I could see he receives it."

"Are you trying to blackmail me?"

"I don't participate in blackmail; I believe in money for services rendered, just as you do. Think of it as a business deal. I own the vote of every Klan member in Colorado, and you need votes from every corner of the state. What better cause could you embrace than our law and order organization, which fights crime and protects the flower of America's white womanhood?"

The pounding in Jim's head grew louder. "You have nothing to offer me, nothing that I would want. Please, take me back to my house."

"Don't be hasty, Senator. The Republican State Convention—which will decide the candidates on the primary ballot—is in a week. Clarence Morley is a certainty, given his popularity among my followers. But there are three old-line Republicans in the mix: you, Robert Rockwell, who hasn't the guts of a flea, and our Lieutenant Governor, Earl Cooley, who can't talk enough about how much he hates the Klan. If the three of you split the loyalty of the few old-liners left, there's a chance that none of you will garner enough votes to have your names on the primary ballot."

Jim said nothing. Mina's name repeated in his head—how, where, why? He had not touched the whiskey, yet the knuckles of his hand had gone white from gripping the glass.

"You've worked long and hard to be governor of this state, Senator Graves," Dr. Locke said. "You shouldn't let an inconvenient secret get in your way. Take your time and think about it. You have a week. And then, once you make the ballot, we can discuss the prospects of your success in the primary in September and the general election in November."

Dr. Locke reached beneath the table to press a button, and the chauffeur entered.

"Please take Senator Graves to his house."

"I'll walk."

"As you wish, Senator," Dr. Locke said.

Outside, a cold wind had picked up, blowing off the peaks that surrounded the town. Jim stumbled through the darkness, not entirely sure which way he should go. Shock had left him weak, disoriented. How had Kathleen found out, and why in hell had she gone to see Mina? Damn her curiosity, her desire to know everything, her inability to keep herself out of trouble. What did she know? What had she been told and by whom?

After losing his way on more streets than he had imagined existed in Craig, he came back to the house he had rented. Inside, Harris waited for him. "I'm so sorry, sir. I wasn't aware that you were leaving again, or I—"

"I was Shanghaied." Jim handed his coat and hat to the valet. "I'll be leaving tomorrow, on the first train. Can you call the house and let them know? And I'd like to speak with Mrs. Graves."

Jim poured a glass of brandy as he waited for Harris. When the valet returned, he said, "Mrs. Graves is at Redlands, sir. Should I ask for someone to go and fetch her?"

Redlands, that damned hole where there was no telephone service. Jim glanced at the clock. It was close to midnight—to send someone now would terrify Kathleen. "I'll send a telegram tomorrow."

The mail slot on the front door of the house clanked. Harris opened his coat to reveal a pistol tucked inside before he called, "Who's there?" No one answered, but a note fell through the slot onto the floor. Harris retrieved it and handed it to Jim.

"Thank you," Jim said. "Nothing more tonight."

As Harris left the room, Jim read the note. "Thank you for visiting with me tonight. It was very enlightening. Please see me at my office once you have made your decision. 1345 Glenarm Place."

It was signed by John Galen Locke.

Trembling with fury, panic, and contempt, Jim crumpled it. The office on Glenarm, which was also Dr. Locke's medical hospital, was said to be obscenely elaborate. It supposedly had a throne guarded by three Great Danes, a solid gold reproduction of the seal of the United States; a collection of ancient swords and vintage pistols; hunting trophies adorning the walls; and a total of six bodyguards for the Grand Dragon.

How demeaning it would be to walk into that office and beg for a spot on the primary ballot. How well the Grand Dragon had scripted and produced this little melodrama.

In the parlor, Jim poured another glass of brandy and walked out onto the porch of the house. The night had cloaked the tiny town in star-studded darkness and silence. Memories flashed through Jim's mind: the house on Corona Street; Anneka's blond hair on the fur of the beaver coat he had bought for her; Mina dancing in a matching dress with her doll; Anneka lying in a sweat-soaked bed, barely breathing, as Mina tried to read to her; telling Mina goodbye before he went to Paris, breaking the child's heart.

# THIRTY-ONE

Kathleen sat on the sofa in the parlor of her house, holding a message from Eleanora in her hands. Eleanora requested that Kathleen meet with herself and Victoria. There could be no question as to what the visit was about—the only mystery was how they had learned about the situation.

She had returned from Redlands yesterday, leaving shortly after Paul. They had spent the warm, sunny day on the red rock ridge that towered over and defined the ranch. From there, they could see the entirety of the Front Range, from Longs Peak to Pikes Peak.

"You can see the taller buildings in Denver over there," she told Paul. "As the crow flies, we're not far from the city."

"It feels a century away, at least," Paul said. "Not at all like the fast and noisy twentieth."

"You once wrote to me that you would learn to fly so you could sail across the Rockies while I rode Napoli below. Do you remember that?"

"I won't fly now, with only one working arm."

"As long as you can still hold me."

Paul brought his arm up around her. "That, Madame, I am ready and willing to do."

She didn't know how to comprehend all that had happened. In love with one man, married to another. Her father had asked her how Jim had failed her. Now, she knew the bitter, unfathomable answer.

Drake hailed Kathleen from the door. "Mrs. Graves, Mrs. Lloyd-Elliot and Madame Graves have arrived."

Kathleen rose as the women came into the room. Eleanora had lost none of her glamor or beauty as she aged, but she had acquired a hard, brittle quality, as if she might someday crack open. On the other hand, Victoria struck Kathleen as immovable. She carried herself as if she meant to charge ahead in any situation. As Victoria and Ellie sat down, Kathleen rang the bell for tea.

Small talk lasted only as long as was required by the rules of polite society. Once the tea was delivered and served, Victoria said sweetly, "We're here because Jim called Eleanora this morning, and although he couldn't give many details, he wanted us to ask you about a trip you made recently to Aurora."

How did he know she had visited Mina? Had Paul contacted him in Craig? She addressed Ellie. "Why did he call you? He hasn't called me."

"I don't believe he wanted to discuss much over the phone." Ellie waved her hand. "It's all been rather confusing for us. Jim says you've found a girl that you believe is somehow . . . connected with him."

"She is connected to him," Kathleen said. "It's Mina Lindstrom."

Victoria blanched at the name, her eyes cast downward onto her tea cup. It was the first time that Kathleen had seen her silenced or intimidated. Ellie took up the conversation. "How did you find her?"

"I received a note from Miss Crawley asking if she and Mary Jane Grayson could visit on a matter of some importance for the election."

"Mary Jane," Ellie mused. "I suppose she's still in the typing pool?"

"She's still at Graves Industries," Kathleen said. "Of course, I agreed to see them—I thought it might be some business of the National Woman's Party. When they came here, Mary Jane told me about Mina and her mother, Anneka. She told me that Mina is Jim's daughter. So, Mary Jane and I went to the place where Mina's living, and I met her. She could be Stephen's twin."

Ellie and Victoria exchanged a look.

Kathleen continued. "So, all that Jim has told me is a lie—"

"Kathleen, please," Victoria inserted.

"He told me that nothing in his past that would harm his political future. He told me that Dr. Locke was threatening him because of me, because I'm Catholic and Irish."

"I can imagine you're upset," Victoria said. "All this has been a thorn in the family's side for years, and it needs to be handled very carefully. I've already contacted Gerald Hughes—you know Gerry, Jim's lawyer from Hughes and Dorsey, who are the best in Denver. Jim worked with Gerry on the Moffat Tunnel, and he can be trusted implicitly."

"Trusted to do what?"

Ellie spoke. "We believe it's best if Mina is sent to a boarding school in the east—"

"A boarding school! She isn't well-educated enough to attend a fancy school! She has some kind of problem with her eyes—"

"Such a thing can be remedied," Ellie assured her. "We'll see to it. We promised her mother that we would do the best for her and the child."

"But you haven't done the best! You haven't even tried! Her mother died—as I understand it—alone, and Mina's been lost for years. And now you have a chance to bring her home—"

"Home?" Victoria asked. "Jim's home has never been hers. I doubt she knows he's her father."

"Which is another wrong that should be righted."

Victoria's sugary voice sharpened. "Kathleen, dear, you need to think about what it means not only for Jim, but for you and the children if this becomes public. There are vicious gossips in this city."

"I can protect my children," she said fiercely. "Mina has no protection but Mary Jane, who is only around her now and then. What if the Dercums decide they no longer want to take care of her? What if they take her out of school and marry her off to some brute twice her age? Mary Jane said that Andy himself is a threat to her—"

"A threat? What do you mean?"

"He's attracted to her, in an adult way."

Neither woman spoke for a moment.

"That is why we would take responsibility for her education and care," Ellie said at last. "Quietly, without fanfare, so that the family's situation is not harmed."

"The 'family's situation' has already been harmed! Why hasn't Jim told me about this?"

"I'm sure he wanted to, but perhaps, he thought it best to spare you from the discomfort of knowing about another woman in his past," Victoria offered. "Surely you understand from the turmoil that Paul Reston has caused between you—"

"That is entirely different—"

"—that some things are best left unmentioned."

"A child is not one of them."

Ellie took the reins again. "Kathleen, I understand. You're angry, you're hurt. That's why you must let our family handle this. We need to be sure that there are no repercussions for my brother. Or for you and darling Stephen and Susanna. And we certainly don't want you to be distressed over this. Jim was twenty-two or so when this all happened—he wasn't the capable and decisive man he is now. And now, we need to handle this in a manner that's kind but discreet."

Kathleen said nothing. Arguing further would do no good.

Ellie rose, assuming that Kathleen's silence was agreement. "I will keep you informed of what I'm doing." She touched Kathleen's arm. "We will see this through."

After Kathleen had shown the two out, she returned to the sofa. She felt restless, unable to settle, her thoughts moving too quickly. She should simply go and bring Mina home. Pay the Dercums, pack up whatever belongings the girl might have, and take her away from them. But that would only add confusion for poor Mina—another stranger, whisking her away to a house she had never seen before. She had to wait—she had to trust—even though every minute that she did, Mina was helpless and lost.

When Jim arrives, she is waiting for him.

He comes inside in his usual hurried state, with Harris and Drake bustling behind him, bringing in his bags, taking his coat and hat, asking if there is anything he needs done. Kathleen fumes—all this fuss and flurry over a man who could easily open his own doors, carry his own bags, hang his coat. When Jim spies Kathleen in the foyer, he says, "Join me in my study. I'll be right in."

She goes into the study and sits in the cowhide chair, every muscle in her body tensed. Shortly after, Harris comes in with a decanter of brandy and two glasses on a tray. "Should I send in tea as well?" he asks.

"No, thank you."

When Jim returns, he has changed from his traveling clothes into a fresh shirt and suit. His hair is slicked back, and the skin of his newly-washed face glistens with dampness. The only sign of his inner agitation is a mild tremor of his hand as he pours a glass of brandy for himself.

"What is this all about?" He sits across from her in the matching cowhide chair. "I've been in the dark far too long."

"You've been in the dark?" Kathleen explodes. "You kept this from me for all these years! And after you told me that you had nothing to hide, after you threw Paul's return—which I had nothing to do with—in my face." She leaps from the chair with such force that it scoots a few inches across the floor. "And my friendship with Julia and Liam and going to Mass—"

"Jesus, sit down. Do you want a drink?"

"No." She takes up a stance next to the fireplace. "Why didn't you tell me about this before we were married? Why have you allowed this girl to be raised by the Dercums, who treat—?"

"Lower your voice. This is as much of a surprise to me as it is to you."

"It's no surprise to you! You have known since the day she was born that you were her father. You should have told me when you met me that you weren't a free man, that you had a prior commitment to—!"

"Stop!" he commands. "You are, as usual, ten steps ahead of me, with your opinions already set. Now, how did you come across this information?"

"I learned it from Mary Jane Grayson."

"Mary Jane? From the typing pool?"

"She and Miss Crawley—"

"Good Lord, Johanna Crawley, that dragon of a woman. How did she know?"

"Evidently, she knew Anneka Lindstrom through the National Woman's Party." Unable to believe that she is defending her former supervisor, she adds, "Miss Crawley was very polite and straightforward with me."

"But how did they find Mina?"

"It was a matter of chance—Mary Jane's brother married into the Edwards family, who owns the dairy. His wife is Essie, and her sister is Judith Dercum. Their sister is Jenny Edwards, who took care of Mina after her mother died. Mary Jane found Mina the first time she visited their dairy in Aurora."

"Good God, I can't believe she's only a few miles away."

"The Dercums have told her that her mother is coming back for her one day."

"Why would they tell her that? She was undoubtedly with Anneka when she died."

"She was seven years old!" Kathleen's words come out as a shriek. "And now, for nearly as many years, she's looked forward to something that can never happen. She suffered one of the greatest losses a child can suffer, and there was no one—no one!—there to help her!"

"This is not the moment for blind sentiment. We need to—"

"Why didn't you marry her mother?"

"I was young at the time, still in college." Jim's voice is tight. "Our affair happened during the summer between my junior and senior year at

Princeton. By the time I learned of Anneka's predicament, my mother had already made arrangements for her, and I didn't interfere—"

"Arrangements? What arrangement could possibly be better than—?"

"Don't interrupt me," he warns. "My mother and Anneka agreed that she could live in a house provided by us, and that she could have whatever she or Mina wanted, as long as she didn't marry or reveal the name of Mina's father. It was never cruel."

"It was viciously cruel! To tell a woman that she cannot love anyone for the rest of her life! To keep her as your concubine, for your own private use?"

"She was not my 'concubine,'" Jim snaps. "Besides, she intended to end the arrangement. She told me that she was to marry someone after the war."

"That was Mary Jane's brother, Ross."

"What happened to him? Was he killed?"

"No, he is very much alive, but Mary Jane says he refuses to do anything about Mina now. And why should he? She's not his responsibility. She's yours."

He takes a swallow of brandy. "Is Mina's situation that bad? Are the Dercums poor? Do they lack the necessities?"

"They aren't poor—they're far better off than I was as a child, but Mary Jane told me that Andy Dercum is a horrible man. He is with the Klan, and he, well, he touches Mina in a way that Mary Jane says isn't right. It reminds me of the way that the soldiers used to touch the French girls on the streets in Creil, as if they were not human, but goods to be handled as roughly as—"

"That's a bit dramatic, isn't it?"

"Why isn't this girl as important as any other child? Would you let Stephen or Susanna be treated as a piece of property? Would you let them be abused and used as—?"

"Oh, for God's sake, Kathleen, stop!"

His shout echoes through the room. Kathleen's chest heaves as if she has been running or crying. Jim swallows the rest of his brandy and pours another glass.

"It's true that Anneka was young when I met her—sixteen and newly arrived from Sweden," he says. "She was exceptionally beautiful, and she was smart and well-educated in her native country. I wanted to teach her about the world, to mold her into a woman who was as beautiful and fine as her face and body—"

"That is exactly what you told me," Kathleen says bitterly. "You said that you'd teach me what I should know to be your equal."

He does not reply, and Kathleen continues, "Anneka was a child, a girl, not that much older than Mina is now—"

"Neither were you when I met you at eighteen," he counters. "I never used my position or privilege to pressure her into a relationship. Anneka and I shared equal amounts of attraction and curiosity and, in the end, passion for each other. Mina was the unintended consequence."

"Consequence! This is a child, an innocent! Why did you let her get into such a situation? Why didn't you take care of her after her mother died?"

"I was in France. Anneka was ill, but so were you and Ellie and Miss Mills. I made the choice I had to make—my God, I was responsible for sending all of you there. I left Mina and Anneka, thinking that my mother would care for them."

"Why didn't she?"

"That's a question that has never been satisfactorily answered."

Kathleen's anger does not abate. "Do you know what Mina's life is now? They treat her like a servant. She cooks the meals and she cleans up after them. She's evidently failing in school and rather than help her, they tell her she's stupid."

Jim takes another swallow of brandy. "I had every intention of caring for Anneka once I came back from France, but she was dead by then, and Mina had disappeared."

"Why didn't you try to find her? You have the best lawyers, you have private detectives, you have whatever and whoever you want at your beck and call. Why didn't you do what was right?"

"I did try to find her after I returned from France. And then . . ."

His voice trails away, and Kathleen comprehends. "And then we married."

"And Stephen was born."

Stephen—the heir to the fortune, the political power, and the family pride. The child who would be everything Jim was not—undaunted by having to live up to an older, dead sibling's legacy.

"And you had started thinking of the state house," Kathleen says.

"I thought of you, and my son, and your welfare—"

"And your mother, who so wants you to succeed in politics—"

"Yes, and my mother, who—you forget—lost two children in the most tragic of ways. I will not disappoint her."

"Yet you've lost Mina just as surely as she lost her own children. Didn't you think of that?"

"It felt so long ago, so far away."

"You need to do right by her. You need to bring her here and raise her as your own, as you should have done on the day she was born. You have a holy obligation, a responsibility—"

"I will soon have a holy obligation, as you put it, to the state of Colorado, to nearly a million people—"

"A responsibility that is tainted in the same way that this marriage, this house, is! Everything we have is built on a lie that you have created. You promised me—you promised!—that there was nothing in your past that the Klan could use against you, and yet your own daughter is living in a Klan household and attending Klan rallies—"

"How do you know that?"

"Because Mary Jane goes with her. She has all but joined the Klan so that she can stay close to Mina and protect her from them."

"Is that how John Galen Locke found out? He was in Craig—I'm not sure whether to threaten me or for other business. Did Mary Jane decide to share her knowledge with him?"

"She wouldn't do that," Kathleen vows. "She and Miss Crawley are loyal to you. Her brother and Andy Dercum saw us leaving the dairy, and they're both Klan members. Paul told me that Locke knew almost as soon as I'd gone—"

Jim whips around. "You told him about this?"

"No, he told me. He's been collecting reports of what goes on at Klan meetings. Locke spoke about my visit at a meeting on Table Mountain."

"When did you see Colonel Reston? I thought you were at Redlands."

"He drove to Redlands to see me."

"And you didn't think of how suspicious that would seem?"

"I'm not the one at fault here. Besides, he had come to see you."

"What were you thinking, going to the Edwards place?" Jim demands. "The whole thing is now public knowledge because of you. You never should have gone there without asking me—"

"If you'd told me the truth when we married, it would have been settled long ago. I would have known, it wouldn't have surprised me. I could have been as discreet as you think I should have been. You promised me that there was nothing—"

"You've said that."

"You've betrayed me in the worst way, by keeping the truth from me, by not trusting me to choose whether I wanted to marry a man who already had a child. You've betrayed Susanna and Stephen, too. They aren't the first, they aren't the heirs—Mina is."

"That, at least, is not true—"

"And your mother and father—they think so little of me, they think me so unfit to be your wife that they barely speak to me! And Ellie—I've always trusted her, and now—all of them have postured and pretended for you so that you could be the great politician, while laughing behind my back—"

"It has never been a laughing matter for any of us."

"Did you love Anneka or was she simply a summer's fling?"

His face tightens into a mask. "Now that the years have passed, I realize that I did, indeed, love her. I would have married her when I came back from France, regardless of my parents' feelings."

"Is that true, or is it just hindsight?"

He turns on her. "Since you're so set on disbelieving everything I say, why bother asking me questions? And how much does this have to do with Paul Reston? What better way to ease your guilt for loving him than to rescue the child of your husband's mistress?"

Kathleen fights the urge to fly at him. "I would never use a child as a bargaining chip."

"You needn't play the saint." Jim lights a cigarette and shakes out the flame of the match. "The irony is, I would have paid this Dercum fellow anything he wanted to keep this quiet, if he had come to me first. He could have been a wealthy man, by all standards. But he went to Dr. Locke with it—and what did he get? A meaningless position in the Klan."

"How do you know that?"

"Dr. Locke told me."

"Doesn't it bother you that Andy can do whatever he wants to Mina? She needs to be in a place where she is safe—"

"Which a good school would do—"

"Which her father should do—"

"And you?" Jim asks. "You wouldn't feel the least bit anxious about my mistress' child coming to live with us?"

"We have enough for twenty children to come to live with us."

"Well, fortunately, I have only the one," he says dryly. "Be realistic, Kathleen. You would like having Mina here no more than I would."

"You never intended to be a father to her, did you? Even if you'd found her after her mother died, you would have put her in a school and let your lawyers send a monthly check to keep her there. You never intended to honor the God-given life that you brought into this world through your own recklessness."

"How very Catholic you are."

She does not deign to answer. "Do you intend to pay Locke what he wants? Have you paid him? If you do, you'll only end up owing him something more. Once you're governor, he'll be sure to collect."

"I've made no decision at all."

"Then, quit. Drop out of the contest. Bring Mina here and raise her. Save your dignity and that of your family."

"Good God, you know that's not possible."

"Why not? Isn't she worth anything to you? When I was in France—"

"Oh, for God's sake, don't bring that up again."

"No, listen, please." She waits for his attention. "You and Ellie taught me about doing good for others. You made it so that I—so that we—could go to France and work for our country. I learned from you—you taught me to sacrifice for my beliefs. Please, don't let that go now, when it is your own child, your own daughter by a woman you say you loved."

"When you put it that way, it sounds like some kind of dime novel."

The conversation is at an end; Jim has always shielded himself against the unpleasant with sarcasm. Kathleen leaves the study and goes to her studio to paint. But she can't focus on the canvas. Taking her sketch pad, she sits outside, near the pond where the house is reflected in the still water. From memory, she sketches Mina's face.

She studies it—the same eyes, the same chin, the same lips as Jim and Stephen, as Eleanora and Victoria. Angrily, she rips it from the sketch book and tears it in half.

At three o'clock, Kathleen hears the sound of the children on the gravel path outside the studio. She packs away her things as they rush into the studio. The two nursemaids linger outside. "Thank you, Miss Brown and Miss Davis," Kathleen calls. "I'll let you know when we come in the house."

She kneels down to take both her children in her arms.

"Mommy, Mommy, look what I have!" Stephen holds up a mason jar with an insect inside.

"What is it?"

"A praying mantis," Stephen says. "Mr. Collins gave it to me. Miss Brown read about it in the cy-cycol—"

"The encyclopedia?" Kathleen asks.

"Cy-col-pee-da."

"Did you say thank you to both Mr. Collins and Miss Brown?"

Stephen nods. "How does it pray?"

Kathleen eyes the insect, which swipes frantically at the glass with its front legs. "I think it just looks like it prays because of its legs." She folds her hands in front of her. "But it doesn't look very happy. Let's find a nice, cool place to let it go."

"I want to keep it—"

"How would you take care of it? What would you feed it?"

Stephen's face closes in stubbornness. "I could do it."

Kathleen kisses his cheek. "I'm sure you could, but it wants to be with its family. Wouldn't you want to be with yours?"

"I want to show it to Daddy."

"Then we'll do that before we set it free."

"He's gone," Stephen says.

"Gone?" Kathleen asks. "No, he just came home. He's in his study—"

"No, he's gone."

"Let's go find out."

Reaching the house, Kathleen knocks on the door of Jim's study. Drake—who always seems to be lurking nearby—steps around the corner from the foyer to inform her, "Mr. Graves has gone to the Brown Palace. Harris accompanied him."

If Harris has gone with Jim, then the stay at the Brown will be a long one. "Thank you," she says.

As the children watch the praying mantis, mesmerized by its struggle to escape, Kathleen fumes. How like him to run, to remove himself from conflict. How like him to leave her with the burden of her thoughts and feelings. How like him to let her fester in the dark while he and his family make plans around her.

Without a doubt, he will pay John Galen Locke whatever he asks for and ship Mina off, unaware of her father's identity, to a boarding school in the east.

# THIRTY-TWO

The evening of the Republican State Convention, Sean and Kathleen traveled to the City Auditorium together. At the grand stone building, lines spilled from the doors.

"Can you imagine?" Kathleen said. "So many people!"

"Let's just hope they're on our side." Sean linked his elbow with hers. "No one's masked or robed. We'll hope they left their guns at home, too."

"Kathleen?"

She turned and found Paul behind her. "Oh, I'm so glad to see you."

Paul and Sean shook hands and exchanged greetings.

Paul surveyed the confusion. "Where's Senator Graves tonight?"

"I'm not sure," Kathleen said. "I assume he's inside."

"I hope we can find him."

But at the door of the auditorium, the frenzy increased. As they approached, it became evident that only certain people were allowed inside. "What's going on here?" Sean asked as the usher at the door refused admittance to a couple ahead of them. "What's the delay?"

"Patrolman Sullivan." A heavy-set man with white hair and a craggy, weathered face approached. He wore a three-piece suit and a crooked bow tie.

"Good evening, Chief Candlish," Sean said. "Is it full?"

"We're turning away trouble-causers." He eyed Paul. "Undesirables."

"Who qualifies as an undesirable?" Paul asked.

"I'd think that you'd be pouting with your boss, D.A. Van Cise, over the fate of the Republican Party, Colonel Reston," Chief Candlish said. "What a shame he chose not to run again. The 'Fighting D.A.' seems to have lost his taste for it."

"I doubt he's done yet," Paul said calmly. "And he isn't the only former soldier at the D.A.'s office."

Chief Candlish smirked. "Mrs. Graves, if you'll step inside, I can help you locate Mr. Graves."

Kathleen did so, expecting Paul and Sean to accompany her. When she turned, a stranger stood behind her, and others were pressing through the door. "Where are Colonel Reston and Officer Sullivan?" she asked.

"It's Klan only, tonight," he said.

"I am not a Klanswoman," Kathleen said loudly enough that heads turned. "And this is a public meeting. No one can be excluded—"

"There's your husband." He pointed toward the stage at the front. Jim stood beside it, talking with John Galen Locke. Suddenly, the Grand Dragon looked directly at Kathleen. He motioned with one hand, pointing out her presence to Jim. Jim's eyes met hers, shamed, surprised.

Chief Candlish placed a hand on Kathleen's elbow. "There's a seat up front for you, too."

"No, thank you. I won't be staying."

She swung around and barged through the crowd, back to the doors, and into the cool, fresh air of the evening. Sean and Paul had disappeared, either let inside or shooed away by the police presence. Kathleen ran away from the chaos to the street, where she hailed a taxi to take her to the Denver Country Club.

She flees to Redlands, driving the Nash on dark, dusty roads. She tells only the children's nursemaids that she's leaving.

Arriving at the farmhouse in darkness, she sleeps poorly in her childhood bed. In the morning, she watches the sun rise in the east. The dove gray sky fades until the sun bursts with orange warmth over the horizon. Kathleen dresses in her father's shirt and trousers and walks far from the house, along the creek. Crouching beside the flowing water, she dips her hands into the cold, pure water and brings it to her lips.

She sits in the shade of a cottonwood that has grown so thick that she can't wrap her arms around its trunk. Removing her boots, she lowers her feet into the creek, wiggling her toes against the cold of the water. She steps back and takes off her flannel shirt. Loosening the belt of her trousers, she slips from them. Dressed only in camisole and drawers, she steps into the water, stepping from rock to slippery rock. Her shoulders and legs prickle with goosebumps.

What a mess this is—a mess in which she is playing a role she has no desire to play. The girl she was, the girl who went to France, had had the world in her sights, as sure as a sharpshooter, but now she seems to have no courage at all. If she were still brave, she would wrest Mina from the Dercums and parade her down 17th Street as Jim's child. If she were still brave, she would take Stephen and Susanna and leave, no matter the consequences. How much she has compromised to keep a peace that hardly seems worth it. How much she has lost in gaining what looks to others to be everything.

She steps out of the water when she can no longer stand the cold. Seeking the sun beyond the cottonwood, she wraps herself in her father's clothes, lies on the warm, fragrant grass, and sleeps in the radiant warmth of the day.

The sun has moved over her head, casting long shadows to the east, by the time she returns to the house. As she walks past the corral, Napoli neighs at her. She strokes his nose and lets him nuzzle her hand in a search for treats. It is only when she turns that she glances toward the house.

Paul sits on the step of the porch.

She reaches out to him. "When did you get here?"

"I arrived a couple of hours ago" He kisses the palm of her hand. "My car's behind the house."

"Did he receive enough votes to be on the primary ballot?"

Paul lays the morning newspapers on the porch. Kathleen picks up one that sports the headline: "MORLEY, GRAVES WIN SPOTS ON BALLOT." She doesn't bother to look at the other headlines.

"What did Jim do to make the ballot?" Paul asks.

"He paid Locke, I'm sure. Larry Phipps did the same to keep his seat in Washington. That's why he has no challengers."

"But Jim has Morley. I suspect Locke will play one against the other until he finds the one who is most likely to do what he asks."

Faintness rushes through Kathleen's head, and she steadies herself against the post of the porch. The world seems to be rocking under her feet. She puts the back of her hand to her forehead and feels heat. "I need to sit down," she says weakly. "Too much sun—"

"How long has it been since you've eaten?"

"I don't know. Yesterday—"

"Come inside. Julia sent food. I put it in your kitchen."

Inside, Paul unpacks a meal of roast beef, tomatoes, cheese and bread. Kathleen rinses and dries plates and flatware and sets the table. "This is lovely," she says. "Julia is so kind."

"Julia is worried and scared. Worried about you and scared for me. She's afraid that I'll become a target once Phil is out of office."

"It's likely to be worse after the election, isn't it?"

"I think so. What did you and Jim decide about Mina?"

"We didn't. His family wants to pack her off to a boarding school, but I refuse to see that happen. She needs a home with her father." She fiddles with the food on her plate before she blurts, "Why do I care so much about this little girl that I'm willing to jeopardize my own welfare and that of my children? Children suffer all over the world—and in much worse ways—than Mina. She's well-fed, and she has a warm house to live in. She's being sent to school, so maybe she can better herself one day. But I can't let go of her—and Jim's right. She's the daughter of my husband's mistress. Why should I feel any obligation or pity toward her?"

"From what you've told me, almost anyone would feel pity for her."

Kathleen looks out the window at the late afternoon sky. The clouds glow orange, the yellow line of sunset gathering along the spine of the Rocky Mountains. She does not want to be alone, to remember what's past, or to think ahead to what will be.

"Will you stay with me?" she asks.

Paul hesitates. "What about—?"

"I don't believe anyone will come here."

Again, Paul does not answer immediately. "Let's walk out and watch the sunset from the ridge above the house. You can think about whether you're sure, whether this is what you really want."

The walk does nothing to change Kathleen's mind. After they return, she leads Paul to the bedroom she had as a child. The cool breeze of evening blows from the open window. The wallpaper is the original pattern of daisies, but the linoleum, lace curtains and electric light fixtures are new. The brass bed is no longer a child's, but full sized, and the dainty walnut bureau and vanity are a matching set. Nothing shabby or worn remains.

Standing on tiptoe, Kathleen kisses him, and joy floods her heart. To be in his arms, to feel his hands on her skin, to smell the scent of his hair and neck. She kisses him again, opening her lips, letting her tongue dart against his. "Your ribs," she whispers, as if they are in a hotel of hundreds of people, not on the lonely prairie in the twilight. "Will I hurt them?"

"No, don't worry about it. But"—he warns—"it's hideous."

"I don't care. I'm with you at last, after all this time."

Their clothes fall away. Paul moves his mouth over her breasts, the insides of her elbows, the flesh of her stomach, and her thighs. The sweetness of his kiss makes her both raw and tender. She runs her hands over him, kissing wildly at his jaw, his neck, his shoulders.

He draws her to him, pulling her onto the bed beside him. She feels as if she—the mother of two—has never been in a man's arms before, as if every inch of her skin is being touched for the first time. Every grazing fingertip, every brush of the lips, every whisper of air from her lungs releases a ripple of pleasure in her body.

Her passion grows, weaving through every nerve of her body. He responds, bringing her to a raging delight, a jubilant burst that fills the hollow of her stomach with shivering golden light. The back of her throat pulses with the rush of pleasure, her tongue tingles. "Paul," she gasps. "Paul—"

His body shudders against hers, and he calls her name into the tangles of her hair. After, they lie motionless, swept by the breeze. At last, Paul rolls away and settles his head on the pillows. She nestles into the hollow of his shoulder and runs her hands over the knobby ribs on his left side.

He lays his hand on hers. "I've been afraid that I've become repulsive."

"Oh, never, never to me."

Leaning down, she kisses her way down the string of welts and scars on his ribs.

He exhales sharply, as if released from some inner prison.

Together, they sink back to the bed.


Kathleen woke in Paul's arms for the first time in seven years when the robin began his monotonous chirrup outside. The breeze had turned chilly during the night, and they had nestled at some early hour beneath the thick covers.

Unwilling to disturb Paul's rest, she remained still for a long time, listening to him breathe, feeling the stretch of his body against hers, and reveling in the warmth of his flesh. This is where she might be if—what? fate? God? chance?—had not turned against them during the war.

She drew a finger down Paul's chest, and he grasped her hand and kissed it. "You're awake!" she exclaimed.

"I have been for a while."

"Did you sleep well?"

"I haven't slept this well since those days in Chaumont. What bird do I hear?"

"It's a meadowlark."

"I could lie here all day and listen to it."

"We can do that, if you like," she offered, kissing just below his ear. "Or we can do something more."

He laughed as he took her in his arms.

He left Redlands that afternoon, and Kathleen returned to the Denver Country Club. She spent the rest of the day in her studio, painting. Her strokes were lazy and carefree—she only wanted to remember—and the colors she chose were bold and brilliant, the shapes broad and open.

Late in the afternoon, Jim stepped onto the threshold of the open door, neither in nor out of the studio. He held a cigarette between two fingers. "Where have you been?" he asked.

"Redlands." She struggled to rid her voice of emotion. "I assume you're staying at the Brown Palace?"

"For the time being."

"I saw in the newspapers that your name is on the primary ballot."

"It is."

She stabbed at the canvas with her paintbrush. "What did it cost you?"

"I told you what the agreement was."

"Money with no obligation to the Klan? But I saw you talking with Locke at the convention."

"He wanted me to speak. I told him no."

"So, first you pander to him and then throw his demands back in his face? You know he'll just ask again and again until you give in. And even if you do, what guarantee do you have that he won't choose Morley instead?"

Jim said nothing.

"So what have you decided about Mina?" Kathleen asked.

"We're still working on it."

"We? You mean, your mother and sister and you?"

"With our lawyer, yes."

"Even though I'm not included in the group, I would like my thoughts on the matter to be known."

"Rest assured, they're known." He looked toward the house. "Was Colonel Reston in Redlands?"

She would not lie. "Yes."

"You won't be happy until I'm brought to my knees, will you?"

"As far as I can see, Locke is the one who's brought you to your knees."

"Jesus, you are tiresome," he said. "You have never grown out of your fantasy of love among the bombs and bullets of war. Paul Reston, the heroic ambulance driver, the daring pilot, and now, the sad, wounded soldier. You've never grown up, you've never become a woman with a consistent and true heart who can love a man who doesn't require pity."

His words cut through her breast. "It's you I pity, not him. He's strong and wise, and he acts with integrity and morals."

"Except for preying on another man's wife."

"I told him I wouldn't see him again."

She had told Paul just before they had parted, although she had known in her heart what she would do since he had arrived in Redlands.

"I can't see you again, you know," she had said. "It's wrong, it's a sin, and I can't allow my children—"

"I wouldn't ask you to, but you know it changes nothing." He had kissed her forehead. "We've been apart for so many years, do you think anything could end my love for you?"

Now, Jim asked, "Why? The sin is done, according to your church. You've violated your wedding vows. You've broken a commandment and jeopardized your immortal, Catholic soul. I certainly hope it was worth it."

"Don't lecture me about the state of my immortal soul."

He stamped out his cigarette butt in the dirt outside the door. "I'll be leaving again after I see the children."

# THIRTY-THREE

Only days after the Klan-only Republican State Convention, Denver Mayor Ben Stapleton won the recall vote by an unprecedented seventy-two percent of voters. In response, Denver District Attorney Philip Van Cise formed a new political party, the Visible Government League, which consisted of one hundred prominent Denver Republicans who opposed the Ku Klux Klan. Working furiously, the League's organizers gathered enough signatures on petitions so that a League candidate, who pledged to have no affiliation with the Klan, would appear on the primary ballot in nearly every race.

Four days before the primary election, the Visible Government League rented the Denver City Auditorium. Colonel Van Cise was to speak on "Morley and the Courts" in an effort to steer Denver's voters toward the League's candidates. For Jim, it was a bitter pill. In the governor's race, the League had thrown its lot in with Robert Rockwell over the anti-Klan firebrand Earl Cooley, banking on moderation over fervency. Jim had felt a wave of sickness when he heard the news. Had he not given into Dr. Locke's demands, he would have been the League's choice.

On Thursday, he went to hear Colonel Van Cise speak. Slipping into the very back of the auditorium, he took a seat high above the crowd in the last row of the shadowy balcony. With the Colonel were like-minded foes of the Klan—Phillip Hornbein, a lawyer from the West Side; Judge Ben Lindsey, whose own seat was in question in this year's election; and Paul Reston, who looked unruffled and sure of himself.

Long before the speakers took the floor, trouble started. Men openly carried firearms on their hips, and the seats near the front were snapped up by sour-faced women. Once the seats had all been taken, spectators lined the walls, two deep, their voices droning in protest.

As a scratchy recording of "The Star Spangled Banner" played, the mob quieted, raising their voices in patriotic song, their hands folded before them. But the moment that Philip Van Cise took the stage, a chant erupted: "Philip, go home! Philip, go home!"

Van Cise shouted into the microphone. "Will the city of Denver be turned over to the Ku Klux Klan?"

"Yes! Yes!" The crowd thundered, drowning out the few voices of dissension. "We must keep this a white man's country!"

Across the aisle from Jim, a woman shrilled her hatred. "You're a failure, Phil! You're a fraud! Go home, go home!"

Colonel Van Cise retreated, and the four men held a conference near the back of the stage, accompanied by a steady volley of boos. Determined, Paul stepped up to the squawking microphone. "The Klan has intentionally disrupted the reputable and honorable party of Lincoln," he called. "It has defiled the Republican party with its secrecy, its cowardly exclusive membership, and its oaths that are at best inconsistent with, and at worse, contrary to the laws of this land. It vows allegiance to an Emperor, and—"

"Cuckoo! Cuckoo! Cuckoo!"

The auditorium echoed with the sounds of a cuckoo clock. Jim looked around, puzzled. My God, what had become of public discourse and civility? How could this be the reaction of adult men and women who held jobs, and attended churches, and raised children?

"Is this seat taken?"

A priest stood in the aisle next to Jim. The poor man's face was beaded with sweat, and his Roman collar was slightly askew.

"Please," Jim said. "Sit down."

The priest took his seat as the cries of "Cuckoo" drowned out Paul Reston's voice. Paul stepped back from the microphone, and Ben Lindsey stepped up with an angry shout. "Where is your respect—?"

"Senator Graves," the priest said. "You may not remember me, but we have met at the Sullivans' home. I'm Father Brendan Keohane, the curate at Blessed Savior, which Kathleen—excuse me—Mrs. Graves supports with her kind contributions."

"Father." Jim shook his hand. "You're brave to appear in clerical clothing in this crowd."

The priest wiped at his forehead with a handkerchief. "I was to meet Fathers Walsh and Kelly from Immaculate Conception and Father Smith from the *Catholic Register*, but I was running late. What have I missed?"

"Only this." Jim took his flask from his pocket. "Would you like some?"

Father Keohane shook his head. "I rely on a much greater power."

Jim replaced the flask. "Do you know what these cuckoo calls are about?"

"Supposedly, Colonel Reston had a mental collapse in France, which led to his being in an asylum for a time. I really don't know any more details, but this is vicious and cruel, poor man."

Jim leaned back in his chair. So Paul Reston's wounds were not simply physical, but mental—which was like offering candy to Kathleen, who was always seeking to save someone. Wasn't that what her fixation with Mina was all about?

The crowd's attention shifted again to Colonel Van Cise, who tried to shout over the noise. A chorus rose up: "California, here I come, right back where I started from—"

"Colonel Van Cise said he would move to California if Mayor Stapleton were re-elected," Father Keohane explained.

"Go home, Phil!" The woman across the aisle from Jim screeched.

Colonel Van Cise plodded on, despite the roar of the crowd. Only a few of his words reached Jim: "ruin Catholic businessmen who are honest and . . . influence judges and juries by stacking them with Klan . . ."

"This is despicable," Jim said.

Father Keohane said nothing, and at once, Jim realized how humiliating it was to be considered one of them, for whom hate for others had replaced every sensible human emotion or logical process.

"What you are doing here tonight is a better argument against the Klan than any I could make!" Colonel Van Cise shouted into the microphone. "Tonight we see the mob, and we see what mob rule means!"

A fresh round of boos filled the auditorium. The woman from across the aisle spotted Father Keohane. "Look! It's a Roman Catholic priest! Get out of here! Get out of our country! Stop tryin' to make real churches illegal! We're the Christians, not you! Stop tryin' to take the Bible from our public schools!"

"Madame," Father Keohane said. "I assure you that the Catholic Church intends to do none of those—"

She pointed a finger at him. "You think the Pope is God! You think that Catholics are above the law, with your wine and your Pope!"

"Ma'am," Jim intervened. "Please, sit down. This is a public gathering. This man is here to listen to the speaker. Please, calm yourself."

"You need to explain yourself, Mr. Graves."

Jim heard his name bounce about the balcony, as other spectators craned their necks to see what the commotion was about.

"Why are you with this filth of Rome?" the woman demanded. "Why are you married to one?"

Jim ripped from his seat, balancing on the narrow step between the rows of seats. "You can call me whatever you like, ma'am, but don't you dare to bring my wife and family into this."

"Ethel, stop," a man beside the woman said. "Leave him alone."

After giving Jim a vicious glare, the woman resumed yelling at the stage. "Go home! Go away, Phil!"

Father Keohane spoke into Jim's ear. "I believe I should go find my fellow priests."

"I have no qualms about sitting here with you," Jim said. "I won't be frightened away by their ignorance."

"Thank you, but I don't want you to be attacked because of me. And please, tell Kathleen that if she or the children need anything from me, I am available. She has always been a bright spot in my brother's and my lives, from the time we were young boys."

Father Keohane picked his way to the door. A hiss followed him, but no one accosted him. Ignoring the crowd around him, Jim focused his attention on the speakers, but his heart thumped in his chest. Father Keohane's offer of aid had glaringly excluded him.

The meeting lasted until one in the morning, when Mayor Ben Stapleton and Director of Safety Rice Means came on stage and ordered that the Auditorium be emptied and closed. As Colonel Van Cise, Phillip Hornbein, Ben Lindsey, and Paul packed away their speeches, the Klansmen bellowed "Onward Valiant Klansmen," one of the many Christian hymns they had rewritten. As the Klansmen filed out, they continued to sing: "'*Oh, we'll cling to the old fiery cross, And exchange it someday for a crown.*'"

Home again at his suite in the Brown Palace, Jim brooded through the next day, the frenzied screaming still echoing his head. This was the side with which he'd aligned himself, the side that sought to take rights from those who disagreed with it, the side that believed it was permissible to attack others' personal histories—a spell in an asylum, a Catholic wife. It was not the side of war heroes, Van Cise and Reston, who had parlayed their honors into civil service, or of Lindsey, the man who had gained national fame for creating the first juvenile court in the nation, or of a brave Jewish lawyer or an indefatigable Catholic priest.

On Friday evening, a knock sounded on the door of the suite. Rather than disturb Harris, who was in the smaller adjoining suite, Jim answered the door himself.

Two fully-garbed Klansmen stood outside. Jim took an involuntary step backward, his heart pounding.

"Good evening, Senator Graves," one of them said. "The Grand Dragon wants you up on the hill."

"I beg your pardon?"

The other knight spoke. "The Grand Dragon has requested that you accompany us to Kastle Mountain. He wants to talk to you."

"I'll speak with him next week."

"I'm afraid you don't understand, Senator. When the Grand Dragon requests you come up to the mountain, you don't refuse."

Kathleen's warning rang in his head: *If you do, you'll only end up owing him something more. Once you're governor, he'll be sure to collect.*

"Tell Dr. Locke thank you for the invitation, but I won't be joining him," he said.

The knight wedged his foot against the door to keep Jim from closing it. "All candidates in this year's election need to come to Kastle Mountain and pledge to the Klan. Dr. Locke says that anyone who doesn't sign his name on the dotted line and agree to keep all the promises he's made to the Grand Dragon will be out."

The other knight grabbed Jim's arm. "Nobody says no to Dr. Locke."

Jim jerked away. "Let go of me!"

The second knight lunged for his other arm, and Jim backed into the coffee table behind him in his attempt to escape. "Get out!"

The door to the adjoining suite burst open, and Harris rushed into the room, followed closely by Blount.

"What's going on here?" Harris demanded.

"So, you've got your fancy man and his pet with you." Addressing Harris, one of the knights taunted, "Be careful that don't rub off on you."

Harris took a step forward, while Blount inched closer to the other knight. The knights' shoulders raised, and one clenched his fist.

"Stop," Jim ordered. "Harris, Blount, stand down." He addressed the knights. "You can tell Dr. Locke that I am not coming tonight or any other night."

The Klansmen looked at one another. "Why would you do that?" one asked. "You're set to win this whole thing, if you just go along with the Grand Dragon. This is the worst mistake you will ever make. The Klan is here for good."

Harris stepped forward, opening his jacket so that his pistol was visible, and the knights retreated. Jim slammed the door behind them. He leaned back against it, unable to move. My God, what had just happened?

When he looked up, his gaze met Blount's. Blount, who had been with him for years, who was the only one allowed to drive the Silver Ghost. Blount, whom Kathleen said had never spoken more than a handful of words to her in the six years she and Jim had been married, yet who could name, explain, and repair every gizmo on every car that Jim owned. And now, he had risked physical harm for Jim, for a man who had, for all intents and purposes, betrayed him.

"Are you all right, sir?" Harris asked.

"Yes, I'm fine," Jim managed.

Harris said, "If there's any more trouble—"

"Thank you, Harris, Blount. No more tonight."

The two left for the adjoining suite. Trembling, Jim made it to the table, where he found brandy and a cigarette. At the window, he looked into the dark street below. Couples strolled, bound for the theater or restaurants in the area, and street vendors plied their wares to tourists and pleasure-seekers. He could not see the two knights. They had most likely slipped off their robes long before they reached the sidewalk.

*Cuckoo, filth of Rome, be careful that don't rub off on you*—my God, what had happened to decency?

He poured another glass of brandy, his fear subsiding into anger. This was his chance. To take over the governor's seat, to see progress made to unite the parts of Colorado that were separated by the difficult and beautiful Rocky Mountains, to see a pipeline built from west to east, to see water brought in from the generous snow pack of the western slope to the thirsty eastern plains. This moment in history, when so much was possible, would not come again.

He picked up the telephone. He wanted to talk to someone, to hear a friendly voice, but he was afraid that Kathleen would be at Redlands, in Paul Reston's arms. Instead, he telephoned Ellie, but there was no answer at the Lloyd-Elliot household. Jim assumed that the Friday night party was most likely in full swing. He clicked off the lights in the suite and sat down in the darkness.

He had no one to turn to.

He was still on the sofa when the sun rose on Saturday morning, and when his political secretary, Nathaniel, arrived full of good news. Waving a stack of papers, Nathaniel said, "After the near riot at the Auditorium the other night, the newspapers are taking a stand on the Klan. The *Colorado Springs Gazette and Telegraph* and the P*ueblo Chieftain* came out in opposition. The *Boulder New Herald* declared that free speech is being destroyed, and fear and strife are taking its place. The *Post* endorsed the entire Visible Government League's candidates—"

"I'm withdrawing from the race," Jim said.

Nathaniel looked up from behind the newspaper. "I'm sorry?"

"I have decided to end my candidacy."

"But with this"—Nathaniel tapped the newspapers—"you could come out strong against the Klan and knock out Morley. He's weak, and he can't think for himself—"

"It's final." Jim turned away from the window. "I'd like to put out a press release."

"Yes, sir." Still in shock, Nathaniel took out his notebook. "I'm ready."

"Say that I believe it's best for my family and for myself to continue representing the neighborhood that we call home rather than trying to attain a higher office—"

He stopped speaking at a sound from Nathaniel. The young man's bottom lip trembled, as if he would burst into tears. "I'm sorry." Jim laid a hand on Nathaniel's shoulder. "I regret disappointing you and all the others who supported me."

An hour later, Jim left the Brown Palace as Nathaniel tearfully telephoned the newspapers and read the release to them. At home, he found Kathleen in the small sitting room that she used during the day. She sat on the floor next to Stephen, who was building a tower of blocks, with Susanna in her lap, her hands holding the little girl's.

"Let's try one more," Kathleen coached. "Let's see if it will stand."

Stephen set one more block on the tower, and the pile swayed, but held.

"Bravo!" Kathleen cried, clapping Susanna's hands in applause.

"Again, Mommy, again!" Stephen shouted.

"Go ahead. We'll hold our breath." She took a gulp of air and puffed out her cheeks, and Susanna imitated her.

Stephen set the block on the tower. It swayed once and fell.

Kathleen cried, "Look out below!" and Susanna echoed, "Loo'-ou-'low!"

As the blocks clattered across the floor, spilling under the sofa and chairs, Stephen spied his father.

He ran toward Jim. "Daddy! Daddy!"

Susanna wriggled her way out of Kathleen's lap. "Daddy!"

Stephen wrapped his arms around Jim's legs, and Susanna embraced one of his thighs in her toddler arms. Jim touched both their heads, stroking Susanna's fly-away red hair. At once, Stephen began to talk, telling his father about his adventures, while Susanna echoed a word or two now and then.

"I will come up to your room and see you in a few minutes," Jim said. "Right now, I need you to go with Miss Brown and Miss Davis. I want to talk to Mommy."

The nursemaids collected the children while Kathleen lifted herself from the floor and sat on the sofa. Once Miss Davis closed the door behind her, Kathleen asked, "Do you want to talk here or in your study?"

"I don't care." He moved to the French doors at the end of the room. "I've withdrawn my candidacy."

Kathleen blinked, disbelieving. "What?"

"I could not—" Jim stopped, but began again, his voice ravaged by emotion. "I will not be part of it. I couldn't stand to be their puppet, to act their fool."

She opened her mouth, but no words sounded.

He turned to leave, but Kathleen flew after him, catching up with him before he reached the door. "What, why?" She grabbed his arm. "Tell me what happened. Did they threaten you?"

"Of course, but that was to be expected. Ironically, it was your lover—"

"Please, don't call him that. Don't use that word."

"You should ask him or Father Keohane what happened on Thursday night at the City Auditorium. It was a valiant show by men for whom bravery is evidently second-nature. It revealed to me all that I am not."

With that, he opened the door and strode down the hall, leaving her dumbstruck behind him.

# THIRTY-FOUR

On Monday, Graves Industries seemed darker to Mary Jane. The hallways echoed with emptiness, and no one pored over the company bulletin board for news or entertainment. The whole place had the feel of shame and a profound disillusionment, as if Mr. Graves' fate adversely affected them all.

On Saturday evening, it had been in the newspapers: "JIM GRAVES OUT OF GOVERNOR'S RACE" and "GRAVES STEPS ASIDE FOR MORLEY." Some of them had given it a humorous twist: "OILMAN COMES UP DRY ON GOVERNOR'S RACE" or "GRAVES DIGS HIS OWN GRAVE."

When Mary Jane came into the typing pool, the girls clustered around her desk.

"Why do you think he quit?" Annabel asked.

"I heard that the Klan paid him to drop the race," Edna said. "They want Judge Morley to win, and Mr. Graves would have beat him."

"Doesn't he want to be governor?" Mavis asked.

"My money's on Teapot Dome," Nancy, the new girl, said. "Every lease I type is for Wyoming."

"Ladies." Miss Crawley had entered the room. "To your machines, please. I won't have idle speculation in my office."

Early in the afternoon, a messenger came into the typing pool to deliver a note to Miss Crawley. As the girls pretended to type, she read it and cleared her throat.

"Miss Grayson, would you come here, please?"

So this was it, then, Mary Jane thought as she walked up the aisle, ignoring Mavis' popped eyes. Mr. Graves must blame her for revealing his secret to Kathleen; maybe he even blamed her for his losing the governor's seat.

Miss Crawley handed the note to Mary Jane. It read: *Please report to Mr. Graves' office at once.*

"You are to take your things, Miss Grayson," Miss Crawley said. "You won't be returning."

"Am I being fired?" Mary Jane whispered.

"I don't know." Miss Crawley lowered her voice. "But I wish you the best, if it is so."

With that dour send-off as her only comfort, Mary Jane left the typing pool and climbed the stairs to the main lobby. The elevator doors stood open, the operator just inside, waiting to take her to the top floor. Mary Jane recalled the last time she had ridden on this elevator. It had been during the war, when she had begged Mr. Spratt to send a letter to Mr. Graves telling him about Anneka's death and Mina's predicament. And now, she was about to be fired for finding Mina again.

Mr. Spratt—still irritatingly at his post—showed her into the inner office. Mr. Graves sat on a leather couch in one corner of the room with a graying gentleman in his forties, who wore a suit that was even more dapper than Mr. Graves' stylish clothing, although he wore shoes rather than exotic cowboy boots. The two men rose as Mary Jane entered, and Mr. Graves introduced him. "Miss Grayson, I would like you to meet Mr. Gerald Hughes from Hughes and Dorsey."

"Pleased to meet you." The words were no more than a whisper as she shook his hand.

"Please, sit down," Mr. Graves said. "Would you like lemon water?"

Her voice shook as she spoke. "Yes, please."

Mr. Hughes leaned toward her. "Miss Grayson, Mr. Graves has commissioned me to ask you to help with an important and sensitive situation. He would like us to go together to the home of Andrew and Judith Dercum and retrieve Miss Lindstrom and her belongings."

"Mina?"

"Yes, Mina," Mr. Hughes said. "Mr. Graves has told me that the little girl trusts you and would feel comfortable in your company."

"Andy and Judith will never let her go—"

"An agreement has already been reached. You don't need to concern yourself with that."

"Where would we . . . where will she go?"

Mr. Graves answered. "She will be coming to my house."

"To live?"

"Yes, to live."

Mary Jane put her hand over her mouth. Oh, thank God, no Catholic orphanage or other dumping ground for unwanted children. "Yes, oh, yes, I will help." Less enthusiastically, she added, "Am I being fired?"

Mr. Graves laughed shortly. "No, why would you think that?"

"Miss Crawley said that I wouldn't be returning."

"For today, Miss Grayson. You won't return today."

Mary Jane gulped out a "thank you," while Mr. Hughes said, "We should go now. I believe the child comes home from school around three?"

"She's usually home by three-thirty," Mary Jane offered.

The Rolls Royce Silver Ghost carried them to Aurora. Mr. Hughes stared out the window, while Mary Jane longed to ask him how this had all come about. Had Kathleen talked Mr. Graves into reclaiming Mina? Had he given up his chance for governor so he could bring her home? How had Judith and Andy reacted to Mr. Graves' offer? When they arrived at the dairy, Mr. Hughes cautioned. "Miss Grayson, when we go inside, would you please help the little girl along as quickly as possible? I suspect our welcome won't be warm here today."

He was right. When Andy opened the door of the house, he stood aside to let them enter without greeting them. Mary Jane caught Judith's spiteful glare as Andy showed Mr. Hughes to the living room. She hurried through to Mina's room.

She found Mina sitting on her bed with tears running down her cheeks. She held Marta in a tight embrace, the doll's smashed face pressed against her own, where it left ugly red welts. A suitcase lay empty and open beside her.

"What's wrong?" Mary Jane sat on the bed next to her.

"They told me I have to go away. They said I can't stay here anymore."

"That's right, but did they tell you where you're going?"

Mina shook her head.

Leave it to Judith and Andy to present Mina with a cruel version of the facts.

"You're going to Mr. Graves' house. To Mr. Yeem's house. Oh, Mina, there will be all sorts of new things for you there. New clothes and shoes, and new toys, and maybe even a new doll."

Mina clung to her doll. "No, I want Marta."

"Then you can keep her, but let's hurry and pack."

Mary Jane gathered as much as she could stuff into Mina's suitcase and her own bag. Carrying the suitcase, she escorted Mina from the house. Mr. Hughes waited for her just beside the door, his briefcase in his hand. As Mary Jane and Mina walked down the path to the car, Judith rushed outside.

"Minnie! You can't leave without saying goodbye!"

Judith knelt down, and Mina returned to hug her, roiling Mary Jane. She could not believe that Judith cared whether Mina stayed or went—unless she was sad that she would no longer have a slave to cook and clean for her.

Once again, the car ride passed in silence. When the Silver Ghost pulled up in front of the Graves' house, Mina asked, "Is this the castle?"

"It looks like one, doesn't it?" Mary Jane said.

"No, this isn't the castle." Mr. Hughes spoke for the first time. "The castle is in the mountains."

Mary Jane arched her eyebrows and made a la-di-dah face, and Mina wringed out an anxious smile.

Inside, Mary Jane and Mina were shown to the sitting room, while Mr. Hughes went down the hall. The sitting room was much smaller and messier than the parlor where Mary Jane and Miss Crawley had met with Kathleen. Toys and books scattered across the floor, while a chalkboard filled with scribblings, a doll house, and a rocking horse vied for space near the windows. Kathleen rose from the sofa as they came into the room.

"Mrs. Kathleen!" Mina said.

"Mina," she said. "How nice to see you again. Please sit down, I'll ring for tea."

Mina balked, and Mary Jane asked, "What is it?"

"Do I make the tea?" Mina whispered.

"You don't need to make the tea here," Kathleen said gently.

Mina sat on the very edge of the sofa. Mary Jane sat across from her in an armchair, while Kathleen took her place beside Mina. The little girl looked fragile and helpless here, in this gaping mansion. Yet she would be far safer here than she had ever been in Judith and Andy's homey and warm house.

The door opened, and Mr. Graves came into the room. "Miss Grayson, Mrs. Graves." He turned to Mina. "Mina."

Mina jumped from the sofa and rushed to him. "Mr. Yeem!"

Mr. Graves took her in his arms. "Oh, Mina, oh, my darling."

Mary Jane smiled at Kathleen, but Kathleen's face had set in a pale, fragile mask as she watched the two of them. Dark circles shadowed her eyes, and lines etched the skin around her mouth. Bringing Mina home must have cost her dearly.

"Where is Mother?" Mina asked Mr. Graves. "Is she with you?"

"Let's sit down."

The tea arrived, and Kathleen said, "Mina, would you please pour for us? You do it so well."

Mina obediently sat next to her father. "Yes, Mrs. Kathleen."

When everyone had a cup, Mr. Graves asked, "Do you remember when your mother was so sick? Remember when I came to your house and we tried to help her get better?"

"I remember, but then you went away."

"That's right. I had to leave for France, because my sister and . . . Mrs. Kathleen were sick."

Mina glanced at Kathleen, but said nothing.

"Miss Edwards and Mrs. Stroop took care of you," Mr. Graves continued. "That's because your mother got so sick that she couldn't get well. She died."

"No, she went away. That's what Miss Judith told me."

"She wouldn't leave you," Mr. Graves said carefully. "Believe me, she would never have left you."

Kathleen spoke. "Mina, your mother was very sick, and she couldn't get better. She passed away, just like mine did. Remember, I told you about my mother when I visited you?"

Mina's face set in a scowl that looked as if it were one kind word away from cracking into a sob.

"May I say something?" Mary Jane asked.

Mr. Graves nodded.

"Mina, do you remember when we met each other outside the church where the wagon with the coffin was? You were with Miss Edwards, and it was a cold and windy day?"

"Yes," Mina said uncertainly.

"We laid your mother to rest that day. We . . . buried her. You, me, and Miss Edwards."

Tears rolled down Mina's cheeks. "But Miss Judith said she would come back for me, if I was a good girl and did as I was told."

As if he could stand no more, Mr. Graves stood and walked to the window, where he lit a cigarette.

"I'm sorry," Mary Jane said. "That isn't true. Miss Judith was probably just trying to be kind to you."

Kathleen moved to the loveseat and took one of Mina's hands. "We would like you to stay with us now, with me and . . . Mr. Yeem and our children, Stephen and Susanna. Your mother isn't here, but I think you'll be happy here."

Mina sobbed. Kathleen put her arm around her and drew her against her shoulder, stroking her hair with her free hand. She shot an imperious look toward Mr. Graves, who came to sit on the other side of Mina. He laid his hand on her shoulder.

Neither of them tried to rush Mina, but once her tears had abated, Kathleen asked quietly, "Would you like to see your bedroom? We haven't had time to do much with it, but I think you'll like it."

Mr. Graves added, "It will make you feel better to know where you'll be sleeping."

The room upstairs was painted a cloudy blue. Everything in it had the smell of department store tissue paper—the chenille bedspread; the stiff, sheer curtains; the freshly polished furniture. Four perfectly starched dresses hung in the closet.

"These are yours," Kathleen said. "If they don't fit, we can have them fixed so that they do."

"See what pretty clothes you'll have?" Mary Jane said. "It will be just like it used to be, with you and Marta and your pretty clothes and things."

"But Mother was there."

Kathleen eyed Mary Jane over the girl's head. "Well, we'll be here now." She pointed toward a woman who stood just outside the door. "And Miss Davis will be helping you out."

"Would you like to have a bath?" Miss Davis asked. "Then you can put on one of your new dresses for dinner."

Mina looked around the room, taking in the beautiful coverlet, the fluffy pillows, and the elegant dresses, and burst into tears.

After Mina was delivered into the hands of the nursemaid for her bath, Mr. Graves thanked Mary Jane for her help, reassured her that she would be welcome at work tomorrow, and left the room. Mary Jane and Kathleen loitered in the powder blue room, while Kathleen discussed what she planned to do with it.

"I don't know what color she'll want it to be," Kathleen confessed. "When I was thirteen, all I wanted to do was to be outside, to ride my horse and draw pictures. Do you know if she has any hobbies?"

"I don't think she's had much of a childhood. She's been expected to take care of the house for years."

"I'll ask her what she wants. Who knows? She may want worms and bugs, just like Stephen."

Mary Jane laughed. As they walked along the lovely landing to the grand staircase, Mary Jane offered, "I'm sorry Mr. Graves had to leave the governor's race."

Kathleen's face tightened again. "We felt it was the best for our children and for Mina. He'll still be at the State Senate, so he isn't out of politics yet."

"Do you think he'll try again in two years?"

"Perhaps. Another time he might be more successful." Kathleen laid her hand on her arm. "Mary Jane, I, we feel nothing but gratitude to you for finding Mina and helping us to bring her home. I've written to Miss Crawley to thank her, as well."

Mary Jane laughed at the way Kathleen winced when she mentioned Johanna's name. "You need to thank Raynelle, too. Remember her? She stocks and cleans the washroom."

"Of course, I remember her."

"She helped me get up the courage to do this."

"I'll send her a letter, then."

"May I come to visit Mina?" Mary Jane asked.

"Anytime you want. Just drop me a note and I'll send a car for you. Would Raynelle come, too?"

"I don't know, but please ask her. What about Miss Crawley?"

A flicker of the Kathleen from the Relief Society reappeared. "Oh, I'm nowhere near that brave, but yes, I'll ask her as well."

Mary Jane laughed. "Johanna and I are on a first name basis now."

"Oh! That's a surprise. Tell me how that happened."

With their heads bent together, they walked the rest of the way to the sitting room, chattering and giggling as if they were girls on their way to the Woolworth's lunch counter.

"What about . . . well, does Mina know that Mr. Graves is her, um, father? I haven't told her, and I don't know if Andy and Judith did."

'We decided that we'd do a little at a time," Kathleen assured her. "She's only just found out her mother is never coming back. It seems too soon to tell her more."

Mina came down from her bath dressed in a champagne-colored gingham dress with a shawl collar and wrap-around bodice. The color of the dress nearly matched her hair, which was brushed neatly back and tied with a bright yellow ribbon. She looked eerily like her mother.

She held Marta in her arms. The governess, Miss Davis, whispered to Kathleen. "She won't let go of the doll."

"Then leave it," Kathleen said airily.

"But the thing is filthy, and it could have lice or some other kind of infestation—"

"I think she's had enough upset for one day."

Miss Davis gave Kathleen a sour look, and Kathleen winked at Mary Jane. Mary Jane's heart filled with delight. She was certain that Kathleen would treat Mina as if she were her own child.

Mary Jane stayed for dinner, eating with Kathleen, Mr. Graves, and Mina. Afterward, the Negro chauffeur who had taken Mr. Hughes and Mary Jane to the Edwards place delivered her home. Ross came out on the front porch to watch as the chauffeur opened the door of the Silver Ghost for Mary Jane. She stepped out as if she were a queen.

"That's Jim Graves' car," Ross commented. "There's only one of them in Denver."

Mary Jane laughed breathlessly. "Yes, it is."

"You'd better get ready. We have visitors."

They were grouped around the living room—Matt and Essie, with pursed lips and piqued expression, and Andy and Judith, who sobbed into a handkerchief. Mary Jane's mother sat in the middle of the couch, between Essie and Judith, while Matt and Andy stood tensely near the fireplace with Avery. Andy glared as Mary Jane came into the room.

Mary Jane's mother spoke first. "What have you done?"

The words resounded in accusation. Ross touched Mary Jane's shoulder, directing her to take a seat in the armchair. She sat on the edge to keep from sinking into the soft cushions "I did what was right."

Judith sobbed. "You took away our Minnie!"

"I didn't take her away! I just made sure she was where she should be, with her father—"

"Her father! He didn't want her in the first place! He never contacted us after the flu was gone! And he married and had a new family, and he became famous, and he probably never even thought about her until you stuck your nose into it!"

"No, it was all a mix-up," Mary Jane said. "He intended for her and her mother to live with him after the war. I don't know if he was going to marry Mina's mother, but he was going to care for them."

"How do you know him so well?" Ross asked. "You've never said anything about being friends with him."

"Mina told me before Anneka died."

Ross glanced away at the mention of Anneka's name, and a fury rose up in Mary Jane.

"What I did was to see a child reunited with her father and her half-brother and sister," she said. "I didn't do anything that anyone in this room wouldn't do!"

She looked toward Andy, whose face had grown even darker and cloudier as she spoke.

He lashed out. "That high-handed prig of a lawyer—"

"Please, watch your language," her mother warned.

"Your high and mighty Mr. Graves only offered us five thousand dollars for her."

"Five thousand!" Mary Jane said. "That's more than most people make in a lifetime! And it couldn't have cost you that much—or even half that much—to raise her. Not the way you treated her—"

"How dare you," Judith said. "We took good care of—"

"Why did you take the money if it isn't enough, or it isn't what you deserve, or whatever you think? Why didn't you say no to Mr. Graves and keep Mina?"

"Because I'm going to tell everyone I know," Andy said. "It's going to be all over town that he took his bastard back—"

"Andy!" Mary Jane's mother protested. "Please, your language!"

"He'll never run for office again. I'll make sure nobody respects him."

"Respect!" Mary Jane cried. "You were teaching Mina to hate other people! You were teaching her—you're teaching your own son!—to call Jews pigs and to dump manure on the steps of their church, and to throw dynamite at the houses in Five Points because black people live there—"

"What's this?" Ross asked. "What dynamite?"

"And who are you going to tell about this?" Mary Jane went on. "Mr. Graves dropped out of the governor's race, and Mina is living in his home. Soon enough, everyone in Denver is going to know she's his daughter, and it won't be because you told them. It will be because he did the right thing."

With a flounce, she left the room. Outside, in the garden at the back of the house, she worked to calm herself. Her whole body felt light and jittery, and she didn't know if she wanted to cry or laugh. She heard the slamming of the front door, and she peered around the corner of the house. Essie led Judith, who was still crying, from the house, while Matt and Andy climbed into the front seat of the car. A moment later, the car roared into the night.

Ross came from the back door of the house. Cupping his hands against the autumn breeze, he lit a cigarette. After blowing out smoke, he said, "Well, you got what you wanted."

His words pushed Mary Jane into laughter. "I don't think I've ever done anything like that before. But—"

"No buts. Our family ties are hanging by a frayed thread just now."

"That isn't it," Mary Jane said. "Do you think . . . when I came home from France, everyone was so ashamed of me. Mom and Dad, and the people I work with—none of them understood why . . ." She let her words trail away, but started again. "If I hadn't come home, you wouldn't have introduced me to Anneka, and I wouldn't have found out that Mr. Graves is Mina's father. I would have thought that Mina was what Judith said she was—a slow-witted, dull little girl—and I wouldn't have fought for her. Do you think I was meant—by God or fate or something—to do what I just did?"

"Mary Jane of Arc, huh?"

"Don't laugh."

"Well, I guess I deserve some of the credit. I'm the one who fell in love with Anneka in the first place." He tossed his cigarette butt into the night. "It doesn't matter what it was, M.J. You did a kind thing."

He squeezed Mary Jane's shoulder before he went inside, and she folded her hands as if in prayer. She could hardly wait to tell Raynelle and Johanna the news.

Mina was safe.

She was home.

# THIRTY-FIVE

After the primary election in September, in which Clarence Morley handily won the Republican nomination for Governor, the Klan leased the entire second floor of the Brown Palace for its headquarters. Grand Dragon John Galen Locke's announced to the voters of Colorado: "We are not Democrats or Republicans, but Klansmen." And in the general election on November 5, Klan Republicans won every office in the state, save two, which were won by Klan Democrats.

As if 1924 hadn't been bad enough, the new year looked to Sean as if it would be worse.

As Christmas approached, he bought a parched, spindly evergreen tree from a street corner vendor and put it up in his room, its trunk stuck in a Mason's jar full of water. He invited Chava to come to his room at the boarding house to decorate it. As he parked the car, he said, "We need to be quiet. I'm not allowed female visitors anywhere but in the parlor."

"I don't want to cause trouble—"

"Oh, you won't. Mrs. Potter claims to be half-deaf, and she's more than that when she wants to be. She never hears the pipes groaning or the dogs barking in the yard or her own radio, which she plays louder than a train whistle. If we go two by two on the steps, like Noah's animals, she'll never know."

Chava's eyes flashed mischievously. Together, they crept up the dark, rickety stairs, Sean whispering bawdy tales about the other tenants as he went. More than once, Chava stopped dead, breathless, stifling her laughter with one hand.

On the third floor landing, Sean struggled to unlock the door in the near darkness of the windowless hall. "There was an overhead light," he whispered. "But it's been burnt out for about six months now." He flung open the door. "Welcome to the Taj-Mah-awful."

The light from the west-facing window illuminated the room's flaws. The delicate bouquets on the wallpaper had faded to gray, and the curtains were drab and frayed. A bed draped with a dull, woolen quilt consumed the tiny space, leaving only a narrow passage on either side. A pressboard bureau tucked against one wall beneath a low-hanging dormer, and a chair and table with radio, hot plate, coffee pot, and a week's worth of groceries crowded against the other. A warped shaving mirror hung over an antiquated washstand. The door of the closet stood ajar, one hinge bent. As Chava looked around, Sean noted with shame what his mother had always told him—he was not the neatest of fellows.

"Isn't this the worst place you've ever seen?" he whispered.

"Yes! Why do you live here?"

"It's cheap." He closed the door behind them and spoke in full voice. "Cheap enough so I can give my mother some help every month. And it's not so bad. The cockroaches aren't any bigger than small cats, and the bedbugs are polite enough to gnaw only at my ankles."

Chava snorted. "*Vi ir greytn di bet, azoy ir vet shlofn.*"

"What's that?"

"The way you prepare the bed, so shall you sleep."

"No wonder I'm awake half the night. *Voilà.*" Sean gestured toward the Christmas tree. "Here it is, soon to be a *pièce de résistance.*"

"It looks like it already resisted becoming a lovely tree."

Sean rummaged through a box of ornaments. "It just needs sparkle."

He tossed some icicle tinsel toward it, but the strands clumped on a branch.

Chava plucked up the wad and separated the icicles, gently hanging them one by one. "I had a friend in Brooklyn who celebrated Christmas. I was so jealous of her. She received the eight gifts of Hanukkah and Christmas packages as well. One year, I stole a glass bird from her Christmas tree. Its body was silver, and it had a real feather for a tail. I thought it the most beautiful treasure on earth. But when my father found it, I got a good lesson in the evils of stealing."

"I can imagine. I wouldn't have been able to sit down for a month."

"Oh, my father never used force on us. He was a talker, a very grave talker, who could make us question the meaning of life with a statement as simple as 'Pass the salt.' None of us wanted to do anything that would earn a lecture from him, because sometimes they continued for hours or even days, spread out between meals and with all sorts of parables and proverbs." She laughed. "I still miss him."

Sean encircled her with his arms. "Well, now I wonder if it was wise to ask you to help me. You just might swipe my tin foil Santa."

She picked up a string of popcorn and cranberries that Alice Colleen had made for his tree. Lifting it above their heads, she cast it around his neck, lassoing him. She pulled on it, drawing him closer to her, but the string broke. Cranberries spilled over the floor, while the popcorn bounced on the rug.

Chava put her hand over her mouth. "Oh, I'm sorry!"

Sean felt the poke of the popcorn against his back. "They went down my neck."

Laughing, Chava stood behind him and brushed at his collar. Popcorn fell to the floor.

"The cranberries rolled all the way down." He unbuttoned his shirt. "Can you find them?"

Standing behind him, she brushed at the spot where the shirt met his trousers. He twisted to watch her. The sun, shining through the window, touched off the auburn of her hair. It wasn't red—not like Kathleen's—but the deep, sweet color of chocolate. "I'll be chasing cranberries around this place for months to come," he said.

Chava's eyes sparked, with the sunlight from the window, with the joy of her own laughter. He thought of how, during the few minutes together they stole each night, he had become acutely aware of her body against his, the way her curves aligned with his, and the parts matched. Fully clothed, he had noted the swell of her breasts and felt the responsive pressure of her hips against his. Fully clothed, she had run her hands along his chest from his shoulders to his waist. They'd acted as lusty as teenagers who petted in cars on country roads.

He turned toward her, and her arms encircled his neck. She was all at once supple, yielding, and his body reacted immediately, swelling and throbbing.

"Touch me," she said.

Her words sent sparks through him. What a woman—to speak so plainly!

"Oh, Chava," he moaned. "The flesh is weak, and mine's no different—"

"It feels firm enough to me," she teased.

His laughter came out as a strangled hiccup.

She caught him unawares with a kiss—lips on lips, tongue on tongue, teeth. He pulled her closer, arching his hips against hers, pressing into her. Her body quivered, and he ran his hands over her back. Her dress was only a thin shift—easily removed. With his tongue, he sculpted the curve of her collarbone. She threw back her head and bared her throat. When he kissed it, she cried out with pleasure.

Sitting on the bed, he pulled her toward him and kissed the rise of her breasts, her ribs and her waist, nipping her slip into his mouth. He blew through the slick fabric onto her skin, which was softly scented with apricot.

"Sean, you . . . Sean," she whispered.

Slipping to the floor, he unbuckled her shoes, and she stepped from them. He traced a finger along the delicate embroidery that twined up her stockings. Unhooking her garters, he caressed the hosiery from her legs. As each inch of soft skin was revealed, he kissed it—bare thighs, knees, calves, ankles. It had been so long since he had done this, and never with a woman who stirred his blood the way Chava did. When he lifted his face, she covered his mouth with hers, her lips seeking his.

"Sean," she confessed. "I haven't ever—"

"It's all right. I know what to do." In France, he had learned how a man could use his fingers to make a woman cry out with passion long before he took his own pleasure, and how he could kiss the most private of places and bring her delight. Things a good Catholic boy would never have learned in America. "But are you sure?"

"Yes, yes, I am . . ."

"Then come here." He coaxed her onto the bed beside him, and they lay full-length, bodies pressed together. Her underthings floated away—slip, bra, garter belt—until she was naked. In the orange glow from the setting sun, he ran a finger between her breasts, then kissed her nipples. Reaching the wealth of hair between her thighs, he stroked with one gentle finger.

"Sean," she moaned. "Oh, Sean."

He pulled his undershirt over his head. Her mouth grazed the tender skin near his Adam's apple. Her fingers slid downwards, and she rubbed ticklish arcs around his nipples. With a rumble from deep within, he grabbed one of her hands and kissed it.

"Tell me what to . . . you know," she said.

"You're doing just fine on your own."

Shedding his trousers, he kissed her palms, wrists, neck and breasts, moving his hands over her, responding to her sighs.

She cast a leg across his waist, and he ran his hand down her thigh to her knee. Inhaling sharply, she whispered, "You must tell me how—"

"Not yet. It's more fun to take it slow. Let me show you."

Taking her hands in his, he taught her, what he wanted for himself. Her hands were soft and strong, unafraid and curious, against his firm flesh. He caressed her with his full hand, his finger slipping inside. She gasped, then covered his lips and tongue again with hers.

Heart of my heart, he thought. Oh, my love.


After they make love, Sean holds Chava, her head on his shoulder, her body against his, their legs entwined, their hands folded together. Night has fallen, and the only light in the room is from the street lamp outside. He kisses her forehead. "You're all right?" he whispers. "I didn't hurt you?"

"No, no, not so much."

"Did you like it?"

"Yes, I . . . Oh, Sean, I never thought it would be like this!"

He chuckles. "I didn't either." Then, he realizes that she is crying. Oh, God, what has he done? His smugness evaporates. "What's wrong?"

"I don't know," she chokes. "I'm happy, don't worry. I'm not sad. I just can't seem to stop the tears." She tries to laugh. "My mind, my thoughts—they're all confused."

"About what? You're not sorry you did this? I would never have done it, if you didn't want—"

"No, no, I'm not sorry. I wanted you. I want you. But I . . ." She buries her face against his neck. "I want so much more! How can I ever go home again, or sleep in my own bed, or look in the mirror, without wondering . . ."

"Wondering what?"

"Without wanting to be here with you. I feel like a piece of silver that has been tarnished for years and is suddenly rubbed clean and shining. I can't go back to being what I was. Don't you see?"

Her body shudders, and he can feel the dampness of fresh tears.

"I don't know," he confesses. "All I know is that I haven't been the same since the day I met you. And it isn't because I've thought of doing this—although I'm happy we did. It's the way you think, Chava. The way you talk—about everything, you know so much and you're so smart. You laugh at my jokes—which I know aren't all that funny. I've been so lonely, for so long, without you. What we've done isn't just, well, it isn't just what men and women do. It's sacred, I think, as sacred as anything I've ever known."

"I feel it, too."

The knowledge thrills him, exhilarates him, makes him braver and more certain than he's ever been before. He kisses her with newfound wisdom.

"Even before I knew you, I wanted you," she whispers. "Is that possible?"

"Anything's possible," he says. "Anything, just now."

# THIRTY-SIX

After Mass on Christmas morning, the Sullivan household was in a ruckus. Amid heaps of discarded wrapping paper, the Keohane children played with their new toys—books and a new doll for Alice Colleen; tops and Lincoln Logs for the twins; a set of alphabet blocks and a jack-in-the-box for Kieran. All of them talked at once—a phenomenon that Maggie had noticed was becoming a daily occurrence—and all of them wanted their grandmother to admire their new toys. Ma sat on the couch, a patient and loving saint to her grandchildren, while silent Pa rocked in his wooden chair. Liam had rolled into the parlor, parking his chair next to the Christmas tree. Again and again, he turned the crank of the jack-in-the-box for Kieran, who shrieked with delight every time Jack sprang out. The baby's—although not a baby, but nearly two—reactions made Liam laugh in a hearty way that Maggie rarely heard these days.

While everyone was distracted, Maggie sneaked into the kitchen. She hadn't had a smoke yet this morning, and the raw energy made her edgy. In the kitchen, she stopped abruptly. Seaney sat at the kitchen table, his elbows propped on it, his folded hands against his forehead, a cigarette poking out from between his fingers.

"What are you doing here so early?" Maggie asked.

He raised his head. "I couldn't sleep." As an afterthought, he added, "Merry Christmas."

"I suppose you don't get to say that much over on the West Side. You don't even have to worry that Santa and his reindeer might slide off the roof."

He didn't smile or reply.

Maggie fumbled in her apron for her cigarettes. "Come out with me on the landing. I don't smoke in the house. I don't like the children to see me."

"A bit hypocritical, isn't it?"

She stuck out her tongue at him—a reflex from childhood—and opened the door that led to the inside landing. The high-ceilinged, boxy store had no heat, and the cold struck Maggie as soon as they left the kitchen. She closed the door behind her to keep the warm air in the apartments. Seaney struck a match so that Maggie could light up. She took a deep breath, blew out a mouthful of smoke, and crossed her arms over her breasts to trap the heat of her body.

"Speaking of hypocrites, are you going to Kathleen's?" she asked.

"Mag," he scolded half-heartedly. "I don't know. Are you?"

"I wouldn't miss it. I have to wonder how many friends Jim has left after all his shenanigans before the election."

What a fuss Jim had caused, pulling out of the governor's race without a clear explanation. Denver's gossip mill had outdone itself scrutinizing it all, until, at last, someone had chanced upon the identity of a Swedish maid, Anneka Lindstrom, who had once worked at the elder Graves' home. After that, it was all about her—who she was, what had become of her, why it had taken so long for this to be public.

When Kathleen had brought Mina to visit the Sullivans, Alice Colleen had fallen in love at first sight with her sweet-faced, Nordic cousin—or half-cousin, or whatever she might be. For hours, she wrote letters to Mina, telling her all about her first grade class and her brothers and herself. For her part, Kathleen had acted nervous around the girl, trying too hard to include Mina in whatever Stephen and Susanna had gotten up to, although Mina was much too old to play with them. Worse, she encouraged the girl to talk about herself, which embarrassed Mina into a red-faced, stuttering state. Poor Kathleen—she tried to be mother, friend, and teacher all at once, and wasn't entirely successful at any of them.

"What do you think of their newly acquired daughter?" Maggie asked.

"Oh, she's pretty enough," Seaney conceded. "But those glasses lenses are so thick, they make her eyes look sort of like a wise, old owl."

"When she's here, she won't let Kathleen out of her sight. She acts terrified of the world."

"Well, since her daddy isn't governor and the Klan's got the state by the scruff of its neck, maybe she should be."

"My, aren't we sour on a bright Christmas morning?" When Maggie received no reply, she added, "I wish you had someone to bring over for the day."

Again, he was silent.

"What's wrong?" Maggie asked.

"There is someone," he said.

"Well, why didn't you invite her over for Mass and Christmas dinner?"

"Because—"

She waited, and then it dawned on her. "It's the Jewish girl, isn't it? The one who tanned your hide the first time you met. What was her name?"

"Chava," he said, with some sort of growl in his throat.

"I knew it! When you vowed never to speak to her again, I knew you'd fallen in love with her!"

"What am I going to do?"

"The question is—what aren't you going to do? If I said to you now, oh, she's evil, they're pagan, and she's bad for you, would you take my advice?"

"Brendan's already told me all that."

"He has? And did you do what he suggested?"

"No."

"Then I win." Maggie laughed again. "Or rather—you and Chava win. How does she feel about falling in love with a Catholic?"

"I don't know. We haven't really talked about it. I think—we both thought it was so unlikely that we would . . . you know."

"Attraction between a man and a woman is never unlikely, regardless of the circumstances. You know what Mrs. James would tell someone who wrote to me with this problem? She would say, love is love, and if you try to deny it, you'll just end up hurting yourself."

"That sounds so easy, but you aren't answering a letter from the newspaper. It's real, not just made up for—"

"My letters aren't just made up to sound good. I give sound advice."

"But I can't stop being Catholic any more than I can stop being Irish, or a man."

"But you can decide which part of you is most important. If it's Catholic, then that settles it—she's out of your life. If it's Irish, well, maybe she doesn't care. But if you start measuring things as a man, isn't your love for this woman the most important thing? If she returns your love, doesn't that overshadow everything else?"

"I don't know," he admitted. "I haven't been to Mass or confession since I talked to Brendan. She's taken me away from the Church, just like he warned me she'd do."

"Oh, poppycock," Maggie said. "Only you yourself can take you away from God or the Church. I'm married to the most ardent Catholic I've ever met. And you know what? I don't go to Mass or confession."

Seaney looked down into the empty, cavernous store. "Don't you listen to Mass when Brendan's here?"

"Well, yes, when I can. All I'm saying is, let Chava worship her God and you worship yours. And when you have children"—he opened his mouth to object, but she held up a finger to shush him—"let them choose what they want to be."

He mulled over the words. "Maybe that's it."

"Oh, so now my advice is real, not just made up?" she asked. "Are you sure that this isn't what you've been hoping someone would tell you?"

Seaney laughed sheepishly. From inside the apartments came the sound of an accordion and a deep male voice.

"Oh, Tony's here," he said.

She flashed him a cross look—how easily he had wriggled out of answering her. "You invited him for Christmas?" she asked. "Isn't this morning for family?"

"I didn't," he said. "Ma probably did."

"Or Alice Colleen." Maggie stubbed out her cigarette. "Neither one of them can resist his charms."

Nor could she. Whenever Tony visited, Maggie found herself making excuses to sit in the parlor and listen to him talk. She liked the way he kept his hands neatly folded in his lap when he spoke, as if he were still an altar boy. His manners, which he would probably claim had been beaten into him by his Mamma, were impeccable.

Seaney and she returned to the kitchen, and Seaney opened the door to the parlor. Tony's hands worked the concertina as he sang "Silent Night" in Italian. Pa and Liam were still in the room, but all eyes were on Tony. The boys and Ma snuggled onto the sofa cushions like so many bunnies, while Alice Colleen sat on the arm. One of Ma's hands held Alice Colleen's, their fingers entwined.

"If you were Irish, you'd be as good as John McCormick," Ma said when he finished.

"Yeah, but I'm Italian, so it's Caruso," Tony said.

"Oh, that's just silly. Give me a Merry Christmas kiss."

Tony bent down and kissed her cheek.

"Jealous yet?" Maggie asked Seaney as Tony favored Alice Colleen with a kiss, and then the boys, who promptly wiped them off. "Ma never asks for a kiss from either one of us."

Seaney laughed—at last—and Maggie caught a flash of Liam's glasses lenses. He watched Maggie as she watched Tony. With a twitch, she stepped back into the kitchen. She never spoke of Tony to Liam, and now that the make-believe exchange with the dog—Perching—had ended, there had been no more incidents where the kids grew too loud, laughing at his stunts.

Around noon, she set the last of the hot dishes on the table. Ma and Pa took seats at the head and foot of the table, with Alice Colleen happily seated between Tony and Sean on one side, and Frankie and Declan on either side of Liam on the other. Maggie carved out a corner for herself next to Kieran. After grace, the conversation turned to chitchat, while the kids interrupted at regular intervals. Funny, Maggie thought, the number of topics that they avoided: Seaney's work on the West Side; Kathleen's troubles; her new stepdaughter; Jim's fall from grace; Maggie's role as Mrs. James; the inanity of the Ku Klux Klan.

As the mashed potatoes rounded the table the second time, Tony asked, "Where did you serve in the war, Mr. James?"

Liam paused, his fork lifted halfway to his mouth. Maggie dropped the biscuit that she was offering to Kieran in her lap.

"Daddy didn't fight in the war," Alice Colleen volunteered. "He was in prison."

"Alice Colleen!" Maggie scolded.

Calmly, Liam said, "That's right. I was sentenced to twenty-five years hard labor at the federal penitentiary in Ft. Leavenworth. And my surname is not James. It's Keohane. I'm Liam Keohane."

Quizzically, Tony looked at Seaney, who had taken an intense interest in the ham on his plate. Ma brought a napkin to her lips, while Pa's face grew rawer. When Tony's eyes met hers, Maggie busied herself with taking a glass of milk from Kieran's hands.

"You may have read about me in the newspapers," Liam continued. "I refused to report to the induction center for the army on humanitarian grounds. The draft falls hardest on the man who is simply trying to make a decent living, such as yourself or myself—I was a bookkeeper for a railroad. It pulls working men into conflicts in which they have no interest, but which are engineered by the titans and rulers of the world for their own gain. It separates man from wife, and father from child. It abuses men by forcing them to be what they are not."

"I don't know nothing about that," Tony said. "I signed up to go."

"I also refused to fight on religious grounds. I believe that God's word is the ultimate law, and that the Sixth Commandment should be followed above all man-made dictates. War enacts the worst barbarism. It is the pinnacle of lawlessness."

Maggie wondered if Tony—with his rough knowledge of English—had caught all of Liam's fifty-cent words.

"They said that God was on our side," Tony said. "We prayed before we fought, and we'd go to Mass when we got out of the trenches. My priest said we should all go and fight for this country, if we wanted to live here."

"Many Catholic priests took that line of argument, as the Church deemed the war a 'just war.' But there were hundreds of us who saw it differently."

"And so they all went to prison?"

"No, most agreed to do non-combatant work for the military. But there were four of us who were Catholic and would not assist in the war. In prison, we were tortured because we would not submit. We were beaten and deprived of the most basic of necessities. I was called a coward and a slacker, although I was neither."

"It woulda been easier to go to war."

"Yes, it would have," Liam agreed. "And for thirty dollars a month, I could have slaughtered my fellow man, as you and Sean did."

Sean started. "Hey!"

"I killed Germans," Tony said. "I did what I was supposed to do."

Liam smiled. "As did I."

"Stop it, both of you," Ma said. "This is Christmas, the children—"

Tony stood. "I'm sorry, Bella Signora Sullivan, Mrs. James. Thank you for the food, but I'll go home now."

He retrieved his coat and left. After the thump of his feet on the metal steps outside faded, silence fell over the family. Pa lit a cigarette, while Seaney picked at his food. Maggie burned with anger—why were men so arrogant? When she caught Liam's gaze, she swore he looked triumphant.

"He left his music box," Alice Colleen said. "Can I go give it to him?"

The concertina lay on the coffee table, a reminder of happier moments.

"Uncle Seaney will give it to him later," Maggie snapped. "Now, eat your food before it's cold."

Alice Colleen sulkily obeyed, but the silence lasted through the rest of the meal. Once the kids had gone back to their new toys, Seaney helped

Maggie carry the plates into the kitchen. He set Tony's plate, which still mounded with food, aside, as if Tony might come back to claim it.

"Why did Tony say that about killing Germans?" She launched the question at Seaney. "Alice Colleen listens to everything he says—she worships him—and he just spilled it all out for her and the boys to hear."

"Liam didn't have any qualms about saying that he'd been tortured in prison."

"Oh, don't even make that comparison—"

"Why not? He never stops going on about it, telling us how much he suffered during the war. Tell that to the men who were at Belleau Woods or Chateau-Thierry."

"Why does everything come back to the war?" she demanded. "I hated it when it happened—when it stripped me of my husband and we lost the store—and I hate it now."

"I didn't start this fight," Seaney said. "And I'm not going to finish it for you."

He left the kitchen, slamming the door to the store behind him. Maggie picked up Tony's plate and dumped the congealed food into the slop bucket, scraping so hard at the plate that she scored lines across it. Why did he think he could disrupt this family again and again? He had wormed his way into their lives with his Italian charm and wit and his silly games with the kids, and he made Ma blush—at her age!—when he called her Bella Signora Sullivan.

Maggie stopped, out of breath. She wished she'd never met him.

She ignored the voice in her heart that responded immediately: That's not true.

That evening, after all the kids are finally settled down enough to sleep, Maggie retreats to her bedroom. Since Kieran has started sleeping through the night, his crib is no longer in his parents' bedroom, but in a corner of Alice Colleen's room. Liam lies in bed, reading. With her back to Liam, she sits on the edge of the bed to remove her shoes.

"I think we should pray for Sean's friend," Liam says. "He believed all the propaganda that our government used to make men into its puppets."

Maggie places her shoes next to the nightstand. "He seems to be doing fine on his own."

"His soul is sadly disturbed by his actions during the war."

Maggie cannot argue that. Silently, she unclips her stockings from her garters and folds them carefully. "Let's see if we can move this next year." She turns toward Liam. "Back to a house like we had when we were first married—"

"Move? Isn't Sean building a house for your parents?"

"It will never be finished, as slow as they are. Maybe I could get a better job for more money, with the *Post* or the *Rocky Mountain News*, one of the bigger papers. And if you could take a few accounts, do some bookkeeping from home. You wouldn't need to go to an office. I bet Judah would help. He'd find some clients for you—"

"Why do you always talk about moving whenever you are upset?"

"I'm not upset, I'm just tired. If it was just you and me, and we had our own things, and—"

"It will never be the two of us again. We have children."

"That's not what I mean. I've lived here my whole life, and I'm raising our children exactly as my mother raised us. I cook on the same stove, I fill up the same old copper bath that Seaney and I used, I'm doing everything just as Ma did it. I want to have my own place, and—"

"What about finishing my book?"

"Maybe it's time to let it go. Maybe it's time for all of us to move past the war and think about the future—"

"I am thinking about the future," he says. "The 'War for Democracy' was won, the 'War to End All Wars' was won. Yet what do you see? Is the world at peace? Is militarism crushed? The English keep an army the size of our American Expeditionary Force in Ireland. America puts men in irons for speaking out for labor laws and human rights. No true democracy would do that."

Maggie pulls her slip over her head. She unhooks her brassiere and dons her nightgown.

"I nearly died, Maggie," Liam says. "I thought I would never see you or Alice Colleen again. Would you think me a better man if I'd joined Tony and Sean in their lust for killing?"

"Why do you call it lust?"

"After Tony's remarks today, what else could I call it? How can a man kill another and then cradle his own baby in his blood-soaked arms?"

Tony, so gentle and playful with her children. Seaney, so sweet and insecure in his love for Chava.

"I want to live honestly," she says. "Not hidden away, not pretending—"

"I'm not the one who is keeping you from living 'honestly,'" he protests. "You are. You've become so worldly, so divorced in some ways from the Church and from me."

"What are you talking about?"

"Your writing, your dealings with the newspaper, and all this talk of moving. It interferes with your family and faith. You use a false name, and you spend half the night in the shed, and the advice you give ignores God, it neglects your faith."

"It puts food on the table."

"That's temporal, a matter of the present. I'm talking about your soul."

"I don't have time to think about my soul," she says wearily. "Now I need to go to sleep. I'm tired."

She lies down, rolling away from Liam. She can feel him beside her, festering, as if the words inside are pushing against the pores of his skin.

But if he hasn't yet spoken his piece, then neither has she. Thinking of the spiritual is a luxury. Only those few who can remove themselves from the messiness of life—priests, nuns, Liam—are well served by it. The rest of us just have to slog through it all.

# THIRTY-SEVEN

"Here are my precious grandchildren! Merry Christmas, my dears!"

Stephen and Susanna skipped across the floor to their grandmother, who reigned over the Christmas day celebration from the tastefully decorated parlor of her home. She embraced both of them, her face snugged between their heads, her eyes closed. Once the hug ended, Susanna sat beside Victoria, while Stephen ran to the Christmas tree, where a model train chugged along an oval track.

"Is this mine?" he asked, as his nursemaid, Miss Brown, slipped silently across the room to tend to him.

"If you want it," Victoria said airily. "There are other gifts over there for you and your sister as well."

At that, Susanna bounced from the divan to join Stephen.

Mina stood to the left of Kathleen, about two steps behind, ready to hide. Kathleen turned to her and placed a hand on her shoulder, urging her forward. Mina took one step, but stalled again. Kathleen moved behind the girl, steadying Mina in front of her with a hand on each of her shoulders. Entering behind his family, Jim sought a space near the window of the room.

Victoria addressed Kathleen. "Merry Christmas, Kathleen, Mina, Jim."

"Merry Christmas," Kathleen replied.

Everyone stared—Victoria, Arthur, Thomas and Ellie, the Crawfords and the Fallowses. The blame for Mina's tumultuous reappearance in Jim's life had, as she had expected, fallen on Kathleen. It hadn't mattered that John Galen Locke had been deprived of breaking the scandal for the benefit of the Klan, for Denver's newspapers had had a feast anyway with the collapse of Jim's political career, chalking up Anneka Lindstrom as just another poor, working girl exploited by a wealthy baron.

No one knew that Mina's homecoming had been Jim's decision.

The evening that he had come home from the Brown Palace, after quitting the race for governor, he had come to Kathleen's room. Stephen and Susanna had long been in bed, and Kathleen sat in an armchair, reading.

"I will be bringing Mina here on Monday," he had announced.

"For good?" Kathleen asked. "Or simply as a transition?"

"She'll live here."

"And they will have no claim on her?"

"They will have no claim on or contact with her."

It was odd, the elation that had come over Kathleen. As Jim explained that he would send his lawyer to fetch Mina, she had been struck by how stripped down and aged he looked without his customary crutch of cigarette or brandy or his glittering friends. He appeared to be a man who had burned bright at one time but whose glory days had passed.

After he had told her the details, he added, "I hope this satisfies your conditions."

Kathleen ignored the jab. "Send Mary Jane to get her."

"Miss Grayson?"

"Mina will be terrified if a stranger comes to take her away. She trusts Mary Jane."

After he agreed, she had thought, See, things in this world can be made right. Things can be changed.

Whether things had changed for the better could still be debated. Mina could be in a room and never be noticed; she could be at the dinner table, or in the sitting room, or in her own room and never make a sound. Stephen and Susanna had accepted her without much question, and Kathleen worried that they thought of Mina as just another servant or employee. She had explained that Mina was their sister, returned after a long absence, but that information, too, had failed to move them. Perhaps they were just too young to feel threatened or jealous, which was a relief, but they also showed no signs of affection for Mina.

After fitting Mina with glasses from the optician's, Jim had hired a tutor to come to the Graves' home to teach her, with the hope that she would catch up to her grade level. Kathleen had glimpsed Mina's literary curiosity—which Mary Jane swore was legendary—one afternoon, when she discovered the girl in Jim's study.

Prowling next to the bookcases filled with Jim's collections of leather-bound first editions, Mina had trailed her hand along the books, stopping now and then to rub a finger across the gold lettering on the bindings. At the ladder that allowed access to the upper shelves, she climbed up two rungs to stroke the spines as if they were pets.

"What are you looking for?" Kathleen asked.

Mina jumped and nearly fell from the ladder. "Mrs. Kathleen!"

"I'm sorry," Kathleen said. "I should have warned you that I was here. Miss Mary Jane said you used to read quite a lot."

Mina nodded without speaking.

"But you stopped reading at Miss Judith's house? Why?"

"She said the only true books were the Bible and those written by Bishop White. She said that made-up stories are sinful."

"Is that what you think?"

"My mother used to read made-up books. And you read them to your children."

"Yes, I read them to your brother and sister. I think we can learn from made-up stories as well as from the Bible. A story set in India, like Mr. Kipling's books, can teach us about that place."

Mina eyed the books on the shelves again.

"These books belong to your father," Kathleen said. "They're about oil and law and history. But we can find books that would be more interesting for you to read. Would you like that?"

"I had a book about a nurse in France named Valerie." Mina's voice was little more a whisper. "I lost it when I moved to Miss Judith's house. Miss Mary Jane gave it to me. I read it to my mother, when she was sick." She touched another spine. "I could learn about the war, where you were, that way."

Mina's blatant offer to please her had touched Kathleen's heart. "Let's see if we can find out the name of the book from Miss Mary Jane. She'll probably remember. There's a bookstore downtown called Pratt's where we might be able to buy it."

Mina had easily accepted that Jim was her father. With only Kathleen present, Jim had told Mina the truth.

"I know," Mina had said.

"How do you know?" Jim asked. "Who told you?"

"Mother did," she said. "She always said that you took care of us the way a father did his children."

"Why didn't you tell Miss Judith that you knew your father's name?" Kathleen asked.

"I told her that Mr. Yeem was my father, but she said that wasn't a proper name and that lying was a sin. So I stopped."

Kathleen's heart had broken at the words. Poor Mina, poor unloved Mina.

Equally troubling as Mina's losses were the things she kept. Despite Miss Davis' constant warnings that catastrophic infection would result from Mina's proximity to Marta, Mina carried the doll around the house and slept with her in her bed. The girl was too old for dolls—that much Kathleen acknowledged—and she didn't actually play with the doll. But Marta was nearly always with her, as if the doll were her own shadow.

Kathleen's offer of a new doll had been resoundingly dismissed.

"May I keep Marta?" Mina had asked.

"Your new doll won't be broken and dirty. She'll have two eyes, and pretty, clean hair. We can put Marta where you know where she is."

"I don't want to put Marta away."

Kathleen supposed that Marta was the only semblance of stability that Mina had. For better and for worse, the doll had accompanied her through her mother's death, to her years settling and resettling with the Dercums, and now, to her father's home.

When Marta was unavailable, as she was now, Mina followed Kathleen. Kathleen had taken the girl shopping for new clothes, although Mina seemed too afraid to choose, making it Kathleen's decision, and she had taken the girl for tea at the Denver Dry Goods' Russian Room. They had been to movies—*Peter Pan* and the most recent films starring Buster Keaton or Harold Lloyd. While Stephen and Susanna giggled, Mina barely smiled. The girl had yet to walk beside, rather than behind, Kathleen.

Jim certainly wasn't helping the situation. His initial joy in seeing Mina had faded into an aloofness that wasn't cruel, but wasn't entirely kind. He asked about her, but he made no move to spend time with her. Then again, since the humiliation of the election, he had not spent much time with Stephen and Susanna either.

At Victoria and Arthur's house, Mina sat beside Kathleen on the sofa. She folded her hands in her lap, clenching them so tightly that the skin almost immediately drained of blood. Kathleen laid her hand on top of them, rubbing lightly to relieve the tension.

"This is for you, Mina." With a tight smile, Victoria handed the girl a wrapped present.

Everyone in the room watched Mina unwrap the present. Inside were a selection of daintily-constructed lace collars. Gently, Mina sifted through them, carefully studying the colors, which ranged from pristine white to fanciful red and yellow flowers.

"Thank you," she said in a small voice.

"Those are lovely," Kathleen said. "Would you like to wear one now? I'll fasten it for you."

Mina chose the white collar, and Kathleen fixed it around the girl's neck, then fussed with it until it hung evenly across her rose-colored dress.

"You look beautiful," Kathleen said. "Would you like to see yourself? There's a mirror in the powder room—"

Mina shook her head fervently, and Kathleen wondered if Judith Dercum taught her that looking at herself in a mirror was vanity. It would not surprise Kathleen to hear that Judith had told Mina she was ugly as well as stupid.

Thankfully, the attention of the guests moved from Mina and Kathleen to a conversation about actors and actresses in the moving pictures. Gloria Swanson, Marion Davies, Valentino, the Barrymores, Jackie Coogan. Relieved, Kathleen took no part in it. Mina nervously rubbed the lace collar between her thumb and index finger until Kathleen was afraid she would snag the fine tatting.

Suddenly, Stephen burst through the room. "Daddy! Look at this!"

Close on Stephen's heels, Susanna echoed, "Loo'! Daddy! Loo'!'"

"Stephen, Susanna," Kathleen scolded. "You've interrupted your grandmother and her friends. Please apologize."

"I'm sorry, Grandmother," Stephen said, while Susanna echoed, "Sowy, Gamudda."

"What is it?" Jim asked.

"Look through the marble. Everything's upside down."

"Up-sye down," Susanna mimicked.

Jim took the marble from Stephen and held it up to the light.

"Would you like to look?" Kathleen urged Mina. "You can go over there."

Mina slid from the sofa and more or less tiptoed across the room. Jim had squatted down so that both Stephen and Susanna could look through the marble. Mina stood at his shoulder.

"Why does it do that, Daddy?" Stephen asked.

"It's the way the light shines through the glass," he said. "Think about light as an arrow flying through the air. The light is free—you can't touch it—but the marble is glass. When the light hits the glass, it can't fly freely anymore. So it bends."

"It's called refraction," Mina said.

A look passed among the adults. Victoria raised her eyebrows, while Thomas muttered, "Hear, hear." Eleanora kept a critical eye on Mina, while Kathleen felt pride. Immediately she chastised herself: as if Mina were a product of her mothering, as if she had the faintest clue what the girl wanted or felt or knew. But she felt vindicated somehow, as if the evidence of Mina's intelligence justified the battle to bring her into the Graves' home.

"Let's go find more," Stephen grabbed Mina's hand. "Come on!"

Stephen dragged Mina toward the corner where the games and gifts were spread across the floor. "Come on, come on!"

Susanna took Mina's other hand. Mina looked toward Kathleen, who nodded. The three ran to the corner to play.

Mrs. Crawford laughed. "I'm certainly glad you know what you're talking about, Jim. We could all do with a science lesson."

"I don't know what I'm talking about," he said. "My daughter does."

Kathleen took in a sharp breath. If he smiled now, if he laughed, if he played the remark as a jest, everyone would follow his example. The tension would break, and the curious and judgmental eyes would land more softly on poor Mina. She would not be seen as the ruination of the man, but as his validated and true offspring.

But Jim dropped the marble in the pocket of his jacket and stalked off into the adjoining library. He would sit in there, Kathleen knew, with his cigarettes and flask of brandy until it was time to go in for dinner.

Victoria said cheerfully, "Oh, my, have you heard the recording of 'Rhapsody in Blue' by the Paul Whiteman Orchestra? It's so very disjointed—as if the composer starts on one idea, then switches to another without thinking it through—"

Mrs. Crawford took over. "I read that the score wasn't even ready to orchestrate—which is evidently very hard—until a week before the premiere. George Gershwin made up the piano parts on the fly, and at one point, he just nodded to let the orchestra know that his solo had ended."

"Isn't that how jazz is supposed to sound?" Eleanora commented. "As if the composer hadn't made up his mind what he wanted to play."

Everyone laughed and marveled at Gershwin's extraordinary talent.

Later that night, after they have returned home, after the children are sleeping, after the servants have left for their lodgings, Kathleen tosses and turns in her bed, her anger still roiling.

She dons a heavy velvet gown and goes down the stairs to the silent main floor. She taps on the door of Jim's study, then enters without waiting for an answer. Jim sits at his desk in darkness. The tip of his lit cigarette glows, the brightest object in the room. Beside him is a glass of brandy.

"What is it?" He clicks on the Tiffany lamp on his desk.

She sits in the chair that faces his desk. "We need to talk about today."

"Did you not get what you wanted for Christmas?"

She waves aside the insult, but her words tumble out. "If you would just treat Mina like you do Stephen and Susanna, everything would change. Your mother, your father, the others—they wouldn't stare at her like she's some Eskimo or Comanche that's been put on public display—"

"Good Lord, Kathleen—"

"They wouldn't pretend that she isn't in the room or that she doesn't exist."

"She did quite well making herself known today, with her smart answer."

"And you didn't even acknowledge it! You didn't tell her that she was right and ask her to tell us more. If Stephen would have said it was a magical pony making the light, you would have praised him for his imagination."

"Your imagination is certainly running at full speed tonight."

Kathleen whips out of her chair. "I don't understand why you brought Mina home if you weren't going to care for her any more than Andy and Judith Dercum did. Oh, yes, she doesn't have to scrub the floors anymore, but she is no more loved here than she was there."

"You seem to have established a relationship with her."

"This has nothing to do with me! You told me you loved her when she was a child and her mother was alive. You were even willing to marry her mother—"

"What else would you have me do, Kathleen? My reputation, my career, my prospects, the respect others had for me—everything is in shambles."

"Then rebuild them. Stand up and say, Mina is my daughter, and she is to be respected as any other child of the Graves family would be. She is a beautiful, smart girl, Jim, and she needs someone—besides me, a complete stranger—to tell her that. If only you would—"

"If only I would! If only I would have told you before we married, if only I would have found her before the Dercums did, if only I would have brought her home years ago—and it isn't only you. From Ellie and my mother, I hear, if only you could have controlled Kathleen, if only she wouldn't have become involved—"

"You have always had more power than the rest of us. It isn't only political or in public. Whatever you say in this family is regarded as the way it is. Use it to make them accept Mina, as they should have done years ago."

He says nothing, and Kathleen grasps at the opportunity. "I'm glad to take care of Mina. I like her, she's a lovely girl. But you have to care for her as well. Take her for a walk, show her your cars, or teach her to play golf at the Country Club." She gestures toward the bookshelves that rise above her head. "Show her the books in here. I've already found her looking at them, she's fascinated by them. She would love the attention from you."

He fiddles with his glass of brandy. "Every time I look at her, I see—"

"Anneka," Kathleen supplies. "Why shouldn't you? She is beautiful and graceful and intelligent—all the things I've heard about her mother. Why shouldn't that be a thing of joy?"

"I never should have left her. I never should have trusted my mother." He takes a gulp of brandy. "I knew—I knew!—on the day I went to talk to her that she had no intention of seeing to Anneka. She and my father were on their way to Inglesfield, and I knew she wouldn't come back to Denver or send anyone down the mountain to check on them. I knew I shouldn't go, but the choice was impossible—you and Ellie or Anneka and Mina."

Kathleen lets the words echo through the study before she says, "But you've been given a second chance. You can't undo the past, but you can right some of the wrong by loving Mina as you'd once planned to do—"

"How do I face her? The deprivations she's suffered are my fault."

"She doesn't realize that, and it's unfair of you to distance yourself from her for reminding you of Anneka or of your mother's negligence. You can free both yourself and Mina from the past by creating an entirely new family, one that accepts her, that doesn't judge her, or tell her she's—"

"Good Lord, you sound like a revival preacher. I don't want to talk about this any longer."

"Think about what I said, please, just think—"

"Goodnight."

She leaves the study. In her own bedroom, she lies alone in the bed. She isn't sure if she made any headway—she's never sure any longer—or if the matter will somehow twist away into something entirely different.

She rolls over and turns out the light.

And so, Christmas passes.

# THIRTY-EIGHT

Late on New Year's Day, Paul sat before the blazing fire in Julia's parlor. A drawing of a lighthouse—primitive but with some sense of structure and color—lay on the cushion beside him. In his hand, he held a letter that he had received only a few days before from Mélisande. Written in her not-quite-native English, it read:

Mon Cher Paul,

Joyeux Noël et bonne année!

I am wishing you the best, etc., and hope that you are well. Alex misses you and has asked when you might come back to France. I have told him that I don't know. When you write, would you please answer his question? If you have no thoughts of returning, it is kindest to let him know.

My sister and I are in Paris for the holidays, but do you know? They have turned the Palais de Glace into a dancing hall where the crowds go nightly to learn the tango, with poorly-washed men treading on one's feet and nearly cracking a girl's spine with the dips. There's some truth to the accusation that Mr. and Mrs. Castle's dancing lessons are a menace to our society. I've had four pairs of my best silken slippers ruined by oafs who've no business dancing the waltz much less the tango or any other dance that requires coordination of the limbs. My goodness, the Black Bottom leaves them in knots.

It is snowing here and quite cold. It reminds me of the time that I went ice dancing on the pond in the Bois de Boulogne. Do you remember it? The police came and told everyone to be gone, but we just laughed and kept on, even as they whistled and shouted that we would be taken away to the jail. We had been through the war, and nothing scared us.

Paul remembered that night well. Despite the bitter cold, Mélisande had been determined to skate on a pond in the woods. They had bundled Alex into as many warm clothes as they could find, and they carried with them heaps of blankets. At the pond, Mélisande had donned her skates and stepped onto the ice. Her skating was nothing like the others who circled the pond, arms flailing, grabbing onto each other for balance. She glided across the ice as if she skated on a daily basis, or as if she were a dancer from the ballet or the Folies Bergère. While the others clomped around the corners of the oval, she stroked past them, one dainty foot crossed over the other to make a seamless arc. She twirled, she spun, she leaped and landed as gracefully as if she were in bare feet.

Giggling, Alex had said, "*Maman est belle,*" and Paul had agreed, "*Oui, très belle.*"

Her cheeks were rosy red in the light from the flaming torches that lined the shore of the pond. Her dark hair streamed out from beneath her beret, and her full skirts flowed as she moved. Paul believed—he still believed today—that this was the girl Mélisande had been before the war. Daring but not yet cutthroat, desirable but not yet abused, bold but not yet jaded. She was joyful, happy, carefree and careless.

The *gendarmes* had arrived soon after, whistles round their necks, to drive the skaters away.

"*Il n'est pas sûr,*" the officers shouted. "*La glace est trop mince.*"

It isn't safe. The ice is too thin.

Many of the skaters cleared the ice, grumbling but cooperative, but Mélisande stood with hands on hips, unmoving. One of the police officers lumbered onto the ice, guiding off the more recalcitrant skaters, his street shoes slipping beneath him. Mélisande waited until he had nearly reached her, then skated at a speed Paul had not yet witnessed toward the dark, foreboding center of the pond. The officer yelled at her to stop, while his partner waded onto the ice, his arms spread for balance. He took frantic steps in one place, à la Buster Keaton, as his feet went out from under him. Laughter filled the park as Mélisande carved elegant figure eights near the center of the pond.

"Are you going to go catch her?" the spectators shouted in French. "Do you have the nerve to chase her? You can't even walk, you fat fools, slipping and falling!"

Mélisande wheeled around and made her way back in a graceful, unhurried serpentine. As she approached the *gendarme* who still stood on the ice, she reached out and touched his cheek, without slowing or altering her movements.

Alex had laughed happily as his mother stepped onto the snowy bank and made her way to the place where she had left her shoes. The crowd shouted "Bravo! Bravo!" as the police officers waddled off the ice and disappeared, evidently too embarrassed to pursue the matter.

"What did you think?" Mélisande asked. *"Que penses-tu? Am I not glorious? Am I not a sylph of the night?"*

That evening, after Alex was asleep, Mélisande had come to Paul, still the fairy, the sprite, the siren, and they had made love in a way that had belied their ramshackle relationship. Desire, passion, an inkling of love—it was one of their happier moments.

Now, warmed by the fire in Julia's parlor, he continued reading the letter:

*I suppose I should not dwell on what once was. Those days seem far away now. We shall be returning to Marseille after the first of the year, and Alex and I will be home with my parents again. You would find me changed, if you were to come here. I am different from the one you knew, more serious, I think, and more of a woman, although I would still skate on thin ice! So you see, I am not completely dull and old.*

*I hope you enjoy Alex's drawing of the lighthouse at Marseille, as he labored over it for some time. Perhaps you can overlook the places where he nearly dug holes through the paper with an eraser in his hopes of getting it right for you. But, of course, I know you will be kind.*

*Mille Baisers,*

*Mélisande*

A thousand kisses. She had never before used that phrase to close her letters; usually she offered abstract affection or fondness. These words signified romance. Even the effort Mélisande had made to write the letter in English, instead of tossing it off in her florid French, seemed unusual to him.

He laid the letter aside and turned his thoughts closer to home. Earlier today, Kathleen had stopped by to visit Julia.

"Happy New Year," she said as she came into the house. "I have presents for you and Julia—cookies and candies that Mina helped me to bake yesterday."

He had kissed her cheek. "Julia will be disappointed she missed you. She's visiting across town."

"I've missed her? I'm sorry. I should have called ahead." But even as she spoke, Kathleen's face lightened, with recognition of the possibilities, a flame of desire, a flicker of unbridled sensuality.

He opened his arms, and Kathleen stepped into them. Closing his eyes, Paul breathed in her scent and warmth before she lifted her face for a kiss. He ran a finger across her lower lip. "I've missed you."

"I've been almost afraid to come here."

"Afraid? For me, this is a moment of sweetness, a gift."

"I vowed not to do this . . . not to come to you again. But I love you so. I want you so."

"And I vowed I would honor your decision." He kissed her forehead. "And I will."

She laughed nervously as they sat together on the divan. "But will I?"

"How are things at home?" he asked.

"Silent, broken, weary. Christmas was strained, although I did my best to keep the children happy."

"And were they?"

"Stephen and Susanna were, but Mina . . ." Her voice trailed away, and she turned to face him. "Is there such as thing as being too obedient? I long to hear her say 'no' just once to something I ask her to do. I almost want her to throw a tantrum—a broken glass or something would be good—or slam the door to her room. Am I crazy to want that?"

"You've always been a rebel, my girl of the Wild West."

She laughed. "What about Alex? Are he and his mother still in Marseille?"

"They were in Paris for the holidays, but they'll be going back to Marseille soon."

"Don't you want to see him again? Isn't your life empty without him?"

"Of course." Paul realized that she was speaking of her own children. "But it wasn't the same with Mélisande and me as it is for you and Jim and your children. We never formalized our relationship. In true French spirit, we never made it binding. And, of course, I'm not Alex's father."

"But aren't you? In the same way that I've taken over being Mina's mother, you were raising Alex to be a good and kind man someday."

"His mother had other ideas."

"But I'm afraid . . ." She began again. "This isn't enough, Paul. Cuddling on the couch when your aunt is gone, as if we are children. Seeing each other now and then at parties or political rallies. It isn't enough for me, and I doubt if it's enough for you, even though you're good enough to say it is. You've been here for a year, and nothing has changed. But I can't offer you more."

It was true. How much longer could he go on loving a woman who could never be his? But he had come here for her, even though he had known that it was unlikely they would be together.

"Do you want me to leave Denver?" he asked.

Her eyes filled with tears. "I don't know what I want. I'm trapped by my own beliefs. I believe in marriage, in family and children, but I also believe in everlasting, perfect love, like we had in France. It paralyzes me, makes me unable to settle down or to act."

He kissed her forehead. "I'm a patient man. I'll wait."

"I would never ask you to do that, Paul. You need to know that I want you to be happy."

"Right now, I only want you."

They had spent the rest of the afternoon together, with Kathleen's head in the hollow of Paul's shoulder and his arms wrapped around her. If this was all she could offer, he would make the most of it.

Later, when she left, Paul had walked her outside. The snow fell in heavy, wet flakes that lofted on the ground and weighted the branches of the towering spruce near the house. The night smelled fresh and damp, the sounds of the city beyond Park Hill muffled by the snow into comforting silence.

Kathleen held out gloved hands to catch the snow. "Oh, isn't this beautiful?"

From behind, Paul wrapped his arms around her and kissed at the snowflakes that landed on her cheeks. "It looks as if we'll have a white winter here as well," he said.

She turned to face him. "As well?"

"Perhaps I should say, again."

As Kathleen had driven away, Paul had realized that he had been thinking of Paris when he had spoken. Of a pond in the Bois de Boulogne, and an apartment above a *charcuterie* on the Rue de Raspail, and Alex playing with an army of cast iron soldiers in Napoleonic uniform.

And Mélisande, drinking too much, smoking too much, wanting too much, and skating on ice that was no thinner than the ice that Paul was skating on here in Denver.

The Ku Klux Klan anointed 1925 by sponsoring a nine-day boxing and wrestling tournament at Cotton Mills Stadium. Word had it that no hoods or robes were to be donned. There was no longer any need for concealment. The Klan was in charge of the city and the state.

At the Denver District Attorney's office, Paul's colleague, Charlie Hague, read from a copy of the *Denver Express*: "Governor Clarence Morley stated: 'In times of trouble the Almighty always sends some men to lead us. God sent us George Washington when we needed a leader in our struggle with England. God sent us Abraham Lincoln to preserve the union. And God has sent us John Galen Locke to lead our city out of its terrible condition of chaos and trouble.'" Charlie rattled the paper as he lowered it. "Oh, my, it sounds as if our new Governor has a love crush on his boss."

"'Every Man under the Dome a Klansman,'" Paul said, repeating the slogan that Governor Morley had chosen for his administration.

Charlie glanced toward the corner office, where the new District Attorney, Foster Cline, was in the process of setting up shop. "Yeah, and maybe in this office, too."

Paul followed Charlie's gaze. The transition between Philip Van Cise, who had despised the Klan, and D.A. Cline, who had been elected with its support, had left everyone in the office uncertain of their futures. Most of the time, they pretended to be busy, hoping they would not be fired.

"But, take heart," Charlie continued. "The eminent Colonel Van Cise left us a parting present." He handed Paul a file. "So, on January 6, Grand Dragon Locke and six others kidnap a boy named Keith Boehm. Kid's nineteen and goes to East High School. They take him to Locke's office and set him up to marry a girl who's eight months gone. The kid's saying now that Locke forced him to marry her at gunpoint."

"Is that so?" Paul leafed through the folder. "He's willing to testify against Locke, then?"

"He says they threatened to castrate him. That'd make me run like hell." Charlie shook his head. "Who knows whose baby it is? The kid says Locke told him he was only helping him to 'do the manly thing.' My guess is that it was somebody else's 'manly thing' that did the damage in the first place."

Paul laughed. "So what happens now?"

Charlie waved a folded letter. "I have an arrest warrant for one John Galen Locke, among others. And guess who issued it? Good old Ben Lindsey."

Judge Lindsey was—after Philip Van Cise—Locke's greatest enemy. "Locke's lawyers will bail him out in five minutes," Paul said.

"Sure, but the newspapers will have a ball with this. It might even replace Jim Graves and his love child on the front page."

"Full steam ahead, Charlie boy."

Shortly before lunch, D.A. Cline, an imposing man with a generous amount of dark hair and a weak chin, stopped by Paul's desk.

"Colonel Reston, would you come into my office for a moment?"

Paul glanced over at Charlie, who looked as if Paul had just been offered his last meal before being executed. Since Charlie had been given the kidnapping case, Paul assumed he was expendable.

When he stepped through the door of D.A. Cline's office, he stopped dead. Mayor Ben Stapleton sat in a chair in front of the desk. Mayor Stapleton rose, and D.A. Cline introduced Paul to him.

"Sit down, Colonel Reston," Mayor Stapleton said

Once Paul was seated, the Mayor continued. "We've asked you here because you come on great recommendation from Colonel Van Cise. You were, from all I've heard, his best assistant."

"Thank you."

"The spy reports that you collected under Colonel Van Cise indicate that the Klan has quite a set-up here," the Mayor said. "It's a well-organized, well-run operation."

As if the Mayor didn't already know that. Paul noted that he took no responsibility for his own contributions to the Klan's success. He'd obviously forgotten the debts he owed to the Klan for being elected—twice—to his seat.

"There are indications of a widespread system of embezzlement, mail fraud, and protection money," Paul offered. "But much of the Klan's momentum comes from making money for its higher-ups at the expense of the true believers at the bottom. The cross-burnings, the attacks on Catholics and Jews and Negroes have always been a smokescreen while Locke and his crew empty the coffers. It claims to be a law and order organization, but it's about as corrupt as the Bunco Gang or the Roma family in Little Italy."

"Paul, we'd like to organize a city-wide raid that focuses on the Klan," D. A. Cline said. "Something like Colonel Van Cise did with the Bunco Gang. And I want you in charge of it, working closely with the Mayor and me. Are you willing to you do that?"

"Yes, sir. But I have to ask, why is this coming to light now?"

D.A. Cline and Mayor Stapleton exchanged looks. The Mayor spoke. "John Galen Locke's influence over the state of Colorado has gone too far. Now that the governor, both long- and short-term senators, and most of the House are Klan, there's a fear that a new government will emerge that will overtake the established one."

"Hasn't that always been the case?"

"The elections made the Klan legitimate."

"Governor Morley intends to dismantle the system of due process in this state," D.A. Cline interjected. "He plans to do away with regulating boards and examiners and others who lend oversight, and he wants to replace them with his own boards and personnel. He wants to deputize his own regulators to manage bootlegging, sidelining the local police and the D.A.'s offices throughout the state."

"So he would create his own private police force? And stack the regulating boards with his own people?"

D.A. Cline nodded. "It's also clear that Denver's police officers under the current Chief of Police are violating Prohibition laws, and letting bootleggers go free. We suspect there are warehouses that have been rented under false names and then used as 'drops,' where contraband and liquor change hands."

Again, Paul glanced at Mayor Stapleton, who had appointed Chief Candlish in a sign of loyalty to the Klan. The Mayor showed no emotion at the mention of the corruption that had ensued once Candlish took over.

"We're asking you to keep complete secrecy," Mayor Stapleton said. "Even from your colleagues in this office until the time that D.A. Cline and I choose to execute the raids."

"Yes, sirs, you can trust me," he said.

After shaking hands all around, Paul left the office. When Charlie eyed him, looking for a clue as to what had happened, Paul simply shrugged. He settled down to look over the paperwork for a minor case, his heart beating and blood flowing, a new horizon in sight.

# THIRTY-NINE

Proposed legislation piled up quickly after the opening day of the Twenty-Fifth General Assembly. In the Senate, the bills mostly dealt with the business of running the state of Colorado. Jim had introduced three that had to do with appropriating money for the oil shale research being done at the University of Colorado by the U.S. Bureau of Mines. The legislation in the House, however, was a different story. The bills introduced there included one to "provide religious training in public schools" and "to repeal the Act to protect all citizens in their civil and legal rights." Nearly every House bill smacked of Klan interference.

On January 13, 1925, Clarence Morley was sworn in as Colorado's governor. The inaugural address was held at the Denver Auditorium, which was jammed with members of the victorious Invisible Empire. Jim squeezed in with the other Republicans senators to listen to the speech, which at fifteen minutes would surely go down in history as the shortest speech ever by an incoming governor. Despite its brevity, though, Morley said plenty. He recommended the elimination of more than fifteen regulatory boards and commissions; the amending of the primary voting law; an alien exclusion act that forbade ownership of property by immigrants; and abolishing the public defender act, which he saw as a waste of money and resources. He also intended to create a Woman's Reformatory to replace the unregulated charitable homes that currently existed.

After the speech, a reception was held at the Capitol for the jubilant Republican lawmakers. Raising his glass of champagne, Joshua Hart, a newly elected senator who was loyal to the robe, said, "Whatever we want is law, boys. The House is ninety-nine percent Klan, a dream come true. The Senate, although not as strong, is solid." He eyed Jim. "You're with us, aren't you, Senator Graves?"

The word, "us," stung Jim. He was no longer trusted by anyone. The old-line Republicans saw him as tainted by the Klan; the Klan Republicans saw him as a weakling, rubbed out of the governor's race by an easily avoided scandal.

"I will vote for legislation that is constitutionally legal," he said. "And that protects and aids my constituents and our state."

"You've had a rough time with it." Hart smirked. "All the trouble around your bid for governor was unfortunate, but you have a chance now to redeem yourself. We want to see an America that promotes only the strongest and the best. We want to see a powerful nation that has no heathen, immigrant filth hanging on its underbelly, dragging it down. That's what we want. What do you want?"

"Of course, I want to see America at its best. During the war, I—"

"The war's long over," Hart snapped. "And those stories have been told a million times. It's a new day and a new way of thinking. While we were off fighting for the Frogs, no one was fighting for us, here, and the Democrats were fast erasing any freedoms that Americans had, while the wops and the dagos were taking our jobs and moving into our neighborhoods. Our goal is to see the rights of white, Protestant America—which have long been trodden on and degraded—restored. We intend to win back our place in this country."

Jim scanned the faces in the room. "As the current Legislature is at least ninety-five percent white, Protestant, and male, that shouldn't prove difficult."

Someone laughed, but mostly his comment was met with glaring silence. As the conversation drifted to other topics, Jim set down his glass of champagne and left the Capitol. Keyed up, he wandered down Broadway. Rather than return to his office on 17th Street, he caught a streetcar bound for Cheesman Park.

Eleanora's butler met him at the door and showed him into the sitting room, where he found Ellie lounging on the loveseat near the fireplace, reading and sipping from a glass of sherry. She wore an ornately-embroidered pink kimono and satin slippers.

She sat up, bringing her feet to the floor. "What brings you here at this time of the day?"

Jim helped himself to the brandy on the sideboard. "I'm already wondering if I'm going to survive very much longer in the Senate."

"What's going on?"

"Didn't you hear the Governor's address on the radio?"

"Of course not, darling," she said. "Until Prohibition is out of force, I can't get my hands on enough alcohol to stomach politics."

Jim laughed. "Well, the legislation that's been introduced in the Senate isn't so bad, but the House is overdoing itself with inanity. They've introduced a bill that only people of the party that won at the polls can become employees of the state. And Orientals are no longer to be allowed to marry."

"Do they think that will stop the procreation of children? What a surprise it will be when slant-eyed children still appear in Hop Alley." She circled a finger around the rim of her glass. "That sounds distinctly like the work of Dr. Minnie Love and her eugenics movement."

She referred to Dr. Minnehaha Love, who had founded the Children's Hospital in Denver, and who was a two-time state representative. Dr. Love had attempted to establish a eugenics institute at the hospital that would lead the nation in the field. The Rockefeller Institute in New York had won the bid, though, and was now partnering with Germany to create its eugenics program.

"It is," Jim said. "Of course, she reintroduced the bill to sterilize idiots, epileptics, imbeciles and the insane. Oh, and there's a bill to outlaw marriages for drunkards and the insane."

"Well, that should effectively end marriage in the state of Colorado," Ellie quipped. "But as an average person, who can do little but hope that my elected representative is sane and sheet-free, I refuse to worry about it."

"It isn't funny. There's a good chance that these bills will become law."

"No, it isn't funny. But why aren't you at home talking to Kathleen about all this? It's her job to care, you know."

"I doubt she has any desire to talk to me."

Ellie plucked a cigarette from her silver case, and Jim leaned forward with a lighter. As she breathed out, she asked, "How is she getting along with Mina?"

Jim lit his own cigarette. "I'm not entirely sure. Because Kathleen is Kathleen, she's hell-bent that Mina be a part of the family, but she's woefully awkward at mothering a thirteen-year-old girl. She treats her the same way she treats Stephen and Susanna, and Mina is far too old for that."

"Perhaps our original plan was best. Send her to a good school in the east so that you and Kathleen can resume your life with Stephen and Susanna. It might even be best for Mina. She'd make friends her own age, and Kathleen could fuss over her from afar and show up on Parents' Weekend to cheer her on in the three-legged race."

Jim bristled at the puerile description of his wife and daughter. "Except that Kathleen insists that Mina have a mother and father."

"Thomas' son, Teddy, has done quite well without either parent in his life," Ellie said. "With his mother dead, and his father absent throughout most of his childhood and now living in America, he's grown up to be a perfectly fine Lieutenant in the British Army."

"I'll remember that if I want Mina to become a soldier."

Ellie waved him away. "You seek advice, and then you are intentionally obtuse."

"Perhaps not intentionally."

After shooting him a look of disdain, she asked, "What about Kathleen? Is she still pining over Paul Reston?"

"The bastard. He came back here for her, you know."

"That was to be expected, I suppose, once he discovered he still had a pulse."

Jim snorted. "Kathleen would never agree to a divorce."

"Or would she? She has always been deceptively good at getting what she wants, considering she's Catholic and a country girl. What about you? You no longer have anything to lose in becoming a divorced man, and anyway, it isn't nearly as damning for a man to end his marriage as it is for a woman."

Her words unleashed a specter in his head—one that he had not allowed to surface. After all they had gone through last year, with Paul's return and Mina's reappearance, it was astounding that he and Kathleen were still married. Yet, how long could things continue as they were? They rarely spoke to each other, and when they did, it usually flared into argument.

"Stephen and Susanna love their mother," he said.

"Yes, but they also love you. And they are young. They will readjust. As someone who has freed herself from an unhappy situation through the grace of the divorce court, I would suggest it. It's much easier to breathe once you're free."

"It took you years—and a world war—to learn how to breathe freely."

"That's true, but most of that was Mother's doing. She would have a more sympathetic reaction to your decision to choose another partner for the marital dance." She sipped her sherry. "Think about it, Jim. There are few valid reasons for living unhappily. Now, if you don't mind, it's time for my nap."

Jim left the house and caught the streetcar downtown. As the trolley arrived at the intersection of Lincoln and 16th, the conductor stopped the car and climbed down the steps.

A wave of protests resounded: "What's going on?" "Is there an accident?" "Has someone been hurt?"

Jim hopped off the trolley through the back. He could walk to his office from here. But as he started north on Lincoln, he saw a blaze of white coming down 16th Street. Hundreds of Klansmen marched, two or three abreast, the parade extending for blocks. They made no sound, keeping as silent as they had in the town of Craig last summer. Their footsteps, not in military synchronization, but individual and varied, echoed against the stone walls of the buildings in a low rumble. Along the sidewalk, people stepped out of shops and offices to watch, while passers-by knotted around parked cars. They, too, grew silent.

So it had come to this: broad daylight, one of the busiest shopping streets in Denver, the Klan well aware that they had immunity from any city ordinance or infraction because they now owned the state government.

He turned toward Lincoln again, but a flash of red hair caught his eye. Across 16th, Kathleen stood with her left arm around Mina's shoulder. Stephen stood in front and slightly to Kathleen's right, with his mother's right arm crossed over his chest. The fingers of Kathleen's right hand touched Susanna, who stood between Mina and Stephen, squarely in front of her mother. Kathleen looked poised to absorb the children into herself if they were threatened, while at the same time viciously lashing out at her attacker.

Beside Kathleen, Mina's face was pale, and her lips trembled. Jim remembered the little girl who had once danced for him and Anneka, gathering up the compliments on her beauty and grace like so many fallen leaves. She had taken the praise for granted, so accustomed to it. God, what had happened to that sparkling, precocious child?

All of Ellie's talk of sending Mina away and divorcing Kathleen—he wanted none of it. In fact, he wanted none of this mockery of law and order that paraded before him, either; none of the defeat and humiliation that awaited him at the State House; none of the pressure and burden of a public life.

What he wanted was to cross the street and stand in defiance with his wife and children.

# FORTY

Kathleen accepted an invitation from Seaney to listen to Governor Morley's inaugural speech, which was to be broadcast over KLZ radio, at the Sullivans' apartments. The plan turned out to be more awkward than she'd expected. Everyone in the room, acted edgy. Aunt Maury and Maggie made too much of a fuss over Stephen, Susanna, and Mina, while Seaney fussed over the glowing tubes of the radio. Liam had rolled his chair out for the occasion, and Uncle Seamus rocked in his favorite chair. It felt to Kathleen as if they'd been discussing her situation—the fall of Jim's career, the revelation of his sinful past, the evidence of it in Mina—before she arrived, and now had nothing to say to her face.

With Maggie's help, Alice Colleen shepherded the three boys and Stephen and Susanna into her room to play.

"Would you like to go with them?" Kathleen asked Mina. "I'm not sure how interesting this will be to you."

Mina shook her head and inserted herself between Aunt Maury and Kathleen on the sofa. Aunt Maury placed a hand on Mina's, but Mina made no effort to entwine her fingers with her great-aunt's.

Seaney fiddled with the dials until KLZ boomed static-free through the room. After the Governor was sworn in, his speech began: "As Governor, I want a conservative administration. I do not want any legislation that will bring on rancor or class hatred. I have no intention of turning the world upside down."

"That's promisin'," Aunt Maury commented.

He continued with the usual gratitude towards those who had elected him, and a list of his proposed legislation. He promised to repeal more laws than enact new ones, and said he could not tell "all he knew," but would do so in future speeches.

"What does that mean?" Uncle Seamus asked.

"It means he has to wait for Dr. Locke to tell him what to do," Seaney said. "Just like Candlish and Stapleton."

An argumentative screech sounded from Alice Colleen's room. Kathleen and Maggie were both on their feet at once.

"I'll go." Maggie left the room.

The Governor's voice resonated from the radio. "I also propose to eliminate from the Prohibition law the right to obtain, possess, or dispense intoxicating liquor for 'sacramental mass.' Experience shows that this exemption is too often flagrantly abused."

Seaney's eyes met Kathleen's. "What did he just say?"

"He said . . . I don't know."

The speech did not last much longer, and Seaney clicked off the radio. "So much for not causing rancor," he grumbled. "He must have a cross burning to go to."

No one laughed. If it had been Jim giving the speech, Kathleen thought, he would have spoken of building better highways and completing the Moffat Tunnel to unite Coloradans.

Maggie came back from the bedroom. "It can't be over yet—I was only gone a minute! What did I miss?"

Liam spoke. "He called for the repeal of the Prohibition exemption for churches."

"What? But that's what most of the Mass is!"

"Yes. In effect, he just outlawed Catholicism."

"But the Episcopalians have never stopped using wine, either," Maggie protested. "And neither have the Jews, right, Seaney?"

"I don't know," Seaney said. "But the government can't dictate whether Mass is celebrated. It's unconstitutional, isn't it? Against freedom of religion?"

"But, as we know, the constitution doesn't always keep us from abuse by those in power," Liam said. "Freedom of religion and freedom of speech are nearly always under strain by fanatics, and that's what the Klan's members are."

Liam's words cast a pall over the parlor. Hoping to lift the mood, Kathleen offered, "Jim will never support something as wrong as this. And he still has his seat in the Senate."

No one spoke, and she sensed the doubt in their minds. Jim would forever carry the stigma of his alliance with the Klan, and the more she defended him, the more it seemed that he was guilty.

A knock sounded at the front door, and Kathleen hoped that it was Jim, come to reassure them. Seaney answered it. Brendan came into the apartments, carrying a sheaf of papers in his hand. "Did you hear it?" he demanded of Liam. "Governor Morley not only took away our right to worship, but our ability to help others. A woman's reformatory! It would be nothing more than a prison for unwed mothers, while our charity homes would be empty."

"We heard it."

Brendan waved the papers. "Father Smith has asked me to look over his response to the Governor's speech before it goes to press in the *Catholic Register*. If we could go to your study—"

"Read it to us all," Aunt Maury said. "We all want to hear it."

Father Smith's article first summed up what Governor Morley had said, then denied abuse of sacramental wine by the Catholic Church. On the subject of Mass, Brendan read, "*It is going to be celebrated, and right here in Colorado. The Catholic religion is not going to be banished, and the Mass is the center of our worship. If every priest and Catholic layman in this state has to go to jail we will celebrate Mass.*" He looked up, the lenses of his glasses clouded. "*This is our stand and let our enemies make the most of it. When they step inside the sanctuary itself, they will find every one of us ready to go to death rather than submit.*"

"That's excellent," Liam said. "Please thank Father Matthew for writing it in our defense."

Kathleen looked at her lap. How had she ended up on the wrong side of all she believed and held dear? Her good acts in France meant almost nothing now, washed away by the passage of time, and her kindness on behalf of Mina had doomed her to endless apology. Her marriage and home life were broken, and her ties with her birth family and the Church of her childhood were strained to snapping. Never before had she felt like such a pariah.

Driving home after lunch, with Mina in the front seat beside her and Stephen and Susanna in the back, Kathleen tried to make conversation.

"Did you enjoy the meal?" she asked Mina. "Maggie's a good cook."

"Those people are Catholic," Mina said in distaste.

Kathleen started, but quickly calmed herself. "Yes, my family is Catholic. I am Catholic."

"Is that why you do that with your hand when you pray?"

"Yes, I make the sign of the cross." Kathleen demonstrated. "In the name of the Father, and of the Son, and of the Holy Ghost. Amen. It's a sign that I have faith in God."

Stephen echoed Kathleen from the back seat, with Susanna miming some of the words.

Mina peered crossly over her seat at them. "Is Father Catholic?"

"No, he isn't." Kathleen decided not to tell her that he had no belief at all. It would open up a fresh can of worms when the first had just been punctured. "He's a member of the Presbyterian Church. Why do you ask?"

"Bishop White said Catholics love the Pope more than God, and that they want to make everyone in America kiss his ring and worship him. She says they'll kill those who don't bow down to the Pope. That man today—"

"Father Keohane?"

"He sounded so mean."

Kathleen wished that Brendan hadn't read Father Smith's article with such gusto. "He's a Catholic priest, a man of peace and prayer. He's taken a vow to hurt no one and to help everyone. And he's a good friend of mine. I think he was just upset—as were we all—over the talk of keeping people from worshipping God in the way they choose. Freedom of religion is a precious right."

Mina's face retained its sour expression.

"Do you think that Catholics would truly kill those who don't believe as they do?" Kathleen asked. When Mina made no answer, she tried again, "Do you think that Aunt Maggie and Uncle Seaney and Great-Aunt Maury would do that?"

"I don't know," she said shortly. "But I don't want to be Catholic."

"Do you remember if your mother took you to church?"

"No, she didn't, but Miss Judith and Miss Essie went to the Pillar of Fire church."

"And did you believe in what you heard there?"

Mina mulled over the question before she said, "You have dances with jazz bands at your house."

Kathleen glanced toward her. "Yes, we like to have friends visit, and we like to hear music played by live musicians."

"Isn't dancing to that kind of music a sin?"

"Why do you think that?"

"Miss Judith told me jazz is the Devil's music, and Bishop White said dancing is sinful and wrong."

"I see."

As if a floodgate had been opened up, Mina continued, "And you drink liquor at your house, and you play cards, and you go to movies. The movies are made by evil Jews who show them on Sunday so Christian people are tempted not to go to church. They are trying to make them lose their souls to Satan, while making more money for themselves—"

"Mina, I'm not sure that's true—"

"And you have Negroes in your house."

Kathleen took in a breath and glanced at the mirror on the dashboard. She should be pleased that Mina was talking at last, but both Stephen and Susanna were listening wide-eyed to the conversation. She wished they weren't here. She didn't want them to think any differently of the people they had known since their birth.

"Yes, we do," she said steadily. "We do all of those things—drink, dance, play cards, listen to music, and go to movies. We don't believe those things are sins. And yes, we do have people whose skin is black who work for us. That is because your father and I believe that those people— Blount and Beryl and the others—are no different than we are. I have red hair, you have blond. You and your father have blue eyes, I have green. Having colored skin is no different than having green or blue eyes or red or yellow hair."

From the back seat, Stephen called, "Look, Mommy, there's a parade!"

People hurried along Curtis Street toward 16th, which was blocked by a uniformed police officer.

"Can we stop?" he asked.

"Of course," Kathleen said, relieved to leave off the conversation with Mina. "We'll park here and walk. Is everyone bundled up? Coats buttoned? Hats and mittens on?"

Holding Stephen's hand in one of hers, and Susanna's in the other, they worked their way down Curtis to 16th. As the parade came into view, Kathleen gasped. A phalanx of Klansmen strode down the street, stretching both ways for as far as she could see.

"Are there horseys?" Susanna asked.

"I don't think so."

Stephen and Susanna quickly grew bored with the silent parade, and Kathleen gathered them against her for warmth. Her stomach churned—should she even be here? Would it look as if she were supporting the Klan—maybe even searching for her husband among the robed—if she stayed? Was it still dangerous for her, or for Susanna and Stephen and Mina? Jim had warned her that he could not protect her, and that was long before he had tussled with the Grand Dragon over the election.

As she opened her mouth to suggest leaving, Mina said, "That's Andy."

"What?" Kathleen asked. "How would you know?"

"Those are his boots. There's Matt, and Avery, too."

All the shoes, marching by in quick time, looked the same to Kathleen, but one of the Klansmen looked directly at her, then elbowed the man beside him. A third one paused as well, all looking toward Kathleen and Mina.

Mina stepped behind Kathleen.

"No," Kathleen said impatiently. "Don't stand behind me. Stand where they can see you. Show them that you aren't upset. Show them that you are proud of yourself and that you're brave and strong."

"They scare me—"

"Then, the best thing to do is to pretend that they don't. Some people think it's funny to scare others, but if we don't act scared, it's no fun for them."

Kathleen laid an arm around Mina's shoulder. She gathered Stephen and Susanna to her with her other hand, and then met the gaze of the three men.

And even though Mina quavered, she stayed put.

That evening, as Kathleen told Mina goodnight, she discovered that the girl wasn't finished with the conversation.

"You didn't let them take me today," Mina whispered.

Kathleen puzzled. "Take you? Do you mean Andy?"

Mina nodded, and Kathleen said, "I wouldn't let them take you. If they'd tried, I would have protected you, I would have"—Kathleen searched for a sincere answer—"asked for help from the people around us. Your father and I worked very hard to bring you home to us, and you won't leave us again."

"You won't send me back because I don't want to be Catholic?"

"No, of course not."

Her eyes teared. "How did you learn not to be scared of them?"

Again, Kathleen searched for an honest answer, without telling Mina that there was far worse to fear. "When I was in France, during the war, I learned that all people—even people like us, who have so much and are so lucky—can be cold and hungry and scared. Some went from having homes like this"—she gestured toward the riches around them—"to living in forests and digging in the ditches for their next meal."

She dabbed at her eyes, and Mina said, "You're crying."

"It makes me sad to remember how cruel and hopeless that time was for so many. It didn't matter to me or the other girls I worked with— including your Aunt Ellie—what they thought, or which church they went to, or how much money they had. We didn't care at all who they were or what color their skin was, only that they needed help. We only wanted to stop their suffering, if we could. That's why I'm not afraid of the Klan. I know that underneath skin color and different ideas about God, we all need to care for each other."

Mina's eyes clouded. "My mother told me we needed to be nice to other people because other people had given us a house and nice things."

Kathleen hesitated. She had long ago decided that the Graves family had damaged Mina and Anneka more than helped them. But at least, Mina was no longer quoting Judith Dercum. "That's a good thing to believe," she said. "Your mother would be proud of you for remembering that."

She kissed Mina's forehead—as she had always done—and rose from the bed. "Now, go to sleep. You have school and studies tomorrow."

On the landing of the stairs, Kathleen tipped her head, listening. From the bustle in the hallway downstairs, she guessed that Jim was in his study.

She knocked on the door, and he called, "Come in."

He sat at his desk, the yellow light from the Tiffany lamp the only illumination in the room. Holding a pen in his hand, he scribbled on a pile of papers that lay before him. Glancing up, he asked, "What is it?"

Kathleen sat down across from him and waited until he gave her his full attention. "We need to talk about Mina."

"What about her?"

"She's so confused. She thinks everything that we do here is sinful, and she thinks we'll send her back to Andy and Judith Dercum if she doesn't do what we want her to do or if she doesn't please us."

"I don't have time for this right now, with all the legislation—"

"But she started to talk today." Kathleen leaned forward. "In fact, she talked more than she has since she came here. I caught a glimpse of who she might be if she felt sure enough to be herself. We can't squander that." As an afterthought, she added, "To be honest, she was a little combative."

"Combative? Was she disrespectful? Or ill-behaved?"

"Oh, no, nothing like that. She stood up for herself, though."

"About what?"

"The evils of Catholicism."

Jim laughed. "Well, if one is going to pick an argument, that's a fair place to start—"

"Jim," she scolded. "You're her only connection to her mother. I can't talk to her about her—I didn't know her." She laid a hand over his to stop him from writing. "I think she needs to mourn her. I don't think anyone taught her about loss or let her grieve." Her words grew bitter. "And you need to tell her that we won't lie to her or change her name or force her to forget who she is. And we'll let her read books, and look at herself in the mirror, and play and dance, if she wants—"

"All right. I'll see if I can get away and take her for a soda or something."

"Thank you."

She rose to leave, but he said, "I saw you today. At the parade downtown."

"We were there entirely by chance. I wouldn't have stopped if I'd known what it was, but Stephen and Susanna wanted ice cream, and I was trying to reach Baur's Parlor." She paused. "Mina recognized Andy Dercum and Mary Jane's brothers."

"How? Weren't they robed?"

"She recognized them by their dairy boots."

"I would never have thought of that." Jim leaned back in his chair. "Kathleen, I don't know if there's anything I can do to atone for the mistakes I made last summer. Klansmen are being appointed as chairmen of the committees, and those of us who are old-line are being ignored. I, especially, am looked down upon, because of my indecision."

"So you won't be at the helm of Industrial Relations any longer?"

"It doesn't look like it." He fiddled with his pen. "The most powerful committee seats have been meted out to Klansmen. I've been named to the City and County of Denver sub-committee—which is a nauseatingly impotent position."

"I'm sorry. I'm aware of how important that was to you."

"I was well suited to it—that's all." He looked at his desk. "I need to go back to work. It's still days from the end of the period for introducing new legislation, and we're already at five-hundred bills. And, yes, I'll see to Mina."

She left, but paused outside the study door. Something seemed different in him. Perhaps it was just that he was busy again in the legislature, or that the oil business and the Moffat Fields still looked promising for the coming year, but he had listened to her—and that was something that had not happened in a long time.

# FORTY-ONE

On a bitterly cold morning in January, Sean reported to the station house for a mandatory meeting. His shift had just ended, and he was anxious to get home, eat breakfast, and sleep. The patrolmen had assembled for the meeting in the station's common room, but the usual chatter and banter was absent. Sean passed through, nodding at his colleagues in greeting. A sealed envelope lay on his desk. He picked it up and slit it open with a file. His knees buckled as he unfolded it, and he sat down.

Illustrations of robed and hooded knights greeted him in both top corners of the letter. The knights carried flaming torches and sat upon robed and hooded horses that reared up on their hind legs. The sprawling letterhead read: INVISIBLE EMPIRE, Knights of the Ku Klux Klan, Incorporated.

In the body, Sean read:

"Dear Sir: We have been requested by one of your personal friends to get in touch with you, and inform you of this organization. And, in view of this request, we are sending you this form. Without delay you will fill in, sign and return it."

The letter was signed, "Very truly yours, KNIGHTS OF THE KU KLUX KLAN." A list of twenty questions followed, asking for personal information, as well as inquiring about heritage and faith.

Nearly everyone in the station watched for his reaction. Walt Wells and some of the others smirked or grinned. In the corner of the office, seated at his desk, Joe Flannery, who had been Sean's partner in more than one raid on a speakeasy or gambling house, sat with his head lowered. Evidently, Joe had received an application as well.

Chief William Candlish entered the room, and the patrolmen straightened up and smoothed down their uniforms. "Thank you for coming this morning," the Chief said. "Especially those of you who have just completed your beat." He eyed Sean before he continued. "I am requesting that everyone who is employed by the Denver Police fill out an application for the Ku Klux Klan. We have been working closely with the Klan in the past year in keeping law and order in this city, and now with the Klan's presence in our State House, we will be receiving even more support from it. Filling out the application will ensure your continued employment here. I will be collecting these at the end of the day. For now, everyone, back to work."

Immediately, Wells sauntered over to Sean's desk. "So, what's it going to be, Seaney?" he drawled. "Are you going to become a Klansman?"

Patrolmen Able and Peters—who were always in Wells' shadow—joined him.

"A couple of questions might cause you some trouble." Able pointed. "Number 15, there, 'What is your religious faith?' Or 16, 'Of what church are you a member?'"

Peters joined in. "Or Number 20, 'Do you owe ANY KIND of allegiance to any foreign nation, government, institution, sect, people, ruler or person?' See, 'any kind' is capitalized."

"You sons-of-bitches—"

"Oh, Seaney boy," Able said. "Now you'll have to confess to using naughty language to your priest."

Sean stood up so forcefully that the legs of his chair squealed across the wooden floor. He unpinned his badge from his uniform and flipped it on the desk, then tossed his baton beside it. Wadding the application in his hands, he said, "I quit. You'll have the uniform back this afternoon."

Laughter followed him from the station. On the steps, Joe Flannery caught up with him.

"Jesus Holy Christ!" Joe said. "You just dumped me in it. What am I goin' to do? I can't afford to quit—"

"Me? I dumped you in it?"

"I thought we'd stick together, watch each other's back—"

"I'm not going to grovel at their feet! I'm not going to play their fool!"

"Maybe they'll let us be if we just fill it out—"

"That isn't the point!" Sean's voice seemed to crack through the frigid air. "They want to humiliate us! They want to walk all over us—!"

"I have five children and another on the way," Joe said. "I can't let them go hungry. You can ask your cousin for money, but I'm not that high on the hog."

Joe whipped away, leaving Sean alone on the station steps. Just fill it out, a voice inside Sean's head said. Let them have their little joke, it won't last that long, and then everything will be back to normal.

Another voice answered: And be the target of their disrespect and contempt? Let them abuse you and mock you? Be forever an outsider, a nobody?

Not for all the money in the world.

He sat in his car for some time, trying to breathe deeply enough to get air into his lungs and to calm his jittery nerves. Jesus, Jesus, everything gone, over, thrown away, as if it had been nothing but an old rag. When he at last unclenched his fists, he found the wad of the application in one.

Starting the car, he drove not to Mrs. Potter's boarding house, but to Sullivan's Grocery. Stealing up through the dark shell of the store, he slipped into the kitchen. As usual, Maggie was there, scrubbing pans.

"What are you doing here?" she asked, up to her elbows in suds.

"I quit my job."

"Why?" She turned toward him, her reddened hands dripping on the floor. Snatching up a towel, she dried them. "What happened?"

He sat at the table and lit cigarettes for both of them, while she took a chair across from him. After he told her of the morning's events, he tossed the ball of the application toward her. "Here it is."

She arched her eyebrows, but made no comment about its condition. Smoothing it out, she read: "12. Do you believe in the principles of a PURE Americanism? 13. Do you believe in White Supremacy?"

After she finished the list, she laid it down.

"Chief Candlish said that everyone has to fill it out to keep their jobs," Sean said.

"I'm sorry."

He put his head in his hands. "I don't know what I'm going to do. I don't know how I'm going to help Ma and Pa. I don't even know how I'll keep my room."

Maggie said nothing, letting the unspoken hang in the air: there was no room for him at home anymore. His bedroom was now Liam's office.

"How am I going to tell Chava?" he mourned.

"Won't she notice when you're not there tonight?"

Of course she would. She would wait for him, as she nearly always did, in the cold shadows along the side of Max and Rachel's house.

"She'll never understand," he said. "She'll think I'm a coward—"

"What would she expect? That you wear your green Order of the Hibernians coat to a cross-burning? If anyone understands humiliation, Seaney, it's the Jews."

"She would expect me to . . . I don't know, stand up for myself." He looked up at Maggie. "She's so smart, and she has a college degree, and her brother is friends with all the important men on the West Side. Maggie, I used to call them Christ killers. I believed it, too, until . . ."

"Until you met a pretty one."

But no, it wasn't that. It was Danhour—that thorn in Sean's side throughout his entire time in the AEF. He'd hated Danhour so much because he'd seen himself in him. Someone who hated just to hate, someone who lit a fire just to see who was burned by it, someone who could bash in the brains of others like an animal gone mad and win a medal for it.

"Maybe it's better if I just don't see her again," he said. "If I just don't show up over there, she'll figure it out after a while."

"Don't you dare do that to her. If you love her, you owe her the truth."

"That's a sure way to end it. I have quite a 'truth' to tell."

Maggie hesitated. "We could open the store again."

"What? How? It's a mess."

"I've been thinking about it." She pulled out the bottom drawer of the larder and removed a stack of papers. "All sorts of things have happened since the war that would make it easier."

"Why would you want to do it? It was a sad living, and—"

"Hear me out." She laid an advertisement clipped from a newspaper in front of him. The ad offered "revolving credit" to customers. "There's something called installment payment now. If you need more than you can afford that week, you don't have to beg the shopkeeper for it. You can charge it to your account and pay a certain amount every month. You never have to pay the full balance, but you have to pay interest—"

"That sounds like a con game to me."

She pursed her lips in exasperation. "The banks are all doing it, and some of the bigger department stores, too. It would be good for our customers—they'd know they'd always have food. And it would be better than what Ma used to do. She just handed out what they needed even if they couldn't pay for it."

"When do you have time to think about this?"

"I let the store go during the war. I let you and Ma and Pa down. I'd like to fix it."

This was a change of heart. Sean had always thought she blamed him for the store's demise.

"Ah, hell, Maggie, who knows if that's true?" he asked.

She sorted through her pages for another advertisement of a white, metal box. "They have electric refrigerators now, so no more trying to store enough ice to keep the meat from rotting. The Kelvinator or this new one, the Frigidaire—"

"Seven hundred dollars! It costs more than a new car!"

"But if we could sell enough meat, it would pay for itself after a while."

"And who's going to butcher? Pa can't slaughter or cut meat anymore. We might as well send him to the Old Soaks Home."

She flicked at the corner of the Frigidaire ad before she answered. "You could do it."

"No." Sean stood. "Jesus, no. I saw enough blood and guts in the war. And where would you get the money for all this? It would take more than any of us have to make the store look halfway decent. The shelves are the ones Grandpa Sullivan built during the Gold Rush."

"I thought . . . We could ask Kathleen for a loan—"

Flannery's words echoed in Sean's head: *You can ask your cousin for money, but I'm not that high on the hog.*

"No," he said. "I'm not begging to Jim Graves."

"Kathleen's a wealthy woman in her own right," Maggie said. "We could ask her to be a partner in the store. Sullivan & Graves Grocery. Or Sullivan & O'Doherty, if she doesn't want to embarrass Jim. Maybe if it were Sullivan & O'Doherty, Uncle Irish would work here."

"Only if we sell bootleg out of the back room."

"That's not a bad idea—"

"Mag—"

"Oh, don't be so stodgy. Think about it, Seaney. We could get our place back in the world."

"You have a place, Mrs. James, as you like to remind me."

"But our place—Ma and Pa's and yours," she said fiercely. "The Sullivans' place. We were looked up to before the war. People were always in the store for one reason or another, and we were proud and respected."

"I don't know. Let me think about it."

He went into the deserted store. Near the bottom of the stairs, he sat down on the next to the last step. Lighting another cigarette, he looked around at the dust and despair. He was back to the place he'd tried to escape from eight years—more than a third of his life—ago.

Maggie wanted to get their place back in the world. But the store had never been his place. It was Grandpa Sullivan's, it was Pa's, it was Ma's. He'd just wanted to be rid of it. Maybe instead of putting a house on the back lot, they should sell the whole shebang and buy Maggie and Liam a decent house where they could raise their kids. Maybe there would be enough left to buy Ma and Pa something, too.

He threw down his cigarette butt, then ground it into the dirty, wooden planks of the floor. Without a backward look, he left.

That afternoon, at the Sheltering Home on the West Side, no one stops him from strolling through the grounds and knocking on the back door of the cottage where Chava teaches. He's dressed—inexplicably—in his clothes for Mass. He has delivered his uniform back to the station, wrapped in brown paper.

The matron, Mrs. Bergmann, opens the door.

Sean turns his hat in his hands. "May I speak to Miss Rosen?"

"Is this important? She's teaching just now."

Sean hears singing in the other room. The song has a distinctive Hebrew lilt to it. For some reason, in this day of bad tidings, he smiles.

"I just need to see her for a minute," he says. "I just need to tell her—"

He stops.

Tell her what? That he is no longer worthy of her—if he ever was?

The singing ends, and Mrs. Bergman says, "Wait here. I'll get her."

Sean stamps his feet and rubs his hands together as he waits in the brutal winter wind. She will reject him, he knows, now that he has no status, no money, no future. What beautiful, wise, and sensible woman wouldn't?

Chava comes into the kitchen. "Why are you out in the cold? Come in."

"Chava, I just came to tell you—"

"The children will want to see you. Come into the classroom."

She swooshes him through, and all at once, he's standing amid a group of children, with Leah holding his right hand and a little girl whose name he doesn't remember holding his left. Mrs. Bergmann retires to the kitchen.

"Look who has come to visit!" Chava says. "Patrolman Sullivan."

"I need to talk to you," Sean whispers.

Chava claps her hands. "Everyone sit down and draw a picture for Patrolman Sullivan of your favorite part of the school day. Take your time, don't rush, and we will be back to look at them in a few minutes."

As the children scurry to the tables to take up paper and crayons, she leads Sean into the hallway, where she can keep an eye on her students. "What is it?"

"I just wanted to tell you I won't be by tonight or any night from now on—"

"What? Why? Have you been reassigned?"

"It's too much to tell you now, but I've lost my job—"

"Did you quit or were you fired?"

Sheepishly, he admits, "I quit."

She puts her hands on either side of his face. "Was it the right thing to do?"

"Yes, I . . . yes."

Standing on tiptoe, she kisses his forehead. "I'll wait for you tonight, and we can talk. Now, come in and look at the pictures. It's a good thing you have extra time. They'll all want to tell you about their drawings."

# FORTY-TWO

As Maggie prepared dinner, she heard a knock on the outside door. She glanced at the clock—it was nearly four o'clock, a strange time for visitors. The sun had dipped behind the mountains in the cold, gray day, leaving the rooms in the apartments gloomy and dim.

"Alice Colleen, answer that for me," she called.

Alice Colleen reported back a few seconds later. "There's a man here to see Daddy."

"Who is it?"

"I don't know."

Maggie's heart lurched. At last, someone had come to accost Liam. A newspaper reporter? An emissary from the Catholic Church, intent on excommunication? A Klansman from the police department, where Seaney had just made dangerous enemies?

She rammed through the kitchen door, all of the children following.

Mr. Ledbetter stood in the parlor.

"Mrs. James!" he said.

Liam rolled out from the hallway. "Ah, Mr. Ledbetter, welcome. I'm Liam Keohane. You know Maggie, my wife. And these are our children, Alice Colleen, Declan, Frankie, and Kieran."

Mr. Ledbetter shook the hand that Liam offered and acknowledged Maggie. My God—what a mess she looked. Whenever she went to the newspaper office, she wore a skirt, jacket, and hat that she had purchased to look professional. Now, her hair was frizzy from the steam in the kitchen, and the dress she wore was a hand-me-down from her mother. An apron—once white, but now permanently stained—was tied lopsidedly around her waist.

"Mommy, the kettle's boiling," Alice Colleen said.

Maggie went to the kitchen, stopping only long enough to lift the tea kettle from the stove. Taking refuge on the landing that led down into the store, she gasped for air. Why would Liam contact Mr. Ledbetter? It was all ruined now—nearly eight years of writing as Mrs. James; of working under her own terms for the *Denver City Daily News*; of having a healthy income outside the home.

Alice Colleen hailed her from inside. "Do we need to fix tea?"

"Yes, of course." Maggie swiped at her eyes before she returned to the kitchen. I can't go back in there, she thought. I can't.

But she did. She made the tea, and, after asking Ma to keep the children, she returned to the parlor. As she poured the tea, her hand shaking so hard that she nearly spilled it, Liam explained, "I invited Mr. Ledbetter here today because my book is almost finished. I'd like to see it published."

Maggie said nothing, but Mr. Ledbetter said, "I'm a newspaper publisher. I don't print books."

"But I believe that a serialization would appeal to your readers. Some of the chapters are difficult to read, because of the torture I endured, but it would be an incentive for your readers to pick up the next edition." Liam laughed lightly. "Something like Dickens did."

"I see," Mr. Ledbetter said uncomfortably.

"There are many people who wonder why we went to war, and many who hope we never go again. My book lays out a simple objection to war that would give people a basis for protesting if our government ever leaned toward engaging in a foreign war again."

"Mr. Keohane, you have to know that you're not a popular figure in Denver," Mr. Ledbetter said. "You've been hung in effigy and told you would be assassinated if you returned to Denver. I'm not sure people want to hear your side of the story."

"I know that I am misunderstood and that many misperceptions exist around my reasons for becoming a Conscientious Objector. But shouldn't the people of Denver be allowed to make up their own minds about me after reading my book?"

Mr. Ledbetter rose. "I'll look at it, but I'll make no promises."

"It's been well edited by my talented wife."

Mr. Ledbetter's eyes barely met Maggie's before he turned toward the door. "Yes, well, I have to get back to the office. I'll be in touch. Good day, Mr. and Mrs. Keohane."

Maggie saw him to the door, but he merely tipped his hat at her before he loped down the outside stairs. As she closed the door behind him, she knew—this was the end.

Turning to Liam, who still sipped from his tea cup, she asked, "Why in God's name did you do that?"

"I assume you're asking why I contacted Mr. Ledbetter?" Liam said calmly.

"You sabotaged me."

"What?"

"You sabotaged me! You ruined my career, you ruined everything!"

"I did nothing of the sort—"

"Mr. Ledbetter is never going to let me keep working for him! He's never going to forgive me for this! Oh, my God, what will I do?"

"I just freed you, Maggie, to do what you wanted. You told me at Christmas that you wanted to live honestly. Now we both can. My book will clarify and vindicate my position, and you can write under your own name, under Maggie Keohane."

"I won't be writing at all now. Don't you see? He can't keep me on staff now that he knows I'm married to . . ."

"To whom?" Liam demanded. "To what? Finish the sentence."

"Liam, I bring in all the money we have. What we eat, what we wear, the medicine for Ma, and for the kids—"

"Sean helps with your mother and father—"

"Seaney quit his job!"

"—and we get plenty of help from Kathleen with toys and clothes—"

"Hand-me-downs! Charity rags from the richest woman in town. She doesn't do it from the goodness of her heart. She does it because we embarrass her. She feels sorry for us—and besides, she has nothing for Alice Colleen. Susanna is too young—"

"Their new daughter will grow out of hers, I expect."

Wiping her nose with the back of her hand, Maggie fumbled in her pocket for a handkerchief, but it did no good. The tears came even after the handkerchief was soaked.

"I had no idea this would upset you so," Liam said. "I thought it was a way to free you from the sin of a lie. Mrs. James is no one, but you, Maggie, are brilliant and beloved by all of us."

"No, Mrs. James is . . . Mrs. James . . . I can't—"

From the hallway, Alice Colleen appeared, trailed by the boys.

"Daddy! Daddy!" she said. "Look at what we made—"

Maggie remembered the dinner she had started. Had the water for the potatoes boiled away? Was the meat just a charred crisp? She hit the swinging door between the kitchen and the parlor so hard that it fanned back and forth, its hinges squeaking.

How could Liam have done this? she wondered. Why would he ruin my career?

Because he has always been jealous of your success, a voice answered.

No, no, it's Liam. I've loved him since I was seven-years-old.

But I'm not that child any longer.

She put her hands over her face. No, no—she wouldn't even consider that. She would never change so much that her love for Liam would fade, or burn out, or die. Liam was the essence of her existence. But how could she reconcile it with all he had done to her?

She forced her way through the meal, and the children's bath times, and evening prayers, and bedtime. Without speaking to Liam again, she went out to the shed to work on her letters.

The first letter set her on edge: "*Dear Mrs. James, I am a young, attractive woman who works in an office as a receptionist. I like my job, and I think I am good at it. My fiancé wants me to stop working after we marry. I don't want to, and besides, his job doesn't pay as much as mine. If I refuse to stop working, will I seem to be nothing more than money-grabbing and shallow? Signed, Not a Golddigger, but Likes to Eat Well.*"

Maggie pounded out: "*Dear Likes to Eat Well: Don't try to be successful or rich. Oh, and don't you dare try to make anything of yourself. Just do what you're told and realize that no matter how hard you try, there is someone who will want to take any gains you make for yourself away from you. And never fall in love. It's not worth it, and you just lose your soul and come out of it someone you've never met before—*"

"Mrs. James!"

Tony stood in the doorway of the shed. "Boy, whoever wrote that letter must have told you he don't like opera but still wants to be kissed."

Maggie ripped the page from the typewriter. "What are you doing here?"

Tony eyed the potbelly stove. "Why don't you have a fire going?"

"Leave it alone."

"But it's so cold—"

"What do you want?"

"I came to get my hammer. I musta left it here."

"Your hammer?" Maggie wheeled around in her chair. "You haven't been here for months, and you're only realizing it now? Go look in the back. It's probably frozen to the head of the last nail you hammered into that stupid house."

He gauged her. "I guess you're still mad at me about Christmas. You should be. I shouldn't of said those things. You love your husband, that's what counts. I'm sorry."

The argument between Liam and Tony seemed so long ago, and hardly important, given today's events. "I wouldn't expect you to understand my husband's and my beliefs, Sergeant Necchi," she said. "But I would have expected you to have some manners at Christmas dinner, to which you were graciously invited as part of our family, at least for the sake of my mother, father, and children."

"Yeah, my mamma woulda taken the mule reins to me for that."

Maggie eyes brimmed unexpectedly. "It doesn't matter. It doesn't . . . I don't know where your hammer is. Just find it and go."

Leaving the shed so he could search, she trudged through the snow to the half-built house. It consisted of four framed walls, and a knee-high brick wall that Seaney had created to test his masonry skills. Maggie brushed the snow off the ledge of the wall and sat on it, her hands on her knees, her eyes on the ground, tears spilling from them.

By the time Tony came from the shed, she had started shivering. Smoke wisped from the chimney of the potbelly stove.

"There," Tony said. "It'll warm up in there soon."

"I don't want to go back in there."

"Well, then, come on. Walk with me. You'll freeze just sitting there."

"I can't take a walk. I have to listen for the kids."

"We'll walk twenty paces that direction, then back, and twenty paces the other way, just like guard duty in the Army. You'll be able to see the house the whole time."

Maggie stood, too restless to remain still. The first twenty paces out and back, she silently counted her steps, but on the second go around, Tony took an extra step.

"That's twenty-one," Maggie said, despite herself.

"I just wanted to know if you're watching, since you don't talk no more."

Tony began to pace in the opposite direction, and Maggie asked, "What's it like on top of a telephone pole?"

"Out here, it's quiet. You know, in Brooklyn, you climb up a pole, and you can look in everybody's window. You see all sorts of things, like ladies in their underwear, and men slapping their wives, and kids stealing stuff."

"Did you ever call the police or try to stop it?"

"It wasn't none of my business. And here, well, when I climb up a pole, you know what I see? Nothing. Nothing at all. Because there isn't nothing out there, just miles of empty land that's not good for nothing."

"It sounds wonderful, to be alone, to see nothing. I think I'll take up pole sitting."

"Why? You got your kids, and your husband, and you got your Mamma and Papi living here, too. And Sean's just over there, and you got your rich cousin. You got your whole family, and that makes you luckier than me. My brothers and me, look at us. Three of us here in America, and the rest back in Italy, and now I'm way out here, and I don't know if I'll ever see any of them again."

"Are you ever afraid you might fall when you climb a telephone pole?"

"Naw, I got my belt and my gaffes."

Anger welled up in her. "Why did you say that to my husband at Christmas? Why didn't you just sit there and be quiet?"

"I don't know," he said. "Maybe 'cuz, we all had to do it, so why not him? It don't seem fair to the ones who didn't come back."

"He believed in—" She started again. "He believes in what he did during the war. He followed the laws of his faith—of your faith, and mine."

"Yeah, and you think he was right, so that's what matters." He stopped. "Hey, Mrs. James, why are you so sad tonight? You got a problem?"

She had wanted to fight, to tell him off for treating Liam as he had, but his reference to Mrs. James brought back the recollection—and the tears—of the day. "I don't think I'll be Mrs. James much longer."

"Why not? Don't you like doing it no more?"

"It's not that, I don't, it's . . . it was all pretend. Look at me—I barely even leave the house. I'm not a society belle like Kathleen or a flapper. I don't go to speakeasies, and I don't go to parties with the bright young people or the theater or movies. I'm stuck here at home—I can't even take a walk because I have to listen for the kids. How can I give advice to people who've lived in the world? Who've traveled or worked? I'm nothing, I'm no one."

"You must be smart to write all those letters, and if people like what you say so much, you must be right."

She laughed weakly. She lifted her chin, and there he was: his lips, his breath, the heat that emanated from him. He kissed her, and she brought her hand up to his face. The stubbly whiskers on it grazed her palm. His arms, full of muscle and life, wrapped around her waist, his hands on her back. He was strong enough that he could lift her from the ground, out of her sorrow and panic—

She pulled back. "Oh, God, no, I shouldn't, no, I can't."

"No, I'm sorry. I know you love him . . . I gotta go, Mrs. James."

He disappeared into the darkness, leaving her to walk the twenty paces back to the house by herself.

In the bedroom, Liam waited for her. She lay down, facing away from him, her eyes still brimming with tears. The feel of Tony's kiss, of his size and weight, of his masculine energy, stayed with her, despite the fact that she'd scrubbed her face and hands with lye soap.

"I'm sorry," Liam said. "Forgive me."

"I don't want to talk about it."

"Tomorrow, we can go to the newspaper office together and speak with Mr. Ledbetter—"

"No!" she protested. "No, I'll go."

"But if I go along—"

She rolled to face him. "You don't understand. The relationship I have with Mr. Ledbetter, it's mine! It always has been. I went to him when you were in prison and asked him for that job—twice. And I got it all by myself, because I was Margaret James! And now, you've put yourself into it—"

"I'm sorry if I've stepped on your toes," Liam said stiffly. "I certainly had no intention of that."

"Never mind. I need to get to sleep."

But as she lay in bed, words flooded through her: You knew how I would feel, you knew that I would resent it, that it would ruin everything—

But that gives you no right to kiss Tony Necchi, her conscience replied. That gives you no right to dash into the arms of another man like some harlot.

The next morning, she dressed in her best suit and drove the delivery truck downtown to the offices of the *Denver City Daily News*. Mr. Ledbetter was in his office, with the door slightly ajar, as if he were expecting her. As she took a chair opposite him, she saw that he had the two *Ladies' Home*

*Journal* magazines open to the pages on which her stories had appeared years ago. Catching a glimpse of the beautiful illustration for the first, "Evelyn's Joy," she felt a wave of sadness. Oh, she'd been so young, so untested and naïve. She'd thought the world was hers to conquer.

Mr. Ledbetter greeted her by asking, "How old were you when you came in here for the first time?"

"Eighteen." Without intending to say it aloud, she added, "You called me 'little girly.'"

"And I told you not to lie to get a job. And what have you done? You've lied for years."

She fiddled with her purse. "I didn't think it would hurt anyone—"

"I assume you didn't know yesterday that your husband had contacted me."

"No, I didn't."

"It's a dangerous game you've played. We looked high and low to get the story of Liam Keohane's release from prison, and all the time, it was sitting in our offices."

"I'm sorry."

"I can't say I blame you for wanting to stay quiet." Mr. Ledbetter looked down at the magazines on his desk. "These are very good. I've always thought you made a mistake giving up fiction writing to be a sob sister. Were you afraid of success? You were going to be one, you know."

"What? No, but I couldn't—" She stopped. "I couldn't stand them anymore. George and Evelyn, I mean. Their lives were so perfect."

"So you've dedicated your talents to dumb Doras and sad sacks. What a shame."

Maggie looked at her lap. "I'll turn in the letters I wrote last night, and I'll give today's to Thalia to finish. Please, would you keep her on? She's been a good assistant, and she'll make a good Thinking Woman. If she wants to keep the name, Mrs. James, I don't care—"

"No, you won't, Mrs. James. You won't do any of that. You're the best thing that's ever happened to this newspaper. You have a following of women that Dorothy Dix would be proud of. Denver's ladies would be lost without you."

Maggie took in a deep breath. "Then you don't mind—"

"Oh, I mind. You'd better believe I mind. You've made a fool out of me—more than once—but I'd rather be a fool than another failed publisher."

"Thank you, oh, thank you."

"You can trust me that this will stay between us, Mrs. James."

"Thank—"

He closed the magazines and reached for a draft in his letter box. "Don't you have work to do?"

At home, Liam met her in the hallway. He had evidently rolled out of his office when he heard her come into the apartments. "What happened?" he asked. "Will you write under your own name now?"

"No, I won't. But I managed to keep my job."

"What did he say about my book?"

"We didn't talk about it."

Liam rolled into his office, as Maggie steeled herself to keep from running after him and apologizing for her curt reply or her success or for just being who she was. In her bedroom, she changed her clothes and went to relieve her mother, who was on the sofa trying to dig her way out of a pile of children. Maggie kissed her mother on the head.

"Thanks for keeping them, Ma." To the kids, she said, "All right, you lot, I'm home. Let Grandma rest for a while."

That evening, she kept watch from the kitchen window on the back lot. Twenty paces in one direction, twenty paces in the other—on which side of the house had Tony kissed her? She couldn't remember—only the darkness, his smell of creosote and Italian spices, the broadness of his chest and shoulders, the way his arms wrapped around her. What had she done? My God, what had she tasted there, in his kiss—sin, adultery, temptation? But also, sweetness, love, desire—all that was missing in her life.

# FORTY-THREE

On a sunny day, Jim made arrangements to take Mina to the mountains. They drove in his Marmon up Turkey Creek Canyon for as far as the car could travel. From there, Mr. Holden, the groundskeeper at Inglesfield, took them into the castle in a light sleigh pulled by two bay horses. Mina nearly disappeared beneath the lap robes that the elderly gentleman piled atop her. By the time they arrived at Inglesfield, the frigid mountain air had given her nose and cheeks a healthy bloom. She looked lovely, as radiant as her mother.

In the emptiness of the Great Room, Mina turned all the way around, gawking at the massive stone walls, the mounted heads of game animals, the grizzly bear rug on the floor. Jim urged her to stand near the fireplace, where Mr. Holden had built a fine blaze. She clutched a cloth bag in both her hands as she followed him toward the warmth.

Jim sat on the stone bench of the fireplace and patted the spot beside him. "One day your mother and I came here for a picnic," he said as Mina sat down. "We'd planned to eat outside, on the terrace, but it was cold and raining when we got here. So we spread the blanket on the floor here in front of the fireplace, and we watched the rain run down the windows as we ate."

He stopped, overcome by the memory. The rain had chilled the stone walls, and the air inside was as cold—if not colder—than it was outside. Anneka had shivered, and Jim had found a pile of buffalo hides that his grandfather had undoubtedly shot when buffalo were plentiful on the plains. He and Anneka had made love on those hides, then had fallen asleep, wrapped tightly within them.

"Your mother liked it here," he continued. "She said this place was from a fairytale, and that she was a queen when she was here. I suppose that makes you the Princess of the Castle."

"A princess!"

Jim pointed to the balustrade surrounding the upper story. "Your mother and I used to play chase along the balcony. We'd run up the stairs here"—he waved toward the grand staircase—"and go around through the bedrooms to there, then into the library, where the turret circles back down to here. The first one to run down the steps and touch the fireplace won."

"Can we do that?" Mina asked timidly.

"You have to know your way pretty well. You can't see them from here, but there are all sorts of nooks and crannies and alcoves up there. Come on, I'll show you."

They mounted the grand staircase and wended their way through the cold hallways of the upper story. Jim showed her all the rooms as they passed through. "Remember to always stay along the balustrade when you can see it," he said.

When they came into the Great Room again, after winding down the spiraling stone steps of the turret, Mina asked, "Can we do that again?"

"Do you know your way well enough?"

She nodded, and Jim shouted, "Then we're off!"

Together, they ran up the stairs, along the balcony, and through the labyrinthine rooms of the upper floor. More than once, Jim urged, "This way!" as Mina hesitated, looking from side to side for the direction. Jim let her reach the turret first, so that when she arrived back at the fireplace, she called, "I won!"

Jim trotted down the last two or three stairs, slightly out of breath. "You're fast."

"Can we do it again?"

He chased her through the upper story again, but this time, she took no false turns. By the time they reached the fireplace, they were both out of breath—Jim from running, Mina from giggling. "I'm the Princess of the Castle!" she sang. "I'm the Princess of the Castle!"

He bowed to her. "Milady."

She went to the windows. "What's down there?"

Jim joined her. "It's a lake."

"Can we walk down there?"

He hesitated. He had not been there in dozens of years. He had never walked down to it with Anneka, who had never asked him about the Graves' tragedy, although she must have known it from the gossip in the kitchen.

"Whatever Milady commands," he said.

Outside, he helped her down the slippery, narrow path that Mr. Holden had dug out by hand. On either side of them, banks of snow towered above

Jim's head. He silently thanked Kathleen for her good, country-girl sense. Mina wore a woolen skirt and sweater, thick hosiery, and sturdy boots. Jim's outfit, which included slick-soled cowboy boots, was nowhere near as practical.

At the lake, they sat on benches of split logs. "We used to put on our ice skates here," Jim remembered. "My brother, Stephen, could skate all the way around the lake without stopping. My sister Elizabeth and your Aunt Ellie would link arms and dance their way across the ice."

"What did you do?"

"I was younger, and I wasn't as sure on skates as they were. Mostly I just skated along the edges."

Even then, before the accident that took Stephen's and Elizabeth's lives, he had been alone, the one who could not keep up with his daring brother, and who was a nuisance to his swan-like sisters. Even then, he was ill at ease in his own family.

Mina fiddled with the drawstrings on the cloth bag she carried.

"What do you have in there?" Jim asked.

"These." She removed a metal pencil box embossed with the Eiffel Tower from the bag. Inside, eight colored pencils lay in a row, some of them worn to stubs. Only the orange pencil was still at full length.

"Mrs. Kathleen gave these to me," Mina said. "She told me a friend gave them to her a long time ago. See, some of them have been used so much they're nearly gone. She said she drew pictures with them during the war to make the hurt soldiers smile."

The Eiffel Tower on the box. The pencils worn to near stubs. These had to be the pencils that Paul Reston had given to her for Christmas in 1917. Jim remembered seeing them when he had visited the girls of the Relief Society in Nice.

"Why didn't you ask her for a new set?" he asked. "These don't have much life left in them."

"I didn't want a new set. Mrs. Kathleen said that when she got them, you couldn't buy them at Woolworth's. They're special. But the orange is a dud."

"A dud?"

"That's what she called it. It has never worked, that's why it's still so long. It doesn't color, it just tears up the paper." Mina took a sketchbook from her bag. "She gave me this, too."

Jim took the sketchbook from her. On the front cover, in careful, even cursive was the name "Mina Maira Graves."

"I see you wrote your name on it," he said.

"Mrs. Kathleen told me to. Is that all right?"

"Of course, it's all right, Mina. It belongs to you."

He flipped through the book. The pictures—some of which had lightly penciled corrections—were stiff and unimaginative. Jim envisioned Kathleen bending over Mina's work, making suggestions and trying to help her with some of the more difficult features. Still, the sketches showed little evidence of artistic talent.

"Would you like to draw something now?" he asked. "The lake, perhaps?"

On a new page, Mina drew a featureless blue oval for the lake. At once, she began to fill it with squiggled lines that looked like waves, even though the lake lay before them calm and still.

The plain blue oval; her uninspired strokes; her lowered head—they struck Jim as unspeakably sad. Why did things crumble so easily, why were they so tenuous? Why were children so often the victims of adult folly? And to try to aright the past was a task that defeated even the best man.

"You used to dance with Marta," he said. "Do you still like to dance?"

Her eyes lit up. "Mother taught me ballet. She taught me plee-"

"Plié."

"Oh, I loved ballet! She said you had to be strong to do ballet, strong and beautiful."

"And you are both of those things," Jim put an arm around her shoulders as Mina went back to coloring in her sketch. "Mina, I know you don't completely understand what happened to you, but I want you to know that I loved your mother very much."

"Did she go to heaven when she died?"

"I'm sure she did."

"But you weren't married to her when I was born."

"No," Jim said stolidly. "We were never married."

"Then I am a b . . . a bas . . ."

"A bastard?"

She nodded, wearing the pencil's point away against the page.

"That's a very unpleasant word that isn't used much today," Jim said. "Where did you hear it?"

"Miss Judith told me that my father was finally coming to get his bastard. She meant me. Clyde called me that, too."

Good Lord, the Dercums and their vile religion, where punishment and intolerance were rife and compassion non-existent. How could such hateful people call themselves Christian?

"It was probably to shame you," he said. "But you shouldn't be ashamed."

"But being a bastard is a sin, and my mother was a sinner. And Bishop White said that God never fails to punish the wicked. They're cast into the terrible fires of hell where Satan waits to—"

"Mina, stop," Jim said. "Stop this. Anyone as good and loving as your mother would not be cast into the fires of hell. She was never wicked or cruel or bad. She was smart, and she cared for others, and she believed in goodness and mercy. Hell, if it exists, is for the truly evil."

"Miss Judith said it's as real as heaven."

"I don't—" He started again. "Have you asked Mrs. Kathleen about this? She knows more about it than I do."

"No! I don't want her to know my mother wasn't married."

"She knows that I wasn't married."

"Oh," Mina said, crestfallen.

"Why are you worried that Mrs. Kathleen knows?" Jim asked. "Has she spoken to you about it?"

"No!" Mina reacted. "No, but . . . I want her to like me."

The last plea, so pitiful, was delivered through the scratch, scratch, scratch of the pencil on the page. Jim reached over and put his hand over hers to stop it. A tear fell on the page and pooled there.

"I miss Mother," she said." I want my mother."

And suddenly, the child who had shown no emotion for months sobbed, repeating, "I want Mother, I want Mother."

Jim put his arms around her. "Oh, my darling."

He kissed the top of her head. The wetness of her tears and open mouth soaked the wool of his great coat.

He looked out over the lake. Mina's cries had startled the birds from the trees. As Jim watched them disappear into the blue sky, he realized the terrible weight of grief: you cannot rebuild, you cannot recover. You are never again a complete person, but a shackling together of whatever pieces you can collect. You will forever long for the quiet depths of the grave, to be at peace with them—the brother, the sister, the mother who died.

Mina had quieted to only an occasional sniffle. Jim reached for his handkerchief.

"Dry your eyes, now," he said. "And we'll go home. You can tell Stephen and Susanna what you've seen today—they've never been here, did you know that? And Mrs. Kathleen will want to see your drawing of the lake."

Mina stood, forgetting about the pencils in her lap, which dropped to the ground. "Oh, no!" She fell to her knees, scrambling in the snow to pick them up. "I can't lose them! Mrs. Kathleen said I could draw whatever I dreamed of!"

As Jim knelt to help her pick them up, he recalled Anneka's disdain for the gifts that he had given to Mina. When he'd inquired what Mina wanted for Christmas, Anneka had replied: *She is a little girl, she does not care for things. She wants dreams.*

Kathleen had given them to her.

He handed her a nubby green. "Here, is this the last of them?"

"Yes."

"Mina." He took her by the shoulders. "I will not leave you. You must trust me, you must believe me. Your home will always be with me, and you will always be my daughter."

He drew her against him, and she put her arms around him. After he released her, she packed the colored pencils and sketchbook into her bag and took his hand to walk up the icy trail to the castle.

After the house in the Denver Country Club had quieted that evening, Jim searched his bookshelves for a copy of the poem, "Prometheus," by Goethe. He had once been able to read it in its original German, but years of disuse had stripped him of a clear memory of the language. Settling into one of the cowhide chairs near the fireplace with a translation, he read: *"Cover thy spacious heavens, Zeus, With clouds of mist—"*

A knock sounded on the door, and Kathleen entered the study. He closed the book as she sat in the matching cowhide chair.

"How did it go today?" she asked anxiously. "Did you have any luck getting through to her?"

"I think so. All in all, it was quite an enjoyable day." He sipped brandy. "Although she did cry quite a bit over her mother."

"It sounds cruel to say it, but that's good. She said you took her to the castle. Why there? I wouldn't have thought—"

"I used to take Anneka there. We would drive up to the castle in the summertime. We'd spend the afternoon making love before the fireplace."

The statement rang through the room. "Where we had our picnic lunch," Kathleen said at last.

Something in her words—the hesitation, the low volume, the lack of expression—made Jim see it as she did. What a stupid boy he'd been, brash and thoughtless—to take his illicit lover to a place of pain and sorrow for trysts. He saw now the vulgarity of it, how sordid and low it had been, especially when compared to her wartime romance of precious moments and constant danger. But he was no longer the young man on top of the world who loved Anneka. He carried the years since her death with him as heavily as Mina did.

"Mina asked me about her legitimacy," he said. "Evidently Mrs. Dercum impressed upon her that she was a bastard."

"Oh, is there anything more they could have told her to make her feel bad about herself? Poor girl."

"She wanted to know if her mother had gone to hell for having an illegitimate child." He shook his head. "The misery that religion introduces into human existence is appalling. It allows for cruelty and judgment, and exclusion and oppression, all in the name of godliness."

"It also allows for kindness and hope," Kathleen said solidly.

Jim opened his book and read: *"I know naught poorer Under the sun, than ye Gods! Ye nourish painfully, with Sacrifices and votive prayers, Your majesty: Ye would e'en starve, if children and beggars Were not trusting fools."*

"What is that?"

"It's the poem I was reading when I met Anneka."

She leaned back in her chair.

"Do you believe that Anneka burned—or is burning—in hell?" he asked. "What's your Catholic assessment?"

"Jim—"

"You're the one who has clung to the Church through all these years. It's only fair you share it with me."

"If Anneka truly repented her sins and asked God for forgiveness—"

"I doubt she would repent—or regret—the sin that gave her Mina. And with that, she's cast into hellfire once more."

"This is not helping the situation," Kathleen said firmly. "We need to make Mina feel as if she's a legitimate member of the family."

"She showed me the pencils that you'd given her." Jim said. "Those are the ones Paul gave you in France, aren't they? Why did you give her those? Why didn't you buy her new ones?"

Kathleen smiled. "She was intrigued by them, and their history. And they'd been lying in that drawer for years. I thought, why not? They were special to me, why not let them be special to her?"

At times, Kathleen's determined kindness awed him. To give such a precious item as the pencils to a child who might—as Mina had almost done today—lose it. What a tremendous gift of the heart.

"I'm afraid she has no artistic talent," he said.

"She doesn't know that."

"I suggested that she learn ballet. She seemed delighted by that."

"That's a good idea," Kathleen acknowledged. "You know I'm doing what I can. But without your help, I'm just floundering with Mina—"

"She wants you to like her."

"I do like her, and I want her to do well. But for months, you've ignored her and dismissed me. And you've done nothing to stop your parents and Ellie and all their friends from thinking that bringing Mina here was my doing. You need to take responsibility and tell the truth—that it was our decision, not merely mine. Mina and I are outcasts, creeping in and out of rooms after you, only acknowledged when we have to be by your mother and sister—"

"Why must you always make yourself out to be a martyr?"

"I resent that I've become a black sheep—more than I was before—for doing what was right. I'd earn more attention from your family if I were the maid, if I were Anneka, bringing in the tea."

Her bluntness strafed him. "And what about Paul Reston, the other thorn in the sadly-suffering heart of our marriage? The night you spent with him—or is it many times, now?—is never far from us. You're no more special than any other woman, Kathleen. You can't expect to keep both a husband and a lover without some consequence."

"I've told you, he is not my lover. We have not—"

"Then what is he to you now? Just a friend? A tea companion? A mah-jongg partner?"

"That isn't what this is about. Why can't we come to some agreement— any agreement—anymore?"

He could keep on—he could continue to bully and badger her about Paul, but where would it lead? Back to separate rooms, separate domiciles, he at his suite in the Brown Palace and Kathleen here or in Redlands. Lethargy swept through him, settling in his bones. This tug-of-war could not continue; it consumed too much of their time, energy, their ability to live and succeed.

"Why don't we go to Stock Show?" he said. "We can stay the night at the Brown Palace."

She looked at him squarely. "I thought you were too busy at the State House."

He shrugged. "I've already introduced my bills. There won't be any serious action until after the end of the introductory session."

"I wasn't intending to buy any stock this year."

"So, we'll go and look it over, and then walk off without spending a dime." He shrugged. "Perhaps we could mend some of the ill will between us, too."

"One night at the Brown Palace isn't going to fix all that's wrong between us."

"No, but it could be a start."

"And then?"

"What do you mean?"

"When we come home, will everything be just as it was before? The next time you're angry or upset, will you run off to the Brown, or to the Moffat Oil Field, or to the Capitol so that you don't have to face it? Will you bury yourself in your work so you don't have to face me?"

"I miss you," he said. "I want us to be as we were before all this mess— all these messes—came into our lives."

His confession—which surprised him as much as it surprised her—felt as if it had opened a vein in him and allowed the blood to pool at her feet. She could either mercifully stanch it, or she could allow it to drain him dry.

"So do I," she said evenly.

"Then let's do it. Let's go away for a day or two."

She twisted her wedding ring as if she were a virgin being propositioned by a roué rather than a woman who had been married to the same man for the better part of a decade. "All right," she agreed tentatively. "I'll speak with the staff."

The day at Stock Show is a great success. After looking over the stock, Kathleen buys new heifers for her herd, while Jim stands aside, watching her browbeat a giant of a man into a lower price. That evening, they eat in the suite, forgoing the boisterous dining room and restaurant downstairs. The waiters bring in an assortment of Colorado lamb, freshly-caught rainbow trout from the mountain streams, and steak from cattle raised on the eastern plains, as part of the seven-course meal that ends in a Grand

Hotel Fizz—a mixture of orange juice, maraschino cherry, sweet cream, and other sweet flavors. Before the waiter adds soda water to make the drink bubble, Jim adds a finger of gin to each.

"To your fine purchase today," Jim toasts as the drink slops over the rim of his glass. "I haven't heard your full-blooded Irish brogue in a while."

Kathleen's eyes are lit by the wine she drank with the meal. "He thought he could hoodwink me because I'm a woman—"

"He will never make that mistake again."

"I know what I'm doing," she says, in a rare and uncharacteristic boast. "He's going back to Nebraska with a year's income in his pocket. His wife will be delighted to see him. Their children will all have new shoes and coats come September."

"I suppose it's no surprise that you'd think first of the benefits for them, and not for yourself."

"Not at all. I'll have some beautiful calves next breeding season."

They spend the evening sitting near the fire and watching the comings and goings on the street below. Spying Jim at the window, one of the revelers signals for him to come down and join the riotous party that has spilled over onto Tremont Place. The man waves a flask until a woman plucks it from his hand. The two disappear into the crowd.

"They're having a fine time," Kathleen remarks.

"Until tomorrow morning, when they wake up with their money rolls gone and their heads aching," Jim says. "Typical Stock Show shenanigans."

At bedtime, Kathleen sits at the mirror, trying to untangle a pearl-encrusted comb from her hair.

"Let me do that." Jim sets about untangling the strands of her hair from between and around the pearls. "How did this thing get so confounded? It's trapped like a fly in a spider's web."

"Confounded?" Kathleen laughs. "Is that the right word?"

"Isn't it? I don't know. I'm not thinking straight."

"Well, confound it."

She dissolves into laughter, with far more hilarity than the joke warrants. As Jim laughs, a spark alights. He kisses the tender spot beneath her earlobe.

Kathleen leans back toward him, still saucy with wit and pride. One of her hands reaches up to his hair, her neck arched and lovely beneath his lips. Her breath quickens, with laughter, with desire, hot on his cheek, and he seeks her mouth, brought to his knees by the sweetness of the moment. She turns toward him, taking his face in her hands, and he runs his hands from her shoulders to her waist before he lifts her and carries her to the bed. They make love beneath luxurious feather-filled comforters, bathed in the golden light of the hotel's diamond-laced chandeliers. In the elaborate room, with its double-doored privacy and its perch above much of the city, they rediscover what they have squandered in each other.

After they make love, they lie in each other's arms. Kathleen dozes, but Jim listens to the revelers outside the hotel. All the bitter words that had passed between him and Kathleen, the accusations and mistrust of last summer—could it all be washed away by desire, tenderness, the elemental workings of the heart?

He trails his fingertips down her arm. She stretches lazily, a sleeping lioness, and draws closer to him. "This is how it should be," she murmurs.

Jim kisses her hair. "You mean love?"

"Marriage."

"Ah," he says, and nothing more.

# FORTY-FOUR

Chava cradled the soft bundle of Hannah in her arms as she sang: *"Shlof shoyn mayn tayer faygele, Makh shoyn tsu dayn kosher aygelekh, Shlof shoyn shlof, In ziser ruh, Aaaaai lu lu lu lu lu lu."*

Sleep now my pretty little one; Slumber on my precious little one; Sleep in peace, the whole night through.

Hannah shivered in her sleep, her tiny, dimpled hands elegantly folded beneath her chin.

"Ten fingers, ten toes," Chava whispered. "How can one so small be so perfect?"

"You need to have one of your own," Rachael teased from where she sat on the divan. "Making a baby is as wonderful as having one. Oh, Chava, what you don't know, and what Judah would like to teach you."

As Rachael laughed, Chava smiled to herself. She did know—so much more than anyone imagined. Sometimes, she dreamed of carrying Sean's child, of giving birth to a son or daughter who could only astound them. Would he—or she—have eyes of piercing blue or deep amber; would he have Sean's raven hair or Chava's chocolate brown; would her face carry the surprising paleness of Sean's skin or the olive color of her own?

Sean would be such a fine father.

"Are you going to Mrs. Bergman's tonight?" Rachael asked. "I wish she would find someone else. I worry about all this going about at night."

"It's only temporary," Chava murmured, although she did not meet Rachael's gaze.

Since Sean had left the police force, he and Chava had had to devise various ruses to see each other. They had decided it was best to meet in Berkeley Park, rather than near Sloan's Lake, now that he had no valid business in the West Side neighborhood. Tonight, Chava had told Rachael that she had to take charge of the children at the Sheltering Home while Mrs. Bergman went to a meeting of a literary reading club.

"Well, be careful," Rachael said. "It's snowing."

"Of course, I'll be careful." Chava kissed the top of Rachael's head. "Don't worry."

Chava laid Hannah in the crib and went into her own room. There, she combed her hair, rouged her cheeks and lips, and puffed her neck and arms with apricot powder. Skipping out of the house, she buttoned her coat against the bitter January wind. The snow was falling in heavy, wet flakes. Taking the streetcar, she traveled north toward Berkeley Park.

She crept up the steps at Sean's boarding house, trying not to alert his landlady. On the shadowy third floor landing, she jangled her metal ring of keys to find the one to his apartment. She had nearly inserted it in the lock when she heard the swish of fabric behind her.

"Hello, Jewgirl."

Chava whirled, the keys flying from her grip. Blocking the stairs was a knight of the Ku Klux Klan. She opened her mouth, but no sound came forth. Frantic, she lunged for the key.

Moving with surprising speed, he bent and scooped up the ring. "So he's given you a key to his place. How handy."

"Give it to me!" She pressed her back against the door of Sean's room. The man towered over her, his hood making him close to seven feet tall. He smelled of boiled onions and greasy meat.

"You have a pretty voice."

"Give it back! Now!"

"You're an impatient little thing. Hold out your hand and say please." She had no choice but to obey. "Please."

He examined the keys. "So you have a key to his place, and a key to your brother and sister-in-law's house, and a key to your school, where you teach the poor, little, tuberculosis-riddled orphans, right?"

How did he know all this about her? Sean would never have spoken about her outside his family. Unless someone had followed him on his beat through the West Side. Someone who knew he stopped every night at the house on Osceola Street. And if they had followed him, then surely, they had followed her as well.

"You're one of the policemen who filled out the application and joined the Klan, aren't you?" she accused, hoping that someone—anyone—would appear on the stairs behind him. "You're a coward—hiding under that hood, scaring women because it's what makes you feel strong."

The Klansman enclosed the keys in his fist. "And I'm doing a good job of it, too, wouldn't you say?"

Please, please, Chava prayed. Someone come up the stairs. Someone, anyone. No light issued from beneath any other door on the third floor, and she couldn't hear any radios or phonographs playing in the dingy house. She could not push past him—to try would be the same as slamming against a wall. Her only hope was to scream. If she screamed, surely someone would hear. Someone would come.

The Klansman read her thoughts. "If you scream, I'll take you somewhere you won't be heard. Now, ask me nice for the key. And don't forget to say please."

Sweat broke out on her back and armpits. "Give me the key."

"Say, I'm a Jew whore."

"No."

"Say it. If you want this." He held out his hand, palm flat, the keys couched in it.

"No!" She grabbed for the keys. The Klansman whisked them away, catching her right wrist with his left hand. His fingers tightened around it, digging into her flesh. She tugged at his hand, trying to free herself.

"You're not very polite." He jerked her closer, wrenching her wrist. "And you aren't too smart either. I knew you'd try that."

She cried out as she fell forward against him. "Let me go!"

"You smell good."

Chava lashed out with her free hand, aiming toward his eyes. Her fingernails only grazed the thick fabric of his hood, and she tried again.

"Jesus Christ!" With a fist, the Klansman knocked her sideways. She fell against the door, smacking her brow on the jamb. Her head reeled, and her eyelid felt sticky and warm. Blood trickled down her face. Desperately, she wiped it away with the back of her hand. Her knees buckling beneath her, she slid toward the ground.

The Klansman grasped her by the shoulders. Pinning her against the door with his left arm across her throat, he snatched at her coat. Chava tugged on his arm with both her hands, tears spilling from her eyes. As her windpipe constricted, she gasped for air.

He taunted in her ear: "You shouldn't have made me mad."

He clawed at her blouse. The light chamois ripped, buttons bouncing on the floor. His hand wandered over her breasts, his fingers snaking inside her bra until the elastic gave way. He pinched and twisted her nipples between his fingers. She whimpered as the pain shot through her shoulders into her jaw. Saliva filled her mouth.

His knee pushed in between her legs, his beefy body weighing against hers, immobilizing her against the door. Her breath puffed from her.

He rocked against her. "Is that what you come here for? To be bedded? Like a cat in heat?"

The fabric of the hood grazed her lips and forehead.

"Your boyfriend's a cocky little shitass. Thinks he knows what's what. But you tell him, this is our city now, and he better watch himself."

Blood vessels burst in her head, causing distended black shapes before her eyes.

He jammed the key into the lock. If she fainted, he would be free to do to her as he pleased, and to leave her there for Sean to find—or worse, he would wait for Sean after he'd . . . You have to fight, she told herself. You have to do something.

With an effort that required all her strength, she squirmed, feebly kicking at him. His grip loosened from her neck long enough for her to grunt out a garbled cry.

"Who's there?"

The voice reached her—perhaps it was only her imagination—through a haze of shooting, red sparks. Help me! Chava cried, knowing her words could not be heard. Please help me! I can't breathe!

The knight opened the bedroom door and shoved her inside. She reeled backward and downward, her skull cracking against something as she fell. Nauseous and dizzy, she scrambled on all fours to the far side of the bed and covered her head with her hands, her shoulders pressed into the mattress.

Minutes ticked by before she peered over the bed. She blinked to focus, her eyes bulgy and popped, her head pounding, her heart beating irregularly. Nothing moved in the silent room. The broken closet door stood open, but the clothes within were blissfully motionless. The Klansman was gone.

She gagged, a foul taste flooding her mouth. Curling into a ball, she clasped her shoulders, crossing her arms over her sore breasts. Her brain burned with the return of oxygen, and the gash on the back of her head prickled with pain. Blood smeared her hair, face and hands. And she was cold, so cold. With stiff fingers, she pulled the quilt from Sean's bed and wrapped herself in it.

The door of the apartment burst open, and light blazed through the room. Oh, God, had he come back to finish the job? Sitting up, she tried to stifle her fear with the quilt.

"Sorry I'm late. They called me down to the station to pick up my last pay, and—"

Sean stopped, dead still, in the middle of the room.

Chava buried her face and cinched the quilt around her with her fists.

"Oh, my God!" He knelt before her, his hands on her shoulders. "Are you sick? Did you hurt yourself?"

"Leave me alone!" Her voice was no more than a hoarse growl.

"Let me see!" He put his hand under her chin, and forced her to raise her face. "What in God's name? Who did this to you?"

She could see out of only one eye, and the back of her head rang with pain. Sobbing, she buried her face against the side of his mattress.

"Chava," Sean pleaded. "Take off the blanket, let me see!"

"No! No, leave me—!"

With a quick tug, he stole it from her, exposing her. The tatters of her blouse hung limply under her arms; the shredded bodice of her camisole and bra flapped downward. The wool of her coat had ragged holes where the buttons had been ripped away.

"Jesus Christ, I'm going to kill him!" Sean ran his fingers down her throat and over her shoulders. "What did he do? You're black and blue!"

"I couldn't breathe—"

"Don't move. I have to call a doctor. There's a phone at the drug store—"

What if the Klansman came back when he saw Sean leave? What if he was waiting in the dark hallway for Sean? "Don't leave me! Oh, God, Sean, don't leave me here alone! He might still be in the house!"

"Chava, who was it? Who did this?"

"He wore a hood and robe! He took my keys, he wouldn't give them back, I tried to fight him, but I couldn't!"

"It was a Klansman? Come on, I have to get you out of here."

"No! I don't want anyone to know—!"

"You can't stay here! You need a doctor! You need to be somewhere safe!" His voice tore at her. "Chava—Jesus God in heaven—come on, now. Wrap the blanket around you. Here, let me help you."

He walked her down to his car, holding her close to him as she stepped along the ice. Revving up his car, he fishtailed down the street to the drug store. Before he went inside to use the pay phone, Chava said, "Please don't call Max and Rachael."

"But—"

"Please, not now."

While Sean went inside, she covered her face with the blanket. How dare that man do this to her? Why would he—?

Because she was a Jew who was in love with a Catholic—such an easy target.

She laid her aching head against the cold glass of the window. To be called a whore, to be treated as one—how shameful it was, how humiliating.

Sean came back with a grim expression on his face and an impatience with the slippery roads. As they careened away from the drug store, Chava asked, "Where are you taking me?"

"Kathleen thinks you'll be safest at the Restons' house in Park Hill. She's calling ahead to arrange it."

"I don't even know them—"

"That's right. They'll never find you there."

# FORTY-FIVE

Faces parade through the richly furnished room in Julia Reston's house where Chava lies in a nest of warm, supple blankets. Through the long night and the next day, while the spruce outside the window sways in a fierce, snow-laden wind, Chava watches faces come and go through her eye that is not swollen shut.

The first face is Julia's, of course, helping her up the stairs, along with Sean. Chava, hobbled by cold and soreness and a terrible weariness, can barely stand upright. Leaving Sean in the hallway, Julia offers Chava a silken kimono to replace her tattered clothes. Chava fumbles with her clothing, her teeth chattering, her body quaking.

"I've asked Paul to call Dr. Erickson," Julia informs her as she turns down the bed covers.

Chava's battered throat has swollen even tighter, and she can barely croak, "I don't want anyone touching me—"

"He's my own personal physician," Julia reassures her. "And a trusted friend. You can be sure that he will be kind and considerate."

"Stay in the room," Chava begs. "Please, stay in the room with me."

"I will." Julia adds, "And I'll contact your family myself to tell them that you are staying here tonight. Your brother does have a telephone?"

"Please don't call! Max will be so angry—"

"He needs to know you're safe. The roads are slick, and he'll worry if you don't come home. Tomorrow, we can tell him about what's happened."

Dr. Erickson looks over the bruises and cuts with detached professionalism. He asks Chava to follow his finger with her eyes—her eye, that is—and looks into her mouth. While Chava clenches her fists, he gently probes the swollen, painful flesh behind her ears, down her throat and on her breasts. He announces that she needs stitches in the back of her head, and near her right eye, where the gash from the door jamb runs just through the end of her eyebrow. "I will do my best, Miss Rosen, to see you have no scar." He rolls up his sleeves and rummages in his bag. "You're lucky he didn't crush your windpipe. The damage is very severe."

"Will I sing again?" Chava whispers.

"Pardon?"

"Will I be able to sing? I teach at the Sheltering Home, and I sing—"

"Do you?" His stern face softens into a smile. "I believe you will sing as well as ever, once the swelling has passed. For now, though, talk as little as possible. Don't strain your voice."

"Can I bathe?" She appeals to Julia. "Please, may I bathe?"

"Yes," Dr. Erickson says. "But don't wash your stitches yet."

Julia holds Chava's hand while Dr. Erickson closes the wound on the back of her head and sews up the painful split in her eyebrow. Chava's eyes sting with each prick of the needle, and Julia wipes away the tears. Afterward, Chava bathes in the tub in a bathroom down the hall, in oils that smell of vanilla. She cannot lean back against the tub's edge because of the stitches in her skull, but sits upright, her sore body erect. She splashes water up on her neck, wincing at even the touch of the washrag. All at once, she recalls the feel of his hands on her neck, and the press of his body into hers, his knee jammed between her thighs. Tears dripping into the water, she scrubs harder, ignoring her aching flesh.

When she returns to the bedroom, she finds Julia tucking hot water bottles in at the foot of the bed. "Sean has asked to come up and see you before you go to sleep," Julia says.

"No!" Chava reacts. "I don't want him to see me—"

"He brought you here, dear," Julia reminds her. "He's seen you."

"No, please, please, not tonight!"

Graciously, Julia withdraws, and Dr. Erickson reappears. He applies a mentholated poultice to her breast and throat to ease the swelling. He props up pillows behind her. "I want you to sleep upright. Don't lie flat. With your breathing so constricted, I'm afraid your lungs may collect fluid."

"I could get pneumonia?"

He pats her hand. "We'll do all we can to prevent it. I'll be back tomorrow."

He administers a dose of laudanum. As the storm rages, Chava falls into a deep, dreamless sleep.

She wakes in the morning when Kathleen Graves carries a tea tray into the room. "Julia thought you might be hungry," Kathleen says. "She sent up porridge and scrambled eggs, soft foods that won't be so hard to swallow. Do you think you can eat?"

Chava tries to swallow, but everything has tightened during the night. The laudanum has worn off, and now her shoulders and neck throb with pain. Even though her stomach rumbles with hunger, she shakes her head. Undeterred, Kathleen sits in the chair beside the bed.

"There's tea with lemon and plenty of sugar," she offers. "The warmth might be good for your throat. It might clear it some."

"Thank you." Chava accepts the cup.

"Miss Rosen . . . Chava, I know we've only met once, but I want you to know that whatever I can do for you and Seaney—Sean—just let me know. Whatever you need or want, just ask me."

Kathleen's offer reduces Chava to tears. "I was so scared!"

"I know. But you're safe now, and you can trust everyone in this house to help you."

"The . . .Klansman"—there, she had said it—"called me vile names. What if Sean sees me that way, now, too?"

"He won't. He's downstairs now. He's been here all night. He wants to talk to you—"

"Look at me! I've never been touched by anyone but Sean, and now someone else has . . . no one has ever done anything like this to me—"

"Shh, save your voice," Kathleen says gently. "The bruises will heal. The swelling, the stitches—they'll be gone. You'll be as lovely as you ever were."

"That doesn't matter!" Pain sears her throat, and she returns to a whisper. "I can feel him. Where he touched me, what he did to me, what he said—I'll never forget it as long as I live."

"Maybe not, but don't forget what's important. You're safe now, and the doctor said there will be no lasting damage. And Sean loves you, no matter what happened last night. Talk to him. You'll see."

"I'm afraid he'll never want me again."

"He's beside himself just now. Won't you talk to him?"

Chava violently shakes her head.

Seemingly resigned, Kathleen lifts a cloth bag from the floor. "Julia thought you might be more comfortable in, um, more traditional clothes. I bought some things at Daniels & Fisher this morning—nightgowns, clean drawers, socks, slippers, and a robe. If they don't fit or if you need more, just ask Julia to call and have more sent over."

"I'll pay you—"

Kathleen lays a hand on her wrist. "Chava, please."

Chava says no more, although tears stream from her eyes again. Kathleen spreads the gowns, delicately embroidered and sewn from the best linen, on the bed. Most of them button up closely around the neck, and Chava realizes at once that they would hide much of the bruising. Suddenly self-conscious, she gathers the loose kimono around her throat. "Thank you."

"Paul wants to know if you'll consider speaking to him," Kathleen says gently. "He wants to make an official report to the District Attorney's office."

"Oh, I could never tell him—"

"Think about it. You've been the victim of an awful crime. It shouldn't go unpunished." Before Kathleen leaves, she kisses Chava gently on the forehead, and Chava senses that she is passing on some message from Sean— or trying to prove to Chava that she is not as hideous as she believes she is.

But she is. Alone again, Chava climbs from bed and looks at herself in the mirror on the dresser. The entire left side of her face is discolored from hitting the door jamb, and the marks on her throat have deepened to purplish-black. Fierce black bruises underscore her swollen right eye. She touches the back of her head where Dr. Erickson shaved her hair. She can feel cold air on the nape of her neck, where her hair used to lie.

A knock sounds on the door, and Julia leans into the room. "Chava, your brother is here. Are you ready to see him?"

"Yes."

Chava returns to the bed. Max bursts in, still wearing his overcoat. His face blanches when he sees her. "Dear God!"

Chava reflexively touches her face. "Max, please, listen—"

"Last night, we received a call from this stranger, this Julia, who said you were staying here because of the snow. Then, this morning, a man named Paul met me as I was opening the store to tell me you were hurt while you were waiting to meet a friend. What is going on? We've been so worried—"

"Max, please." Her throat pulsing painfully, she explains to him about the previous evening, leaving out so much—so much!—that horrifies her yet. Tears drip onto the fine linen of her nightgown, until the wet cloth sticks to her chest. Shivering, she pulls her robe closer around her.

Max's wrinkled forehead beads with sweat in the warm room. Still, he does not remove his coat. "And this friend you were meeting. It was a man?"

"Yes."

"All those evenings you said Mrs. Bergman needed your help, you've been meeting a man?"

Chava rubs her forehead, accidentally tugging the stitches in her eyebrow. Quickly, she pulls her fingers away. "Yes."

"You've been lying to us? You've been sneaking away to meet him, telling me, telling Rachael"—his face twists—"that you're at the Home? How could you do this? How could you betray our trust?"

"I chose to meet him! I wanted to be with him—"

"Who is he? Is it this Paul?"

Chava swallows painfully. "No, it's not Paul. It's Sean Sullivan."

"The Catholic patrolman? What sort of man is he to encourage a decent woman to engage in such disreputable behavior?"

His harsh question releases a wave of guilt and revulsion in her. The question is not what kind of man Sean is—he is always honorable and good at heart—but what kind of woman would do as she'd done. One, she fears, who has no dignity or self-respect.

Max stands and walks to the window, his back to her. "Rachael has treated you as her dearest friend, her sister. She's trusted you to take care of Hannah, like a second mother. What am I to tell her now?"

The throbbing in her body flares. "Please, Max, Rachael and Hannah are the world to me! Don't make them think badly of me."

"I won't have to." He turns to face her. "When will you be well enough to come home? I'd like you to leave here as soon as possible. This afternoon?"

"No! Look at me! I can't let Rachael see me this way—"

"I want you away from him."

"But Julia and Paul and Kathleen, Sean's cousin—they've shown me nothing but kindness! And Dr. Erickson—he's trustworthy and nice, too. Let me stay here until I can hide what's happened to me—"

"Chava, you brought this on yourself. By lying, by breaking the laws of our faith, by being shameless—there is no one to blame but you."

She rolls away from him, her knees drawn up to her chest to stave off the pain in her heart and lungs and head. Sobbing, she does not hear Max leave, but only stirs when Julia speaks: "Chava, dear, I have another dose of laudanum for you. It will help you to calm down."

After Julia gives her the drug, she slips away into sleep.

# FORTY-SIX

Sean sat in his car, hidden in an alley. Shadow spread over him, the only illumination a patch of streetlight draped like a shawl over the passenger's seat. He shivered—the temperature had dipped below freezing—and rubbed his stiff fingers. Stuffing his hands into the pockets of his coat, he settled back against the seat to wait.

Across Curtis Street, the lighted marquee of the Kool Kozy Kafe blinked and buzzed. Tinny music blared as customers came and went from the cafe, and the sound of laughter, clinking glasses and jumbled conversation sliced through the frigid air. Cars sped along Curtis, and the trolley rumbled over the tracks, blocking his sight at times. Still, Sean kept his eyes on the black Oldsmobile that belonged to Walt Wells.

He had already been here for two hours. He hadn't eaten today; he hadn't bathed or changed clothes since yesterday morning. The stink of his sweat and the rankness of his breath pierced the bitter air in the car. Two days beard growth scratched along his chin, and his feet were numb in his thin leather shoes. He didn't care. With merciless clarity, the events of the last twenty-four hours crashed in on him. Finding her huddled in his room, her vomit strewn across the floor, her face—so beautiful, so perfect—ripped and beaten. He had never felt so helpless, so worthless. After he had taken her to Julia's, he had sat listlessly on the couch in the living room, staring at Julia's paintings until the vivid images burned in his brain, and he dreamed of them as bruises on Chava's throat.

He knew immediately who had done this: Walt Wells. No one else would have held such a grudge against him, or needed to prove his superiority so badly, or felt that he was above the law. Wells fit the description that Chava had given of the Klansman as huge, and he was the only one, besides Able and Peters, who called Sean "Seaney" at the station.

But Chava—why wouldn't she see him? Why wouldn't she speak to him? She blamed him, he knew. And it was his fault. Why had he ever thought it safe to meet her at his apartment? Why had he ever thought he could speak to her, much less court her, without putting her in danger? Yet he couldn't bear to be shut out of her life, without a chance to apologize, to try to make it right. Last night, after Paul and Julia had retired, he had crept up the stairs and knocked at the door of Chava's room. There was no answer.

He'd awakened this morning when the maid, Rosa, had walked into the parlor to light the fire. "Excuse me," she'd said, her eyes wide with surprise. "I didn't know anyone was in here—"

"Sorry." Sean had hauled himself off the sofa, where he'd slept, and to the bathroom at the end of the hall. When he had come out, his grizzled face splashed by cold water, the house was alive with movement. Paul, greatcoat buttoned tight, shoveling a path to his car through the snow outside. Julia, cooking in the kitchen, while the displaced maid cast quizzical looks toward Sean. And Kathleen, newly arrived, her coat crookedly buttoned, her hair a mess of curls, looking as if she had stumbled directly from bed.

"Oh, Seaney, I'm so sorry," she said.

"See if she'll talk to me," he had begged. "Please, get her to talk to me."

But Kathleen had failed, as Julia had. Chava refused to see him.

Well, all that was done. He'd seen to that. After Max Rosen had arrived, ripping through the Reston house with the vengeance of God, Sean, Paul, Julia and Kathleen had waited silently in the parlor. When Max reappeared, his voice carried a deadly weight. "I will be back to pick up my sister this afternoon."

Paul accepted the challenge. "She's welcome to stay until—"

"No, I think it would be best to take her home."

"I'll have to check with Dr. Erickson," Julia said. "It's so bitterly cold outside, and he has expressed some fear of pneumonia—"

"Thank you." Max dismissed her. "But I'll see she has proper care at home." Scanning the faces in the room, he added, "And I would appreciate it if none of you attempted to contact her again."

Sean emerged from his torpor. "Now, wait a minute—"

Max's sharp gaze honed in on him. "You, sir, I believe, are responsible for this. I ask you, please, not to try to see or talk to my sister again."

"I'll take responsibility for what happened to her. It was my doing, yes. But it's her decision whether or not to see—"

Max offered his hand. "I ask it for my sister's safety."

And suddenly, the whole foolish thing crashed down on his head—Catholic boy and Jewish girl, Romeo and Juliet all over again, stupidity and folly. He ignored Kathleen's murmured, "Seaney, don't." Without speaking, he shook Max Rosen's hand.

What an ungodly mess he'd made of things. At one time, his entire life had been mapped out like a road through a valley, straight and unswerving. Marriage in the Church, a large and noisy family, the store bringing in cash—and then the war left him in pieces that didn't fit together any longer.

He squinted as three figures emerged from the Kool Kozy Kafe. One of them—judging by the hulk and swagger—was Wells. The other two had to be Able and Peters. Sean whipped from the car. "Wells!"

"Faith and begorra!" Wells imitated an Irish accent. "Seaney Sullivan. Come to turn in your Klan application, are ya now? Come to beg for yer wee job that makes ya feel like a big man?"

"Shouldn't you be in church?" Peters asked. "Worshipping the Virgin"—he waggled his eyebrows—"Mary?"

The others laughed, and Sean charged. He caught Peters just under the chin with his right hook, knocking him backward a step or two. Peters folded like a paper bag.

"You little runt!" Wells roared.

Sean bounded forward again, fists flailing in Wells' face, but Able and Peters, recovered now, caught him. Holding him by the arms and shoulders, they hung on tight as Sean twisted and jerked to free himself, cursing all the while. "You son of a bitch, you bastard—"

Without speaking, Wells stepped forward. Putting all his massive weight into it, he punched Sean in the gut. Sean sagged, the pain robbing him of breath, flowing up through his ribs into his neck. For a moment, the street went black. Wells' next strike caught Sean in the jaw, sending a ringing through his head. Blood and saliva filled his mouth. He gagged, unable to breathe.

"What've you caught, Walt? Looks like a Papist rat!"

Men poured out onto Curtis Street from the Kool Kozy Kafe.

"Come on, Walt, why are you messing around with this bastard? Take him up on the mountain and show him the score."

Able and Peters wrestled Sean toward the Olds. Other men ran for their cars, cranking them up and racing the engines. As Peters opened the car door, Sean wrangled his way out of Able's grasp. On the street again, he found himself face to face with Wells.

"You son-of-a-bitch," Sean hissed. "You had no right to touch her, you had no reason to bring her into this—"

With all his force, Wells shoved Sean. Sean's feet went out from under him, and he splayed across the ice, landing hard on his tailbone. Peters delivered a kick to Sean's ribs. The pain from his chest and backbone riveted through him, and he choked on vomit. Furious, he rolled and jumped upright, intent on pursuing Wells, who stood only a few feet away, laughing.

"Lose your fish dinner, Mick?" Able asked.

Sean brought up his fists, ready to go around round.

"Walk away, Sean."

The voice came from behind him. Sean whirled around. Paul emerged from the shadows of the sidewalk beyond the street lamp. Sean wiped the blood from his chin, and spat out a bloody wad of snot.

"Colonel Reston!" Wells spat. "What the hell are you doing here?"

"Everyone needs to go," Paul said. "Leave immediately."

Paul stood his ground, a head shorter than Wells, and less than half his weight, but with an authority that made Peters and Able scurry out of the way. Some of the others scattered, either going inside the café or spinning their cars out onto the street. It was obvious that none of them had counted on any form of the law showing up tonight.

"We were just going home to our wives and children when this ass jumped me for no reason," Able said innocently.

Paul eyed Wells. "From what I witnessed, this man"—he gestured at Sean—"was assaulted, and brutally at that."

Wells said nothing, but started for his car. Able and Peters ran behind him. Wells' car spun on the ice as he drove away. Once he'd rounded the corner onto 15th Street, Sean bent over double, grabbing at his stomach. "Jesus," he huffed. "How did you know where I was?"

"Kathleen called me. She was afraid you'd do something foolish. Let's go back to my place. You probably need a doctor."

Sean's gut ached as if it had been flattened by a streetcar, but fury rose up in him. He had just proven to Wells—and to half the Klan—that he was exactly what they thought he was: a stupid, good-for nothing Irish bum.

"I don't need anything," he said. "I just need to go home."

"You think you're going to win this by fighting it out on the streets? What happens to you when you end up in the Denver jail, guarded by those three?"

"I don't care what happens to me."

"No, but, lucky for you, there are others who do. Now, come on."

With Sean in the passenger's seat of the Packard, Paul drove to the Reston home. As Paul ushered him through to his study, Sean glanced at the Devil's den of paintings on the wall of the parlor. He never wanted to spend another night in this house.

Paul retrieved a bottle of Scotch and poured two glasses. Handing one to Sean, he said, "I promise you, Sean, I will see Wells prosecuted."

Sean threw back the Scotch in one swallow. "On what evidence? He was wearing a hood and robe. Chava never saw his face. And I'll bet you my life's savings that Wells has an alibi from some of his Klan buddies for last night."

Paul sipped at his Scotch. His lawyerly calm infuriated Sean.

"Why don't you let me take care of it?" Sean asked. "It'll be a hell of a lot faster, and save the taxpayers some money. And you'll have the successful conviction of Wells' killer to your credit. You can go down to your office now and write out the charges. Make sure it's murder, first degree, premeditated, with malicious intent. And it's Sean Murphy Sullivan."

Paul ignored him. "The D.A.'s office is closing in on the Klan—"

"And when is that going to happen? When every Catholic in this town's been put out of business? When all the Negroes up in Five Points have had their houses blown to pieces? When all the Jewish girls have been raped by jackals like Wells?"

"You need to think—"

"Did Chava talk to you?"

Paul hesitated, as if he wouldn't deign to answer after such a rude interruption. "Yes," he said at last. "She told me all she could about it."

"You're lucky."

"She's scared. She's afraid you won't find her attractive anymore. That you won't want her now that someone else has . . . touched her."

"She told you that?" Sean asked, affronted. "When she wouldn't even see me! She told you something so private?"

"She told Kathleen and Julia, woman to woman."

"Well, it's not true! She should know me better—"

"Then tell her."

"You forget, I've promised her troll of a brother that I won't talk to her."

"Give them time." Paul corked the Scotch bottle. "How long has it been since you've eaten? How long has it been since you've been warm? You need to clean up, take care of yourself. Let me make us some—"

Sean stood, his head reeling from the Scotch, his body aching. "I'm going home."

"To your boarding house?" Paul asked. "Why don't you stay here again, or let me call Kathleen—?"

"No, I want to go home. Will you take me to pick up my car?"

Reluctantly, Paul agreed. Sean retrieved his car from the alley near the Kool Kozy Kafe and drove to Berkeley Park. At Mrs. Potter's house, he unlocked the door, expecting to see the mess of the night before. But the rag rug covered with vomit was gone, and the bed was neatly made with a chenille spread that looked expensive and new. A basket of food sat on the table—fruit, cold cuts, cheese, a tin of shortbread. A bag of coffee beans stood untouched beside it.

Kathleen must have been there.

Still, Sean could catch the whiff of sweat and fear and rot, the smell of the trenches in France, of places where the unspeakable becomes reality.

Without undressing, he laid back on the bed. The humiliation of the encounter with Wells rose up in him like bile. My God, why had he walked away? He should have killed Wells, he should have spent his dying breath doing it. He had failed Chava again.

He rose to turn out the overhead light. On the sharp corner of the bureau, he noticed a couple of Chava's hairs. This must be where she struck the back of her head. He wound them around his finger. Every day of his life he had prayed, and every day he had tried to be a good Christian. And what had God done? Mocked him—by making him a "hero" alongside Danhour, that bastard. Tricked him—by sending him a woman who would never be the right one even though she was the perfect one. Shamed him— by making him unable to save her from the most disgusting act a man could commit toward a woman.

Jesus, Jesus, he cried silently, what do you want from me?

Turning off the lights, he stood at the window, Chava's hair still in his hands, his muscles tensed, his body strafed by cold and hunger and pain. His cut lip and swollen jaw pulsed. Leaning his forehead against the cold windowpane, he wept, while elaborate frost flowers blossomed on the glass from the warmth of his breath and tears.

# FORTY-SEVEN

The phone rang—again and again. Maggie sat up in bed, listening to it jingle away in the kitchen, far from the warmth of the bed. She had just taught Alice Colleen how to answer it, and the little girl ran for it every time it rang. But she was sound asleep this late at night.

Maggie threw aside the blankets and shuffled through the dark house. "Hello?"

"Maureen, ya must send Seaney over right away!" Father Devlin's heavy accent greeted her. "Somethin's happened to Brendan!"

"It's Maggie, and Seaney's not here anymore—"

"Oh, right away, Maureen, right away! It's somethin' terrible—"

Other voices sounded, and Father Devlin hung up the phone.

Maggie looked stupidly into the ear piece, as if she could see what was happening. The kitchen door flapped open and Liam limped in on withered legs. "What's going on?"

"We need to go down to the church. Something's happened to Brendan. Get dressed while I wake Ma and ask her to watch the kids."

By the time Maggie returned from waking her mother, who took several shakes to rouse, Liam was gone. She grabbed her coat and ran onto the landing of the outdoor stairs. Halfway down, Liam struggled to carry his rolling chair.

"Liam!" she cried. "Come back! Give me a few minutes to—"

"Help me down the stairs."

"It's bitter out here. Let me get dressed, and we'll take the truck—"

She caught him as he started to fall. "Leave the chair."

With his arm over her shoulder and his other hand on the railing, Maggie walked him down the stairs, then dashed up to bring down the rolling chair.

After she dressed, she jumped into the delivery truck, but it wouldn't start in the bitter cold. On foot, she followed Liam's tracks through the snow, catching up with him just as Blessed Savior came into view. The lights blazed from the sanctuary. Maggie squinted—one of the stained glass windows was broken.

Inside the church, Father Devlin met Liam and Maggie in the corridor near Brendan's study. "Oh, Maggie, Liam, 'tis terrible. We found him in the west alleyway, lyin' on the pavement, his head bleedin' a puddle beneath him—"

Brendan's study teemed with men Maggie hadn't seen, except in passing, since before Liam went to Fort Leavenworth. Dr. Thorp, Ed Barry, Danny MacMahon, who had lost both Frankie and Donnell in the war, Mr. McKenna—these were the men who had voted to expel Liam from the Knights of Columbus. They stared at him as if they did not recognize him.

Liam plowed through to where Brendan lay on a small sofa near the window, his head propped on a pillow. The left shoulder of his pajamas was saturated with blood. Mrs. McKenna, the only other woman in the room, called, "Come take this, Maggie. I need to find more blankets. The shock, you know."

Maggie accepted the blood-soaked cloth. Brendan's face was the color of the pillow, so pale, it seemed to have no features—no lips, no cheekbones, no eyes. He breathed in shallow hiccups. She turned the rag over in her hand and applied the clean side to his left temple. A jagged slash zigzagged from his forehead to his chin, so raw and pulpy that Maggie's stomach turned.

"Brendan, brother, I'm here." With Brendan's hand clutched against his forehead, Liam began to pray, his words barely audible.

"Do you know where Seaney is, Maggie?" Dr. Thorp asked. "Can you bring him here? We need to report this, and it won't be to that idiot who's patrolling here now."

She shook her head. "He's not with the police anymore."

"How can we find him? We need him—"

"He's waking up," someone said.

Brendan's eyes flitted open, closed, and opened again. Someone dimmed the light on the lamp, and he blinked a few times. "What—?" he murmured. "Am I—?"

"What happened, Brendan?" Liam asked.

Brendan swallowed a number of times before he whispered, "I heard noise in the alley. They were children, searching in the trash behind the church."

"Children?" Liam asked incredulously.

"Thirteen, fourteen years old, I would guess. One said, Where's your wine, drunkard priest? Where's the wine? One had a piece of pipe, and—"

"Good God!" Dr. Thorp said.

"What happened to your face?" Liam asked.

"I don't know. God forgive them."

No one spoke for a moment, and then Dr. Thorp said, "Danny, Ed, help me get him to his bed, and I'll examine him properly. I suspect some ribs could be broken."

The men carried him to the rectory, which was directly behind the church building. Liam and Maggie followed. After Brendan was laid in his bed, Dr. Thorp asked everyone to leave as he examined him.

In the hallway, the men lit cigarettes and leaned against the walls.

"They were the children of Klansmen," Mr. Barry decided.

"How do you know?" Danny asked. "The streets are filled with juvenile offenders, thanks to Ben Lindsey. They could have been Jewish gang boys."

"The Jewish boys have their own wine to steal," Maggie pointed out.

Danny eyed her coldly, and Liam rolled away, heading toward the parlor. Maggie weighed whether to follow or to wait for Dr. Thorp's report.

"I'm surprised the two of you have never moved," Danny said sourly. "I thought Liam was warned to stay away from Denver."

"Well, we're still here," Maggie said gaily, and then she caught the eyes of the others in the hallway—accusing, vilifying, unforgiving. She turned away. In the parlor, she found Liam sitting before the cold fireplace.

She sat in the chair beside him. "Come out, it's cold in here."

"I cannot believe the proliferation of evil in this world! After killing so many just a few years ago, nothing has been learned, nothing has changed." He looked at Maggie with tears in his eyes. "They attacked a man of God and left him to die."

She laid her hand on his shoulder.

"You don't think it had anything to do with me? Because of what I did in the war? You don't think it's—?"

"It was because this is a Catholic church," Maggie soothed. "And Governor Morley just told the entire state that Catholic churches have wine that the priests use for obscene purposes. It was an invitation for priests to have their brains beaten out."

Liam winced at her bluntness. "Maggie, please—"

"Well, that's what happened, isn't it?" Anger swelled in her. "It's stupid to think it's anything else. I'm tired of everyone tiptoeing around pretending things are different."

She stopped, uncertain what she meant by the last sentence. Why was she so angry? And with whom? With Liam, or Brendan, or the whole lot in the hallway? She wanted to throw something, to kick something, to do as much damage as the vandals had.

"We should go back and see what Dr. Thorp has to say," she said.

They arrived in the hallway outside Brendan's bedroom just as Dr. Thorp was giving his diagnosis. "Father Keohane has a fractured rib, and the possibility of concussion. I stitched up the wound on his face, and his eye should be all right once the swelling recedes. Mrs. McKenna will stay until—"

"I'll stay with him," Liam said.

"But Fiona can—"

"She needn't stay. I can take care of my brother."

Silence filled the hallway.

"Liam," Maggie interceded. "You need someone who can fetch things for you. Mrs. McKenna knows where everything is—"

"She may stay if she likes, but I'm also staying."

"He's asleep right now," Dr. Thorp said. "I gave him a sedative. It would be best if you came back in the morning."

Without another word, Liam rolled himself into Brendan's room. Maggie followed. Brendan lay in the bed, breathing hoarsely.

"Close the door," Liam ordered. "He needs quiet."

Maggie latched the door. "You can't sit here all night. It's chilly in here. At least, let me bring you a blanket."

"He has never left me, and I won't leave him. And if he's suffered this, then I shouldn't complain about not having a blanket."

"Come home with me now and we'll talk to Seaney in the morning. Maybe there's somebody honest left at the police department."

"I'm staying here."

"I have to go home, Liam," she said. "Ma can't handle the boys—"

"Go ahead. I'm staying here."

Liam arrives home later that morning, after the household is teeming with children and the smells of cooking from the old black stove in the kitchen. Ed Barry helps him up the outdoor stairs and into the parlor. Liam's head hangs as if he hasn't the strength to hold it upright.

"Liam!" Maggie cries. "Are you all right?"

"I'm tired, that's all."

"How is Brendan?"

"He's still sleeping," Mr. Barry answers. "Dr. Thorp is there with him now. But, Maggie, keep Liam home. This has done him no good."

After Maggie thanks him, Mr. Barry settles into a chair in the kitchen for a cup of tea with Ma. "We've set up a patrol to guard the church through the coming nights," he tells her. "And we're fixing the broken windows and locks now. They broke four windows and tore open two doors—"

"Have mercy on us," Ma says. "Who would do such a thing?"

Stiff after so many hours in his chair, Liam shivers uncontrollably. Maggie helps him to the bedroom and takes off his shoes and clothes for him. She covers him up, then fills every water bottle in the house from the kettle and packs them around his body.

By the afternoon, Liam has a fever. Maggie sits by the bed and keeps a cool cloth on his forehead while her mother tends the children. By morning, his cough has turned to wheeze. She calls Dr. Thorp, who comes somewhat begrudgingly from Brendan's bedside, to listen to Liam's lungs.

"I think he has caught a cold from his exploits the other night," Dr. Thorp says.

"Should we take him to the hospital?"

"Oh, no, no, it's nothing serious."

"But with his frail health—"

"It's best to care for him here. I'll be back this evening."

That afternoon, as Maggie sits by Liam's bed, as unwilling to leave him as he was to leave Brendan, she hears voices. Seaney's and Ma's, of course, but also others. Alice Colleen tiptoes in to say that Aunt Kathleen has come to pick her and the boys up, and that they are going to ride in her big car to her big house for an adventure.

"We get to stay until Daddy is better," Alice Colleen whispers. "Aunt Kathleen helped us pack our clothes. And she says that we can play with Stephen and Susanna and Mina, and we can pet the horses in the stables—"

Alice Colleen goes on, naming the fun that Kathleen has promised them, but Maggie ceases to hear. Liam's breathing is growing more labored.

That night, long after Dr. Thorp has given Liam something to help him sleep, Maggie wakes from the chair where she has been sitting all day. The silence in the house haunts her—usually, she can sense the children breathing, their hearts beating through their dreams. Taking up her pencil, she starts to cull through the letters that Seaney picked up for her at the newspaper. Maggie doesn't want to delegate too much of the work. Mr. Ledbetter just might decide Thalia makes a less problematic Mrs. James than Mrs. James.

But the questions in the letters are stupid, written by thoughtless people who know nothing of true suffering. Wedding etiquette, problems with mothers-in-law, tussles with neighbors over barking dogs. Have any of these people ever truly lived? Have they ever loved or known true sorrow?

She wanders out to the parlor. Ma sits on the sofa, darning socks for the kids, one of the many jobs that she's shouldered for Maggie. A single lamp lights her work. Her hair, which still streams down her back, is plaited in a braid as thick as a fist. Around her shoulders, she wears an old-fashioned shawl with a traditional Celtic weave. She could be a fisherman's wife awaiting her husband on a stormy coast in County Cork.

Maggie sits down beside her, her hands idle in her lap. She watches her mother darn another hole, shoring it up against the insistent toes of the growing boys.

"I'm afraid, Ma," she says.

"Our Mother Mary will see us through."

But all Maggie's sins flock in her head. Even though she's claimed for years now that she supports Liam's choices, she hasn't. She's resented his demands on her time and energy, especially as more children arrived. She thinks of the kiss she shared with Tony. She had wanted him to touch her, to hold her, to make her laugh and forget—oh God, what made her do something so shameful and sinful?

She begins to cry. "I haven't been the wife I should have, that I wanted to be. I wanted to be so perfect—"

"Shush, now, there's no need for that—"

"I've been so busy, I've been so wrapped up, and I'm so sick and tired of it all." She stops. "What happened to me? To who I wanted to be?"

"Aren't ya doin' what you want, writin' for the paper?"

"I don't know," Maggie says. "Let me lie down."

Her mother starts to move, but Maggie says, "Don't leave. Let me lie in your lap."

Eyes closed, she whispers into the rose-scented warmth of her mother's skirt. "They didn't even remember him. Dr. Thorp, Mr. Barry, the others—they looked at him as if they'd thought he was dead. And Danny MacMahon asked why we hadn't left town. After all they did to us—kicking him out of the Knights, boycotting our store, ruining us—they acted like it was an affront that he wanted to be there for his brother."

"Ah, *fuist, fuist.*" Her mother strokes her hair and sings, a lullaby from long ago: "*Sleep, sleep,* grah mo chree, *Here on your Mamma's knee, Angels are guarding, And they watch o'er thee—*"

And just as she had when she was a little girl, Maggie falls asleep.

# FORTY-EIGHT

Paul knocked at the door of the room in Mrs. Potter's boarding house. The door creaked open, and Sean appeared, his clothes crumpled, his face unshaven, and his hair uncombed.

"Colonel Reston!" Sean exclaimed.

Paul caught a wave of sour breath. "Good afternoon, Sean, may I come in?"

The room was a messy wallow that reeked of unwashed flesh and sorrow. From what he could see, Sean had spent the time since Chava's attack sitting in a wooden chair next to the window, smoking. Cigarette butts overflowed from the ashtray onto the floor, amid crumbs and crusts of half-eaten meals.

"How are you?" Paul asked.

"You can see." Sean swept a pile of junk from a wooden chair. "Sit down."

Paul sat on the chair, while Sean took his place next to the window.

"I'll come right to the point," Paul said. "I'd like you to work for me at the D.A.'s office. We need leg men—people to collect information for us."

"Information about what? Are you after the Bunco Gang again?"

"No, we're going after the Klan."

Sean said nothing, but his appearance changed. He combed through his greasy hair with his fingers, and straightened up, so that his chest was no longer concave.

"It's probably no more pay than the police department," Paul said. "But I need someone I can trust to keep this in complete confidence."

"Why would you ask me?" Sean eyed him warily. "I haven't always been . . . this isn't because of Kathleen, is it?"

"Kathleen knows nothing of it. I want someone who has a personal grudge against the Klan, and I suspect you'd like to see justice for Chava and all the other women who've been brutalized by them."

Sean's gaze dropped to the floor, and Paul let him mull over the offer in silence. Paul had visited Chava a few days ago, citing official District

Attorney's business. He had conducted the interview with Chava under Rachael's supervision, while roly-poly baby Hannah cooed happily on the floor. It was an odd affair—all eyes on the baby, who reaped smiles and words of praise whenever she glanced up. Yet the looks exchanged between the two women and himself were solemn, the tension unmistakable.

Chava's face had healed some, the bruises now purple and yellow blotches, yet Paul could see the whisk of scar through her eyebrow. Her hair was neatly bunched at the nape of her neck to hide the spot where Dr. Erickson had cut it away. Her voice, so damaged by Wells' attack, was still rough and hoarse.

After the conversation had ended as uncomfortably as it began, Chava had followed him out onto the screened porch, leaving Rachael behind. "How is your teaching?" Paul had asked.

"I'm not teaching now. I'm not working. I . . . they . . . I was afraid my looks would scare the children."

"Surely you'll go back to it."

"Yes, I hope to." Then, as if it hurt her to say the words, she asked, "How is Sean?"

"Not well, according to Kathleen." Paul added gently, "Is there anything you'd like me to tell him?"

"I don't know how—" Her words faltered when Rachael appeared at the door. "I have to go," she whispered. "Please, please, come again."

And she had disappeared into the Rosen home, leaving Paul alone on the porch.

Now, Sean's forehead furrowed. "You think there are others like Chava? I thought—"

"That it was just revenge or a sour trick? There are undoubtedly other women like Chava who are too scared or embarrassed to report what's happened to them."

"And you think that you can stop them? I thought Foster Cline was one of them."

"So do most people, but he has a rabid dislike of our new governor."

"And Stapleton? Who's to say that he won't just turn around and sell the entire D.A.'s office to the Klan." Bitterly, he added, "He sold the Denver Police Department to them."

"That's a chance you'd have to be willing to take. It's a chance I'm taking, too." Paul softened his approach. "Sean, I saw her. She's as miserable as you are. If you still care for her, you need to be fighting, helping, trying—not sitting here falling into despair."

Sean studied his grubby hands before he looked directly at Paul. "When do you want me to start?"

"As soon as you have a shower and a shave, and as soon as you get this place and yourself in order." Paul used his Colonel's voice, the one that brooked no argument. "When you're ready, come to my office. I'll introduce you to District Attorney Cline."

Darkness had fallen by the time Paul arrived at Julia's house in Park Hill. As he entered the kitchen, wiping his snowy shoes on the rug, Julia met him. "You have a visitor," she said quietly.

"Kathleen?" He hadn't truly seen Kathleen since the beginning of the year, when she had visited on New Year's Day. During Chava's brief stay at the Reston house, Kathleen had been in and out, and they had never really had time to speak to each other alone. But if she were here this late in the evening, something must be wrong at home.

Julia shook her head. "No, it is your wife."

Paul reared back in disbelief. "Mélisande? Is Alex with her?"

"Yes."

Relief rushed through him. He had worried that Mélisande might abandon Alex in a fit of temper or addiction.

She waited for him in the parlor. She seemed smaller than he remembered—no more than five feet tall, and so thin that her cheekbones formed sharp ridges in her face. The span between her shoulders was mere inches, giving her a tragic, fragile appearance. But her dark hair, cut to her chin, was thick and wavy, and Paul remembered well how her dark eyes could snap with mischievous wit.

Before she could speak, Alex ran forward and wrapped his arms around Paul's waist. "Papa Paul! Papa Paul!"

Paul hugged the boy against him. *"Combien tu as grandi!"*

*"Oui, Papa Paul, je suis grand et fort!"*

Alex struck a muscleman pose, and Paul laughed. When Alex returned to hug his legs again, Paul rubbed his head. "Big and strong you are," he agreed.

In English, he asked Mélisande, "When did you arrive? I thought you were going back to Marseille."

"I changed my mind." She glanced at Alex. "I wanted Alex to see the country of his father."

"Did you meet with the McKenzies?"

She shook her head. "We docked in New York, and we went to the Long Island"—Paul smiled at her awkward phrasing—"but they were not willing to see us."

"Fools."

"Alex." Julia held out her hand. "Would you like to come into the kitchen? I believe Rosa baked a cake today. We can have it with cocoa."

"He doesn't speak much English," Mélisande said. "I have not been faithful about teaching him both languages."

"*Ça va,*" Julia said. "*J'ai vécu à Paris pendant de nombreuses années.*"

"*Ah, oui, pardonnez-moi.*" Mélisande laughed. "I'd forgotten that you once lived there. Before the war—oh, you were so fortunate to see it then."

Alex followed Julia to the kitchen, chattering in his native tongue. Mélisande and Paul sat together on the sofa, speaking softly in French.

"He has missed you so much," Mélisande said.

"And I've missed him. Why have you come here? Do you need money?"

"Of course, but that is not why I've come." She waved it away. "I needed to see you again."

"Why? You left me without a backward glance in Paris when I needed you the most."

"Oh, I know, I know. I am sorry. We didn't do a good job caring for Alex or for ourselves. We were so undone by the war for so long."

"Are you still drinking? Are you still using heroin and cocaine?"

"No, I have finished with all that. It is not good for Alex."

He did not know if he could believe her. "I'm not the man you knew any longer. I have a good job here, and I've settled in well. I'm contented with my life."

"But you came here for Kathleen, *non*?" she tossed back. "Yet you aren't married to her. She isn't here with you. Why not?"

"It isn't that easy. She's married to an important man. A divorce would cause a calamity for their family."

"Then what do you have here?" She laid her hand on his. "Paul, I was so excited to see my parents and sister again, but my parents—after what happened to my brother—they have grown old and without any sort of joy. And my sister, who was the mistress of a German officer for so long—she is also without hope. I couldn't stand it. It is no way to raise a child, no way for me to . . ."

She lifted her chin. "There was no way for me to stay away from drink or anything else in Marseille. It is a place of refugees, a place where no one is safe because they have never known safety. And it is poor—everyone is so poor, because no one belongs there. Italians and Corsicans, who know nothing but violence, and Russians who escaped from the Bolsheviks, and Armenians who left because of hunger. The Vietnamese live in filthy shacks, and the Arabs and Africans come from across the sea on every boat, and they have nothing—no money and no way to make it but to steal and sell themselves. We—my family, which once had so much pride and power—we are just so much debris that has washed up on the shores."

Paul relented. "I'm sorry."

"I could not breathe there. We were so close to the sea, but all I could smell was the rotting docks, and the fumes from the ships sailing in and out, and the ocean waves washing up again and again with their load of filth and scum, and I could not help but think of the endlessness of it all—"

She shivered. "I was afraid I would be caught in it forever. So I decided I would come here. For Alex, for my beloved Alex."

Paul weighed her words. She sounded sincere—and he knew her well enough to know that she did not hide her emotions well—but he still felt the sting of the betrayal in Paris.

Julia and Alex returned from the kitchen. A tick of chocolate clung to Alex's lips. Mélisande wiped it away with her handkerchief. "Was the cake good?"

"*Oui, Maman.*"

"I am going to take Alex up to bed," Julia said. "The guest room is freshly made up. You may choose to stay in there. It's right next to the smaller room where Alex will be sleeping."

"Thank you." In French, Mélisande addressed Alex, "I will be right up to tuck you in, *mon amour.*"

"*Oui, Maman.*" Alex embraced her, then turned to Paul. "*Bonne nuit, Papa Paul, je t'aime.*"

"*Je t'aime aussi,*" Paul said. "*Dors bien.* Sleep well."

After Julia left, Mélisande's voice turned desperate. "You can see Alex is healthy and happy. I have protected him in every way I can, but we can't keep being prisoners of the past. Paul, no one believes the Belgians. They don't believe that the Germans killed thousands—hundreds of thousands—or that we were forced into labor camps and prostitution by them. The French think only of themselves, and the British have washed their hands of us. There is no one to help us. We have been left with nothing—not even the barest of hopes. Our country is ruined, and we have nowhere to call home."

He recognized the truth in her words. Belgium, that hapless neutral country, had been pounded by the great armies of Europe and America again and again until virtually nothing remained.

"It's late, too late to talk about this tonight," Paul said. "Do you want to stay in the guest room?"

"Where would you like me to be?"

He sensed the tension in her body, as if this moment would cement their future. If he refused her company, it would signify a permanent breach. If he accepted, it would offer them both hope.

He held out his hand. "*Allons-y, Madame Reston.*"

Upstairs, Mélisande lay to his right in his bed, away from his bent and knobby ribs and his faulty left arm. He encircled her with his right arm, drawing her against him, and she rested her head in the hollow of his shoulder. As he moved his hands over her body, she said, "Wait."

He retreated, but did not roll away from her. He wondered if she still felt an aversion to his bulging ribs and stiff shoulder.

"I miss this so," she said. "Being held, being safe and at peace."

"We were never at peace in Paris."

"No, we were not. I was . . . I was lost, and you had no will to love anyone but her—a dream that had left you behind. She left you behind, Paul."

"We were both left behind."

"I was trying to do what the war had not done. It had not killed me, only taken everyone and everything I loved. So I wanted to die, too. And the men I met, the men I saw, they were never—"

"They weren't Kenny."

"*Non, pas du tout.*"

"Neither am I," he said bitterly.

"*Non, mais tu as toujours été le meilleur homme.*"

No, but you were always the better man.

Later, after Mélisande falls asleep, Paul leans against the window frame in his room and looks out into the night. The day has left him shaken—Sean's degraded state, Mélisande's sudden appearance. He can't trust her—perhaps he'll never trust her—but she's right. Kathleen is unattainable, a dream that left him behind. She will never leave her children; she will never undergo the humiliation and ostracism connected with divorce; she will never break the vows she made. He has always known that there was no future together for them. Jim had already laid claim to her heart before Paul met her in France.

"Paul?" Mélisande whispers from the bed. "What are you doing?"

"Just thinking."

"Do you still have those dreams?"

When he lived in Paris, he had been plagued by dreams that varied from night to night, yet which always carried the same message: failure. One night, he would attempt to reassemble a broken china cup with shards so finely splintered that gaps and cracks remained in the shell. Other nights, buttons would not slip into fabric holes, doors would not latch, automobiles would not start, or shoelaces eluded his grasp. Some nights, fields could not be reconstructed, trenches could not be filled and erased, and nothing rooted in the barren, blasted soil. On the worst nights, bodies could not be sewn together, and doctors were impotent, worthless. Limbs scattered, unclaimed, unclaimable.

Always, always, he woke to find himself bathed in sweat and tears.

"Not since I have been here," he says.

*"Bon, j'ai détesté te voir si triste."*

I hated to see you so sad.

"Have you slept with her?" she asks.

"Yes."

"Then, she is your mistress?"

"She isn't the kind of woman who would be comfortable in that arrangement."

"Of course, an American and a Catholic—"

"And a mother with two young children she adores and her husband's illegitimate daughter that she is raising as her own." He turns toward her. "Much as I've done with Alex."

"You think I am being *déraisonnable*? A shrew?"

"I'm wondering why you would come halfway around the world if that's what you have in mind. I didn't know that you still thought enough of me to be jealous."

"I'm not jealous."

"Then what is this?"

She pats the pillow next to her. *"Reviens au lit."*

After he lies down again, she whispers in French, "The war ruined everything and everyone who witnessed it. There is nothing more to understand." She sits up so that she can look into his face. "But Alex was born after it, and he has never seen battle or wounded men dying on the roads, and I will not take him to Verdun or Rheims or the other ruined places to honor those who died for such a senseless cause. I don't want him to know anything of it. Paul, I beg you, I cannot let him be touched by the despair of Marseille and my family and Europe. I cannot let him live the way I have."

"What do you want from me?"

"You are strong, you are doing well—I can see that." She speaks in English. "Let me stay with you. Let me raise Alex as our son—with you as my husband, as Alex's protector and my lover. If I have you, I can be strong, too. I cannot be her—I cannot be Kathleen—but I know you, Paul, as she does not. I have no false ideas about you, just as you have no false ideas about me. Please, we could be happy. We might even fall in love."

# FORTY-NINE

Jim fiddled with a pen as he listened to Senator Hart speak at the podium. They were so smug, so sure of themselves. He surveyed the men seated at the polished wood tables in the Senate Chamber. Above them, the chandelier sparkled with the brilliance of one hundred fifty-five electric bulbs. A polished wooden railing designated the viewing gallery, lit by floor to ceiling windows that made the two-story room feel airy and warm.

Jim stretched his tensed muscles. The deadline for introducing legislation for consideration during this session had passed at midnight last night. Next week, the Senate would adjourn for its first party caucuses in what was referred to as "lull time," when Democrats and Republicans would meet separately to consider the bills that had been introduced. In the party caucuses, the vote tallied would be binding on all members of the party, regardless of personal sentiment. That was the way the General Assembly had always worked. But now, the Klan controlled the Republican caucus and could easily pass its own legislation. Jim could oppose his fellow Republicans until he drew his last breath, and it would make no difference. Under the rules, his vote would be identical to the majority's.

Unless they were stopped. Unless the Klan was stopped.

Jim reached into his suit pocket for his handkerchief to wipe the sweat from his palms. His fingers touched upon something hard and round. He pulled from his pocket the marble that had so enchanted Stephen on Christmas day at his parents' house. As Hart rambled on, Jim fondled the marble. He remembered the clumsy explanation he had given Stephen for the phenomenon before Mina had surprised everyone by calling it by its proper name: refraction.

Jim raised the marble high enough to catch the light from the banker's lamp at the table. Through it, he could see a world turned upside-down.

And suddenly, the answer came to him. He nearly laughed aloud—it was so simple, so elegant, so devastating. Why not turn the Senate upside down?

398 • LAURIE MARR WASMUND

Why not redraw the lines, reestablish the loyalties, realign the parties? After all, it was John Galen Locke who had proclaimed before the election that his candidates were not Democrats or Republicans, but Klansmen.

Why not continue that distinction through the law-making session?

We are not Democrats or Republicans, Jim thought, but foes of the Klan and members of the Klan.

He closed the marble in his fist.

After the Senate adjourned for the weekend at noon on Thursday, Jim waited for the flurry of last minute leave-takings to die down before he sauntered through the halls. As he'd hoped, he found the senators from Colorado Springs, David Elliott and Louis Puffer, talking together in Elliott's office. Colorado Springs prided itself on its liberality, on its refusal to stoop to radical politics. With only a cursory knock, he insinuated himself into the room. "Good afternoon."

"Senator Graves." Senator Elliott's greeting was barely warm. "How can I help you?"

"I have a proposition for you, one that might well benefit the state of Colorado, as well as anyone with an eye toward a political career."

"We stay clear of the Klan in our neck of the woods," Senator Elliott warned. "You've been flitting like a butterfly from one side to the other. Where do you plan to land?"

Jim forced himself to speak casually. "Governor Morley's going to be pushing the administration's first bill through as soon as he can to prove his and Locke's power. Our friends in the House will let it sail. So will the Senate unless we stop it."

"How?" Senator Puffer asked. "We're going to be trampled as badly as the Democrats, especially since most of us have been excluded from the committees."

"Unless"—Jim tempered the excitement rising in his voice—"we join the Democrats."

"Join the Democrats? Senator, you're out of bounds—"

"Consider the numbers." Jim leaned forward. "There are nine old-line Republicans who are anti-Klan. Added to fourteen Democrats, we'd have twenty-five votes. A majority."

"Yes, but—"

"We'll refuse to attend the Republican Party caucus. We'll sit in with the Democrats instead."

"A bi-partisan caucus." Senator Elliott mulled it over. "It would be worth it to see the look on Billy Adams' face."

Both Jim and Senator Puffer laughed. Billy Adams was the Democratic leader in the Senate. He had first been elected 1888, before most of the current crop of senators had been born. Known for his feistiness and bluster, he was also known for making things happen. Only a couple of years ago, he had received money to start Alamosa State Normal School, a college in the poor, forgotten southern part of the state that he represented.

"Have you asked anyone else about this?" Senator Elliott asked.

"I came to the two of you first," Jim said. "Your voices have been the loudest since the old-line Republicans were shut out of the committee appointments, but I know there are others."

"Henry Toll would be a sure bet," Senator Puffer said.

"And John Kelly from Salida."

"And Samuel Freudenthal, of course," Jim added.

All three of them laughed. Samuel Freudenthal, the state senator from Trinidad, was the only Jewish member of the state legislature.

As the two Senators tested the theory, Jim's faith in the plan grew. This was it—this was the way to upend Morley and Locke and humiliate them before the people of Colorado in the same way that Jim had been humiliated by his run for governor.

At last, Senator Puffer said, "There's a possibility it would work. If we have enough guts."

"That's always the question, isn't it?" Jim remarked. "Maybe we can capture a few committee chair appointments if we stick to our guns."

As Jim had hoped, Senator Elliott recognized the chance for glory. "We'd have to start right away," he said. "We'll have to work fast—over the weekend. Let's decide who contacts whom—"

And so, it began.

Word spread immediately, as Jim had known it would. Whatever else it was, the Klan was superbly organized, and communications traveled so quickly that by Friday morning the telephone lines in Jim's office on 17th street, as well as the number of visitors he received, had grown nearly unmanageable for both Joel and Nathaniel. Early in the day, Joshua Hart visited, along with a cadre of scowling senators and House members who intimated that Jim's political career would suffer a death blow if the "insurgency," as it had rapidly become known, continued. Hart promised that he would be a pariah, a no one, by February.

"I doubt my feelings will be hurt much by that," Jim replied.

That afternoon, as the winter sun began to sink over the hazy, snow-capped mountains, Jim called Kathleen to say that he was staying at the Brown Palace. "I suspect it will be a rough weekend," he said.

"May I join you?"

He felt a rush of pleasure. "By all means. You've always been good in a fight."

She had already arrived at the suite by the time Jim left his office. Harris and Kathleen's maid, Beryl, were setting up the accommodations—unpacking clothing, setting out jars of cosmetics or creams, restocking the bar that held Jim's prized liquors. Although Kathleen sat demurely in an armchair, reading the afternoon newspapers, Jim could not stop moving. His heart felt enlivened, young again, and he paced, only pausing to light another cigarette or to refill his glass of brandy.

Kathleen shook the newspaper for a better view. "How much risk are you taking in attempting this?"

"Does it matter?" he asked. "If we can get a couple of Committee Chair appointments, we can control what passes to a full Senate vote."

"So, you've become a gambler now?"

"I've always been a gambler. After all, I married you, my sweet."

After a coy smile, she went back to her newspaper. Jim paced to the window again as a knock sounded on the door of the suite.

He raised his eyebrows. "Here we go."

Harris answered, bringing back a rolled copy of the *Protestant Herald*, the Klan's rag. Just below the masthead, was a black-bordered box with the headline, "The Roll of Dishonor." Grainy photos of the state Senators involved in the coup had been hastily crammed into the box. Jim's head and shoulders appeared larger than the others. "Cut this list of TRAITORS out for future use," the caption advised. "It will come in handy. These are the Colorado legislators who are against patriotic measures and laws." A handwritten note accompanying the newspaper read: "Sent to all loyal Klan members in Colorado."

"Good Lord," Jim said. "That didn't take long."

"Let me see it." Kathleen held out her hand. "'Patriotic measures and laws'? No one is going to believe this."

"The Klan faithful swallows what it's fed, without chewing."

Not more than a half hour later, someone else knocked at the door. Jim opened it to find Governor Clarence Morley and Grand Dragon John Galen Locke. The two made quite a pair; Governor Morley was thin and weak-chinned, with spectacles that gave him a nervous, owlish air, while Dr. Locke was portly and thick-jowled. It was well-known through the legislative houses that Governor Morley was a true believer; he would push the Klan agenda without reservation. Already, he had been dubbed "Dr. Locke's charwoman" by the Denver newspapers.

"Good afternoon, Senator Graves," Dr. Locke said. "May we have a moment of your time?"

Graciously, Jim asked them into the suite. "Dr. Locke, Governor Morley, you remember my wife."

"Mrs. Graves." Dr. Locke nodded toward her. "It's nice to see you."

"Please, take a seat," she said. "Would you like seltzer water?"

Governor Morley declined, but Dr. Locke accepted.

Kathleen went to the bar to pour the drinks. As she handed the glass to Dr. Locke, he said, "I'm afraid, Mrs. Graves, that you'll find our visit somewhat dull compared to the legendary parties that you and your husband give. The Governor and I wouldn't be offended if you chose to leave."

"Thank you for thinking of me," Kathleen replied. "But I'll stay."

Dr. Locke's eyes flashed at the whiff of sarcasm in her voice. "I hope your children are well," he said. "Your son and your daughters?"

Jim caught the drawl on the word "daughters," but Kathleen didn't betray any emotion. "Thank you," she said. "They are all well, and growing so quickly, we can't keep up."

Dr. Locke's attempt to fluster Kathleen having failed, he switched targets. "This week has been very entertaining in the Senate chamber, hasn't it?" he asked Jim. "You and David Elliot and Louis Puffer in your little conclaves—"

"Spelled with a 'c', in this case," Jim said dryly.

The doctor chuckled. "So you've planned a rebellion in the Senate. How does your constituency feel about your efforts to subvert the legislative process? Do they care that their duly-elected Republican representative is now vamping with the Democrats?"

"My constituents want their duly-elected representative to uphold the Constitution of both the state and the country by assuring that the laws passed don't infringe upon individual rights."

Governor Morley sharpened his blade. "I have something here that might interest you." He floated a typed document across the coffee table. Jim picked it up. It was a list of names. At the end of each name was a typed religious affiliation—CATHOLIC, JEW, or PROTESTANT.

"What is this?" Jim asked.

"These are the names of professors at the University of Colorado," the Governor said. "I have informed President Norlin that I will withhold funding from the college unless he dismisses the men and women who are listed as Catholic or Jew. We cannot allow these people to keep indoctrinating our young people in their un-Christian ideas at a state-funded institution."

Jim flipped to the second page of the document, trying to determine if the Governor's threat was sound. Morley could not stop passage of funding in the legislature, but he could refuse to sign the bill.

"President Norlin has already refused to eliminate the offending professors, believing that he is taking the higher ground," Dr. Locke said. "Unfortunately, if President Norlin loses funding through his stubborn refusal, your shale oil projects through the Bureau of Mines will be in jeopardy as well. However, I know you have some rapport with him. Didn't you serve together on the America First Committee under Governor Gunter?"

"We did," Jim acknowledged.

"Perhaps, then, he will listen to you."

"May I ask a question?" Kathleen inserted daintily.

Dr. Locke smiled condescendingly in her direction. "Of course, Mrs. Graves. You're welcome to join the conversation."

"The University of Colorado has educated many of the engineers and doctors and lawyers who practice in this state," she said. "In eliminating funding for it, aren't the true victims the people of Colorado? Where will the next professional class be educated? Where will parents send their children to college? After all, the Catholic and Jewish professors will most likely find jobs elsewhere, in other states, perhaps, but our high school students will find their options limited."

Governor Morley looked flummoxed, but Dr. Locke's eyes gleamed, as if he knew he was pulling the biggest hoax on the state of Colorado that had ever been conceived.

"Then we'd better hope it doesn't happen, hadn't we?" he said. "By the way, Mrs. Graves, are you aware that the house intends to pass a bill that requires all students to devote part of the school day to religious classes? How will that sit with the people of your faith?"

"My guess is that the Catholic Church will embrace it. I've never known it to shy away from educating its members."

"It won't educate them if there are no parochial schools," Governor Morley said. "There's a bill to require all students to attend public schools, and I'm determined to see it pass."

"By the way, how is Father Keohane from Blessed Savior?" Dr. Locke asked. "I heard he had some trouble lately."

"Drunken priests," Governor Morley said in disgust. "They deserve what they get."

The shock of Governor Morley's crassness swept over Kathleen's face, and she exclaimed, "Father Keohane was terribly wounded! That shouldn't happen to anyone, regardless of their—!"

Jim stood, rage rising from his gut. "This conversation is at an end, gentlemen. I will show you out."

"I'm sorry we upset you, Mrs. Graves," Dr. Locke said. "Our apologies."

He hefted his weight from the divan, and Governor Morley squirreled along after him. After closing the suite door behind them, Jim sought his cigarette case from his pocket. His hands fumbling, he struck a match and lit a cigarette.

"I don't believe I've heard that many threats all at one time in my entire political career."

"I can't believe he would say that in front of me!" Kathleen fumed. "I can't believe they would attack the Church in my—in our—home. This man is our leader, the state's most important—"

"Dr. Locke is our leader and the state's most important figure," Jim corrected. "He may as well be sitting in the Governor's chair and presiding over the legislature. So, now that you've had a taste of what's in store, do you want me to continue?"

"Yes, I want you to continue! I want you to make sure that they don't have their way! I want you to stop them, to see them ruined, to—"

He laughed. "I've never known you to be so blood-thirsty."

"I'm so angry! Brendan's health isn't strong to begin with, and to—" She stopped, as another thought occurred to her. "Will you be all right? Will we?"

"Yes," he said. "If this works, we will be quite all right."

*******

Late that afternoon, Jim stopped by his parents' house in Cheesman Park. Announced by the butler, he found his mother and father reading in the library. He kissed his mother on the cheek in greeting and nodded toward his father with a "good afternoon."

His mother rang the bell for tea. "What brings you here in the middle of the day?" She trilled a nervous laugh. "I hope it isn't calamitous news."

Jim took a seat in an overstuffed, velvet-upholstered chair. "We seem to be living in a calamitous day and age."

Never one for chitchat, his father asked, "What's all this we're seeing in the newspapers about an insurrection in the State Senate? Your name is connected to it."

"That's what I've come to explain." Jim detailed the events of the past few days—his decision to approach David Elliott and Louis Puffer; their refusal to caucus with the Republicans; Governor Morley's and Dr. Locke's visit to him at the Brown Palace.

"Both of them came?" his father asked.

"I don't believe Governor Morley makes a move without his master."

"This is a travesty. How the people of Colorado could have elected such a political stooge . . ."

His father's voice trailed away, and Jim knew what he was thinking: If only his own chances had not been dashed by Mina's discovery, Jim would be governor.

"Well, they did, and now our task is to limit the damage."

"Is it in your best self-interest to continue?" his mother asked.

"Perhaps not." He thought of Kathleen's blazing encouragement. "But that has long been a moot point. The more germane point is that this is the correct and necessary thing to do."

The tea came, and the conversation paused as his mother poured. Once she had served, his father asked, "They won't drag the story of how you were forced to take in the little girl through the papers again, will they?"

Wishing for a glass of brandy, Jim set the tea cup on the end table next to the chair. For whatever reason—whether a belated anger toward Morley and Locke, or simply the product of years of keeping the peace—his temper flared. "Her name is Mina, Father, and I'd appreciate if you'd call her that."

His mother offered a conciliatory, "Jim—"

"And I wasn't forced to take her in."

His father parried. "Your wife—"

"My wife's name is Kathleen, and I'd also appreciate it if you would refer to her by that name. We have been married for six years now. And I brought Mina to my house because I'd always wanted her there."

The confession—spoken in a breathless gust—jolted his entire body. How long he'd denied himself this simple admission; how long he'd pretended that losing Mina was regrettable, but not a profound event in his life. He had mourned her loss, he discovered, as much as he'd mourned for Anneka.

"I would have married Anneka after I came home from Paris if she'd still been alive," he said. "I had promised Mina that she and her mother would come to live with me. In fact, I would have married Anneka when she was first pregnant if I hadn't been so selfish and immature. I loved her, and I've always loved Mina. I'm just now seeing the child she was, before she was damaged by the Dercums' inane zealotry and prejudices."

"I have apologized more than once," his mother said edgily. "I was so afraid for Eleanora. And then, to have to send you to France to help her, with the Germans shelling the ships on the Atlantic—what more could you expect of me? Both my children were in peril." She shivered. "And I was . . . not myself at Inglesfield. We should not have gone there."

All at once, Jim understood. Revisiting the place where his parents had lost half of their offspring while the other two were in crisis—it must have provoked a collision of memory and fear that was overwhelming. Sympathy for his mother flickered through him.

"There is no point in discussing this," Jim said. "But Mina is my daughter, and she is, for all intents and purposes, Kathleen's daughter as well. And unless Kathleen chooses otherwise, she will be my wife for the rest of my life, and our children—Mina, Stephen, Susanna, and any others that come—will be my legal and fully-privileged heirs. You'd do well to accept that."

No one spoke, and Jim wondered at how the conversation, meant to clarify what was happening in the Legislature, had come to this. But he stood behind the ultimatum—he would no longer tolerate his parents' disdain toward the family he had created and which he loved so dearly.

His mother cleared her throat. "Mina is a nice girl. It's a pity about her eyeglasses. They detract from her looks."

With an exhale, he accepted the olive branch. "They also allow her to read works far beyond her years. She regularly raids my library. I think she's been reading Gibbons' *Decline and Fall* as a bedtime story."

His mother laughed.

"She's fascinated by science, too." Jim turned to his father. "You'd like her, Father. She's very logical in her reasoning and precise in her conclusions."

His father said nothing, and Jim saw him as he was—deflated, flat, broken, a man who had been so stymied by life that all he had was a well of bitterness and dashed expectations. I could be him, he thought, if I allow it. He could let all his failings and disappointments—Anneka, Kathleen's infidelity, his failed political gambit—overtake and rule him.

But he would not. Not as long as he had Stephen and Susanna, not as long as he had Mina.

Not as long as Kathleen was beside him.

His mother spoke. "You must bring Mina over tomorrow for tea. Just the two of you, please. It will be a privilege to spend time with our granddaughter. Won't it, Arthur?"

There was no answer, but it no longer mattered.

Jim had won a great victory.

# FIFTY

Everything in Sean's life had assumed a dreariness that he could not shake. Nothing felt right—not the hideous room in Mrs. Potter's boarding house, and not his visits home to see Ma and Mag, or his visits to Mag's kids, who were farmed out to Kathleen. And certainly not his job with the D.A.'s office, which had proven ridiculous and dull. He drove around and looked at buildings—and that was about the extent of it. He wrote down names of who rented which apartment or what company occupied which warehouse. Stupid stuff.

Even the Church, where he'd always found some sort of solace, had failed him. He still attended Mass daily, yet it seemed to have little effect. If anything, he left feeling angrier. How had God allowed Chava to become a victim in all this? Sweet, pure, innocent Chava, who did so much good in her life. Just yesterday, Sean had driven to the Sheltering Home. He parked where he could see the preschool cottage through a slice between buildings. When the children came out for their morning recess, he leaned forward in anticipation. Another teacher had accompanied them, followed by Mrs. Bergman. Chava was nowhere to be seen.

Sean's sole comfort in it all was that Wells and the others down at the police station would be wondering what he was telling the D.A. about them. Paul seemed to trust D.A. Cline—and by tenuous extension, Mayor Stapleton—and to think that Cline would act against the Klan now that its power had been so sorely tested in the legislature.

By Jim Graves, no less. By a man as false as a two-headed nickel.

The headlines had blasted the news throughout the city and state: GRAVES PUTS KIBOSH ON KLAN LEGISLATION: *Senator One of Five Rebels To Caucus with Democrats* and REBELLION IN SENATE BREAKS KLAN SPELL: *Governor Morley Unable To Coax Republican Insurgents Back To Fold*. To Sean, it seemed like all Jim had done was to throw the adult equivalent of a temper tantrum, the same as he might do if there was a speck of dust on his precious Rolls Royce Silver Ghost. But Jim's strategy had worked. Evidently the legislature was in uproar and the Klan was scrambling to pass even a shred of its legislation through the Senate.

Now, Sean parked his car in front of Julia Reston's house. Paul had asked him to stop by after dark to share the information he'd collected that week. Sean knocked at the back door of the house, glancing behind him at the shadowy garden as he waited for someone to answer. Everything was silent—and Sean wondered if all this sneaking around were necessary.

Miss Reston opened the door. "Why, Patrolman—I guess, it's Mr. Sullivan now—come in."

Sean tipped his hat. "Good evening, Miss Reston."

"It's so good to see you." She closed the door behind him. "You're looking well."

He thanked her. Looking well was one thing. Being well was another.

As she led him into the parlor, a little boy zagged through the room, a Steelcraft toy airplane in his hands. His lips together, he made the sound of a motor as the plane swooped up and down. "Brrrrrrit, brrrrit!"

A delicately-boned woman with dark hair and eyes followed the child, speaking in French. The sound of the language took Sean back to France, to the trenches, to that time in his life that had both made him who he was and forever broken him.

Miss Reston spoke. "This is Mélisande, Paul's wife, and that"—she gestured toward the boy, who was sorting through a pile of toy airplanes— "is their son, Alex. This is Sergeant Sean Sullivan."

As Sean shook Mélisande's hand, he wondered if Kathleen knew that Paul had a French wife tucked away in Park Hill. Kathleen had never mentioned her to Sean, and the woman certainly hadn't been here on the night Sean had brought Chava here. Plus, he only had to look at Alex, with his blondish hair and soft hazel eyes, to see that the child was not truly Paul's.

As if she had read his mind, Mélisande said, "Alex's father was a pilot in the war and was killed only three days before the Armistice. Were you in France during the war?"

"I was."

"Did you fly with Kenny and Paul?"

"No, I was in the trenches."

"Ah, a Doughboy. Were you wounded?

"No," Sean said, feeling the familiar dread at speaking of his escapades in France.

"Then you were one of the lucky ones."

"It didn't seem that way."

"Anyone who was there will remember the suffering," she said. "Anyone who was there will be forever haunted by it."

Sean opened his mouth, but no words sounded. Paul's wife—with her sharp cheekbones and thin hands—struck him as just as odd as Paul's trouser-wearing aunt. Kathleen adored both Paul and Julia, but Sean found it all disturbing—Julia, who made no effort to hide her attraction to women; Paul, who had legendarily risen from the dead; and now, this woman who appeared just as much of a ghost as her son's father was.

Thankfully, Paul came into the room, saving Sean from making a reply. Paul wore a white shirt, vest, and his tie still cinched at the neck, with a silver tie clasp adorning it. The sleeves of his shirt were rolled up to his elbows. Alex ran toward him, calling, "Papa Paul! Papa Paul!" Showing Paul something on the airplane, Alex rattled on in French, losing Sean in the first few words.

Paul explained something in French, and the child ran up the stairs, the plane in mid-air. Mélisande said, "It was nice to meet you, but it is Alex's bedtime."

Miss Reston stood. "And mine as well."

Sean bade them goodnight. Once they had gone, Paul and Sean retreated to his study. Paul brought out the decanter of Scotch that he had shared with Sean on the night after Chava's assault. As he handed Sean a glass, he asked, "What do you have for me?"

"Not much," Sean said. "I mean, I have the reports, but there's nothing earth-shattering in any of them. Just a bunch of comings and goings."

"Comings and goings are exactly what we need to know about."

"Well, I guess I'm not Sherlock Holmes or Father Brown, then."

Paul laughed. "We aren't looking for the Hound of the Baskervilles, either. You're doing fine, and it might seem pointless to you to record these addresses, but we're putting the puzzle together with what you give us."

"So you're making progress? You'll be able to indict some of the Klan?"

"More than you'd guess." Paul sifted through the notes that Sean had given him. "You'll appreciate that the U.S. Treasury Department has taken an interest in Locke. Seems the good doctor hasn't paid taxes in a few years."

Sean shook his head. "All those dollar-fifty cuts from the ten dollar Klan membership fees must add up to a pretty penny. But nothing came of that kidnapping charge and forced marriage a few weeks ago."

"No, that one slipped away from us, but the newspapers had fun with it." Paul laid Sean's reports aside. "They loved the fact that Governor Morley paid Locke's bail, and that Ben Laska—the bootlegger from the West Side—is representing him. It's a circus, but it's also damaging the Klan's reputation. According to our spies, members are starting to lose faith." Paul sipped from his glass. "Have you seen Miss Rosen?"

"No, I . . . I don't think she would want to see me."

"Why not?"

"Because there were already so many obstacles between us. My family, hers. My faith, hers. In one way, Wells did us a favor because I wasn't strong enough to end our relationship myself."

"Walter Wells committed a crime that shouldn't pass with impunity," Paul said sternly. "You should visit her. She's essentially homebound. She's lonely, and her brother and sister-in-law are very effective jailers."

"That I know." Sean snorted. "So you've seen her again?"

"Yes, I visit on behalf of the D.A.'s office. I think you should see her."

"I don't know how I can. I can't just waltz up to Max Rosen's house and ask for her now, can I?"

"You've been meeting her on the sly for months. The two of you can figure it out."

Sean swished his glass of Scotch. He supposed he could somehow lure Chava into the same old trap—meeting in the alley beside the Rosens' house or at Sloan's Lake. He could mire them both in deceit and guilt again. But what good would it do either one of them? All the old problems were still there, simply heaped over by new ones. It was no way to live, no way to love.

"She should marry someone from her own church," he said. "That would be best for both of us."

"Would it?" Paul rose, signaling that the meeting was over. "I'll be in touch in a few days."

From the Restons' home, Sean drove to Sloan's Lake. Parking along its frozen shore, he tried to spy across the street to the Rosens' house on Osceola. It was too dark to see anything, especially in this neighborhood that put itself to bed by eight o'clock. Besides, he didn't want them to think that he was a Klansman planning to defile the synagogue. He started the car and left.

Unable to face going home to Mrs. Potter's, he drove past Sullivan's Grocery. The sign above the abandoned store looked ghostly. In the apartments above, a single light shone—probably Mag writing her letters. It was too late to knock or intrude. Sean parked his car next to the delivery truck and walked behind the store to the half-built house. Much to his surprise, it was still standing—given his neglect of it, he figured the wind and snow would have collapsed the frame by now.

He squinted. Someone was back there.

"Hey."

Tony sat on the half-built brick wall that he and Sean had put up last fall to test their masonry skills. With all that had happened since the first of the year, Sean hadn't seen Tony since Christmas, when he'd stormed out of the Sullivans' dining room after finding out that Liam had refused to serve in the army.

"What are you doing here?" Sean asked.

"I come to see if I could scare anybody up." Tony nodded toward the darkened apartments above the store. "What happened? Why isn't Mrs. James out here working?"

"She's not working outside anymore. Her husband's sick."

"Her typewriter's still there."

Sean lit a cigarette. "She's writing her answers in pen, then taking them—that is, I've been taking them—to her newspaper office for her assistant to type. It's all been a mess. I'll be glad when Liam is better."

"What happened to him?"

"He did something that he thought was heroic," Sean said dryly. "He wheeled himself out into the freezing dead of night and down to the Church." He told Tony about Brendan's attack and Liam's insistence on staying with his brother. "He caught a cold, which has just gotten worse and worse."

"That's rough," Tony said. "But I can see why he'd want to be with his brother. Did they catch who done it?"

"No," Sean said. 'But it's most likely Klan."

"That's why we have the Roma boys. They keep the Church safe." Tony stretched out his legs. "I'm sorry I ruined your Christmas day. All those kids—I hope they were okay."

"Don't worry about it. It's pretty much the way it always goes when Liam starts talking. I can't stand the sight of him either."

"Naw, that's not right. Your sister loves him. She's stayed with him. They got kids."

"Mag is his greatest defender. She won't allow a word against him."

Without commenting, Tony gazed toward the dark apartments. "Why aren't you working tonight?"

"I got fired."

Tony laughed. "What'd you do?"

"It's what I didn't do." He told Tony of refusing to fill out the Klan application. "And then, well, I threatened to kill one of the other officers."

Tony waved it away. "If you'd wanted to kill him, you woulda, like you done all them Germans. What'd he do to you?"

Sean started to explain in careful, measured tones. But the more he spoke, the more insistent the words became. Anger poured out of him— she had been nearly raped, she had been hurt enough that she'd lost her job, her career, the livelihood that she'd trained for and loved.

Tony mulled over his words. "You never told me you have a girl."

Sean took a couple of breaths, trying to calm himself. "Well, I don't any longer. We saw each other for nearly a year, or . . . not a year, I don't know. The only ones who knew are Mag and Kathleen."

The statement wasn't exactly true—Jim had met Chava at the art exhibition, and, of course, the Restons had hosted her—but he hadn't the energy to explain it all.

"And she's a Jew, huh?" Tony blew out smoke. "After you fought Danhour all the way through France so's you could be Catholic."

Sean laughed. "Yeah, I guess I'm a hypocrite, like just about everybody else I know."

"But you're not gonna see this girl again?"

"No, it's all over between us."

"But you're still in love with her?"

"I always will be."

"So why not tell her?" Tony said. "You two might as well be married 'cuz both of you are already going to hell for the other one."

Sean managed a weak laugh. "All that's left between us now is dust and destruction."

"So turn it into something else."

"How? I can't undo what's done, and when I tried to get justice for her, I ended up on my ass in the middle of Curtis Street."

"You gotta make her think she's more important than any of that."

"You sure are a romantic."

With a laugh, Tony rose. "Naw, just Italian. Hey, tell Mrs. James that I'm sorry about her husband. She'll probably throw a pot of boiling oil at you for it, but she should know all the same."

"Sure," Sean said. "Do you want to work on the house once it warms up again?"

Tony shrugged. "Why not? Neither one of us's got nothing else to do."

# FIFTY-ONE

The surprise was how much Julia liked Mélisande. Day after day, when Paul returned from the District Attorney's office, he found the two women in the kitchen. Mélisande had assumed the job of cooking dinner, replacing Rosa, while Julia sat at the kitchen table, smoking cheroots and speaking in her beloved French, which was rapidly losing its rustiness. Alex played either in the corner of the room or in the parlor on his own. Charlie Hague, Paul's colleague at the D.A.'s office, had dubbed the arrangement, "*La Famille Frenchie.*" In his flat Midwestern drawl, it became, "Lah fam-EE Fren-CHEE."

In private, Julia sought to allay Paul's concerns about Mélisande. "She came all the way from France for you, Paul," she said. "Perhaps she isn't your perfect mate, but the fact that she's here shows some sort of dedication to you."

"I'm convenient, Julia, and she knows I love Alex."

"If she had wanted convenience, don't you think she could have found someone in Marseille? But she sailed the ocean blue in search of you."

Paul had laughed at the singsong rhyme. He had to admit that he enjoyed having a woman in his bed, basking in her warmth at night and waking up beside her in the morning. Mélisande no longer expressed any revulsion over his physical state, although Paul still hesitated to reveal his left side. She openly enjoyed their time together, too—walking in City Park; going to the moving pictures with Alex; partaking of the legendary crab cakes at the Denver Dry Russian Room; or attending plays at the America Theater or the Isis. She had yet to express any regret that the few parties they attended in Denver could not compare to the glamor of Paris.

She was not the jaded, scornful girl he had met on the night that Kenny had fallen in love with her at first sight, nor was she the troubled, angry soul of the years when she and Paul had lived together in France. Instead, as she danced around the kitchen, chopping and steaming and baking, she reminded Paul of the woman who had skated on the frozen pond that night in Paris, traveling beyond what was reasonably safe, but with such grace and flow that one was mesmerized into believing that she was weightless and ethereal.

What had Alex said about her that night?

*Maman est belle.*

*Très belle,* Paul had agreed.

A knock on the back door of Julia's house interrupted Paul's thoughts. Sean waited on the stoop. Inside, Paul led Sean to his study. Papers spread across the mahogany desk. Law books and folders heaped to one side.

"This is getting to be quite the operation," Sean remarked as he laid his reports on the desk.

"So it is." Paul poured their customary glasses of Scotch. "A successful one, I hope."

"Does it bother you that Jim got there first?" Sean asked. "That he stole the show before you even got on stage?"

Paul took a sip of Scotch. Just this past week, the impasse in the Colorado General Assembly had come to a head, and the newspapers had crowed with delight over the battle that ensued. The House had passed a bill abolishing the State Board of Charities and Corrections, but a test vote in the Senate doomed the bill. All nine of the old-line Republicans had joined the insurgency started by Jim, and the Republican State Chairman, John R. Coen, had thrown his support behind them. The Republican Party shattered into two distinct factions: pro-Morley and anti-Morley. In the ensuing chaos, in which Governor Morley had threatened and fumed and crosses had burned throughout the city, a true coup had transpired. Senator David Elliot forced his way into the Chair for the State Affairs and Public Lands Committee, which received one-half of the bills. The Finance Committee, which received one-third named Louis Puffer as its Chair. And the Calendar Committee, which scheduled all bills for debate in the Senate, had gone to Jim. He now had the power to let legislation that he found objectionable wither away and die.

In essence, he now controlled the Senate.

"Any blow against the Klan is welcome," Paul said. "And Jim dealt Morley a doozy. But he hasn't the power to stop the corruption and crime. You don't realize how large our operation has become. The list of names I've compiled number more than one hundred—"

"One hundred! Are all of them Klan?"

"Not all, but a nice percentage is. And I suspect that some of the initial one hundred will give up names and information as well. You'll appreciate that Governor Morley's private secretary looks to be guilty of mail fraud."

"From sending out all those Klan pamphlets on the state's dime, I'd bet."

Paul laughed. "But the number of suspects has actually become a problem. We have no existing enforcement team, and no money to hire the people we need. As you know, we can't trust the Denver Police. Phil Van Cise used Colorado Rangers—"

"The highway patrolmen?"

"Yes, but there were only thirty or so Bunco Gang members arrested that day. We need to have as many deputies as there are criminals—maybe more—to help us carry out simultaneous raids before word gets around and the Klan closes down its schemes."

"The Knights of Columbus would be proud to help."

Paul shook his head. "That would only lead the Klan to claim that the Catholic Church was behind the raids. We have to make sure that the secular and established law of the country is recognized as the primary enforcer."

"Sad to think that you can't find a hundred honest men in a city this size."

Paul laughed again. "I need an army—"

"Wait," Sean said. "The army."

"The Colorado National Guard? That would require Governor Morley's cooperation."

"No, the American Legion. Almost all the talk I've heard in the Legion Hall has been anti-Klan."

It made sense to Paul. The majority of Klan members had sat out the war, mostly because they worked in factories or farmed and were considered temporarily exempted from the draft.

Sean's enthusiasm bubbled over. "I could probably recruit twenty or so from the Legion myself—"

"This investigation is still under tight secrecy," Paul cautioned. "Let me talk with Mayor Stapleton and D.A. Cline. You may have come up with a solution to our dilemma."

After Sean left, Paul sought out Mélisande. He found her beyond the French doors that led outside from the parlor. On Table—or Kastle—Mountain in the west, the three gasoline-powered crosses burned, flaring in the frigid air, at the usual Wednesday night meeting. Paul stood behind

Mélisande and encircled her with his arms. She wore a fur-lined velvet coat embellished with ample ruffs of fur around the cuffs and hem. The fur collar was so lavish that Paul had to smooth it away to find her face.

She leaned back against him. "Is he gone?"

"For tonight."

"Why does he come here? Why don't you meet him at your office?"

"I'll tell you soon enough." He looked up at the burning crosses. "I wonder what causes essentially responsible, basically decent men to join a group that invokes violence and hate."

"Don't you see? It is the war."

"The war? It's been over for six years."

"But everyone in the world—*tout le monde*—learned to hate, then, and they feasted like vultures on the stories of poison gas and bodies pinned on the barbed wire—"

She gasped, as if in tears, but her voice was clear when she spoke again.

"We all became used to it. We would read the newspapers—what's happened now? Oh, look, such a terrible battle, and so many killed, and in such terrible ways, too. So, when it ended, what was there to do? We couldn't go back to the way it had been—no, that was impossible, but we had to do something with our longing for blood."

If she was right, it was a sad commentary on human nature.

"So we found other enemies," she continued. "Those who cannot—or will not—defend themselves. *Les Catholiques, les Juifs, les Nègres*—they are easy to find, are they not? They have no armies or strong men to protect them. It is like the Germans with Belgium."

"Most Klansmen weren't soldiers."

"And it is the ones who did nothing whose hate burns fiercest, *n'est-ce pas*? Because they were not there, they don't know the horror of it all." Her contempt spilled over. "Why do you want to live here? Why do you want to stay? Is it for her?"

The bald question stabbed at Paul. Why did he live where his only knowledge of the woman he loved was through the escapades of her husband? What kept him here? A need to punish himself for having failed so many— Kenny, Kathleen, the dead of the battlefield—or a true longing to be here?

"I need somewhere to call home," he said vaguely. "Julia is here."

"So is she." Mélisande turned to face him. "It wasn't just hating Marseille that brought me here. After you left France, I realized that I should never have let you go. I had been stupid, childish, I had let you go without telling you what you meant to me, and I'd let you go to her, too. We had—*je ne sais quoi*—we fed off of something in each other. You kept me from wanting to die, and I, or at least, Alex, gave you back some semblance of being alive. But we didn't give it enough time to work."

"Three years," Paul said bitterly. "Three years we went back and forth, never happy with each other, never happy with ourselves—"

"We could not live where I had loved Kenny," she said bluntly. "But neither can we live where you love Kathleen."

Paul said nothing.

"Surely, every time her cousin comes here, every time you see him, you must think of her."

Of course, he did, of course. At times, he wanted to ask Sean about her, even though he doubted Sean would have an answer. "We don't discuss her."

"How can we have anything when she is here? If you want her, then, go and be with her! If you want Alex and me, then let's go where we can be free."

She was right. Sean's words echoed in his head: *Does it bother you that Jim got there first? That he stole the show before you even got on stage?* There was no future for him in Denver, nor had there ever been. Certainly, he would finish his time at the D.A.'s office in fine shape, and he supposed he could build a private practice of his own, but the knowledge that Kathleen and Jim lived only a few miles away would always overshadow whatever success he had.

Mélisande laid her palms against his chest. "I want you to myself. Is that so wrong? Perhaps we never imagined we would be with each other, but why shouldn't we be? Why shouldn't we enjoy each other?"

"What will change?"

"I have already changed. When we were in Paris, I hated myself. I hated the world. But now, I only want to love Alex and you. You are a good man, wise and decent, and you can teach Alex to be as strong and gentle as you are."

Her sincerity caught him. He knew her well enough to know that her words came out as sarcasm if she feigned earnestness.

"When I was in college, I thought I would live in Boston," he said.

She kissed his chin. "Where is that?"

"On the east coast, nearly the full continent from here. It's nearer to New York."

She kissed his ear lobe. "It is a nice city?"

"It's a nice city. It's much older and more established than Denver."

"And there is no Ku Klux Klan?"

"I don't know about that. Prejudice runs through every city and state. But Massachusetts has a strong history. It bred abolitionists before the Civil War."

One of her fingers touched his bottom lip, sending a thrill through him. "And Alex would live in a peaceful neighborhood in Boston, *oui*? There would be no crime or drugs? He would grow up without fearing he would be killed if the Germans rise up again?"

"Do you think the Germans will?"

"I believe they are capable of every evil under the sun." She put her hands on either side of his face. "Oh, Paul, isn't it what you would want, what we should want? Isn't it what every little boy should have? And his grandparents—perhaps you could talk them into seeing him if we lived nearer to them."

"That's important to you, isn't it?"

"We have no family here. Only you and Julia. I want more for Alex."

She kissed him, lifting her thigh to bring her body closer to his. Beneath her coat, she wore only a thin shift. He caught her leg in one hand and pressed into her. A low moan rose from her throat.

"Aren't you cold?" he murmured.

"*Fais-moi l'amour,*" she whispered.

As he kissed her again, he considered her proposal. A new city, a new job, a devoted wife at his side and a brilliant child or children to love—*La Famille Frenchie* built in earnest from the commitment of himself and Mélisande to Alex and to each other.

"Let's get married," he said, his lips still against hers.

"*Quoi?*" She pulled back in surprise.

"I want you as my wife, my legally entitled wife. I want to adopt Alex so that he is my rightful heir."

Her eyes filled with tears. "We have seen the very worst in each other," she whispered. "Now we will be the very best for each other."

# FIFTY-TWO

As Easter approached, the weather turned. The days grew warmer with the coming of spring, and the meadowlarks returned to the prairie beyond Berkeley Park. Around the lake, blackbirds trilled in the cattails and reeds, their red-capped wings flashing in the sun.

Maggie threw open the windows of the apartments above the grocery store to clear out the miasma of winter. The only rooms that remained sequestered and dark were her parents', because the light aggravated Ma's headaches, and Maggie's own, where Liam still shivered through the day.

As she fixed morning tea for Liam, she sent Alice Colleen and the boys out to the back, where the remains of the Liberty Garden, abandoned after the war, sprouted rogue dill, squash, and pumpkins. Carrying the tea tray back to him, she found him gazing out the window at the children.

"Are they bothering you?" she asked. "I can—"

"Let them play," he said. "It's such a beautiful day."

Maggie walked to the window to look down on them. Alice Colleen appeared to be directing the boys to run in a circle—a futile endeavor. Frankie wielded a stick as if it were a sword, while Kieran squatted down to play with something—most likely an insect—on the ground. He picked it up, his hand moving toward his mouth. Maggie knocked on the window pane, and Alice Colleen squinted upward. Maggie gestured that Kieran was about to eat something, and Alice Colleen hurried over to scold him.

Liam coughed, his body trembling. "When our boys are in the prime of their manhood, in their twenties, they should be fathers and husbands, earning a living at satisfying work, embracing their faith with honor and devotion. But I'm afraid that mankind has yet to learn its lesson. I'm afraid that ten, maybe twenty years from now, no one will remember the war."

"Surely the world won't have forgotten by then," Maggie soothed. "England and France and Germany have lost a whole generation of men. They don't have fathers and husbands now, so how would they have enough sons to go to war again?"

"Europe lost three million men in the Napoleonic wars and still had enough to fight a few decades later. And America has plenty of sons."

"Frankie and Declan will be twenty in 1941, and Kieran in 1943. There will be plenty of us still around who'll see to it that there isn't another war."

As the weather grew brighter, Liam's condition worsened into pneumonia. His fever spun upward, and he coughed out blood into a spittoon that sat beside the bed. Maggie slept beside his bed in an upholstered chair that she had moved from the parlor to the bedroom. Liam slept more and more, his returns to the conscious world marked by less and less clarity.

Beside him, Maggie prayed. She begged God to help, and when that failed, she turned to Liam himself. "Please, Liam," she whispered to him as he rasped through the night. "Please, don't leave me. I can't bear to be here alone, without you. I've loved you my entire life."

"Maggie," he murmured. "Maggie, my love."

"Liam, stay with me, don't leave me—"

"Let them know," he said. "Let them know that going to war would have broken my spirit. It would have stolen my soul from me. Resisting war never did; what they did to me never did. I've lived my life with no sorrow or regret because I never killed another man or caused harm to another human being."

"I will," she choked out. "I promise, but please, don't—"

"God will bless you. You're strong, you're capable, and Brendan and Judah will help you whenever you need it."

"But I need you—"

"My beautiful Maggie, my dearest companion."

On the night that Liam passed, it was in peace and silence, with Maggie holding his hand, and Brendan nearby, awaiting his brother's last breaths. Maggie laid her head against the mattress and sobbed, while Brendan performed last rites. Giving Brendan some time alone with Liam before she woke the children and her parents, Maggie wandered into Liam's study. Beside the Corona typewriter, Liam's manuscript was neatly tied with a blue, silk ribbon.

She laid her head against the manuscript, cradling her face against her sleeve to keep tears from staining the pages. She had resented it, this bulky book that day after day consumed her time with Liam. Then again, he had been gone from her for so long—ever since he had decided to battle President Wilson rather than the Germans—that she barely remembered the man who made up silly limericks about her name, or read poetry to her as they sat on the banks of Berkeley Lake, or kissed her in the shadows beneath the stairs to the apartments. She barely remembered the brawny and athletic man she married.

Even more elusive were memories of the seventeen-year-old girl who married him.

She heard the children stirring and went to tell them the news. Alice Colleen dutifully knelt and prayed, her rosary in her hand, while the twins fell silent in puzzlement, and Kieran showed no comprehension at all, but whined for breakfast.

"Daddy is with God now," Alice Colleen said. "He is in heaven."

"Yes, he is in heaven."

And if ever a man deserved to reach heaven, it was Liam.

As Brendan saw to the funeral arrangements, Maggie closed herself in Liam's office, armed with fresh sheets of paper and a pen. When she came out, late in the afternoon, she drove the delivery truck through the radiant warmth of spring to the offices of the *Denver City Daily News*.

Mr. Ledbetter answered her knock on his office door without looking up from his work. "What is it, Mrs. James?"

She sat in the chair in front of his desk. "My husband died last night."

He abandoned his editing. "I'm sorry."

"I'll see to it that Thalia has enough to write until I—"

"Don't worry about that. We'll run repeats or we'll find some that were cut. Miss Grant and I will take care of it."

"Thank you," she said. "But, I, I'd like to ask a favor of you."

He leaned back, his suit coat rumpled around him. "What can I do?"

"With my husband's death, I know that the past will be dredged up again in the newspapers, and I know what they'll print. They'll call him a slacker and coward, and they'll dishonor him and, by extension, his children, who have nothing to do with his crusade." She opened her purse and took out a folded sheet of paper. "Would you be willing to print an obituary that told the truth of his life?"

"Let me see it."

Maggie slid the sheet toward him. As he read, she imagined the words along with him:

"Liam Hennessey Keohane was born August 5, 1897 and died peacefully on March 30, 1925 from pneumonia. Mr. Keohane was a good father to his four children, Alice Colleen, Francis Hennessey, Declan Patrick, and Kieran Seamus, and a loving husband to his wife, Margaret Mary. He was also a faithful member of the Roman Catholic Church. He believed that God's will is inexorable and unconditional, and that the only Army on earth should be an Army of Peace. This led him into conflict with the U.S. Government during the world war. Because of his nonviolent resistance to war and conscription, he was arrested, tried, and convicted in civilian court as well as court-martialed by a military court. Sentenced to twenty-five years in Fort Leavenworth, a sentence that was later commuted by President Wilson, Mr. Keohane endured hardships and humiliation for his dedication to his convictions, including solitary confinement, bread-and-water starvation, and brutal beatings, which destroyed his health. Still, he was never defeated or broken. His faith persisted until the end of his life, and he taught his children to love God and the Catholic Church . . . "

Mr. Ledbetter laid it on his desk. "I'll print it as is, no edits. If anyone challenges it, they'll have to see me."

"Thank you."

"What will you do with his book?"

"I'm thinking of writing to the new American Civil Liberties Union."

"That's a good idea."

She started to leave, but Mr. Ledbetter said, "Mrs. Keohane, I am truly sorry for your loss." Bitterly, he added, "That war took and took from us, and it will be decades—if ever—before the wounds heal."

The funeral at Mt. Olivet, northwest of the city, takes place on a perfect spring day. Maggie stands between her father and Uncle Irish, while Brendan, who still moves gingerly after his beating, buries his brother with dignity and Catholic grace. Seaney comes, of course, and Kathleen and Jim and their three children. From Blessed Savior, Mrs. MacMahon and a few others attend, honoring Liam's friendship with their dead sons. Perhaps the most distraught mourner is Judah Rapp, who never doubted Liam. Judah's eyes behind his thick glasses are red-rimmed and weepy, as if he cannot mask his sorrow.

At home, Maggie finds that the safest place for her just now is the kitchen. In the bedroom is the bed that she shared with Liam, where they conceived their children and where he took his last breath. In the study is Liam's manuscript, neatly tied and ready to be read by someone, by anyone. In the parlor stands the home altar where Liam led the entire family in prayer before going to bed every night.

She hears the children's voices outside. They are near the half-built house with Seaney, who is unloading some lumber. Evidently, construction has started again on the house, although there is no need now. The twins can move into Liam's study, once it's been cleaned out, and Alice Colleen and Kieran will each have their own rooms.

Except . . .

She places her hands on her stomach. Only a couple of weeks ago, she had realized that she is pregnant again. The baby must have been conceived before Liam contracted pneumonia. That would make her nearly a third of the way to having another mouth to feed. How did she ever become this—a widow, with five children, and barely in her mid-twenties?

She hears a deep, resonant voice. Tony has joined Sean and the children at the house. He's explaining something to a very serious-looking Alice Colleen. He hands the little girl a hammer. Maggie slides the window above the sink open an inch or two to listen in on the conversation.

"What don't you like?" Tony asks Alice Colleen. "Bugs or worms—"

"Miss-kee-toes," Alice Colleen replies.

"Okay, then. Pretend that nail's a *zanzara* and hit it."

She gives it a feeble tap.

"Naw, that *zanzara* is still gonna bite you," Tony says. "He's gonna bite you right"—he pinches her nose—"there."

Alice Colleen giggles, enthralled. "What's a *zan*—?"

"*Zanzara,*" Tony says. "It's a better name for your mosquito, because it's Italian. Right?"

He defers to Frankie, Declan and Kieran, who have been playing with trucks and pails in the nearby pile of excavated dirt. Curious, they wander over to where Tony and Alice Colleen stand.

Tony says, "Okay, try it again."

Alice Colleen brings the hammer back in both hands and gives a mighty whack. Whether or not she hits the nail, the board vibrates with the blow.

"Now, see!" Tony takes the hammer from her and finishes the job. "That's the way you do it. You wanna try, Frankie? Declan? Come on, then."

As the boys eagerly line up, Alice Colleen spies Maggie at the window. "Mommy," she shouts. "Sergeant Neck-ey is teaching us how to build a house. Come down and see what I did. I hit a nail!"

Maggie nearly shushes her from habit before she remembers that there is no need. Liam, with his sensitivity to light and noise, is gone. Tony's gaze follows Alice Colleen's, and this time, Maggie's instincts aren't so easily handled. She steps back from the window, seeking the shadows, while her face burns with heat from the sight of his black eyes. She has not seen him since he kissed her, or she kissed him, or whatever happened. She doesn't know how she will speak to him again. She can't flirt with him, as she once did, but neither can she pretend that she has forgotten that night.

The boys join in Alice Colleen's request. "Come down, Mommy," they call, in various degrees of unison. "Come down and see!"

Shout, Maggie wants to tell them. Yell, scream, let out all the noise you've kept in for so many years. Be free, be children, be *alive*. For your father, for me.

Tony straightens up, the hammer hanging from his right hand, his weight shifted from the leg where the bullet lodged during the war. He wears a rough, rust-colored shirt, its sleeves rolled up around his elbows, and a tweed cap on his head.

"Come down, Mrs. James," he says.

Maggie's body trembles, as if his voice is a force of nature—wind and water, light and warmth. "Give me a minute," she calls.

As she passes through the parlor, she catches her reflection in the mirror on the sideboard. Her skin is pale, and bags have formed under her eyes from lack of sleep. Her hair is neither curled nor properly cut—it hasn't been in months—and her stained dress is nearly a rag. She had told Liam that she wanted to live honestly, that she wanted to rid herself of secrets. She had told herself that she wanted to be free, on her own. And that is what she is now. Why, then, does it feel so much like despair?

Alice Colleen waits for her at the bottom of the wrought-iron steps outside the apartments, which are wreathed in the shadow of the grocery this early in the morning.

"Come see!" Alice Colleen calls. "I hit the nail!"

Tony and the boys stand in the sunshine just beyond the steps. As Maggie descends, Tony doffs his hat. "I'm sorry your husband died," he says. "I'm sorry for pretty Miss Alice and all your boys. You all loved him, and I'm sorry."

Maggie's composure crumbles, and she pinches her nose between her thumb and index finger to stem the tears. "Thank you," she manages.

"Mommy, don't cry again," Alice Colleen says. "Come see. It will make you happy."

"Don't cwy, Mommy, don't cwy," Declan says, and Frankie and Kieran echo him.

"Brave Mrs. James," Tony says quietly. "You take care of all these people. Now let them take care of you."

The expression on his face is neither bold nor flirty, but kind and sincere. She knows at once that she can trust him to weather her sorrow and grief.

"Come on, Mommy," Alice Colleen pleads. "It's fun."

"Show me, then."

Taking Alice Colleen's hand, Maggie steps out into the sunshine.

# FIFTY-THREE

He had never spent an Easter weekend this way.

Sean paced back and forth along the stained wooden floor of the Denver District Attorney's Office. He bounced on the balls of his feet, thrust his hands in his pockets, pulled them out again, and ran fingers through his sticky hair. Outside the window, the rising sun reflected against the golden dome of the Capitol across Civic Center Park. The dome muted a rosy orange, then bright red, as the sun burst forward in the sky. Saturday morning had come—and he'd yet to see his bed.

Behind him, Paul processed another arrest warrant, answered a telephone call, stamped and filed two or three documents, and slurped down a cup of coffee. The mountain of paperwork in Paul's basket nearly toppled onto the floor, and more was being deposited by the minute. His secretary, Mary, bustled in with another file. "Gambling hall on Wazee, Colonel," she said merrily. "Thirty arrested."

Cradling the headset of the telephone between his neck and shoulder, Paul responded to her with a generous wink that made her grin. His colleague, Charlie, scooped up the report. "Here comes the Easter Bunny," he crooned as he carried it away.

Sean rubbed at the stubble on his face. Neither he nor Paul—nor Mary nor Charlie—had slept in more than twenty-four hours; he had not seen his room at the boarding house since Thursday night. D.A. Cline and Mayor Stapleton had spent Friday night sequestered in the D.A.'s private office, from which cigar smoke billowed every time Paul opened the door.

What a stroke of brilliance it was to choose Good Friday to raid the city's dicey properties. Traffic through the establishments was down—minimizing customer arrests—and yet the operators and managers of the gambling halls and betting rings were in full attendance. Everyone was taken by surprise—who would suspect a police raid on the weekend of the most important Christian holiday of the year? So far, the raids had netted more than two hundred arrests of bootleggers, prostitutes, and gamblers, many of them Klansmen. Much to Sean's amusement and gratification, fourteen Denver police officers—ten of them avowed Klansmen—had been arrested in the crackdown. Sean's former supervisor, Sergeant Denton, was one of them.

Now he understood what he had been doing for the past two months, as he blindly recorded the comings and goings at rickety warehouses and abandoned stables. He stood in awe of Paul, who had managed the clandestine operation nearly to perfection.

"We're almost finished," Paul said. "With this round, anyway."

"I've been awake so long, I can't remember where I live," Sean groused.

Paul laughed. "Just one more arrest, and then we'll call it a night."

"The two of us, then? We're going out together?"

"Yes."

They drove together to a house on Grape Street in Paul's Packard. The neighborhood was one of brick bungalows, pleasant patches of green lawn, and trees that had grown tall enough to offer some shade. Paul parked down the block from a home that was neatly kept, with a child's tricycle on the path leading to the front door. Sean noted that another car waited at the opposite end of the block. Mayor Stapleton had taken Paul's—and Sean's— advice and deputized more than one hundred American Legionnaires for this weekend's raids. Paul signaled to the Legionnaires before he pulled his briefcase from the back.

"What's this?" Sean asked. "Doesn't look like a house of ill repute to me."

Paul handed him a file folder. "No, it's a private home."

Inside the folder was an arrest warrant for Walter Wesley Wells on multiple charges of fraud, graft and profiteering committed as a member of the Klan's Vice Squad. "Good God," Sean said. "You did it."

"Did you think I wouldn't?" Paul slid from the car. "Come on."

Paul rapped at the door, waited, then knocked harder. After all, it was barely six-thirty on a Saturday morning. Sean fidgeted beside him, a range of emotions coursing through him. Fury, disgust, something akin to hatred, exhilaration, smugness, the sweetness of revenge—he could hardly control himself. He shifted from foot to foot. Beside him, Paul warned, "Take it easy, Sean. We don't want to bungle this one."

He was right. It was about Chava now—about an Old Testament eye for an eye and a tooth for a tooth. He had to stay calm for her.

When Wells finally came to the door, he was dressed only in an undershirt and his trousers. His suspenders drooped over his shoulders, and his black hair was tousled. He scratched sleepily at it. "What the hell?"

"We're here on behalf of the District Attorney," Paul said calmly. "We need you to come to the office."

"I haven't done anything—"

"I have a warrant." Sean waved it before him. "Signed by Judge Hawkins."

Wells read it. "So this is all you two little pissants could come up with? I'm going to call—"

"Chief Candlish has no authority in this situation," Paul said. "This action was taken by the Denver District Attorney's office, under District Attorney Cline, at the request of Mayor Stapleton."

Wells shook his head. "So Stapleton's blown the other way, huh? Let me get dressed."

"Walt?" A woman's voice rang from the back of the house. "What's going on?"

"It's all right," he called back. "I have to go downtown." With that, he disappeared into the bedroom.

The bastard, Sean thought. Not even brave enough to tell his wife the truth. Mrs. Wells came from the kitchen, wearing a pink housecoat. With blond hair in pincurls and soft green eyes, she would, in better circumstances, be pretty. She carried a baby, wrapped in a blue flannel blanket. "Feeding time," she said, steadying a bottle with one hand. The baby sucked contentedly at the nipple. "He's three months old today."

Three months. The words slapped Sean in the face. On a night just three months ago, Wells had stood in the hallway of his boarding house, hooded and robed, and torn off Chava's blouse. And all the while, this woman waited at home, either on the brink of giving birth to her husband's baby or holding his newborn in her arms.

"Would you like some coffee?" Mrs. Wells asked. "I can heat it—"

"No, thank you," Paul said graciously.

"I'm sorry, I don't know your names."

"I'm Colonel Paul Reston, Assistant District Attorney. This is Sean Sullivan. He's also with the D.A.'s office."

"Ma'am," Sean murmured politely.

"District Attorney?" She eyed the warrant in Sean's hand. "Has Walt done something wrong? Is he in trouble?"

Sean's breath caught in his throat. Oh, wouldn't he like to tell her about the coward's courage her husband had whenever he donned a hood and robe. Wouldn't he like to tell her how her husband had beaten and mauled a woman he'd never seen before and would never see again? But he felt Paul's eyes on him. He wouldn't disappoint him. Gently, he said, "You need to speak to your husband, Mrs. Wells."

"Walt?" she called, and the bottle slipped from the baby's mouth. He fussed, tiny fists in the air, his cry a steady upward siren. "Walt? What's going on?"

Wells came from the bedroom, donning his coat as he walked. "I'll be home in an hour. Don't worry, Aggie." He kissed her forehead before he went out the door.

And then, it was finished. So simple, so uneventful. Wells scooted the tricycle out of the way as he walked down the path, but otherwise, made no unexpected movements. The two Legionnaires escorted Wells to their car and waited while he climbed into the back seat. In silence, Sean and Paul watched the car drive away.

As they walked toward the Packard, Paul said quietly, "You did well in there, Sean."

"Thank you."

"He's right, you know. He'll post bond in an hour. But Mayor Stapleton has promised that any member of the Denver Police force who is charged in this raid will be immediately suspended. He'll lose his job."

Sean's bitterness overflowed. "Maybe then she'll find out what kind of man she married."

"Do you really hope so? Look behind you."

Sean glanced over his shoulder. Aggie Wells stood yet at the door of the house, her face haggard and confused. She bounced the crying baby in her arms. A girl with brunette ringlets pulled at her mother's waist. A boy of about five huddled nearby, already carrying extra weight on his large frame, like his father.

Oh, God, if they knew, how much sorrow would it cause? A lifetime—for all of them. Chava would never want that, no matter how much she had suffered.

Paul opened the door of the Packard. "I'm hoping for conviction on at least a couple of counts. It's the best I can do. I know it isn't enough, but—"

"It's enough." He'd waited so long for this, for justice and retribution, for revenge. It should feel like victory, but all he wanted now was to sleep,

Chava next to him, with her warm body and scented hair and soft skin. He wanted to bury his face in her beauty and forget the world. Exhaustion spread through his limbs, dropping them like lead. He ducked into the passenger side of the Packard.

"Want some breakfast?" Paul asked cheerfully.

"Don't you need to get back to the office?"

"Oh, they won't process Wells for a while yet. And if he has to wait, it won't hurt him any."

Paul parked the car before a diner near the Capitol building.

As they climbed from the car, Sean asked, "Do you think this will be the end? Surely the Klan won't survive now, what with the legislature's change of heart and all this crime—"

Paul shook his head. "John Galen Locke is still the most powerful Grand Dragon in the United States. He has money, influence and plenty of loyal members. Although Ben Stapleton's done a turnaround, just as Jim Graves did, they have plenty of politicians in their pockets. They're down just now, but not beaten."

"Down, but not beaten," Sean mused. "I know all about that."

In his room at Mrs. Potter's boarding house, he showered in the shared bathroom and shaved and dressed for bed. But, although he had felt bone-tired at the D.A.'s office, he had no desire to sleep. All the excitement of the weekend, all the adrenaline that had pumped through his heart as the deputies brought in Klansman after Klansman, made his thoughts race. He thought of going home, of telling Mag about it, but she was still a shadow of herself, mourning for Liam. As for Kathleen, well, she had Jim's accomplishments to celebrate.

When the sun began to set, Sean darted down the steps of the boarding house to his car. He drove to Sloan's Lake, where he parked squarely in front of the house on Osceola Street. After he knocked on the door, he waited, his eyes on the mezuzah on the frame.

Max answered, a frown pulling at his lips.

"May I see Chava?" Sean asked.

For a moment, Sean thought Max was going to shut the door in his face. Instead, he asked, "Isn't this a sacred time for you? Isn't tomorrow Easter Sunday, the resurrection of your Messiah?"

Behind Max, Chava appeared. Sean had forgotten—how could he?—how lovely she was, how striking her amber eyes were, how full her lips.

Speaking over Max, Sean asked, "Can we go for a cup of coffee? It's just a short distance away, and I promise we won't be gone long—"

"Yes, I'm coming," Chava said, and squeezed past Max.

Once they were in his car, he asked, "How are you?"

Her voice was polite and steady, offering nothing. "I've started working with Mrs. Lorber, making phone calls and writing letters to raise money for the Sheltering Home. I'm very good at what I do. I make calls all over the country, to some of the wealthiest American families." She added, "I've spoken with Kathleen. Did she tell you?"

"I haven't seen much of her. I hope she gave you a bundle."

"She did—much more than I expected, considering that we're not—"

"Catholic?" Sean parked his car before the coffee shop. "Don't be fooled. Kathleen has her own rules about how the world should be run, and religion doesn't have much to do with it. She used to sketch cartoons of the priests during Mass."

Chava laughed. The bell on the door of the coffee shop tinkled as they entered, and the proprietor, a burly Greek with English as thick as the coffee he made, came from the back. Sean signaled "two" to him. No other customers graced the shop, much to Sean's relief. He'd had enough of jabbering and noise this weekend. Chava slid into a booth, and Sean sat across from her. Soon, the proprietor set two cups of steaming coffee and a plate of sticky, honey-drenched pastry before them.

Chava reached for the sugar, and Sean cautioned, "Taste it first. It's usually sweet enough."

"How did you come across this place?"

"I don't spend my entire life in Berkeley Park, you know." She smiled at the joke, and Sean continued, "It was the perfect place for a cup of coffee after I came off duty in your part of town. Halfway between the West Side and my room."

He noted the yellow smudges that still blemished her right cheek and the reddish puff of scar in her eyebrow. She wore a lace collar that buttoned closely around her neck. He wondered what damage hid beneath it.

"I'm sorry about your brother-in-law," Chava said. "Judah told me he had passed away."

"Yeah, poor Mag, I don't know how she'll keep all those kids in food and clothes now. I'll keep giving what I can to our parents, so she doesn't have to worry about them." He ran his finger around the rim of his cup. "I'm glad you're doing well."

"And you? I know you're with the D.A.'s office now. Colonel Reston told me."

He dipped his spoon into his cup. "You'll see what we've been up to once the newspapers blast it all over the city. But I wanted you to know first, before you saw it there—we arrested Walt Wells this morning."

"For what?"

"For collecting protection money from businesses run by Negroes in Five Points, among other things. He claimed it was a 'special tax' for those people who needed more protection from the Klan." Sean swallowed a sip of coffee. "It wasn't for . . . It wasn't for what he did to you."

"Oh."

"I just wanted you to know. At least, he'll lose his job. Mayor Stapleton has promised. I know it probably isn't the way you wanted it."

"I just wish it had never happened."

Suddenly sickened by the smell of the sweet, heavy coffee, Sean pushed his cup away. "I've relived that night a hundred times," he blurted. "I've remembered how you looked. I didn't see every bruise, but those I did, I've thought, How did she get that? What did he do to her to cause that? And I've hated myself. It was my fault that it happened, and—God!— if I could, I would endure anything, I would die, to undo it—"

"It wasn't your fault. It was mine. I should have been smarter—"

"No," he said bitterly. "I was a fool. I never should have put you in that spot, meeting you like that. Those games we played were stupid. They were sinful and prideful, and they made us lesser people than we are. They made us the kind of people Wells and the others can laugh about—"

"Games?" Chava snapped. "Was that all it was for you?"

"Of course not, but hiding it from our families and sneaking out at night—it was stupid. My God, Chava, I tried to kill Wells! I went out, damned and determined to do it, because I thought he'd taken from me the only worthwhile thing I'd ever had—"

"Oh, Sean, no!"

"But it was you who took it away. Why wouldn't you see me after it happened? Why did you disappear? Do you hate me?"

Her voice was so soft when she spoke that he had to lean forward to hear her. "Do you want to know what it was like in the days—the weeks—after it happened? Every hour, I'd look in the mirror, hoping to see my eye open and the bruises fade, but they just got uglier and darker. And when I closed my eyes, all I could see were his hands reaching for me." She inhaled, as if the recollection still had power over her. "The only thing—the one thing that kept me alive was Hannah. Holding her, whispering to her—she saved me."

"Have you been to church—I mean, the synagogue?"

"No, I have not. And you? Surely you've been to Mass?"

"I have, but everything has . . . changed."

"What do you mean?"

"I want your forgiveness more than I want God's." The words caused Sean a nearly physical pain. "I want you to love me more than I want to love Him."

"You needn't choose. I would never ask you to give up your faith."

"I have chosen, though." He glanced toward the proprietor, who impatiently eyed them from behind the counter. "We should go. It's getting late. I don't want to upset your brother and sister-in-law."

Standing, he threw down some coins for the pastries and coffee. In silence, they walked to the curb where he'd left his car, Chava hugging her sweater against her, as if she needed to shield herself from him. Without speaking, Sean closed the passenger door behind her. He started the car and drove west. Although night had cloaked the street, Chava watched out the passenger window, her face hidden from him.

Sean could not think of how to start a conversation with her; he couldn't think how to atone for what had happened to her. He longed for her to launch into a story about one of her children at the Sheltering Home or the Russian-speaking peasants who were learning English from her.

As if she had sensed his anguish, she broke the silence. "I want you to know—" Her words were barely audible. "I haven't kissed a man since the last time you and I . . . I've barely spoken to one."

Sean's heart stalled, with hope, with fear.

She forged onward, her voice sounding as if she had to push the words out from deep within. "I don't know if I can. Not because of what happened to me, but because of you."

"Because of me?"

"I don't want another man to touch me." She reached for his arm, and his muscles tensed under her touch. "I don't want anyone else. I never have."

Her words pierced his heart. What was she to him? he thought again. What he had always wanted—a woman who thought, believed, and loved just as he did. Everything, everything. He twisted the steering wheel, turning away from West Colfax and toward Berkeley Park, to the street where Mrs. Potter's boarding house stood on the corner.

"What are you doing?" Chava asked.

"Just give me a minute." He parked in front of the house. "You need to come to some sort of peace with what happened to you. We both do."

"You want me to go inside?"

Sean touched her arm. "Don't be scared."

Reluctantly, she followed him up the stairs of the boarding house, her hand in his. As they approached the landing, she glanced fretfully toward his neighbors' doors, toward the shadowy hall where Wells had hidden.

Suddenly, she clasped his hand in both of hers. "I can't—"

"Let me show you something," Sean clicked on a wall switch. The hallway glowed with light. "I changed the blasted bulb myself. I had to bring over Pa's ladder to do it—"

Chava stepped onto the landing, her eyes focused on the wooden jamb where her eyebrow had split. The soft pine was dented and scraped from the violence of the impact.

A whimper escaped from her. "You can see where I fell."

"You've come this far," Sean said. "Only a few more steps and you'll be past it. And it'll be over and done with forever."

She eyed the door. "Did you have the locks changed?"

"Oh, yes." He coaxed her gently with a hand at her waist. "But mind you, I still don't have a maid."

She took a step into the room, taking in the new rug, the new bedspread, the accoutrements that Kathleen had brought over. "It doesn't look the same," she said. "It doesn't feel the same. What have you done?"

"Kathleen did some redecorating. You're all right, then?"

"I don't know."

Sean closed the door and leaned back against it as Chava tentatively made her way across the room. She stepped around the worn shirts puddled on the floor, the stack of outdated newspapers, and the pillows kicked from the unmade bed. She ran a finger over the tangle of rosary beads on the dresser.

"Do you still love me?" she asked.

"I always have." He laughed weakly. "I fell in love with you on the night we met, when you said your name, so fierce and angry. I'd never met anyone as proud or contrary as myself, and I knew I would never be able to do without you."

Without warning, tears flooded from her eyes. "Oh, Sean, I just wanted to love you, I just wanted to be loved by you. Why couldn't they leave us alone?"

Sean hurried over and took her in his arms, shushing her. She pressed her cheek against his chest, and he murmured against her hair. "Shh, shh, it will be all right."

"Do you feel the same as you did about me?" she whispered. "About my . . . my body?"

Sean made no reply. *Turn it into something else,* Tony had said, and although Sean hadn't had a clue what he was talking about, he knew what he would do now. Moving as slowly as he could, he pushed back her hair until the right side of her face, which had been so ravaged, was revealed. Carefully, he kissed her eyebrow, where the scar nestled, then her temple, and her right eyelid, which had once been swollen shut. With unhurried deliberateness, he kissed his way along her cheekbone and down her jaw. His mouth circled around to touch hers, lightly and softly, but all the same, summoning a moan from her. She parted her lips to receive a deep, complete kiss, but, instead, he laid his finger on her mouth.

"Wait," he said gently.

His kisses trailed down her throat, stretching across her collarbone and into the hollow of her shoulder, and she took in a gasping breath. Tenderly, he cupped her breasts and kissed them, reclaiming for both of them every part of her that had been bruised and battered.

# FIFTY-FOUR

Oh, it was as if the heady, happy days of the Harding administration had returned! Once again, Kathleen and Jim were the toast of the town. At a party at the home of one of Denver's *crème de la crème*, the parlor filled with elegant figures dressed in ensembles ordered directly from New York, abundant flower arrangements, and the finest of cigars and pre-Prohibition wines. A horn player caressed jazzy pieces from a saxophone, accompanied by banjo, trombone, and drums. Beneath a dazzling chandelier, much of Denver's society sparkled in jeweled hairpins, gold lamé, and beads and bangles. Arthur and Victoria Graves, long silent and semi-reclusive, were in attendance, along with Ellie and Thomas. Kathleen noted wryly that Victoria's blonde hair had grown silvery and glamorous, no gray in its finely coiffed bounty. Her mother-in-law beamed, the queen, the mother of the prince.

Only yesterday, the legislature had adjourned a strenuous two days late without too much harm to the state government. Tonight, Jim spoke to the party-goers as he stood next to feisty Billy Adams and others from the Senate. "One of Denver's most esteemed newspapermen—I won't mention names, but he works at the *Denver Post*"—everyone laughed at the hint that it was Frederick Bonfils—"said that a legislature which 'does nothing is a good one.'" He waited for another laugh to echo through the room. "In that, the Twenty-Fifth is the best assembly that this state has ever seen."

"Hear! Hear!" came the response.

"The House thought it was a race," Billy said. "They rushed legislation through without a word of discussion—a brand new tax system was put in place that way. Some of them even admitted that they didn't know what they were passing, but because the Governor had called on them to pass it, they did. But when it came to the Senate, Senator Graves had a different plan."

He ceded the floor to Jim again.

"We took our time to consider every detail," Jim said. "That is why we spent seven days considering a bill to increase the number of administrative employees in the Senate from three to six at a grand cost to the taxpayers of twenty-four dollars a day."

Laughter echoed through the room, and Jim sent a devilish smile toward Kathleen, who stood near the punch table.

"Eighty-five percent of the more than one thousand bills introduced in January never made it out of committee," Billy announced. "Of the few that did, it's now a crime to pick a columbine"—he waited for the laughter to die down—"and it's now legal to exterminate prairie dogs! So, have at 'em, fellas!"

Jim laughed. "And although the Governor proposed abolishing thirty-seven boards—in order to create new boards that were stacked with Klansmen—the only state board that was abolished was the Board of Horseshoe Examiners."

Billy topped off the celebration. "So the Invisible Empire has been foiled and spoiled by our extraordinary bi-partisan effort. Let's drink to that!"

Applause rounded the room. Jim raised a cup to calls of "Cheers" and "Atta Boy!" The band broke into "For He's a Jolly Good Fellow." As the chorus grew more raucous, Kathleen thought of the accolades that Jim had received—the flowers from former governor William Sweet, the Democratic incumbent who was ousted by Morley last November; a card from former Senator Shafroth; and a box of cigars labeled "Not CYANA" from Billy himself.

But there were also threatening notes and angry phone calls. Kathleen had answered the phone one morning to hear a woman's voice call her an Irish whore and claim that her children were nothing but maggoty bastards. When she'd told Jim, he'd advised, "Let Drake or Harris answer the phone. Neither one of them is the gentleman he pretends to be. They'll know how to handle it."

On a visit to Mina, Mary Jane had told Kathleen of her brother, Avery's, disenchantment with the Klan. "He says that over half of his klokan have quit," she said. "And he's thinking of quitting, too. He says that the Royal Riders of the Red Robe—you know, the group that allows Protestants who weren't born in this country to be members—lets in too many who look Catholic to him."

Kathleen had laughed. "What does a Catholic look like?"

"I don't know, but after all the hullaballoo of the Good Friday raids, he says he's going to burn his Klan stuff—his little Klan Bible and his robe and everything else. He says it's boring and stupid, anyway."

"What about Andy Dercum?" Kathleen asked warily.

"It will take more than a few bad apples to make him quit. He has far too much fun driving around in his robe scaring people." She pondered, then added, "You know, it's just like putting a sheet over your head on Halloween and jumping out and scaring your friends half to death. We all outgrew that, but Andy and Matt haven't."

The merriment at the party resumed, with the band kicking into a lively version of Gus Kahn's "It Had to Be You." About halfway through the song, an audible sigh resonated through the room, followed by renewed chatter. All attention fell on the entryway to the ballroom, which was elevated above the dance floor by a series of steps.

There, Paul was handing a weighty fur coat to the butler, along with his own woolen great coat. Beside him stood a small, dark woman who wore a skin-baring satin shift with exquisite beadwork from top to bottom. The beads metamorphosed from a dark, sensual red to shimmering silver near her hips to flashing onyx near the hem of the dress, which ended just above her knees. Silver chains adorned with garnets looped from her shoulders to her elbows, and a sparkling tiara graced her dark hair. In stark contrast, Paul wore a black tuxedo with white tie.

Eleanora appeared at Kathleen's elbow. "Who is that?"

And even though Kathleen had never seen Mélisande, she knew. The girl—the woman—was no taller than Mina, but with her heavily-kohled eyes and wine-red lips, she carried an exotic, almost Egyptian beauty that outshone every other woman in the room. Why hadn't Paul told her? Why hadn't Julia? She hadn't seen either of them since the year began, but surely the news should have reached her somehow.

"It's his wife," she replied, a dull ache inside.

"His wife?" Ellie asked. "From Paris? The dress certainly came from there."

Kathleen made no reply. She had not anticipated the shock of seeing Paul with someone else, of knowing that he lived with and made love with another woman. Even more painful was the expression on his face. His smile was bright and warm, his eyes happy. *They are in love,* she thought— but no, Paul had told her their relationship was one of convenience.

"Hey, look, it's the other hero of the KKK wars!" someone called. "Tell us about the Good Friday raids, Colonel!"

Paul easily took command, accepting a glass of punch from a waiter, while Mélisande glittered beside him, a crystal cup in her hand. "We arrested more than two hundred bootleggers, gamblers, and prostitutes. Fourteen patrolmen were suspended by Mayor Stapleton, including two sergeants and ten patrolmen. All but two of them were also connected with the Klan. The arrests for an array of crimes focused heavily on members of the Klan Vice Squad." He waited for laughter to round the room. "And we expect to make more arrests any day now."

"So, ladies and gentlemen," Billy called. "Raise your glasses to the Denver D.A.'s Office, which has proven itself more than capable of taking down the Klan!"

The band crashed into another round of "He's a Jolly Good Fellow." Kathleen kept an eye on Jim, standing almost elbow to elbow with Paul. He maintained a practiced smile on his face, generously sharing his moment of glory. And, after the applause had waned, Jim accompanied Paul and Mélisande to where she and Ellie stood. When Paul introduced Mélisande, she dipped gracefully at the knees.

*"Madame, Monsieur,"* she said. "I am pleased to meet you."

Jim welcomed her in French. *"Enchanté, nous sommes ravis de faire vôtre connaissance."*

*"Merci,"* Mélisande replied.

Jim introduced Ellie, who continued the conversation. "When did you arrive in Denver? Did you come into the country through New York?"

The two of them escorted her to the punch table to fill a glass, chattering in French, while Paul looked on in shrewd amusement.

An awkward silence fell between him and Kathleen.

"I didn't know she had come to Denver," she said at last.

Paul told her of Mélisande's and Alex's arrival. "Both Julia and I were shocked that she'd come, but it's turning out quite well for all of us."

Kathleen's heart shifted. He looked younger; the residual sorrow from the war had vanished from his face and shoulders. "I'm so happy for you."

He faced her. "I should tell you that once I've done as much damage to the Klan as I can at the D.A.'s office, Mélisande and I will be moving to Boston. I've secured a job there through some of my former contacts at Yale."

The words struck Kathleen with a physical force. "Oh, Paul, oh . . . is it with the same firm as you were to work for before the war?"

"No, that opportunity passed me by years ago. But this one should be stable and challenging."

"What about Julia?"

"I think she'll join us. She'll appreciate being closer to New York and the artists there."

Kathleen's heart fell again. "I'll miss her terribly."

Paul looked toward Jim, Ellie, and Mélisande. "We lost each other years ago, Kathleen. And every step we take closer to the people we love—Jim, your children, Mina, Mélisande, Alex—takes us farther apart from each other."

She could not deny it. Perhaps Paul had forever laid claim to her heart, but her children and Mina had irrevocably stolen her soul. And Jim, who had been with her throughout nearly every major step in her life—her loyalty and devotion belonged to him.

"We have to be happy," Paul said. "For all those who died in the war, for all those who never had the chances to walk or love or laugh or grow old as we will—we have to make the most of the life that we have. We have to live well, we have to love well. For them."

"*We will remember them,*" she said.

"Pardon?"

"It's the poem by Laurence Binyon. '*Age shall not weary them, nor the years condemn. At the going down of the sun and in the morning, We will remember them.*' I learned it after Cambrai." She blinked away tears. "I'm truly happy for you and for Mélisande and Alex."

"And you? Jim seems to be restored to his former glory."

She glanced toward Jim who, along with Ellie, was still charming Mélisande. "We're doing well. The children, especially Mina, too."

"I'm glad," Paul said. "How is Sean these days?"

"He brought Chava over to meet Aunt Maury and Uncle Seamus the other day," Kathleen said. "I was there, too, and there was some confusion about whose friend she was—Aunt Maury seemed to think she was mine. It will take her some time to admit that her son has fallen in love with a Jewish woman, but I don't think she'll stand in the way of Seaney marrying someone he so obviously loves."

"And Miss Rosen's family?"

"Seaney says that her brother will let him in the house now without his wife and baby fleeing to another room, as if Catholicism is catching."

Paul laughed. "They're both headstrong and stubborn enough to make it work."

The party lasted until well after midnight, filled with more accolades and congratulations to Jim for his work in the Legislature. During the drive home, Jim did not speak, yet when he pulled into the driveway, where Blount waited to take the car back to the garage and Drake waited to take their coats and hats, he signaled to the two men to stay back. They retreated beneath the portico.

"What is it?" Kathleen asked.

"Paul Reston is a man in love, a man who's newly found love," Jim said. "He has all the confidence and geniality of a man who has found someone who believes in him as much as he believes in her."

His words were neither gloating nor resentful. He spoke softly, as if he were trying to break the news to Kathleen as gently as possible.

"I know," she said. "They're moving to Boston soon—"

"How does that sit with you?"

"My life is here, with Stephen and Susanna and Mina. My life is with you."

"And your love?"

"How can you ask me that? I'm proud of what you've done. You've effectively shut down the Klan and—"

"That isn't what I asked. Who do you love, Kathleen?"

She thought about their long history: she had met Jim when she was so young, and he had bent the rules of the Relief Society so that she could go to France. That in itself had bonded them, as fellow rebels, as those for whom rules were less important than experience. Then, there were the dark days after the war, when her heart had been ripped from her by Paul's death. Jim had been with her through that, too. Her father's words ring in her ears: *When has he ever failed you?*

"When I loved Paul—" She swallowed back the emotion in her throat. "I was so young, so innocent, so . . . stupid in so many ways. I loved that part of me, I loved that time in my life—and, I don't know, I'd return to it in a moment if I could. But I can't, of course, and I'm not that person any longer, and I've known that, and Paul has known that since he returned to Denver. I told him the first time I saw him that I couldn't go back to him, that I was committed to you. You have my love. It's yours and our children's—and that includes Mina."

"And not as a second or a consolation?"

"No," she said sincerely. "Not at all. In the past year, you have become the leader, the example, the man of honor and strength that you always wanted to be. And it wasn't by fighting the Klan in the legislature either. It was taking Mina into our home." She paused. "You proved to me that you are the man I've always wanted. Someone I could respect and love, and who would respect and love me."

Jim lit a cigarette, then rolled down the window of the car. The breeze, still cold in mid-April, circled through the cab, and Kathleen caught the fresh, ripe smell of the breaking buds on the trees in the garden. Spring, just outside the window, almost within reach.

"Last summer," he said soberly, "when I was in so much trouble around the election—when I had brought so much trouble on myself, that is—all I wanted was you. But I was afraid of the truth, of how I'd abused everything that we had. I was afraid that you would tell me at any moment that you were leaving with Paul because you had discovered how weak I was, that you couldn't forgive me—"

"I was angry—"

"The fear of losing you was far greater than the fear of anything that John Galen Locke or the Klan could do to me. It didn't matter in the end that they'd found out about Mina; they would have found another way to intimidate me. I could survive losing the governor's seat—I did survive it. I couldn't have survived losing you."

He leaned over and kissed her cheek. Without waiting for her reply, he signaled to Blount and Drake, who rushed forward to open the car doors.

The next morning, she wakes when the children charge into her room.

"Get up, Mommy, get up!" Stephen plows his way onto the high-set bed, while Susanna struggles to climb on until Mina gives her a boost. Beryl enters the room with a breakfast tray, which she sets across Kathleen's lap.

"Thank you," Kathleen says to Beryl. Laughing, she asks the children, "What's all this?"

"Daddy says we're going to the castle today. As soon as you have breakfast and are dressed, we can go."

Stephen plucks a berry from the fruit cocktail on the tray. Susanna, as always, imitates him.

"The castle?" Kathleen asks.

"The castle in the mountains," Mina clarifies.

"As soon as you eat and are dressed," Stephen says again. "So hurry!"

The three of them watch her, measuring each bite to see how much is left. At last, Kathleen sets aside the tray. "I'm finished," she says. "Now, everyone shoo so I can get dressed."

As she is changing, Jim comes into her room. "I see you managed to fend off your wake up party," he says dryly.

Kathleen laughs. "What brought on this idea?"

"I want to go where no one will find us. No newspapers, no telephone, no visitors. Where we can be assured that we're alone."

"Redlands—"

"Redlands has a road that leads right to it. It's far too easy for a reporter to find. Inglesfield has the advantage of distance, a mostly impassable road, and heraldic gates. The only thing missing is a moat."

She laughs again. "How long do you plan to stay?"

"We'll see how long the food lasts. Drake is coordinating all that. Tell Beryl what you want her to pack and leave her to it. The Holdens will open the castle for us, but some of the staff will be coming up later today."

The entire family squeezes into the Marmon, a dove gray 1924 model that has a back seat wide enough for all three children. As Jim guides the car up the still snowy roads through Turkey Creek Canyon, Mina tantalizes Stephen and Susanna with stories of the castle.

"I'm the Princess of the Castle," she informs Stephen.

"The Princess?" Stephen asks. "Daddy, what am I?"

"The Prince of the Realm, of course," Jim says easily.

"What's a realm?"

"Everything you see."

"What is Susanna?" Stephen asks.

"The Princess of Redlands," Kathleen suggests.

Jim flashes a smile—his most charming—in her direction.

"Father used to race with my mother through the castle," Mina says, and Kathleen half-turns to listen. "They ran up the stairs and through the rooms to the turret and back down to the fireplace. The first to touch the stones won."

"Who won?" Stephen asks.

"I don't know," Mina said. "Who won, Father?"

"Whoever was quickest," Jim says vaguely.

"Can we race, Daddy?" Stephen asks.

"Of course."

The fire has already warmed the Great Room from frigid to chilly when they arrive. Kathleen gathers coats, mittens, and hats that are discarded as the children run into the castle, primed by Mina to expect fantastic things. Their first activity is to shout into the cavernous, stonewalled room, laughing hardily when the echo returns to them. The race takes place once Jim shows them the route through the castle. As they slam doors and shout and careen in and out of the upper rooms, Kathleen stands by the window in the Great Room, looking down at the lake. The more the castle echoes with Stephen's, Susanna's and Mina's voices, the more distant the past becomes.

Mina and Stephen clatter down the spiral stone steps of the turret and run to the fireplace.

"Touch it!" Mina calls to Stephen. "Touch it, and we win!"

Stephen lays his hand on the stone ledge, claiming victory. Mina, who no longer walks but dances whenever she moves, performs a series of pirouettes across the room, singing, "I'm the Princess of the Castle."

"Mommy, we won!" Stephen runs to Kathleen.

"Oh, come here, you." Kathleen hoists him onto her hip.

He gives her a peck on the cheek.

Kathleen holds out her free arm to Mina, who swirls into the embrace. "I love you, Mrs. Kathleen."

The top of Mina's head is just under Kathleen's chin. She will be taller than Kathleen when she's a woman. She is big-boned—she has too much Swedish blood to ever be a dainty ballerina—but she carries her mother's magnetic beauty and stoic intellectual bent.

Kathleen kisses Mina's hair. "Ah, Mina, my sweet, sweet girl."

She looks toward the turret. Jim stands on the steps, Susanna in his arms. Kathleen's view of him is blocked by the low-hanging stone lintel that connects the turret to the main building. She sees his trouser legs and elaborate boots, with Susanna's lace-up boots and the hems of her skirt and petticoat at his waist, but their faces are hidden. She knows that Jim has a full view down the steps to where she and Mina and Stephen stand in the Great Room. He has overheard the conversation.

"Go to the kitchen," Kathleen says to Stephen and Mina. "I can hear Cook and the others. I'm sure they've brought goodies for you."

Breaking from her, the two run toward the far end of the room.

Still in Jim's arms, Susanna wiggles to be free, and he trots down the remaining steps and into the room. He sets Susanna on the floor.

"Wait for Susanna," Jim calls.

Mina extends a hand. "Come on!"

Susanna scampers across the room.

Jim strides up to Kathleen and takes her face in his hands, kissing her on the lips. Behind them, the children giggle naughtily.

"Go on!" Jim says. "Or I'll have to chase you again!"

They run, screaming in terror and delight.

"You'll have to keep that promise, you know," Kathleen says.

"I know, but there's no harm in prolonging the agony."

He kisses her again. She brings her arms around his neck, and he embraces her, his hands on her back. "The joke is on me," he whispers. "It always has been, for you've always been far more than my equal."

"I would argue that."

"Of course you would."

That night, they settle into the castle's high-ceilinged rooms, the beds freshly made, a fire in each fireplace. Kathleen worries that the unfamiliarity of the place, the shadowy corners, and the chill of the mountain air will keep the children from sleeping, but they are exhausted by the day's excitement and energy. Stephen and Susanna share a room, with Miss Brown nearby in an adjoining one. Mina has her own room, one that is fit for the undisputed Princess of the Castle.

When night falls, it is with a deep, sedate silence. The moon rises, high and full, in the night sky. It shines through the windows of Jim's and Kathleen's bedroom, outlining her hand as it lies on Jim's bare chest. His face is peaceful in slumber. After a long while, Kathleen dreams of reunion, of people living and dead—her mother and Hank, and her father, and Helen and Henri, and Ellie and Thomas, and Brendan, Liam, and Chava, and the full Sullivan clan. She dreams of Jim and their children. And Julia and Paul—of course, of Paul. All of the people she has loved, or who have made her life what it is. Outside, surrounded by bright stars, the moonlight washes benevolently over the mountains, unsullied for now by the blaze of the Klan's crosses.

# *Thank you for reading the White Winter Trilogy!*

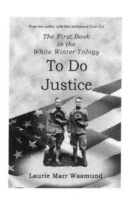

## *To Do Justice*
Three young Irish-Americans encounter the turmoil of a world at war and embark on a journey that will forever change their lives, their country, and the world.

## *To Love Kindness*
In spring, 1918, the Americans mount their greatest battles against the Germans. For Kathleen, Sean, and Maggie, each passing day threatens to take from them the things they love most.

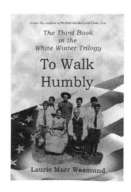

## *To Walk Humbly*
The war is over, yet in Colorado, a more daunting foe has awakened: the Ku Klux Klan. A new battle begins for Kathleen, Sean, and Maggie—one in which the stakes are even higher.

Contact me at
**lost.ranch.books@gmail.com**.

## Help others enjoy this book, too!

### *Share it with others!*
Pass on your copy to friends and acquaintances.

### *Recommend it!*
Please help other readers find this book by recommending it to your friends, book groups, libraries, and discussion boards. If your book group is in the Rocky Mountain region, contact me at **lost.ranch.books@gmail.com** to discuss the possibility of an author visit!

### *Review it!*
Please tell other readers why you liked this book by reviewing it at Amazon or Goodreads. If you write a review, send me an email at **lost.ranch.books@gmail.com** so that I can thank you with a personal reply.

*Visit lostranchbooks.com
for more information.*

# AUTHOR'S NOTE

The number of resources used to write *To Walk Humbly* quickly exceeds the space I have to acknowledge them. I relied heavily on Robert Alan Goldberg's *Hooded Empire: The Ku Klux Klan in Colorado* for information about the incredible relationship between the Ku Klux Klan and the state of Colorado. The article, "Colorado Under the Klan" by James H. Davis, published in *Colorado Magazine,* clarified the Klan's political agenda. "Women of the Klan: Racism and Gender in the 1920s" by Kathleen Blee presented an eye-opening discussion of the Klan's phenomenal rise in Colorado. Dorothy Schwieder's article, "A Farmer and the Ku Klux Klan in Northwest Iowa," published by the State Historical Society of Iowa, gave me an insider's view of the Klan, as did *Inside the Klavern: The Secret History of a Ku Klux Klan of the 1920s*, edited by David A. Horowitz. I also thank my sister, Patsy White for providing detailed notes on a lecture on the Ku Klux Klan in Colorado by former State Senator Dennis Gallagher.

The Klan's philosophy is best explained by Bishop Alma Bridwell White of the Pillar of Fire, whose collection of speeches is published in *The Ku Klux Klan in Prophecy.* Kristin E. Kandt's article, "In the Name of God: An American Story of Feminism Racism, and Religious Intolerance: The Story of Alma Bridwell White," probes the tangled relationship between Denver's independent-minded women and the Klan.

For information about the historical figures of the time, I used mostly online sources. One exception is Philip Van Cise, my favorite historical hero. His autobiography, *Fighting the Underworld*, is not only raucously entertaining but genuinely informative. Alan Prendergast's article in *Westword*, "Phil Van Cise: Scourge of Denver's Underworld" provides a fine overview of his life. My gratitude also goes to Philip Van Cise's granddaughter, Cindy Van Cise, who spent two lovely hours with me talking about her grandfather.

The Colorado Historic Newspaper Collection provided information about the Moffat Tunnel, and the Moffat oil field. It also gave me access to the *Denver Jewish News* and the *Denver Star*, the newspaper of the African-American community in Denver. Through the Archdiocese of Denver Digital Repository, I was able to read issues of Matthew Smith's brilliant *Denver*

*Catholic Register*. Among other sources, I consulted Jeanne Abrams' "'For a Child's Sake': The Denver Sheltering Home for Jewish Children in the Progressive Era" for information about Denver's generous West Side Jewish community. I gleaned information on the Teapot Dome scandal from both newspapers of the time and from James Leonard Bates' *The Origins of Teapot Dome: Progressives, Parties and Petroleum, 1909-1921*.

Please see my website at lauriemarrwasmund.com for a complete list of sources. One disclaimer that I must make concerns the character of Liam Keohane. Although I used the life of Denver conscientious objector Ben Salmon as the model for Liam's experience during the war, Liam's personality and actions after the war come entirely from my own imagination.

Cynthia Norrgran and Linda Burnside read early drafts of the manuscript for me, and Candy Putch read the final manuscript with a sharp and consistent eye. I am indebted to my editor, Mark Putch, whose ability to think critically and creatively far outweighs my own. Thank you, Mark, for the hours, energy, and intellectual intensity that you put into this project.

Sadly, my mother, Wilma Marr, did not live to read the last book of the White Winter Trilogy, but I know that, as my best editor and biggest fan, she would be proud to see it in print. Again, my deepest gratitude is to my husband, Bill, who supports me in whatever I do. Thank you, my love.

Made in the USA
Lexington, KY
06 November 2019

56689134R00251